Making a Scene

Based on the author's decades of teaching, pedagogical and theatrical research, and his professional experience as actor and director, *Making a Scene: Creating a Scene Study Class for Actors* offers a pedagogical approach to rehearsal scenes as a primary tool for diagnosis and actor improvement.

This volume carefully lays out the case for thinking deeply and critically about the nature of every facet of an acting class: the environment of the classroom, the choice of material for performing, diagnostic tools for responding to scene sessions, and means for engaging all students. This study includes suggestions for a teacher's philosophy towards the work; a justification for implementing games, improvisations, and etudes; suggestions for resources for exercises both basic and complex; and a brief discussion on approaches to period styles material and connecting it to contemporary student life and issues.

Addressed to both the beginning theatre teacher and the seasoned educator, this will be an essential book for anyone seeking to update their work with performers in private studios, high school settings, or in higher education.

Bill Gelber is Professor of Theatre at Texas Tech University who teaches acting, directing, pedagogy, and period styles, including Shakespeare and his contemporaries.

Routledge Advances in Theatre & Performance Studies

This series is our home for cutting-edge, upper-level scholarly studies and edited collections. Considering theatre and performance alongside topics such as religion, politics, gender, race, ecology, and the avant-garde, titles are characterized by dynamic interventions into established subjects and innovative studies on emerging topics.

Flora Fantastic
From Orchidelirium to Eco-Critical Contemporary Art
Corina L. Apostol, Tashima Thomas

Applied Theatre and the Sustainable Development Goals
Crises, Collaboration and Beyond
Taiwo Afolabi, Abdul Karim Hakib, Bobby Smith

Dancing Shakespeare
Ballet Adaptations of William Shakespeare's Works from the Eighteenth Century to the Present
Iris Julia Bührle

Teaching Dance Improvisation
A Beginner's Guide
Matthew Farmer

1000 Ways to Ask Why
Introduction to Dramaturgical Thinking
Emily LeQuesne

Making a Scene
Creating a Scene Study Class for Actors
Bill Gelber

For more information about this series, please visit: https://www.routledge.com/Routledge-Advances-in-Theatre-Performance-Studies/book-series/RATPS

Making a Scene
Creating a Scene Study Class for Actors

Bill Gelber

LONDON AND NEW YORK

Designed cover image: Cover Art by Steve Wood

First published 2025
by Routledge
4 Park Square, Milton Park, Abingdon, Oxon OX14 4RN

and by Routledge
605 Third Avenue, New York, NY 10158

Routledge is an imprint of the Taylor & Francis Group, an informa business

© 2025 Bill Gelber

The right of Bill Gelber to be identified as author of this work has been asserted in accordance with sections 77 and 78 of the Copyright, Designs and Patents Act 1988.

All rights reserved. No part of this book may be reprinted or reproduced or utilised in any form or by any electronic, mechanical, or other means, now known or hereafter invented, including photocopying and recording, or in any information storage or retrieval system, without permission in writing from the publishers.

Trademark notice: Product or corporate names may be trademarks or registered trademarks and are used only for identification and explanation without intent to infringe.

British Library Cataloguing-in-Publication Data
A catalogue record for this book is available from the British Library

ISBN: 978–1–032–81179–6 (hbk)
ISBN: 978–1–032–81184–0 (pbk)
ISBN: 978–1–003–49852–0 (ebk)

DOI: 10.4324/9781003498520

Typeset in Bembo
by Apex CoVantage, LLC

Contents

Acknowledgments	*vii*
Introduction	1
1 Philosophy	11
2 Further Thoughts	26
3 Considerations	36
4 Picking Materials for Scene Study	51
5 Script Analysis	60
6 Coaching: Beginning	75
7 Coaching: Categories	88
8 Coaching to Inspire Emotions	104
9 Coaching Habits That Don't Serve	119
10 Coaching: Character	133
11 Feedback	155
12 Exercises, Etudes, and Games	170
13 Styles	183

| 14 | Styles: Shakespeare | 196 |
| 15 | Conclusion | 227 |

Appendix 1. Diverse Classroom Plan — *229*
Appendix 2. Open Scenes — *230*
Appendix 3. Grading Rubric for Acting Period Styles — *233*
Bibliography — *235*
Index — *241*

Acknowledgments

First of all, I want to thank my Teaching of Acting students over the past several years: without your consent to test these ideas in a pedagogical setting, as well as your contributions to the subject, this book would not exist.

To the wonderful editors at Routledge, Laura Hussey, for taking interest in my book and, with Swatti Hindwan, for shepherding me through the publishing process.

To my research assistants Bradley Frenette and Rengim Melis Kose for reading and commenting on portions of this book; your feedback was invaluable.

To my parents Morris and Betty Gelber and my grandparents, Frank and Lelia Beth Powell, who served as my models for what teaching might be.

To Kelly, Kirk, Bethany, Dan, Steve, and Mike for moral support.

To my sons Devon, Alex, and James, who unknowingly served as some of my earliest teachers and continue to make me proud.

To the folks at J&B Coffee, who supplied me with caffeine early every morning as I wrote in the back corner of the store.

And finally, as always, to Deborah Suzanne Gelber, the best teacher I know.

Introduction

It is not uncommon when we begin our careers in education to teach our students as we were taught. This fallback position can be particularly fruitful when our own teachers were adept in their own right, with expertise learned from their teachers. On the other hand, we can discover that our training did not adequately prepare us pedagogically – that, in our early days as instructors in the classroom, performing well and developing superior performances in others proved to be two very different things. After long experience we make the work our own, and even if we pass on earlier practices and traditions of working, keeping effective techniques and methodologies alive, the line becomes blurred between what we have invented and what we have adapted from others.

I began teaching acting as a graduate student in 1988 at the University of Texas at Austin. Our supervisor gave us a template for how to proceed in the instruction of a non-majors course, based around Uta Hagen's classic text, *Respect for Acting* and its various object exercises. I dutifully followed the syllabus, but before my first days of class, as an exercise I also took a pad of paper and listed all of the things I wanted the students to know by the end of such a course. At that time, I imagined the hypothetical scope, the breadth of what I might offer in the future. I then arranged that list in a sequence and filled a calendar with lessons. This was an early attempt to consider what would be, for me, the essential components that represented a foundation for teaching acting.

After many years, I continue to question my priorities: what I should be teaching now to meet the challenges of the times, how I should respond to the changing makeup of each generation of students, and how I will use the current research available to me concerning education and the arts, including neuroscientific studies of the brain during performance. I have my failures, I still get a sense of imposter syndrome, and I have struggled at times with a sense of burnout, but I continue to regroup and recover by seeking opportunities to grow and develop as a teaching artist. I have written this book in part to review where I currently stand and where I still want to go, to remain the lifelong learner I have always aspired to be. Since I see theatre as an essential element for a healthy society, I continue to create an environment for myself and my students that supports this view. This gives me motivation for teaching, the sense that there is a higher purpose: the study of human beings and the recreation of their behavior onstage as a means of allowing the audience to see themselves more clearly, to identify with others, and to empathize with people in situations outside their own experience.

Whether the reader is just beginning a teaching career in higher education, wants to recalibrate a curriculum they believe has grown stale over time, or questions why and how to go about teaching or coaching in the current climate, the topics throughout this book suggest avenues for exploration rather than a blueprint that must be strictly followed to guarantee success. If an accompanying result of the concentration on matters advanced and basic is that seasoned teachers rethink or renew their approaches, this is also a welcome outcome. This particular book is based on the idea that beginning teachers will use the material here to practice coaching in a classroom setting with students: creating a comfortable environment for each other, selecting material, applying tools – exercises, games, or etudes – responding to and diagnosing rehearsals, and doing so with a philosophy towards the work.

In some ways the easiest course to teach, with the least amount of preparation, is a scene study class. After all, the students can pick their own material to perform, rehearse outside of class, and present their work to the teacher, who can walk in, watch their scenes, respond until the end of the period, rinse, and repeat. Latterly, the teacher can also choose the material, using a common play for all students, relying on a previous knowledge of the piece to inform his work, no review of the literature then being required of the instructor. The teacher provides feedback to the performers, and they leave class convinced they are advancing towards a long and successful acting career. The most experienced teachers may worry less about classroom management; with their classrooms as studios and their reputations as adept purveyors of artistic knowledge, they may be afforded the curtesy of attention – the students granting them an authority that creates an atmosphere of respect and motivates those present to put in the work.

This scenario is a characterization now practiced less and less. The guru who holds their students enthralled is a cliché, now more a dramatic device or a source of humor in movies and television. Teachers of great ability not only make great strides in helping their students to acquire craft, but they share with those students the secrets behind what they do. They make the students collaborators in the process. In this way, the students become independent lifelong learners in the field, no longer reliant on hand-holding.

When the magician waves his hands, we do not see the long hours of practice and experience that lead to the successful completion of a trick. The skilled actor, too, uses technique to the point that their work seems effortless. In the same way, when the teacher performs their own magic on a student, transforming the subject into a more capable performer, we are unaware of the training and experiences that led to that moment. Withholding such information may be essential to the magician's livelihood, but for the teacher to pretend that there is some arcane secret behind what they do is to miss an opportunity to impress upon the students the work involved in creating a role and to share the reasoning behind methods that have been effective, further imprinting the lessons in the students' minds.

That is the purpose of this book – to share with those who are interested some of the ways in which a scene study class might be created and run, but also the thinking behind the means whereby the teacher guides the student to improve. A warning: this means extra work on the part of the teacher and coach, including self-reflection on the process and a willingness to continue to grow and learn regardless of what stage the practitioner has reached in their career. This dedication to such work can be effective, student-centered, and highly rewarding.

Also a caveat: this is one perspective on creating a scene study course. Though this book contains a series of open-ended questions which encourage the teacher to consider how they would like to conduct their classes, and I have suggested some answers to these questions – i.e., given a number of examples of my own – I want to stress that I do not consider this a definitive way of working with student actors. There are as many methodologies as there are teachers, and actors all have different ways of working – including means which lead to successful careers with no official training at all. If the book is of any use, it may be as a reminder to teachers to continue to ask themselves the same questions I have asked over the years in my pedagogy class, The Teaching of Acting, and as I coached the students, both undergraduate and graduate, in my classes and onstage in productions at Texas Tech University.

The book begins with the idea that an acting teacher should periodically do a reassessment of what and why they teach, continues through a discussion of the environment created by teachers based on their attitudes towards the students, and moves through the basics of script analysis and scene selection to a number of sections on diagnosing and coaching actors at work. One chapter gives particular emphasis to the nature of feedback, including the role students may take in offering perspectives on the scenes they observe. Games and improvisations are introduced as a further series of tools to aid in student development, and the book concludes with chapters about coaching material outside of contemporary realism.

Chapter Overview

Chapter 1: Philosophy

A philosophy encourages the instructor to consider why they teach acting and what they feel is important when doing so. After all, one must have goals in mind supported by the reasoning behind them and an attitude towards the work that informs it. In this book, the simple answer is that the teacher is working on the entire person, a student who lives in the world and interacts with many different people every day, who seeks to understand his fellow human beings in a way that will lead to empathy and cooperation. The teacher's goal is to encourage that lifelong learner who is always curious, always seeking new and more effective ways to work, and reasons for doing so. In this way, they are also instilling in the student a love of craft which will serve them if they decide to enter the profession. An offshoot may be that the student will succeed and have tools to aid them in professional situations.

The book proposes that a difference exists between coaching and directing and that this distinction is important to consider while teaching a scene study class. In brief, the terms are used to define the teacher's approach: in the directing mindset, the teacher may feel the need to offer answers and seek results; coaching, on the other hand, is understood here as an attitude towards the work that involves proffering questions and encouraging continuing development through process. In the latter case, the teacher is modeling the questions that the students will begin to ask themselves.

The teacher is encouraged to delve deeply into a text for the clues that suggest how to play it; to identify the specific aspects of acting that apply to a particular scene at a particular time; to replace habits that no longer serve the student with better habits that will.

Chapter 2: Further Thoughts

Here is an exploration of some of the speed bumps that arise as the teacher considers their philosophy of theatre and of acting. One discussion concerns a self-fulfilling prophecy: when the coach guides the student to produce a particular result, the coach may see a result they want to see, regardless of whether it has actually appeared. Another is the concept of failure as a learning tool, both for the student and the teacher. The figure of the guru is invoked as a cliché that no longer serves as an effective persona in today's schools: whether conservatories, public schools, or institutes of higher education.

Chapter 3: Considerations

In this chapter, means are suggested for identifying a student's initial beliefs about acting and to determine which diagnostics will serve as assessments of previous learning. Here the initial setup for a scene study class is discussed with a number of suggestions, non-exhaustive, to aid in creating an atmosphere of creativity in which the students work together to discover what works and what doesn't for each individual. This includes how to give constructive and specific notes; how to keep all students engaged, whether onstage or not; how to stress process over product; how to create a balance between the introduction of new concepts and tools and the implementation of scene work; what to teach and what to leave out; setting up the space for coaching – how and whether to divide the room into performers and audience; and managing time, based on a prescribed schedule, such as how many rehearsals should be held in or out of class, how much time should be provided for overall performances, how many scenes the students will work on and why. Important goals include encouraging the students' curiosity about the field – its history, its influences, and its growth over time – and increasing a student's interest in the study of human beings through their behavior.

Chapter 4: Picking Materials for Scene Study

This chapter concerns plans for choosing scene materials: whether the instructor or the student will choose what material to explore; whether one play will be examined, or scenes from different plays, one-acts, sketches, or original material, and the reasoning behind those choices. Here an emphasis is placed on the idea that the instructor will guide scene selection, to heighten student investment and to accomplish training or improvements that the teacher and student perceive as essential given the time available. The belief here is that the instructor initially selects and casts each scene for individual students. This also means the teacher must have a depth and breadth of knowledge about plays and playwrights from all different genres and styles, with particular emphasis on 21st-century work. It also means that the teacher will habitually seek out new work that will be most conducive for particular goals.

Chapter 5: Script Analysis

An important skill for both teacher and student cannot be stressed enough in the study of text-based plays: various means for analyzing a script, and how such a practice can give the students countless clues for realizing a role. It is possible to take scenes out of context or to choose scenes that are written specifically for scene study, but this chapter encourages the theatre practitioner to begin work by taking advantage of what the author has offered the reader, exploring well-constructed plays of the type that students may encounter in the future, and understanding the context, especially the past as it influences the characters in the present.

Coaching the Scenes Is Divided into Five Parts

Chapter 6: Coaching: Beginning

Various methods for coaching are now considered, including side-coaching; taking on an advocate persona; and how to begin a session, whether in dramaturgical discussions or immediately putting the scene on its feet, agreeing on the event of the scene, and other means for easing into the work. It is understood that the pressure of beginning can create tension in the actors, and that the more the coach can create a calming atmosphere to focus the student, the more effective the instruction is likely to be.

Chapter 7: Coaching: Categories

Of particular importance is the creation of categories for diagnoses which allow the teacher to quickly determine where they will concentrate the work, whether this comes after an initial run-through or as part of a stop-and-start process of discovery. Another consideration concerns how the coach will serve as an audience: how vocal they will be in their responses or how contemplative and unintrusive.

Chapter 8: Coaching to Inspire Emotions

This chapter proposes that each actor produces the character's feelings in their own way, and that teachers have disparate means of training them to do so, even if these methods are based on similar principles, such as those proposed by Konstantin Stanislavsky. This discussion is not exhaustive by any means, but it offers some basic principles for experimentation by the acting teacher and coach.

Chapter 9: Coaching Habits That Don't Serve

The premise of this chapter is that students have brought certain habits to the work that they relied on to avoid fear and tension in front of an audience, whether of patrons or peers. These habits outlive their usefulness the further these students progress in their work, as they realize that vulnerability, openness, and impulse-based responses are keys to living a creative life on the stage. Certain behaviors, although comforting, serve as constraints to openness and receptivity, preventing the students from being affective – i.e., allowing the given circumstances to produce emotional responses and truthful behavior.

Chapter 10: Coaching: Character

It is possible to separate character study from the actor's work on themselves. William Esper used two separate year-long processes for each. Given the time constraints of the class and the scope of the course, the teacher will sometimes be working in both areas. This also depends on the teacher's own approach to the work. We are all, in a sense, characters – that is, different personalities with different agendas, different attitudes, and different life choices. This chapter explores the connection of the actor to the character through personal work which aims the actor towards imagining the motives behind actions, including those they would never take in real life.

Chapter 11: Feedback

The goal of this chapter is to consider pedagogical strategies for offering feedback and to suggest how the students, serving as an audience for each other, can contribute to the feedback process: how student peers will evaluate each other, including possible teacher prompts for the student audience; how to maintain an atmosphere of reflection, a tool which has long-term benefits; how to maintain an attitude of process over product even at the conclusion of work on a particular scene. This chapter emphasizes goals: those of the teacher, but particularly of the student. Lloyd Richards's concept of goal-driven student work and teacher feedback is stressed here as a means of concentrating on particular areas of growth – in the scene and in the student. Tools are suggested for student review and reflection throughout the course. A philosophy of grading is also discussed: the difficulty of grading the subjective, and how to make the grading more equitable, with an emphasis on student dedication to the work and growth that can be evaluated.

Chapter 12: Exercises, Etudes, and Games

This chapter introduces tools and exercises as aids to the study of scenes: skills that emphasize such concepts as observation, personalization, and imagination, as well as psychological paradigms which may affect the character's behavior. The chapter will discuss the use of improvisations and etudes, means for acting out previous circumstances, connecting the actor and the situation, and adding physical activity. The use of games will be discussed as they apply to acting training and the improvement of particular parts of the actor's craft. The chapter will also consider the timing for implementing tools and exercises, whether the work is interwoven within study of the scenes themselves or introduced separately as general concepts.

Chapter 13: Styles

Though period texts are often taught in courses of their own, scene study classes are sometimes eclectic, dealing with many different styles and genres, especially when the opportunities for such studies are limited by the range of courses that may be offered. This chapter offers perspectives on period drama for the teacher and actor, with an eye towards connecting contemporary acting theory with classical texts. The aim here is to begin a conversation on coaching heightened language texts: to provide resources for various period pieces, to consider the reasoning behind studying certain genres, to implement specific methodologies, to encourage students to engage in dramaturgical research, and to marry the actors' mindset with that of a role in classic theatre, with examples of how classical acting has been realized by expert practitioners.

Included within the scope of this brief study is a section on the principles of comedy, both its nature and the means whereby it enters into a relationship with the audience and produces amusement. These techniques are further additions to the craft of acting that may or not be included on a menu of basic acting matters, where the emphasis is on an internal psycho-physical system, for example, rather than on external techniques, where the latter are sometimes considered hollow displays of temperament and shameless appeals to the crowd for approval.

Chapter 14: Styles: Shakespeare

This chapter contains a more detailed discussion for coaching a particular period style: Elizabethan and Jacobean acting. Verse speaking skills are explored as well as techniques for handling the material by both professional Shakespearean actors and in the classroom. Resources are also provided for the scenes, and suggestions are made for a full course of study. This chapter addresses, and attempts to assuage, the actor who fears that they are not up to the task of playing roles in Early Modern English.

Chapter 15: Conclusion

What this book doesn't do:

1. It won't promise that scene study will lead directly to professional acting work, although this may be an offshoot of the study.
2. It doesn't cover a wide variety of methods but does suggest how the course may be adapted. It approaches certain tools and methods from a particular point of view.

3. It doesn't concentrate on devised work or performance studies, considering these as separate matters, worthy of their own courses. This book is text based, i.e., it deals with play texts.
4. Skill sets that can be taught with greater breadth in their own courses – such as voice, speech, clown work, dialects – are referred to, but not explored in great depth. Even so, the use of breath and ways to encourage the physical embodiment of character are important parts of diagnoses and coaching.
5. Though various ways of working are considered, this book deals primarily with the idea of intent and focuses on behavior that reveals feeling and thought, whether with realistic plays or plays with heightened text, with the understanding that other methods have a different concentration, and that the work of Konstantin Stanislavsky – the basis for much of the discussion – is dismissed outright in some quarters.[1]

The influences of Russian actor, director, and teacher, Konstantin Stanislavsky[2] (1863–1938) on acting teachers in the 20th and 21st centuries can still be felt.[3] He was the first practitioner to codify ideas about the nature and realization of acting on the stage: "Stanislavski, who had scaled the heights in his creative work as a director and actor, was also remarkable in that he made a proper study of its basic laws."[4] He did this through his careful observation of the outstanding performers of his era.

When he was watching the best actors work, he tried to isolate the special features that made their acting great art: the means by which this was achieved; which method they used when working on a role; what their overall artistic process was; and whether it was possible, once the elements of acting had been defined, to create a technique by which ordinary actors, through hard work and daily training, could overcome their limitations more easily, and perfect and refine their technique.[5]

Stanislavsky was the first to put a form to an actor's preparation for performance. And he never stopped studying human beings, never tired of experimenting with new ways of working to discover a process that was applicable, viable, and teachable. His teacher was the world around him: "There is no System. There is only nature. My life-long concern has been how to get ever closer to what is called 'The System,' that is, to get closer to the nature of creativity."[6] He continued to explore what it meant to live in a creative state on the stage. His model is still the foundation of many acting training programs today, as it is in this book.[7]

This book also questions the notion, still used by those who diminish the art of teaching, "Those who can't, teach." Coaches who have a load of professional experience, who are themselves brilliant actors in the field and who can demonstrate what to do, cannot necessarily explain how they are doing it. Later in the book, this phenomenon will be discussed under the topic of "expert blindness" – the ability to skip steps in a process because of one's expertise in it. To master any field is to reach an unconscious competence – the ability to do something without thinking about it. What the professional offers on a basic level is modeling, an important tool for teaching – an example of the thing to be mastered.[8] This is an invaluable part of the teaching process. With a pedagogical approach, a teacher with varying levels of professional experience can return to the beginning of the learning process, offering in sequence the steps, no matter how small, that will lead the student towards mastery.

One initiative in education in America during the 1980s was the idea that, to improve teaching, each teacher should major in the subject that they would be offering to the students. This idea seemed to hold great promise until a study was done of the work by Japanese teachers, whose students outperformed American students in math and science. Rather than taking inordinate numbers of classes in those disciplines, as was suggested by U.S. education departments, the teachers took more *methodology* classes – courses in *how* to teach.[9]

The study of scenes is a rewarding experience for teacher and student alike. The parameters for a study, and the means for teaching it, are endless. The possibility of constant revision is encouraged, even as our world changes and with it the mindset of our students. To ignore these developments is to enter a dimension of irrelevancy and create an atmosphere that discourages interest in the benefits and excitement of working carefully on oneself and on the thoughts, motives, and desires of others. Reinvention and continued research into new methods of learning and theories behind the acting process will instead promote enjoyment and dedication in the student actor – a worthwhile goal in any course of study.

Note: particularly when it is difficult to distinguish between the actor/student and the teacher/coach, I alternate pronouns between he/him/his, she/her/hers, and they/theirs. There is no design involved in picking one or another, but I avoid obvious stereotypes wherever possible. I use student, actor, and performer interchangeably, as I believe that material may apply to all of those parties.

Notes

1 Though this book has some basis in practices proposed by Stanislavsky, the author is aware that other means of realizing performance are important. This is in part because Stanislavsky's ideas are steeped in historical thinking that does not specifically address the changing makeup of our classes or the way in which the world is interpreted by the Global Majority. See Siiri Scott and Jay Paul Skelton, eds., *Stanislavsky and Race: Questioning the "System" in the 21st Century* (London: Routledge, 2023). Other resources are included in the Bibliography.
2 The spelling of the name Stanislavsky varies according to whether it is anglicized or not. "Konstantin Stanislavsky" will be used by the author, while other forms, such as "Stanislavski," will retain that spelling in accordance with the cited author.
3 Even as the work must be adapted or its relevancy questioned by those who find it dated or inappropriate. See Scott and Skelton, *Stanislavsky and Race,* particularly chapters 1, 2, 4, 7, 8, and 9. On the other hand, practitioners and teachers such as Professor Baron Kelly embrace Stanislavsky's work as a key component of their own. See Baron Kelly, *An Actor's Task: Engaging the Senses* (Indianapolis, IN: Hackett Publishing Company, 2015).
4 Vasili Toporkov, *Stanislavski in Rehearsal*, trans. Jean Benedetti (London: Bloomsbury, 2014), 160.
5 Toporkov, *Stanislavski in Rehearsal,* 160.
6 Sharon Marie Carnicke, *Stanislavsky in Focus, 2nd Edition: An Acting Master for the Twenty-First Century* (London: Routledge, 2009), 66.

7 See his seminal works: Konstantin Stanislavski, *An Actor's Work: A Student's Diary*, 1st Edition, trans. Jean Benedetti (London: Routledge, 2008), formerly published as *An Actor Prepares* and *Building a Character,* and *An Actor's Work on a Role*, trans. Jean Benedetti (London: Routledge, 2009), formerly published as *Creating a Role*. These three volumes were edited and translated by Elizabeth Reynolds Hapgood.
8 This distinction doesn't take into account the many actors who are exemplary teachers, both by example and through their ability to teach craft.
9 Such practices as *jugyōkenkyū*, professional development for teacher improvement, continues today. See "A Different Approach to Teacher Learning," *APMreports*, August 26, 2015, https://www.apmreports.org/episode/2015/08/26/a-different-approach-to-teacher-learning-lesson-study

1 Philosophy

Why someone decides to teach acting has myriad answers. One of the strongest is that at one point the teacher realized they had something to offer the actor that would be of use, that they could enact changes in the students before them through the study and practice of the process of acting. Perhaps they were in a production as an actor and thought, "I know what that person needs and the director isn't giving it to them." Ideally, rather than interposing between the director and the other actor, they waited until a situation arose elsewhere that allowed them to work with an individual or a group of people outside the confines of a production. They had a knack that led them more to directing/coaching than to acting. In another instance, at a certain point in a performer's life, they may have a desire for a different lifestyle: a family, a steady job with benefits, a stable, non-migratory existence.[1] A position in academe would fulfill these requirements while allowing them a continuing engagement in the art they love. Or an actor may decide that the vagaries of the profession are exhausting, the odds of making a living even as a recognized artist continue to be low and are dependent on conditions outside of his control; however, he realizes his experience is valuable as a conduit and model for others who want to pursue a career in the field. He decides to share his love of the art with others, even if he himself has been discouraged.

Ultimately, the why of teaching is a spur to treating the discipline with the respect it deserves. Rather than using a career in education as a fallback position, someone entering the teaching field should give themselves a larger goal, one that excites them with the possibilities of student- and self-improvement, the pursuit of excellence in an educational forum. The following discussion suggests ways of thinking about the teacher's mission – leading to a deeper sense of purpose and articulating a credo with a series of basic beliefs about what should be taught and how.

Basic Tenets of the Work

Why an acting class? Wallace Smith saw two criteria for any course to be included in the curriculum: "1) The subject is fundamental to the lives of people. 2) The subject cannot be taught somewhere else, as part of another subject."[2] The study of humans by human could not be more fundamental to a person's well-being and

DOI: 10.4324/9781003498520-2

understanding of the world. Since acting involves the intense study of human behavior as it may be presented onstage, it is one of the most important studies of all. Answers to acting problems can be found in anthropology, sociology, and psychology. However, only acting gives those subjects context within the frame of recreation in performance.

Every decision a teacher makes when creating a scene study course says something about their views of acting, the theatre, and teaching in general. They may be modeling a certain form of professional behavior. They may approach the craft of acting with a view to making students independent practitioners. They may share their own experiences as performers. They may emphasize one form of theatre over another. They may start with basic ideas as a foundation for the work, or they may concentrate on certain actor problems within the scenes themselves. They may give their students a sense of social responsibility. They may stress the importance of acting as an art form. What they emphasize and what topics they leave for others to teach will be one of the foci within this overall study. Finally, instructors must ask what they want to instill in their students and how they will go about doing so. Olympia Dukakis felt she was teaching to "three kinds of actors: the ones you teach skills to, the ones you teach craft to, and the ones you prepare for a life in the theatre."[3]

Curiosity is an important facet to be instilled in both the student and practiced by the teacher, who should be fascinated by the people she is working with. The teacher should be curious to know who the students are and how they imagine and create. The teacher should be interested in the actors' development and include this as part of her goals. The teacher should motivate the actors through a sense of play – even when the work itself, and the material, is deeply serious, the study of acting can be an enjoyable process.[4]

Coaching Versus Directing

Realizing that every director, just like every teacher, works in different ways, whether in a movement-based form such as Suzuki, Laban, or Viewpoints, or in a psychophysical form used by practitioners of Stanislavsky-based work, acting teachers must consider whether their responses to student work take the form of direction in its strictest sense of manipulating all elements of a production, including the actors, or will treat the students as self-directed learners. Even if the coach leans towards skillful questioning, leading questions may aim the students towards a specific conclusion or interpretation. This is a form of directing. Coaching here is distinguished from directing through an emphasis on querying the students in a different way, to guide them towards their own conclusions, eliciting rather than imposing interpretations and solutions to acting problems.[5]

Just as a scene class can be reduced to the bare minimum – a series of scenes that the teacher responds to – so a teacher as director, especially one who has trained as an actor, can make the coaching process very simple and quick. Such an individual can show the student exactly what to do and how to say the lines, but barring this dictatorial approach, they can still offer quick solutions rather than give the students the experience of learning through self-exploration. The benefit to a directorial approach is that teachers can draw on their own experience as experts in the field to model or impose behaviors they want the students to emulate. This is also a streamlined approach, with less concentration on the details and less feedback required. Teachers with a director mentality may make statements and offer direct suggestions that can quickly be implemented by the students or drilled until they satisfy the teacher. This takes less time than the alternative, or coaching approach, and is finally product oriented.

To treat the actor as a marionette whose strings are pulled to make it move, or a vessel into which knowledge is poured, means cutting off the personal options that a unique individual will give to the role. Instead, the actor will be forced to give his mind and body over to a master manipulator. Yes, it takes far less time, but it doesn't make the actor self-sufficient. Instead, he is beholden to others outside of himself, who continue to offer instructions from production to production or from scene to scene. It is as if he is guided on a journey through the desert, stripped of all technology, but the navigator refuses to show him the map. If the navigator disappears, and takes the map with them, he is lost. He must trust the navigator knows the best route and that eventually he will reach some kind of destination. Once he has finished the course, he realizes he has been offered solutions to particular problems but no overall plan for applying principles to new problems. Having reached one destination – the realization of a performance of a scene – he must rely on the next navigator with a new map to lead him towards new goals in further scenes and plays. In *Master Teachers of Theatre*, Wallace Smith concludes that, in directing high school actors in this way, he has cloned many versions of himself and ignored the uniqueness that each of his students could have brought to their roles: "Before I could see the stage, I heard my voice sounding out in several pitches! Stepping around a screen at the entrance, I saw myself in different costumes and two sexes."[6] He was appalled to realize that he had been "manipulating my adolescent puppets to do it my way in order to win [a state play contest]."[7]

A director is finally product-oriented because, ultimately, the show must open. The director asks for results within a certain time frame because it is part of the business. The show must go on in front of an audience, even if that audience is made up of other students in the classroom. The final version of a scene in class is a performance, and the students are in danger of concluding that all the work that can be done on that material has been accomplished. It is the realization of a scene used to check off a list of accomplishments; the parties can now move on.

This does not mean that the teacher can't offer suggestions that will help the actors to move forward in their work, for example, if the students are still trying to understand what the scene is about or have missed a key to a character relationship. They may have created a groundplan for themselves that prevents certain moments from happening. At this point, the coach asks, "May I offer something?" This is still a way of concentrating the student's attention on particular areas of work while asking them for permission to adjust what they are doing. As long as the teacher explains her reasoning, the actor continues to receive knowledge that will benefit them in the future.

What's missing in the directorial mentality suggested earlier is the wonderful moment when the actors come to their own solutions. Teaching of a different kind happens, and deeper exploration of roles and material can take place. The actors reach their own epiphanies that in turn have a stronger and more memorable impact. This does not mean that the coach has no plan for how to help the students with particular scenes. The homework must be done so that the teacher understands what is required of the role. However, the teacher doesn't have to show off their own learning. Instead, they can give the students the opportunity to go through the same process the teacher went through to reach their own conclusions, even if these are conclusions the teacher wanted them to reach. This was Lloyd Richards's approach: "I like the actor to discover for himself what I intend for him to discover. When he discovers it, it's his."[8] Richards saw the other approach, in which he told the students what he wanted, as an imposition, so he used a more subtle means of getting what he wanted by guiding students towards the answers: "When I impose it, it's mine for a time, so I am always trying to, I guess you call it 'feed,' people or actors so that they discover in a way things I would like to discover."[9]

This method requires patience. As Richards's former student A. Dean Irby notes, "You [the teacher/director] very clearly know – you have a strong idea, let's just say, of what the answer is. But how do you restrain yourself from telling the actor or the student what the answer is? How do you phrase it? How do you articulate it in a way that they find out what the answer is?"[10] To have all the answers as a teacher isn't the point; it is to lead the students towards self-direction, to be unnecessary to their future success.

Stanislavsky appreciated actor/teachers, and when speaking with a fellow director, he complimented him on his ability to serve as a model for performance, "You see, Sakhnovski, you are very good at 'demonstrating' to actors. You, undoubtedly, have talent. You should try to act."[11] However, he had a caveat: "But 'demonstrating' to actors seldom gets you very far."[12] Stanislavsky compared his own approach to fishing, "You have to learn to lure them with the right 'bait.' That is the art of the teacher-director."[13] The bait involved being "aware of what will tempt them and under what circumstances."[14] This meant understanding the kind of actors he was working with. He divided them into two types:

> There are actors of great imagination, and all you have to do is point them in the right direction, and there are actors whose imagination needs to be stirred all the time for them to develop and grow. Don't confuse these two types, or apply the same method to them.[15]

The teacher as coach guides the actors towards solving their own problems. She asks the right questions so that the actors can come to their own conclusions but also, and more importantly, learn what questions need to be asked. The coach thus remains process-oriented even up to and including the last viewing of each scene, suggesting that the work is never finished and there is always more to learn. This is a delicate process and, even with the best of intentions, it is easy for any coach to fall into a director role. Sometimes, the best course of action seems to be to offer a new solution. Or sometimes the coach will ask questions within which the answer can easily be found; these questions presuppose they have a solution in mind. The ability to couch a question in such a way as to leave the actor's options open, but to lead them towards the text, keeps the coach from falling into a directorial role.

One famous theatre practitioner who continued to teach as he directed, purveying actor training during the rehearsal process, was Lloyd Richards. Even as he directed professional productions of August Wilson's plays, Richards embodied the coaching mindset: "'Solicit' and 'elicit' were used to describe his goals when working with actors, and 'impose' indicated action that was antithetical to his working philosophy."[16]

Ron Van Lieu, one of Richards's former students, agreed and practiced this approach with his acting students: "They are always in rehearsal. They are never presenting. In rehearsal you are solving problems and the performance is part of the process."[17] He didn't want his actors to settle on snap judgments, but to understand how better and more effective solutions might arise over time.

There may come a time when a teacher asks a question and the student gives an answer with which the coach disagrees.[18] The coach's response to this is important. If the teacher is not enthusiastic or is noncommittal, the student intuits that they have put a foot wrong. At this point, they will either hesitate to give further answers or doggedly defend what they have proposed. However, they should feel free to explore any idea for the discoveries they will make and be encouraged to seek further options even after initial solutions seem to serve. In this way, they will learn how to distinguish between the quality of the solutions they consider.

The students' ideas may come from previous knowledge the teacher hasn't been made aware of. This previous knowledge may act as an invisible barrier to further instruction unless the students are asked to explain the reasoning behind their decisions. In his book *What the Best College Teachers Do*, his study of highly successful educators, Ken Bain found that "the teachers we encountered believe everybody constructs knowledge and that we all use existing constructions to understand any new sensory input."[19] These mental models have to be recognized and addressed by building new "mental models of reality."[20]

This is done using the concept of "expectation failure." The idea is that, if the student uses a faulty mental model that doesn't work when applied to a new situation, the student will then see that what has been useful in the past no longer serves; their beliefs, which have been limited to some circumstances but not all, have to be expanded or adjusted. Creating a system failure by offering a tougher acting problem to solve – where their current knowledge and experience won't solve it – and then showing them how to consider the problem in a new way, may help them to see that they are at the very beginning of the journey towards mastery of craft. Failure, though it has the potential to be discouraging, can actually be self-motivating as long as the student is in the right mindset: "Motivation is likely to remain high if the student explains his poor performance in terms of controllable and temporary causes such as inadequate preparation, insufficient effort, or lack of relevant information."[21] If instead the student sees their failure as one they can't control, they won't take responsibility for what they can do to succeed.

When the coach asks the student to consider behaviors or events that are brought out in the text, the student may find that his original idea cannot be reconciled with the author's idea. What he expected to find didn't parse with the original answer to the coach's question. This expectation failure creates "a situation in which existing mental models will lead to faulty expectations, causing their students to realize the problems they face in believing whatever they believe."[22] It is important that this practice be handled delicately. It is not a game of "gotcha" in which the teacher shows their superiority and greater knowledge of the text to the detriment of the student's answers, based on the processes as they understand them at that time.

The coach must tread lightly and delicately because "their students may find so much emotional comfort in some existing model of reality that they cling to it even in the face of repeated expectation failures."[23] The teacher prepares the groundwork, without judgment, for the student to adjust their mental models without feeling attacked. The hope is that this will motivate the student to acquire a new habit and reject an old one.[24] As a teacher responds to each new generation, and to each particular group of students, student responses will widely vary.[25] The teacher must familiarize themselves with the latest studies about the people they teach.

Ideally, the coach has some familiarity with each student's mental model, but this is more likely to happen if they probe the student for their thoughts in the moment. The coach might ask the student to elaborate on their answer and then ask questions that will explain where the student's thinking comes from. For example, the student may admit that they cannot relate to the character at all and has been concentrating on the role's negative traits at the expense of positive actions the character may take. This narrows their view of what is actually a more complex individual. The coach can ask the student about particular behaviors the character displays in other scenes in the play that contradict a biased or limited view. This aids the student in becoming an advocate for the character, a strategy that leads to the actor's understanding if not sympathy for the character's unfortunate decision or actions.[26] It also shows the character to be more complex than initially thought.

Or the student may believe that they understand a character's motivations and mindset based on their own 21st-century views. If the play was a contemporary one, their mental model would make sense. However, because the scene is set in the past – for example, the 19th century – the student is unfamiliar with the different mores and manners of that time that influence the character's actions in ways that would make them unusual today.[27] The coach can simply ask the student to look for clues as to how people behaved in that era to see if this is fruitful and give one example unrelated to the particular question already asked, while pointing the student towards historical resources.

Finally, the coach can accept the student's answer with reservations, replying: "Based on your initial reading of the text, this makes sense," and then going on to ask further questions, the emphasis being on modeling the questions for consideration rather than on their answers.

"Think Like a Person, Not Like an Actor"

"Think like a person, not like an actor" is an apothegm that Ron Van Lieu uses so that actors will "get connected to the given circumstances of the character and stop monitoring the effectiveness of their acting so that their concerns are those of a human being."[28] In this way, they aren't calculating how they are perceived by spectators, but are listening as people, connecting with other people onstage who can aid them in accomplishing their goals or who act as barriers to their ultimate happiness. A sense of what is true in life guides them rather than stage rules that are purely technical. They aren't looking for a laugh from the audience or self-monitoring. Instead, they are evaluating their partner as they would in real life.

In *Life in a Mid-Shot*, Les Chantery reminds us that the labels we use affect how we perceive ourselves: "[I]f you call yourself an actor, then you start to see the world as an actor."[29] Instead, the actor must see characters as human beings who are living life spontaneously. His conclusion: "You are therefore in the art of being human," and to "look at the script through our actor lens, we may not be making the most human choices that an audience identifies with."[30]

Chantery uses the principle of re-naming to create a mindset for actors when working on their roles. He changes the word "scene" to "situation" or "conversation." This takes the concept out of the theatrical realm and into reality. If actors are working on a scene, they are using language that retains the sense of being a character in a play. However, "if human beings are in dialogue with each other, it's not a scene; it's a *conversation* between people in a *situation*."[31] The actor then has more choices because there are no wrong ways to deal with a situation or a conversation, just more or less effective ways.

How often are the actors' choices about how they will look to the audience? How often do they work towards effects that will be impressive rather than honest and true? Human beings aren't concerned with this type of behavior. They are too busy trying to accomplish actions that will support their desires and combating threats to their success and/or happiness.

How this happens comes from personal experience or the observation of others. As Michelle Shay noted in rehearsals with Lloyd Richards, "Lloyd would not let the actor do anything that distracted from where the focus of the scenes was supposed to be."[32] She found this a difficult undertaking because the actor is often looking to make an effect: "You'd get frustrated because there is a level of simplicity and a level of serving the ensemble, which is not always easy, because you might want to do something that had more flair to it."[33]

A concentration on living the life of a character is based on experience. When a teacher tells young actors that they don't yet have experience, it's not that the actors are untalented or aren't capable, but because certain life events have not yet occurred. Actors, as they grow older, will draw more and more from their own lives as they learn to grieve the loss of their loved ones, enter important relationships and commitments, have children, and experience pains and ailments. They will be able to draw on all these experiences in an honest way. They will realize the deeper implications of certain events. "Richards definitely began by helping actors free themselves of their public personas and trying to get at their true creative natures."[34]

Mike Nichols expressed this idea when directing as, "What is this really, when it happens in real life? Not what is the accepted convention . . . but what is it really like?"[35] Nichols saw the events in drama as consisting of three types: Fights, negotiations, or seductions. Sometimes the student can confuse what is happening. What seems a fight is actually a seduction. What is considered a seduction is actually a negotiation. Nichols was famous for putting his finger on exactly what the play's events were. He was planning on training as a therapist but ended up turning his curiosity about human behavior into delicate diagnoses of character and the discovery of truthful situations not immediately evident from a surface reading of the play. It allowed him to closely observe what was real life and what was fake.

Lee Strasberg stated the idea thus: "In life, life itself is a sure standard, because if you deal with life unreally, it reacts in such a way that it forces you to correct."[36] Actors can work to illuminate what it means to be human. The actor does this "by embracing the degree of vulnerability that the character doesn't have any choice but to deal with."[37]

Speaking in First Person or Third Person

How the performer speaks of their character is their way into playing it. When an actor uses the third person to describe the character they are working on, they may be trying to distance themselves from the character or avoiding close identification. It may be that they have not yet identified with who they are playing. To encourage the actor to connect to the character not just intellectually but physically and emotionally, the teacher may suggest using the first-person address to lead them in this direction. If the actor is still more comfortable speaking in third person, the teacher may give notes while referring to the actor's character in the second person: "Why do you say that?" rather than "Why does she say that?"

The Importance of Reflection

Time must be set aside to review what the students have learned, discuss the work's deeper implications, and give further examples of how the new discoveries could be used. The students should be able to apply what they have learned to new problems, new characters, and new scenes and plays, and they should be able to do so on their own. The teacher is aiming for not only retention of the learning, but a lifelong interest in the subject that inspires the former student beyond the classroom setting.

Keith Johnstone created a series of behaviors for improvisors and listed ways in which they could be acted. He called it Fast-Food Stanislavsky.[38] One list, a caveat for the guru, is called, "To Be Thought Intelligent." Items include: "Correct people," "Know everything," "Use complex sentences," "Interrupt," "Adopt serious attitudes," "Analyze everything," "Cite authorities," "Lecture," and "Name drop."[39]

Responsibility to the Other Actor

The bonding that actors can have in a theatrical enterprise can become very strong in a very short amount of time. This kind of bonding can first take place in the classroom, where a group of supportive people work on a mutually agreed task: the improvement of their minds, bodies, and artistic souls.

Philip Seymour Hoffman was asked, "How do you save yourself if the other actors are staring at you and nobody's home?"[40] That is, what if the actor is giving their all and the other actor is not?

He said a surprising thing. He said, "You just save them. You have to love the other actor on the stage; you have to, ultimately. How you love the other actor is actually by succeeding in your goal and affecting them the way the play is asking you."[41] If the work is going to come first, then everyone is engaged in the same problems, and the attitude should be, don't let someone fall; help them up. Hoffman felt he could get the other actor back on track, that it was his responsibility to engage the other actor to the point that he did receive a response. "'Cause if somebody's trying to save you, they're loving you with their complete conviction to affect you appropriately for that play, moment to moment."[42] He was modeling an artistic ethic.

Declan Donnellan, in his book *The Actor and Target*, takes the onus off of the partner: "It is the actor's challenge to believe, more than his partner's problem to convince him."[43]

School Priorities

In public secondary schools, as well as higher education institutions, the students are torn between the various duties they have as part of a theatre program. Not only do they have challenging assignments for each course, but they may be cast in school productions or student directing projects; if they are in BFA programs in state schools – as opposed to conservatories – they may take classes unrelated to the art of theatre, in the sciences, mathematics, or composition. Given a choice, they will prioritize their work on productions outside of class. Robert Benedetti reminds himself this natural inclination is an obstacle to thorough classwork: "In the minds of students, the demands of production will always outweigh the demands of classes, and the most rigorous class experiences can be rendered meaningless by production work that is inconsistent with class principles."[44]

However, all is not lost. Teachers and students may see the productions as laboratories for applying what the students have learned, but the performance season can also suggest the techniques that need to be taught in class in order to successfully realize those shows. Robert Benedetti asks the teacher to notice the disconnect in the student's mind between class learning and work on a production:

> "They could do it in class, why didn't they do it on stage?" we ask, and the answer may be that they did not really learn it in the class because they did not feel the absolute necessity to learn; production provides that necessity.[45]

If classwork can be tied to production work, when the teacher is also the play's director, or if the faculty work together on the skill sets the actor needs to play the role in which they have been cast, a symbiotic relationship is created which benefits all concerned. This means that the acting and directing faculty also work together on a curriculum and are aware of the material that is being taught in those classes.

Exposing the Personal

The actor can be asked to consider the moments in their lives that might relate to the moments in the scene, but these thoughts don't have to be shared with the teacher or the class. It is not the teacher's business to prod the actor to confess where the behavior or feelings come from. They can remind the actor to consider what worked about it and to ask if they can reproduce it in the future. As long as the actor effectively puts the experience into their own body, the rest is none of the class's business. The coach shouldn't rush the actor to deeply express themselves, but early on may simply point out what emotional behavior might be needed for the scene. Regardless, some students may feel, for whatever reason, that they reveal too much of themselves. This is because the nature of an acting class, as opposed to the rehearsal room or the public performance, can be more intimate. A cohort of actors who take many classes together may know each other well enough that they compare the character's behavior to the actor's own.

The student observers may not realize when an actor is able to give in to the character's feelings and actions completely. When they fail to recognize the difference, they may judge the actor rather than the character. The actor too may be afraid that what they do will be mistaken for a truth about themselves. On the other hand, during a stage performance, the actor is protected by the fact that the audience is concentrating on the story, and what the character, not the actor, goes through. In this situation, within the persona of the character, the actor can feel more free to reveal parts of themselves. One method, championed by Stanislavsky and given primacy by Lee Strasberg at the Actor's Studio, goes deeply into the performer's past. It is one way of working that has its benefits as well as its limitations.

Affective Memory

Affective Memory is a powerful tool still used by actors or teachers who have a background in the Method. Lee Strasberg felt it was an essential part of the actor's process and the primary means for living a role. It was Stanislavsky who learned of the idea in the works of Théodule-Armand Ribot, a French psychologist. Ribot believed people have "a capacity for storing and recalling 'affective impressions' that works alongside our other forms of memory."[46] These impressions come from memories of the five senses that are attached to "our pleasant or painful states,'"[47] and may be "revived in two ways – by provocation, or spontaneously."[48] In the latter case, one memory may remind us of another. In the former case, the provocation is provided by the coach, who asks the actor to review a moment in their lives, recalling every sensory impression connected to that moment, until the actor finds the strongest impression – i.e., the one that brings the feelings of that moment back – and uses it as a trigger for recalling the emotion in performance.[49]

William Esper's insistence on imagination as being the ideal way to tap into feelings is based on his rejection of Affective Memory.[50] This type of work requires the actor to recall their own feelings and use them as a means of replicating the emotions required of the part. Instead, Esper substitutes the actors' daydreams: "Affective Memory has a number of cards stacked against it. First it isn't something that human beings do naturally, whereas most actors have been daydreaming all their lives."[51]

Affective Memory is limited by the actor's own experience. In the first place, the actors may not have encountered those particular feelings in their own lives yet, and second, feelings they have towards others change over time, so that these changing memories may no longer be effective; the actor no longer relates to those particular incidents in the same way. As a teenager, the actor may be devastated by how they are treated by a peer, whereas years later, from an adult perspective, they don't find this moment important at all. Esper also believes that Affective Memory leads to further introversion by many actors who are already introverted. Finally, Stanislavsky, who first used Affective Memory, abandoned the practice later in his own work.[52]

Everyone Is Welcome: Ensemble Building

All should feel that they belong in the room and are equally valued, an idea that the teacher should project, but also encourage the class to embrace. The bonding that actors can have in a theatrical enterprise can be very strong in a very short amount of time. This kind of bonding can first take place in the classroom, where a group of supportive people work on a mutually agreed task: the improvement of their minds, bodies, and artistic souls.

The Importance of Observation and Experience

The actor grows in experience as he encounters the vagaries of life and draws lessons from them. Until these things actually happen to the actor, some behaviors in a play will not make sense: the death of loved ones, good and bad relationships, the ups and downs of adulting, marriage, and committed relationships.

In the meantime, the actor supplements their experience through observation: one of the most important tools in the actor's arsenal. The everyday world offers a myriad of behaviors to add to the actor's library – specific and truthful examples that the actor may store away for future use in character work. These differentiate the character they are playing from other human beings and bring a spark of recognition to the audience member who recognizes the behavior. For example, if a character absentmindedly rubs the area above their upper lip, the audience member who has shaved off a moustache recognizes how, for a time, they missed their facial hair and continued to stroke the area in remembrance of the missing whiskers. Or an actor has a ritual such as shaking out a napkin before placing it in the lap, or an actor ties their shoelaces in a particular manner, including the many ways the shoes can be laced.[53] In each case, acting in general ignores the many possibilities to further reveal the character.

Ultimate Aims

The study of acting leads to a deeper understanding of the human condition and of the self, sympathy and empathy for other human beings, better communication skills, teamwork, socialization, and collaboration. All are achievable goals in a scene study course. What isn't guaranteed is that a trained actor will be successful in the professional world. Though the master's program in acting at Yale was considered one of the best in the nation, the head of the program, Ron Van Lieu, whose former students often went on to successful careers, did not consider this his primary aim. His feeling was that, given a sense of craft, his students might enter the profession with a mindset of acting as an art and with a series of useful skills: "You are either a school that targets what is marketable or one that tries to teach them to be effective craftspeople in the art of acting, and the industry will deal with them."[54] This means that the teacher's measure of success can be an actor's step-by-step process of accomplishing specific goals that aid in their development. The measure is not, "I nailed that scene and now can play it anywhere, including professionally."

The Ego Versus Confidence

By ego is meant the exaggerated sense of one's talent or skill. Students will sometimes confuse ego with being confident: they conceitedly overestimate their abilities and miss the lessons that might help them to become better artists. They can begin to see theatre as a means of showcasing their talent rather than as an artistic endeavor designed to reveal the audience to itself. When Charles Laughton was asked why he acted, he replied, "People don't know what they are like, and I think I can show them."[55] Konstantin Stanislavsky encouraged his actors to see their work as part of a bigger mission, the creation of art works that ennoble the human spirit. He made it a tenet of his work that, "We must love the art in ourselves, not ourselves in art."[56] Laurence Olivier found ego to be useful when daring to perform great roles but did not take for granted that he was fortunate to be acting them: "I think the most difficult equation to solve is the union of the two things that are absolutely necessary to the actor. One is confidence, absolute confidence, and the other an equal amount of humility towards the work."[57] Finally, Sam Mendes, director of many actors in film and theatre, noted: "Confidence is essential, but ego is not."[58]

To be overconfident is to feel that there is nothing left to learn. Unfortunately, this can happen with the youngest or most untrained of students. They believe that their natural ability compensates for their brief time as actors. There are very few geniuses in the theatre, and those who are asked about their methods, work from instinct, and are unable or unwilling to explain how they arrive at their performances. The student, no matter how talented, is usually not a genius. As Stanislavsky noted: "A genius is a rare occurrence, and it is much better to tell yourself, once and for all, that acting is difficult, and what is difficult can only be overcome by persistence and application."[59] What fools many observers into thinking that they can act is the way that an actor's abilities make the work seem effortless, although there is often much preparation and years of dedicated training behind it. "Unfortunately, there are few who understand this, because acting seems so simple and easy from the outside. And the more accomplished an actor's work is the simpler and easier it appears."[60] No one would think of picking up a violin and beginning to play without any training or practice. Not so with acting.

Finally, the philosophy here is to think of the class sessions as workshops for the scene. Particular skills may be emphasized, goals created for the actors in advance, specific techniques for conditioning forces or constraints may be practiced, the text may be explored for its usefulness as a spur to inspiration, and the creative state encouraged.

With an initial sketch of philosophical matters, it is all the more important to consider the challenges to come, possible minefields that may appear with acting students in higher education, including oft-repeated practices that may have outlived their usefulness. The next chapter will propose failure as an important tool for learning, a warning about certain attitudes towards teaching, the students' previous experiences as an invisible factor in future learning, and a brief discussion of the changing nature of students we encounter in contemporary institutions of higher learning. These matters, and possible alternatives, solutions, and suggestions, will be further scrutinized in subsequent chapters using a pedagogical mindset to bolster my arguments.

Notes

1 The Teacher Development Program, under the auspices of the Actors Center in New York, was created for this purpose: as a means of training professional actors for the teaching field.
2 Wallace Smith, "Theatre in Secondary Schools," in *Master Teachers of Theatre: Observations on Teaching Theatre by Nine American Masters*, ed. Burnet M. Hobgood (Carbondale: Southern Illinois University Press, 1988), 181.
3 Olympia Dukakis, quoted in Ellen Orenstein, "Shaping the Independent Actor," *American Theatre*, January 1, 2008, https://www.americantheatre.org/2008/01/01/shaping-the-independent-actor/
4 For example, see Chapter 12, "Exercises, Etudes, and Games."
5 A major exception to this idea is the need to demonstrate or model physical movement to the students for emulation; words won't do there.
6 Hobgood, *Master Teachers of Theatre*, 174.
7 Hobgood, *Master Teachers of Theatre*, 174. In Texas, the University Interscholastic League offers high schools the opportunity to receive points for all extracurricular activities: including the one-act play. As many as 1700 high schools in Texas participate in these contests, and the degree to which those teachers have been trained varies widely. In that circumstance, students have come to my college classes who had a range of experiences, including being directed to imitate their teachers through line readings and prescribed movements. These same students would begin to direct each other, because they had been allowed to do so in public school. At that level, the line can be blurred between directing and coaching.
8 Lloyd Richards, *Working in the Theatre* #125 Playscript/Director, City University of New York: The American Theatre Wing Seminars, 1987, https://www.youtube.com/watch?v=WSv-AXg9D0Q
9 Richards, *Working in the Theatre* #125.

10 A. Dean Irby, quoted in Carla Claudine Francis, "Preparing Birds to Fly: Lloyd Richards and the Actor" (dissertation, University of Missouri, Columbia, 2013), 166.
11 Toporkov, *Stanislavski in Rehearsal*, 71.
12 Toporkov, *Stanislavski in Rehearsal*, 71.
13 Toporkov, *Stanislavski in Rehearsal*, 71.
14 Toporkov, *Stanislavski in Rehearsal*, 71.
15 Toporkov, *Stanislavski in Rehearsal*, 71.
16 cfrancis blackchild, "Lloyd Richards in the Classroom," in *The Great American Stage Directors, Vol. 3, Kazan, Robbins, Richards*, ed. Harvey Young (London: Bloomsbury Methuen Drama, 2021), 117.
17 Ron Van Lieu, Teacher Development Program Notes, June 2012.
18 At any age, the student may question the teacher's authority, feeling that they have nothing new to learn. See Chapter 3, "Considerations," under "Challenges for Acting Class." This can also be a healthy practice, and one the teacher can encourage rather than take personally as a questioning of their authority. See Conrad Cohen, "A Jewish Journey: Stanislavsky's System; to the American Method," in Scott and Skelton, eds., *Stanislavsky and Race*, 106. Cohen points out the efficacy of dialogic teaching as a means of Jewish learning.
19 Ken Bain, *What the Best College Teachers Do* (Cambridge, MA: Harvard University Press, 2004), 26.
20 Bain, *What the Best College Teachers Do*, 26.
21 Susan A. Ambrose, Michael W. Bridges, Michele DiPietro, Marsha C. Lovett, and Marie K. Norman, *How Learning Works: Seven Research-Based Principles for Smart Teaching* (San Francisco: John Wiley & Sons, 2010), 78.
22 Bain, *What the Best College Teachers Do*, 28.
23 Bain, *What the Best College Teachers Do*, 28.
24 See Chapter 2, "The Craving Brain: How to Create New Habits," in Charles Duhigg, *The Power of Habit: Why We Do What We Do in Life and Business* (New York: Random House, 2013), 31–58.
25 See, for example, Tim Elmore and Andrew McPeak, *Generation Z Unfiltered: Facing Nine Hidden Challenges of the Most Anxious Population* (Atlanta, GA: Poetry Gardener Publishing, 2019), that enumerates seven characteristics of this group including: "They are more PRIVATE," "They are more ANXIOUS," "They are more RESTLESS," "They are more TECH SAVVY," "They are more NURTURED," "They are more ENTREPRENEURAL," and "They are more REDEMPTIVE." See pages 43–48. Emphasis Elmore's and McPeak's.
26 See the section "Being an Advocate for the Character" in Chapter 10.
27 See the discussion on Presentism in Chapter 5.
28 Van Lieu from Teacher Development Program Notes, June 2013.
29 Les Chantery, *Life in a Mid-Shot: A Premier Acting Coach's Tools for Auditions and Self-Tapes* (Australia: Les Chantery Studio Pty Ltd., 2022), 113.
30 Chantery, *Life in a Mid-Shot*, 113.
31 Chantery, *Life in a Mid-Shot*, 117. Emphasis Chantery.
32 Michelle Shay quoted in Everett C. Dixon, "Lloyd Richards in Rehearsal" (dissertation, York University, Toronto, ON, 2013), 123.
33 Michelle Shay in Dixon, "Lloyd Richards in Rehearsal," 123.
34 Dixon, "Lloyd Richards in Rehearsal," 121.
35 Mark Harris, *Mike Nichols: A Life* (New York: Penguin Press, 2021), ix.
36 Robert Hethmon, *Strasberg at the Actors Studio: Tape-Recorded Sessions* (New York: The Viking Press, 1965), 80.
37 Van Lieu from Teacher Development Program Notes, June 2013.
38 See the entire list in Keith Johnstone, *Impro for Storytellers* (New York: Routledge, 1999), 343–353 (Appendix One).

39 Johnstone, *Impro for Storytellers*, 347–348.
40 Philip Seymour Hoffman, interviewed in Rosemarie Tichler and Barry Jay Kaplan, *Actors at Work* (New York: Faber and Faber Inc., 2007), 347.
41 Tichler and Kaplan, *Actors at Work*, 347.
42 Tichler and Kaplan, *Actors at Work*, 347.
43 Declan Donnellan, *The Actor and the Target* (St. Paul, MN: Theatre Communications Group, 2002), 37.
44 Robert Benedetti, "On Acting," in *Master Teachers of Theatre: Observations on Teaching Theatre by Nine American Masters*, ed. Burnet M. Hobgood (Carbondale: Southern Illinois University Press, 1988), 100.
45 Benedetti, "On Acting," 101.
46 Isaac Butler, *The Method: How the Twentieth Century Learned to Act* (New York: Bloomsbury Publishing, 2022), 63.
47 Butler, *The Method*, 64.
48 Butler, *The Method*, 64.
49 See a further discussion on Affective Memory in Chapter 8, "Coaching to Inspire Emotions."
50 See the discussion on Affective Memory in Chapter 8.
51 William Esper and Damon DiMarco, *The Actor's Art and Craft: William Esper Teaches the Meisner Technique* (New York: Anchor Books, 2008), 214.
52 Esper and DiMarco, *The Actor's Art and Craft*, 214–215. For a discussion of other methods and approaches, see Chapter 8, "Coaching to Inspire Emotions."
53 To give himself a sense of disorientation when he was playing Vincent Van Gogh in Vincente Minnelli's film *Lust for Life*, Kirk Douglas left his shoes untied.
54 Van Lieu from Teacher Development Program Notes, June 2012.
55 Bertolt Brecht, *Brecht on Performance: Messingkauf and Modelbooks*, eds. Tom Kuhn, Steve Giles, and Marc Silberman (London: Bloomsbury, 2014), 153–154.
56 Toporkov, *Stanislavski in Rehearsal*, 1.
57 John Cottrell, *Laurence Olivier* (Englewood Cliffs, NJ: Prentice-Hall Inc., 1975), 403.
58 Bennett Marcus, "Sam Mendes's 25 Rules for Directors," *Vanity Fair*, March 11, 2014.
59 Toporkov, *Stanislavski in Rehearsal*, 162.
60 Toporkov, *Stanislavski in Rehearsal*, 162.

2 Further Thoughts

Just as teachers acquire a variety of methods for training the actor, their students will come to class from so many different backgrounds that they are rarely in the same frame of mind to receive the teacher's instruction. In the updated edition of *How Learning Works*, the authors ask their audience of teachers to consider who their students are: "Because learning requires integrating new knowledge and skills with one's current worldview, the maturity, identities, and experiences students bring with them into our classroom affect their learning profoundly."[1] In future chapters, techniques will be offered to address some of these issues; for example, if students are given the option to choose their own scenes or guide their teachers towards the types of material they would like to work on. The first days of class are particularly important, as teachers begin to learn how the students would like to be addressed, where they come from, what their interests are, how they feel about performance, and what challenges they may have when revealing themselves through a character onstage or taking on another persona different from their own.

Even from the standpoint of previous stage experience, each student will have spent distinct amounts of time acting in front of others, while the quality of those experiences will also vary. Some student actors have natural talent, some are amateur performers in community theatres or have extensive hands-on experience in local high schools or churches. Some have studied – on their own or in class – various acting methods by such teachers as Uta Hagen. Some have no background in theatre at all but are curious to see where their interest in the art will take them. Others may seek to emulate their favorite stars or have been impressed with the fame and fortune that comes to those rare individuals who are successful on a national or international scale. All of these students will encounter obstacles to their goals and dreams.

Unfortunately, students have not always had productive or even safe experiences in an acting classroom. These students have suffered in the name of "making them stronger," or "breaking them down to build them back up." The guru system – in which the teacher plays head games with the student, denigrating them to begin with so that they make "incredible progress" throughout the semester because of the coach's command of the art – can be attributed to many factors, including the teacher's own experience as a student. This same teacher may withhold information about their own thinking so as to seem omnipotent. However, the teacher as strict taskmaster who believes in being "brutally honest" about the student's work is an old

DOI: 10.4324/9781003498520-3

model that students no longer respond to. If this so-called honesty ignores the students' personal experiences, or serves as an excuse to criticize their physical appearance, or is manifested as an unhealthy interest in the students' personal lives, or entails complete loyalty to the teacher's own classwork at the expense of courses by other faculty, the students may report their instructor to upper administration, accusing the teacher of mental and physical abuse. The old-school, tough-love approach is no longer effective as the students acquire greater agency. This is a healthy development that seeks to correct the power dynamics in the classrooms of the past.

The instructor's insistence on perfectionism and rejection of learning through trial and error can be part of this mindset. Such a teacher will never be satisfied with the students' work and will penalize missteps – rather than celebrate accomplishments – even if in embryo. The student can become discouraged if they feel no progress is being made; even if there are signs of improvement, the teacher may ignore or dismiss them because they are laser-focused on a much larger goal rather than the small steps that slowly but carefully lead to that goal.

In the 21st century in particular, the teacher and coach must be sensitive to student issues that have come to the fore, such as a student's unwillingness to recreate intimate situations with people they have just met; the lack of respect afforded to their cultural backgrounds; an ignorance about their developing identities as the marginalized, who are rejected by a patriarchal system that still gives primacy to the cisgender white male; and unspoken messages that they must conform to societal norms and ideologies they cannot relate to their own struggles. The kinds of behaviors or misunderstandings that have been taken for granted in the past must now be addressed, through training and ongoing dialogue between students and their instructors, as well as instructors and their administrators. This discussion, and the implementation of new strategies of teaching, are long overdue.

The following thoughts are intended to prompt further reflection rather than to offer definitive answers to these complex subjects.

Failure

Perfectionism can be replaced with the principle that failure is a valuable teaching tool. Making mistakes is the best teacher, and the students should be discouraged from thinking they have done something wrong. Instead, by trying various solutions, they slowly eliminate those options that are less successful.[2] As Niels Bohr once remarked, "An expert is someone who has made all possible mistakes in one field and there are no more to make."[3] From the students' mistakes the teacher can begin to diagnose what isn't working and to offer other ideas. Over time, the teacher learns to spot what might be holding the student back or leading them down an unproductive path. With a class that is about process, with an emphasis on the play under consideration, experimentation is encouraged; the classroom is about trial and error, and the problem is how best to serve the playwright, showing a respect for their work and an attention to detail by exploring and realizing the narrative scene by scene with the understanding that there are many possible options for applying craft to the work. This opens up the range of choices the actor has and reminds the actor as student not to settle for the first solution that occurs to them. There are no wrong answers in the mindset of experimentation, just those that better serve the work.

Lloyd Richards had this philosophy: "To me, being wrong, or what one might call 'failure of a moment,' is just the step before growth."[4] The answer to the problem may be just around the corner: "Growth comes one step after failure and understanding the nature of that failure, and out of that you understand the next step you should take."[5]

When an actor forms an opinion about the character, the only failure may be in not doing the extra work to fully realize the role, in particular, reading the full script. For example, as far as the actor understands from their knowledge of a scene, the person they are playing is acting altruistically. However, previous scenes and circumstances may reveal that ulterior motives are in place. Or the actor may have missed the stage direction in an earlier scene that the character was actually wounded in battle. If the current scene happens only a day later, that information – as a given – is now omitted, but would be helpful to explore as a continuing, external obstacle. Finally, the actor may make a snap judgment about a character that keeps them from identifying with the character's behavior or ignoring those positive or negative sides of the character that the author also wants to bring out. In each case, the actor will learn more the longer they live with the script and the role.

The fear of appearing foolish can be diminished by reminding the students that foolishness is a useful state for expanding the range of possible, spontaneous behavior, that is, returning to a state of not knowing, "the fertile void from which all creation springs."[6] The fertile void George Leonard refers to is a state of emptiness that allows room for fresh thoughts to appear. It is a form of nescience that has positive effects on future learning. Leonard points to Abraham Maslow, the famous psychologist, who "discovered a childlike quality (he called it a "second naiveté") in people who have met an unusually high degree of their potential."[7] It is inevitable that, if an actor wants to test the limits of what is possible for a role, they must go too far – i.e., play the fool. The teacher encourages an attitude of support from the class, creating a non-judgment zone where students understand that experimentation means thinking outside the box, promoting ideas that on the surface seem ridiculous – and may even fall flat – but lead to the answers they seek.

From the teacher's point of view, whether the student takes to the training or not may have to do with timing: either the student is ready to take in the information, or it may be some time – even years – before the student realizes the import of what they have been taught. This means that the teacher need not take the student's reluctance personally. All the teacher can hope for is that the actor will commit to the process, with the understanding that each offering may not work for everyone.

Don't Try So Hard

A topic Keith Johnstone found fascinating was how the very nature of the theatre experience as a construct would affect the actor in a negative fashion. He noticed how actors would change when they entered from the wings: "I could see them step into the light like this terrible radiation. Then they came back [offstage] and relaxed."[8] It was if they entered a poisonous landscape that began to sicken them, prompting an unnatural behavior. This was because of their stage fright: "We have to start by talking about fear. People are afraid to perform."[9]

One particular pressure was the need by the actor to try harder and harder to reach perfection, a counterintuitive measure: "When you come to perform the task, if then you are doing your best it puts you in a bad state. You can't be a better performer than you actually are."[10] His answer is surprising: "You should try to be average. If you come out to impress us, you're doing to look like an idiot."[11] The actor second-guesses himself: "You try to think ahead, or you look back, 'Did I do that right?' Then no one can work with you because you are either looking forward or back."[12] It is the same mindset when coming onstage to make the audience laugh: "If you come on to be funny, you have to rely on the audience."[13] Instead, "You should come on to do something, preferably to make a relationship with somebody else."[14]

Trying to be average actually improves a performance: "The fear's not necessary. It wrecks your work. It's connected with wanting to be good. Wanting to be the best. That's stage fright."[15] Johnstone wasn't being perverse; his insistence on this principle was for the actor's benefit: "When I tell you to be average, it's because I want you to be really good."[16] The actor can quickly recognize when they've reached an inner judgmental attitude: "How do you know you're doing your best? You add extra muscle tension."[17] If the student recognizes tension is actually encouraged as a sign of working hard, they use this as a strategy to avoid attention from the difficult teacher: "How do you show your teacher you are doing your best? You look like you're suffering. Then the teacher will go punish another child."[18]

By asking an actor to be "just a bit boring,"[19] Johnstone took the pressure off the actor to deliver a perfect performance. This led to better results. For the perfectionist, if something went wrong, the number of mistakes could spiral out of control. As Stephen McKinley Henderson noted of Lloyd Richards's class: "So it wasn't something that you were trying to get right, it was something you were trying to get true."[20]

Stanislavsky spoke of great effort almost a century ago as a hindrance: "And another thing: the less you try, the better you reach your audience."[21] He explained why the actor tended to force themselves to improve: "What does 'try harder' mean? It means trying to woo the audience, that the audience is the object. That is one of the actor's greatest vices."[22] He was responding to the trend in naturalism that placed a fourth wall between the actor and spectator, drawing the audience in as voyeurs to the stage action: "It is better not to notice the audience than to 'woo' it."[23]

The idea that the actor changes when they step onto the stage has been remarked upon by several theatre artists. According to Johnstone: "Max Reinhardt would audition people in the seats. He'd ask them to go onstage, and he'd keep talking to them. If they changed, he probably wouldn't take them."[24]

Declan Donnellan tells the story of the old actor at the Moscow Art Theatre and his dog: the dog would accompany the actor to rehearsals and sleep through them. "Strangely, every evening, just before the actors were to finish, the dog would already be at the door, leash in mouth, waiting to be taken home."[25] Stanislavsky realized that the dog was responding to the change when the actors "started talking like normal human beings again."[26] The dog was sensitive to the distinct difference between acting and natural behavior – the creative state Stanislavsky sought, in that instance, led to falsity through theatricality.

When the Coach Is Wrong

Failure as a tool for the student is also useful for the teacher. Elia Kazan, in speaking of his directing, wrote: "Those words, 'I was wrong, let's try it another way,' the ability to say them is a lifesaver."[27] The teacher can admit to and even celebrate mistakes on his part because he joins the students on the journey towards better solutions. He can also ask the students to suggest alternatives. The work moves on.

The student recognizes when the teacher doesn't have the answer but staunchly insists on being the person of authority. This destroys the trust the teacher had previously created, contradicting the basic principle of failure as a tool in learning. The student will be more likely to play it safe in the future, since being right seems to be a priority for the teacher.

If the coach offers some advice that actually blocks the actor, confuses them, or leads them in an unproductive direction, the coach should admit it. If the coach starts to say too much about a scene when the actors are anxious to work or because the actors need to discover something for themselves, the teacher should realize this and stop talking – they can even remark, in effect, "Forget what I just said." The teacher should learn to read the actors' responses. The students display physical signs of subtly checking out. The teacher should be aware when giving the actors answers or directing them too much and shut it down. They should also let go of a bad idea.

The Guru and the Abuser

The teacher who refuses to acknowledge their own mistakes is the guru type. A teacher might also be a guru if they keep their methods to themselves. They have all the answers, but they don't share how they arrived at these answers. This allows them to have an authority in the classroom, but the students don't learn how to ask the right questions for themselves.

Jane Tompkins in her essay, "Pedagogy of the Distressed," admitted that at first, she wasn't in the classroom to promote learning but taught as way of "(a) showing the students how smart I was; (b) showing them how knowledgeable I was, and (c) showing them how well prepared I was for class."[28] She compares this to a performance she was putting on, "whose true goal was not to help the students learn but to act in such a way they would have a good opinion of me."[29] She realized that she was driven by the imposter syndrome, the fear of being discovered as a fraud, but this was at the expense of educating and instead modeled "how to cover up and show off."[30]

Everyone has their reasons for being in the classroom: a paycheck and insurance benefits, a chance to remain close to a field they love, the need to work in a social rather than isolated environment, a desire to make a mark on young minds. The downside is a loss of perspective: a sense of what the job really requires and how it can be important to the lives of students and teacher alike.

Teachers who create fear in the room, teach from ego, and encourage competition between their students, also establish a counterproductive, rather than safe and productive, environment in which to work. There is no place in the academy for instructors who teach from a place of humiliation. Though some students respond to this as an attitude they have dealt with in the past – perhaps even at home – this treatment has limited value, especially if the teacher is trying to establish an environment of trust. The actors have enough to be tense about, since performing in front of their peers is one of the hardest things they do. Humiliation as a teaching technique is no more effective in the classroom than in the home. In the classroom, it is terribly invasive and suggests that the teacher doesn't trust the students to reach their own conclusions. It is also psychologically suspect. Terry Schreiber is adamant about this: "Teachers who think that they have to be cruel in order to teach should go into therapy themselves and explore their destructive, sadistic tendencies."[31] Forcing the actor to share their private thoughts, their past failures, or their embarrassing or shameful moments presupposes that the class is being devoted to a therapy session with someone who hasn't trained to be a therapist.

Celebrate Difference

Dealing with the unique person in front of you means eschewing a cookie cutter approach and adapting to the individuality of each actor. Great directors of film and theatre are known for their ability to meet each actor at the actor's own level of experience and background: to reach an understanding of process with them on an individual basis.

The teacher looks for the individual strengths within the student. Mike Nichols felt, "You have to have an instinct that will tells you what will turn each actor on."[32] When encouraging character work involving inner imagery, the director must remember, "The images are different. The things they imagine are different."[33] This means that the teacher seeks to uncover the actor's inner resources, how their unique identities, backgrounds, and beliefs may serve the role: "There is no right way [for an actor]: you pack your own bag."[34] The teacher reaches a level of understanding about the student in order to connect them to the work: "When you understand what is in this particular actor's imagination, then you have to feed into that and call on that."[35]

Beware of Self-Fulfilling Prophecies

The teacher must be constantly alert to the effects they are having on actors. One unintended consequence is the lack of an effect: the teacher wants to believe that their work is showing results when, in fact, they see changes in behavior that aren't actually there because they are looking so hard for them. Their proposals become a self-fulfilling prophecy. They fail to notice what actually happens, rather than what they want to see there. If no results can be observed, the teacher should try something else. One way to identify a directing note is that, when the actor tries the suggestion, it seems imposed by the teacher.[36] It's as if the student were indicating: I was told to do this for effect. The teacher should be willing to own the mistake and let it go. If the teacher continues to work this note, they are ignoring important information helpfully provided by the actor: if they are doing their best to fulfill the teacher's coaching and something isn't working, then the note doesn't work. The actor may also implement the note half-heartedly, instinctively realizing its lack of efficacy.

What to Emphasize

The teacher may feel that they must know and teach much more than is possible in one course. They should remember that they have resources in other colleagues with those specialties and that the students can be referred to these practitioners or take courses that deal in the specifics of those disciplines. The teacher of acting is a specialist in the same way – of acting. No one can cram so many different disciplines together into one class. This can be a relief, since trying to use an all-encompassing approach to performance can lead to a lack of concentration on essentials in the mistaken belief that everything the actor needs to know should be offered in one or two courses, even if – or especially – the teacher is unqualified. At the same time, educators can continue to develop as teaching artists by taking classes and certifying in various disciplines such as the Alexander Technique or the Feldenkrais Method or Fitzmaurice Voice Work, with the understanding that one workshop does not an expert make.

Don't Ignore the Actor's Previous Stage Knowledge

Sometimes actors come to class with previous stage experience and particular techniques they have learned on the job, while other actors in their class may be unfamiliar with it. At the same time, the students may have experiences that lead to unproductive thinking of which the teacher is unaware. In each case, the teacher may or may not discover that this knowledge affects the student's current perspective in class.

The teacher can use a diagnostic to determine a student's previous knowledge, even creating a list of common stage practices, to identify skills and beliefs the students already have, especially those that, in the long run, will prevent them from moving forward with the teacher's own training for them. A diagnostic instrument might include theatre terms, such as "finding your light," "upstaging," "cheating out," or "beats." It might test the student's knowledge of such basics as stage directions. It might ask the student what approach they use for connecting to the emotions of a character. The teacher wants not to reinvent the wheel, but to build on what the students already know and remediate where necessary.

The New Canon

If a student in your course would like to work on material that speaks to them and their own lives, there should be an understanding that the teacher can learn as much

Further Thoughts 33

as the student; an unfamiliar culture and the behavior associated with it is fascinating to explore, and the whole class benefits. In a sense, the teacher returns to the classroom: they become aware of what they don't know and take certain steps to educate themselves on how to proceed. For example, with an August Wilson play, the teacher, as a white cisgender male, may fall into a trap of thinking of the characters as oppressed by society, rather than as people who are doing their best to make their lives productive and joyful despite whatever obstacles are in their way. The former belief operates from a negative rather than a positive mindset, and the teacher mistakenly begins by exploring a defeatist attitude, which they won't necessarily do when dealing with characters they recognize. The principle of being an advocate for the character applies to all characters, familiar or unfamiliar.[37]

At the same time, the teacher can only speak to their own experience, to teach what they know. When working on new material, they are not expected to become experts in every form of theatre. Though the teacher may not have a cultural background in BIPOC plays, they can at least work from a dramaturgical view and do the kind of homework that is required for playwrights with which they are familiar but have no personal experience, like Anton Chekhov or Moliere. Regardless of the material, there are certain facets of the human condition that affect all characters. These are the disappointments, the triumphs, the tragedy, the joy, the difficulties, that each person experiences as they grow and change throughout their lives.

It is important that the diverse student make the decision to work on certain roles, rather than having them imposed by the teacher because of the student's background. The latter suggests to the student that they are being given a role because of their race – as if the teacher is somehow doing them a favor – but are instead making them representatives of an entire group. If the student is asked to play a character out of their range of experience, they may consider this "code switching," a transition from their own culture to a so-called normative culture with "pressures to conform in their speech, attire and behaviors."[38]

Teaching the old canon by the dead European white male may not appeal to the developing student. However, its worth still lies in its existence as a prototype for later plays and playwrights. Stephen McKinley Henderson stresses the value of older texts when he says, "It is only right that we should be versed in the steps that led us to our contemporary theater."[39] This is because, "It's important to see how long we've been trying to have a dialogue about the nature of being human, about how we've been grappling with the same issues as the ancients."[40]

This is a much larger subject than is covered here.[41] Teachers will continue to adjust to the changes in society as they adapt the language of teaching to include the underrepresented majority. Resources are expanding. Innumerable books, workshops, and meetings are being offered as educational aids.[42] Teachers are asked to question their own biases from a non-defensive position, with a willingness to consider alternative perspectives.

These topics are but a few of the many that the teacher may consider. The point here is to think ahead to the kinds of challenges that may arise due to the very nature of an acting class. The teacher should imagine other cases not introduced here as a means of heading off problems before they arise. Just as a law student examines precedents – the cases that have already been argued – to compare them to future legal actions and suits, so the teacher can think back to their own experiences as students, recalling methodologies that worked or didn't work in the classes they attended, or reflect deeply on their successes and failures as teachers of acting.

The next two chapters will concentrate on specific facets to consider when setting up a class and, in particular, how material is chosen for the work at hand. The latter should never involve arbitrary decisions, as the material to be studied affects the entire nature of the process of each session.

Notes

1 Marsha C. Lovett, Michael W. Bridges, Michele DiPietro, Susan A. Ambrose, and Marie K. Norman, *How Learning Works: Eight Research-Based Principles for Smart Teaching* (Hoboken, NJ: John Wiley & Sons Inc., 2023), 2.
2 At the same time, Ron Van Lieu reminds us, ""Right to Fail" doesn't mean you [the student] have the right to be irresponsible or incompetent." Van Lieu from Teacher Development Program Notes, June 2012.
3 Niels Bohr, quoted in Dan Rothstein and Luz Santana, *Make Just One Change: Teach Students to Ask Their Own Questions* (Cambridge, MA: Harvard Education Press, 2011), 15.
4 Richards, *Working in the Theatre* #125.
5 Richards, *Working in the Theatre* #125.
6 George Leonard, *Mastery: The Keys to Success and Long-Term Fulfillment* (New York: Plume, 1992), 171.
7 Leonard, *Mastery*, 174.
8 Keith Johnstone, author's notes from "Ten Days with Keith," a Keith Johnstone workshop in Calvary, July 17, 2017.
9 Johnstone, "Ten Days with Keith," July 17, 2017.
10 Johnstone, "Ten Days with Keith," July 17, 2017.
11 Johnstone, "Ten Days with Keith," July 17, 2017.
12 Johnstone, "Ten Days with Keith," July 17, 2017.
13 Johnstone, "Ten Days with Keith," July 17, 2017.
14 Johnstone, "Ten Days with Keith," July 17, 2017.
15 Johnstone, "Ten Days with Keith," July 17, 2017.
16 Johnstone, "Ten Days with Keith," July 17, 2017.
17 Johnstone, "Ten Days with Keith," July 17, 2017.
18 Johnstone, "Ten Days with Keith," July 17, 2017.
19 Johnstone, "Ten Days with Keith," July 17, 2017.
20 Stephen Henderson quoting an adage of Lloyd Richards in Francis, "Preparing Birds to Fly," 118.
21 Toporkov, *Stanislavski in Rehearsal*, 147.
22 Toporkov, *Stanislavski in Rehearsal*, 147.
23 Toporkov, *Stanislavski in Rehearsal*, 147.
24 Johnstone, "Ten Days with Keith," July 17, 2017.
25 Declan Donnellan, Introduction to Konstantin Stanislavski, *An Actor's Work*, trans. Jean Benedetti (London: Routledge, 2008), ix.
26 Donnella, *An Actor's Work*, ix.
27 Elia Kazan, *Kazan on Directing* (New York: Vintage Books, 2009), 246.
28 Jane Tompkins, "Pedagogy of the Distressed," quoted in Parker J. Palmer, *The Courage to Teach: Exploring the Inner Landscape of a Teacher's Life*, 20th Anniversary Edition (San Francisco: John Wiley & Sons Inc., 2017), 28–29.
29 Palmer, *The Courage to Teach*, 29.
30 Palmer, *The Courage to Teach*, 29.

31 Terry Schreiber, *Acting: Advanced Techniques for the Actor, Director, and Teacher* (New York: Allworth Press, 2005), 36.
32 Mike Nichols interview on *The Charlie Rose Show*, August 7, 1992. For a discussion on imagery see, for example, the discussion on Stanislavsky's Method of Physical Actions in Chapter 8.
33 Nichols, interview on *The Charlie Rose Show*, August 7, 1992.
34 Nichols on *The Charlie Rose Show*, August 7, 1992.
35 Nichols on *The Charlie Rose Show*, August 7, 1992.
36 See the discussion on coaching versus directing in Chapter 1.
37 See the discussion Being an Advocate for the Character in Chapter 10.
38 Lovett et al., *How Learning Works*, 16.
39 Stephen McKinley Henderson, quoted in Ronald Rand and Luigi Scorcia, *Acting Teachers of America: A Vital Tradition* (New York: Allworth Press, 2007), 183.
40 Henderson, *Acting Teachers of America*, 183.
41 A list of references will be included in the Bibliography. See also Appendix 1, "Diverse Classroom Plan."
42 For further books on the topic, see the Bibliography.

3 Considerations

The instructor has considered a philosophy, a credo, that guides the work. The next step is to make decisions about how to set up the classroom, what to teach and in what proportions, what kind of material to select or approve for the growth of each actor,[1] and how many exercises to include; but also whether to introduce or review foundational aspects of the craft, and what kind of training to omit completely.

The instructor may not have control over factors such as the makeup of the class: students' backgrounds, their motivations for taking the course, their likes and dislikes, their familiarity with dramatic literature, or their priorities; the nature of the classroom, such as its size, acoustics, its proximity to other classrooms, whether it has a sprung or tiled floor, a stage, mirrors, the amount of light and what kind; the length of each class period; the previous experience of each student – what can be built upon and what has to be unlearned; the male-identifying to female-identifying ratio; and the students' initial goals, which may run counter to the instructor's own.

What the instructor can take responsibility for includes the class groundplan – where the actors will work, where the coach and student audience will observe each session; the instructor's overall methodology; the scope and sequence of the course – the range of skills and the order in which they are studied; where and whether remediation will occur, such as the addition of etudes or exercises that address specific problems that arise;[2] classroom rules, including the use of electronic devices and theatre etiquette; the pace of instruction; the use or absence of warmups; the insistence on standards; the resources available to the actors; and how to engage students who will monitor the process while their classmates are rehearsing.

Setting Up the Environment

Where the instructor will position themselves in the room is based on a number of factors. Will she stay in one place throughout the session, quietly making note of student progress; approach the actors for side-coaching or private suggestions; vary locations, moving easily through the space as necessary to point out particular details for both performers and observers; or model process by calling out questions from the audience space for the benefit of the entire group? Will he sit behind the students, so that he can monitor the behaviors of the student observers, or sit in front,

DOI: 10.4324/9781003498520-4

creating a more intimate connection to the performers? This is partly based on the personality of the teacher as well as the teacher's goals during a particular session. The teacher may be more comfortable with the separation from the actors created by his position in the audience. The teacher may find sitting in the front row of the audience allows her to concentrate without the distraction of the students around her. The teacher may be worried about their students checking out and ignoring their peers, doing homework for other classes, or talking off topic, rather than serving as a supportive audience who are also learning by watching.[3]

As to the students' workspace: will the area for rehearsal always be the same, or can it vary? Does the space contain a stage? Audience seating? How will the other students be placed? Will the observers sit in rows facing the actors, delineating a performing space? Will some other configuration be used? Can this vary according to the work on a particular day? Do the students have the option of using different spatial arrangements based on the nature of the scene work?

Resources

The teacher may provide students with supplemental reading lists for further information about acting, theatre history, and self-improvement. Students should have access to set pieces, props, and costumes. When resources are limited, teachers should consider how students can approximate what they need to realize the character and stage the scene. Resources include set pieces, props, costumes or clothing, mats, and other equipment.

Sets

The teacher should think ahead and, before the course begins, ask for necessary furniture, supplying as many of the actual items as possible to be stored in the classroom, such as sofas, a bed, different types of chairs, doorways, flats, platforms, and step units. Francis Hodge, in *Play Directing: Analysis, Communication, and Style*, offers a list for use by his directing students.[4] These can easily be shared with the acting classes.

Props

Teachers should do their best to provide specific props that aid the actors in recreating life onstage or find suitable substitutes. The students can be asked to bring props from home. The teacher can talk with the prop or scene shop and ask for certain items.

Can the teacher discourage the use of miming, or will this be a way of training the imagination? In terms of both sets and props, the principle here is that, though mime is a useful skill for the actor to have, it is not the primary focus of the class. By providing tangible, physical items, the teacher removes another challenge to the actor during scene work.

Clothes and Costumes

If necessary, the students can bring their own clothing, but they should not have to incur further personal expenses. They are encouraged to dress formally or informally within their means depending on the role's requirements. If the students will be participating in physical and vocal exercises, they should expect to bring clothes they can work in.

If the teacher has a good rapport with the costume shop and costumes are available for scene work, they should apprise the costume shop supervisor in advance of their clothing needs. The shop may be able to provide character shoes, skirts, coats or jackets, and sometimes even period pieces for styles classes, such as ruffs, doublets, top hats, tunics, capes, or cloaks.

If the budget is limited, the students should try to approximate the silhouette of the character and the way in which the clothes constrain or release the body. The distinction between their formal and informal attire can create a new attitude or deportment. As costumes can be important tools for creating character, Elia Kazan asks directors to pay close attention to what makes a person's wardrobe unique: "The best way to study this again is to notice how people dress as an expression of what they wish to gain from any occasion, what their intention is."[5] Models are readily available that reveal how mood affects a character's choices: "Study your husband, study your wife, how their attire is an expression of each day's mood and hope, their good days, their days of low confidence, their time of stress and how it shows in clothing."[6] Sometimes it is enough for the character to be "buttoned up" or restricted by what they are wearing. Having the right shoes makes a huge difference.

Mats and Other Materials for Safety

If the class involves tumbling, stage combat training such as falls, lying on the floor for breathing exercises, and other such practices, the teacher should do their best to create an environment conducive to the health and safety of the actors, purchasing or borrowing materials that provide softer surfaces than are to be found in classrooms with linoleum or wood floors. Depending on the training, the students may also need to purchase or be provided with items such as yoga mats, bolsters or blocks, stage-worthy weapons, rope, foam balls, balloons, and neutral or character masks. Having a place to store all items helps to declutter the space and allows for ready access.

Ritual

The teacher should consider how the environment of the classroom mentally prepares the students for work. Establishing a routine for concentrating the actors avoids the time wasted on watching as they release their various tensions and feelings brought from outside, either earlier in the day or just before the class begins.[7] The primary purpose here is to cleanse the mind of outside interferences and to concentrate on the work at hand. The students should not only warm up their bodies and voices, but put their minds in the proper space to receive from the teacher and from each other, letting go of the outside world and entering a world of the artistic self.

Daily check-ins allow the students to share how they are feeling that day. The students have the opportunity to elaborate or not, or even to pass on this opportunity. In this way, the teacher knows how to approach each individual during the class period, showing care for how the actor's previous circumstances may be operating during the work.

Hugh O'Gorman, co-executive director of the National Alliance of Acting Teachers, establishes a "space between," which he refers to as "a creative mystery and the direct result of disciplined, rigorous practice of a repeated technique over time."[8] Like a martial arts student who steps onto a map, the student follows a pattern when entering the classroom, crossing a permeable barrier between the outside world and a space in which artists can create. O'Gorman calls this "crossing the threshold."[9] He asks the students to imagine that they already possess everything they need to act. They establish an invisible line to cross, becoming that persona who is willing to "show up" ready to work,[10] capable of absorbing and embodying everything the teacher has to offer. Michael Chekhov describes how such a change in atmosphere will "facilitate and speed the absorption of the technique, which in turn will facilitate and speed your professional work."[11] O'Gorman uses mindfulness practices to prevent the mind from interfering, from interrupting the zone of concentration.[12]

Rituals are also helpful in that the students always know what to expect when they arrive. This routine is something they may begin to do on their own without prompting from the teacher. No time is wasted in explanations or focusing attention.

Off-Task Behavior

What rules the teacher will set up to guarantee attention and not distraction – from late students; students off task; outside noises or activities; or unforeseen events, such as fire drills, ongoing health problems, or accidents – will depend on school or departmental policies and on the personality and discrimination of the instructor. With an eye to journaling, the teacher must consider the distractions that electronic devices offer the students. With the introduction of computers and cellphones, off-task behavior has grown exponentially. The teacher may ask students to take notes with paper and pen or pencil – not out of nostalgia, but because it is hard to determine whether the students will confine themselves to that activity rather than communicate with friends or classmates off topic.

Making the space a no-cellphone zone is difficult but may be necessary for full attention by the students, and monitoring their behavior is difficult when the teacher is trying to focus on scene work. On the other hand, the teacher may consider strategies that take advantage of smartphone technology, using apps such as Kahoot and Quizlet.[13] The teacher may want to discourage students from pulling up their scripts on their phones – the text is hard to read, they can lose their places, and it is harder to establish contact between the actors. They have returned to an area of prime attention: the digital screen.

When asking for peer feedback, call on students from various areas of the classroom to maintain on-task behavior. If the use of electronic devices is discouraged during a class session, any sounds from those items should lead to some penalty. For example, an instructor may give students an initial number of extra points at the beginning of the course and subtract points from a student for each infraction. The teacher should remind the students to respect the delicate work being attempted and how easily it can be disrupted.

If a student becomes ill, has an accident, or suddenly feels unsafe in the classroom, the instructor must act immediately. At that point, the lesson must be put on hold until the problem is solved. However, the teacher should have a plan in place to bring students' attention back to the work at hand. It may be that a quiet discussion about what has been accomplished so far will be useful or, if the event has a profound effect on the students – consider the news of 9/11 – the class can be suspended for the day. The best-laid plans can be suspended for the mental and physical health of the students. The "show must go on" mentality need not apply here.

Initial Diagnoses

The teacher can create a survey, asking questions about previous learning, student expectations for the course, their definition of successful performances, acting teachers they felt were most effective in the past and why, how they approach a part, what they feel is the most difficult facet of acting a role, how they go about engendering the emotions of the character. The teacher can create and distribute a questionnaire asking each student what they would like to work on in themselves and why, what they have identified as personal challenges, or what is missing from their training. The teacher can meet with other faculty to discuss mutual students they have taught and/or directed.

Performances

The teacher can ask for an initial performance by each student. A prepared monologue or scene may serve as a diagnostic tool. The teacher may ask the students to bring in work early in the semester to gauge where they are in their processes.[14] A number of teachers use the poems from Edgar Lee Masters's *Spoon River Anthology* to introduce the actors to the class but also to determine where they are in their journey as theatre artists. All of the poems are epitaphs for people who have died in the city of Spoon River, Illinois. They are little gems of character. The teacher learns about the student even from the poem each one chooses. Another excellent resource is *Humans of New York: Stories*. As Brandon Stanton photographed hundreds of people on the streets of New York, he began to interview them. Both the book and the website are excellent sources for monologues.[15]

Peer Critiques

Respect for each other is particularly important among the acting students. The actor finds himself in a vulnerable position when working in front of peers. A negative attitude can grow unless it is addressed immediately. The teacher serves as a model for how responses will be offered after work is presented.[16] Impracticable versus constructive feedback has to be identified through teacher examples and non-examples before it appears. For example, a general note based on the quality of the work may encourage the students, but it doesn't speak to specifics. If inappropriate behavior affects others in the class, it must be addressed as soon as possible. If a student creates an unworkable situation for the group, he may be asked to drop the class. If, for some reason, students are late to class, they are not to interrupt the work, but to enter the classroom after the students have presented. The students are excited when they know the answers to the teacher's questions, but if the teacher is only addressing the actors, the observers should refrain from offering their thoughts at that point. Each individual student is being prompted within a scene to consider the types of questions being asked as well as the implications for the scene in those answers.

By stressing theater etiquette, the coach can also encourage certain attitudes towards the work, or a certain decorum in the class – they can share their philosophy of theatre. Surprisingly, if the students respond effusively to each other's work, this might be counterproductive if the feedback is focused on the student rather than the student's efforts. Will the instructor allow applause at the ends of run-throughs? Though the teacher can either encourage or discourage student observers from laughter or applause during or after the session, this is also about philosophical issues. For example, while the teacher may stress the process, encouraging applause suggests that a performance or product is desired. Also, such responses can backfire if every scene doesn't receive the same enthusiastic response or the applause is perfunctory. Such feedback becomes less effective as time passes.

Warmups

The teacher should determine how much time they can devote to warmups. If the class is 50 minutes, 10 minutes of warmups takes up significant time. Warmups may be introduced on a regular basis, especially if the class is 80 minutes or longer, but this is up to the discretion of the teacher and the way in which they establish a creative atmosphere in the classroom. The students enjoy such activities as a way to ease into the work, shaking out the cobwebs and getting the blood and oxygen flowing. Warmups also instill in the students a sense of ensemble. Theatre games are often used for this purpose but can also be used to work on other facets of the acting craft.[17]

Determining the Number of Scenes to Coach

The number of scenes and how often they are rehearsed depends on the number of students in a class, how much time the teacher will use for feedback, and how many times the teacher feels each scene should be worked. Having a large number of students may limit the amount of time the teacher has to explore scenes thoroughly, to reflect on them with the students, and to offer thorough and specific feedback, including questioning to guide the student to look for solutions, or to ask the students about their intended goals. Trying to squeeze too many scenes into the course, the teacher will quickly reach the point of diminishing returns. Though classes often require a minimum number of attendees to "make" – i.e., to justify their inclusion in the semester – if the teacher has any say in it, she can keep that limit at a reasonable number. The instructor can base the ideal number on how many days are available versus how many scenes they want to work on in the course of the semester, and how many sessions they would like to hold for those scenes. Given 16 weeks of class with an average of three hours per week, ten students would be the maximum number in ideal conditions if the instructor wanted to work at least two scenes in three or four sessions each, if each session was the length of a class period.

All scenes should be scheduled in a certain order. If the order is disrupted for any reason, there are alternatives.[18] The length of scenes can vary, but five to seven minutes of material gives the actors much to work on.

Introducing Exercises

The teacher must balance teaching new concepts and exercises with scene work, determining how much to emphasize of each and in what order they should be introduced. What specific tools will they offer? Will they introduce these before, during, or after the coaching sessions? Exercises are introduced at the instructor's discretion based on the need to cover concepts that will advance the scene work sessions. The teacher can begin with exercises that will build on each other and apply directly to the scene work. Or they can leave room in the schedule for exercise days when the work will address different problems the whole class may be having. The teacher will note when more than one student is having trouble. At that point, either re-teaching, remediation, or the introduction of a separate lesson and/or exercise can be used. In particular, the use of exercises will remind the student that the class is process-oriented. What will the instructor teach, and what will they leave out? Play to your expertise. You don't have to teach everything. Remember also that students have other resources, including entire courses for the training of technique, and specific technical skills such as voice and movement. Also, time will tell the teacher how much can be covered within the course; the teacher will get a feel for the pace of the class as they continue to teach it.

Homework

Homework should include other types of reflection and preparation. The students should be reviewing the notes they received in their last session. They should be determining goals for their next session. What do they want to achieve the next time they meet, either in private or classroom rehearsals? They should be working on analyzing their scenes in relation to the whole play. They should be establishing connections to each other and to the given circumstances, work that they can do in advance to bring into the class session. And, of course, they should use time away from class to learn their lines.

Memorization Methods and Deadlines

Students will consider memorization the major homework they have for the scene, so it is important to give them a deadline. To wait until the last rehearsal of the scene is possible, but the second session would be better, when they've had a chance to work on initial events, relationships, actions, or whatever the teacher starts with for familiarization. They will know the entire play at that point, so they will have in mind what given circumstances are operating. The earlier students have scripts out of their hands, the sooner than can pay complete attention to each other and respond to what their partners give them. They cannot read each other if their eyes are glued to the page.

William Esper felt one way to do this was to learn the lines without any particular feelings or intent, to avoid making choices about how the lines should be said. In this way, when the actor was responding naturally to his partner, they would have the lines to use as part of the response.

Even then, as a counterargument, Stanislavsky "was terrified of letting an actor say the lines too soon. The danger, for him, was that the lines lay in 'the muscles of the tongue.'"[19] This resulted in flat, empty readings. He felt his actors would tend to retain those readings, making it difficult to adjust according to the given circumstances. Instead, by letting the work guide the understanding of the text, "the lines would always be living, organic, clear," because they were based on "genuine intentions, needs, clear inner images, clear thoughts, out of which a character can be created."[20]

William B. Davis takes the approach of studying what the lines are for: "Why do you say what you say, exactly what you say, at the exact moment that you say it? If you know the answer to this question, you will know the line."[21]

Engaging the Observers in the Work[22]

Without specific activities or objectives, observers may tune out when they are not the actors in the current session. The teacher models the attitude that all sessions are useful to the student actors, including the observers. By giving them particular foci, the teacher can lead them towards self-critique as well. The work consists of problem-solving, and even the final session of each scene is process. The students should be working on particular principles that have been introduced by the instructor. Here are some possible activities for the observers during an acting session:

Journal Entries

Students are asked to keep class journals making daily entries on the course work. At the end of each class period, the performers can answer such prompts as: name three strategies the teacher used to coach the scene; how the scene changed from the beginning to the end of class; what goals the teacher had; what goals the student participants had; what the primary focus was for today. The teacher can also assign student observers to each actor to follow the process of the session and then give feedback that the students can include in their notebooks.

Play Reading

The students can all be assigned the same play to work on together so that everyone will be literally on the same page with certain parameters: the play should have scenes that vary according to the number of actors and the proportion of male-identifying and female-identifying persons; the play should contain enough scenes that each group of students can do a unique scene if possible. The actors can be asked to pick a character that they'd like to play; they are then motivated by their own interest. The scenes should be within the students' abilities to perform. Some plays that have been used in this way are *Ah, Wilderness* by Eugene O'Neill, *The Dining Room* by A. R. Gurney, and *Pipeline* by Dominique Morisseau.

Summaries

Before the session begins, have the participants describe the context of the scene to the rest of the class, including the previous circumstances. The director can supplement with any missing but necessary information.

Audience Analyses

Have the observers ask analysis questions of the participating students, including given circumstances. Once the students know the type of work the instructor is doing and begin to analyze themselves, ask them to refer to their learning when giving critiques to their peers. Each day, call on random students who have been watching so that everyone knows they need to be prepared to answer. Make students part of the scene, for example, as commentators for or against each character, as the chorus in Greek scenes, as extras, or as parts of etudes.[23]

A Safe Space

A primary purpose of a diagnostic might be to create an environment that is comfortable for the actors, a place where they can count on the support of those in the space when they are in a vulnerable state. Terry Schreiber feels that this is key to creating a safe environment: "The best way to keep the atmosphere safe for the actors is to first have a general awareness of each actor's past and sensitivities."[24] Schreiber does this through separate meetings with each actor outside of class. "Ask that she privately tell you if she has any issues or fears that should be known beforehand."[25] If the student hasn't shared this information with the teacher, or the student isn't aware of particular trigger points, the teacher must use their intuition and trust their instincts about how the work is going. At the same time, the teacher should not be so intrusive as to serve as a trigger or make the student uncomfortable.

The Pace of the Work

The teacher may have a plan that day but abandon it when a more productive opportunity clearly offers itself. The obstacles that confront college and university professors include the pressure to test everything, to seek fast rewards, to be efficient. Instead, the process needs to be a careful one, without regard to parameters such as the amount of material to be covered or the speed in which it is covered. Students will argue that in the real world, they won't be given such time, with professional rehearsals as short as three to four weeks. But this is all the more reason for working slowly before they are thrown into that environment and mindset. With familiarity, with knowing what tools to apply, the actor will be able to find solutions in less time in other, professional situations. When the teacher is dealing with concepts of identity, with their concurrent habits that do not serve but have been inculcated, they are responding to concepts such as emotional vulnerability – the types of work that are difficult based on the students' previous experience; they are encouraging deep change in the student. This can't be rushed. Some actors will consider the last week leading up to the performance to be the time when they will do their best work. However, the entire process leads to a performance, not saving their best work until the dress rehearsal and suddenly changing gears, as if the performance itself were a separate entity unrelated to the work done in rehearsal.

What to Say When

The teacher may have many suggestions but may overload the student with too many aspects to work on. Scheduling more than one rehearsal to offer help allows the teacher to concentrate on a few valuable proposals at a time. Sometimes the most articulate suggestion can be counterproductive; it may be a fascinating insight and at the same time intellectual in scope. That is, it doesn't inspire the student to change. By the same token, a very simple note can be the key to opening up a performance. Working with the same actors on a regular basis can lead to a shorthand, a tacit understanding of what is wanted. The key is, was it helpful? Knowing a play well – perhaps even having directed it – can enable the coach to let go of his previous decisions about how it would be staged and examine it anew with a fresh group of people, their uniqueness as actors leading to a distinct and surprising interpretation. This can be one of the pleasures of working on some of the same scenes over the years with different groups.

Challenges for Acting Class

The following are some situations that may or may not arise, with a brief discussion on each. It is important that, when challenged, the teacher remains unruffled. Often in areas when a student acts out, it has nothing to do with the class or the instructor. The fact is that coaching during a session will solve many of these challenges.

46   Considerations

1. The actor believes that they "know it all" and won't take your suggestions.
2. The actor seems disconnected or has a belligerent attitude in class.
3. The actors haven't read the play beforehand.
4. The actor has a habit that they can't seem to break.
5. The actors don't like the scene you have picked.
6. The actor objects to the content of the dialogue they have to say (based on religious principles, because it includes profanity, or personal biases, because it proposes political views with which the actor disagrees).
7. An actor doesn't want to touch (kiss, slap, hug, etc.) the other actor.
8. The actors refuse to work with each other.
9. The actor has no goals for the day.
10. The actor hasn't incorporated previous notes.
11. The actors haven't worked on the scene outside of class.
12. The actor doesn't seem to be able to "raise the stakes."
13. The actor can't let go of the feelings that have arisen from the scene.
14. The actor can't personally relate to the situation.
15. The actor is extremely tense (about performing or in general).
16. There are too many actors in my class for the amount of time available to do more than one session for each scene and give feedback.
17. Not all of the actors are on the same skill level.
18. Someone's acting partner doesn't show up for their in-class rehearsal.
19. One of the acting partners doesn't show up for the final presentation.
20. Halfway through rehearsals, one of the actors is injured and/or gets sick and has to drop the class. What can be done with the missing actor's partner?
21. An actor forgets to bring their scene text to class.
22. The actor has an ADA requirement (uses a wheelchair, is sight-impaired, is on the spectrum).
23. The actor loses their voice and/or wants to rest it for an evening show.
24. The actor can't remember lines or the actor ad-libs lines, is not word perfect.

Following are some possible responses to these challenges. More important are each teacher's consideration of these issues before they arise.

1. Young actors who have been the stars of their high school drama departments or of their community theatres may feel that what has worked for them in the past has been successful, so why improve? Acting has come easily to them, so they can take the process for granted and "wing it." However, as actor and teacher Michael Woolson notes, "Always remember that those who argue their limitations get to keep them."[26] The adage "You won't know until you try it" is applicable here. The teacher doesn't have to insist that hers is the only way, but the student won't know whether it is effective unless they give it a chance. It is difficult for actors to let go of methods that make them comfortable, but the teacher should encourage them in the spirit of experimentation to do so.

   One way to get the student to let go of preconceived notions is to put them in a situation where their current thinking won't work – in other words, an "expectation failure."[27] The teacher can also relate their previous knowledge to new learning. The student may be on the right track but lack certain elements of the process that will make their ideas more effective. When a student uses a particular method, Michael Chekhov suggests that the attitude should be, "I should like to see what [this means of working] gives me"[28] rather than that the means will be used to automatically produce something. In other words, "I am the master of the method, it is not the master of me."[29] On the other hand, one must not dismiss the possibility of deep engagement with the student on various issues or that the student has a valid perspective, even if it is not one's own.[30]

2. The recalcitrant or absent actor may be operating from several different outside forces, such as working between classes to afford school, bad dietary choices, lack of sleep, depression, alcohol or drug abuse, complicated home lives, or problems with roommates. Navigating these troubled waters without intruding on their private lives is difficult, but if their behavior is affecting their work or the work of classmates, the in-class behavior must be addressed privately as soon as possible. Some behaviors are against university policy, such as attending a class under the influence, and the repercussions may be out of the teacher's hands.
3. If this is the homework, then the actors can still be asked questions about what is happening in the play and the scene. This will guide them towards the reading the teacher now must insist they do. An official type of homework, with clear instructions, may be assigned and graded.
4. See Chapter 9: Coaching Habits That Don't Serve. An actor hangs onto a habit because it has worked in the past and makes them comfortable. They rely on it. Replace this habit with another that better serves the actor.
5. The teacher avoids this by asking what kind of work the actor would like to do.[31] The teacher can offer more than one scene, or the teacher can find a new scene to do. The key is to find out what the objection is about. You may convince the student the scene is worth doing despite their reservations, but the student should not be pressured. Students are sometimes gun-shy after watching bad versions of great works or failing at scenes that haven't been studied properly in the past.
6. There are two schools of thought: one is that the student may work on a different piece that doesn't offend them; the other is that theatre itself is meant to challenge preconceptions, and working on material with which they disagree is a learning experience. The course may come with a content warning in the syllabus so that expectations are clear, and the student can decide if he wants to withdraw from the class. This is a delicate matter, as the teacher must be sensitive to student concerns of marginalization or trauma triggers.
7. With the exposure to abuses by those in positions of power leading to the institution of Intimacy Choreographers, the teacher must work carefully to make everyone safe and not push the students to do things they have issues with. The teacher is encouraged to learn more about intimacy coaching. It is possible to stage moments that are effective and still allow the students control over the situation, and actors may be allowed some time to privately check in with

each other about areas of the body where they don't mind being touched. The teacher can also choose material for those students that doesn't contain intimate actions, although the student should be aware that these situations will arise in plays and make plans for handling them, making sure not to be pressured into doing things they find triggering or extremely uncomfortable because they are under-rehearsed. At the same time, the students should be enjoined to practice these moments not on their own, but with supervision.

8. If the students are asked in advance for scene suggestions, they will sometimes mention who they would like to work with and who they wouldn't. Sometimes, their reticence to work with someone is that they have done so many scenes with that other student already and would like some variety. On the other hand, they may have a relationship with the scene partner with which the teacher is unaware. It's best to respect their requests without calling attention to them.

9. When teachers make it a routine to ask about students' goals for a scene and insist on actors choosing work that will make the best use of their time in each session, the students tend to police themselves. It is a habit that the teacher can inculcate in the student, and one they can carry with them in the outside world.

10. The teacher should insist that the actors take notes at each session and also have peers take notes. All of these can be collected and, after teacher vetting, sent to the student. The teacher can set aside time at the end of class to re-emphasize particular notes that were pertinent to that day's session.

11. This usually relates to item 9. The outside rehearsals are the appropriate time to reflect on and incorporate notes, and to expand on them. New ideas and new goals should be brought to the class. Again, the teacher should consistently ask for them.

12. Raising the stakes involves a commitment to the character's needs and the importance of succeeding in their goals. Sometimes the character's goals aren't clear, or the actor cannot relate to them. Stressing how important it is for the character to succeed and how terrible it would be if they failed sets the actor on the road towards empathy. Find analogous situations the actor can relate to, or even tell a personal story about yourself if appropriate.

13. Great stock is put in the ability to lose oneself in feelings. Find a ritual for the actors to let go of those feelings. For example, after an exercise, an actor can move to a wall and press against it to release that energy, or can have a discussion that decompresses them. Remind them that their feelings do not define them.

14. The actor may be encouraged to find analogous situations that give them similar feelings and at the proper strength or to imagine themselves in new situations and see what behavior arises. The actor has either observed or experienced many situations, but the imagination is a great aid in this process.

15. Check for tension in the actor's body. The teacher can address it through relaxation techniques. The students are encouraged to concentrate on the character or on the other actor rather than themselves. Giving the character an activity is also useful. If they perform everyday routines that are appropriate under the given circumstances of the scene, this will concentrate their attention on doing.

16. Do larger scenes of four or more characters, but with adequate material to work on for each character. Concentrate on introducing tools that can be applied to one or two scenes.
17. A diagnostic at the beginning of the course will identify some missing education. The lack of skill is most likely to arise as the actors put scenes on their feet. The feedback can be a reminder of work to be done by the experienced actor and new work to undertake as the neophyte.
18. The teacher can still work on the material with one of the partners. The other will receive a lower grade for missing their scheduled rehearsal. Or the teacher can ask another group to work that day and come back to the scheduled scene later. The teacher can also assign monologues to all students so that work can still be done if a partner is missing.
19. If the teacher is limited by the number of students and emphasizes work on one or two scenes, the last scene will take on greater importance for the student. The teacher should offer more than one day for the final session of each scene, even as a summing up of the work, rather than as a performance. If a student is missing one day, they may go another. If the student will not be present for any of those days, the teacher may ask another student to read in for the actor who is present. The peer should be in the session space rather than in the audience.
20. If the teacher knows further in advance about an absence – due to an illness or family emergency – the teacher can offer the remaining actor the choice of working on a monologue for their final presentation or offer extra credit to another student to partner with them in whatever capacity is possible.
21. Have extra copies of the scene for yourself, but do not let the actor keep them after the session. Rehearsal points may be subtracted for missing scripts.
22. The teacher should contact the ADA office for instructions and advice and make every effort to accommodate the student.
23. The scene can be substituted for another scene on the schedule or can proceed as planned with accommodation by the teacher as necessary. The silent student can still serve as a reactive target for the other actor.
24. The teacher can either set an early deadline for lines to be memorized or work on the scene moment to moment so that the lines are repeated frequently. Ultimately, this is homework for each student outside the parameters of their off-site rehearsals with their partners. The teacher can also suggest memorizing techniques, such as using the voice memo features on their phones to tape their rehearsals to listen to on their own, or to tape their cues with space for their own lines. Many techniques are available.

It is incumbent on the teaching artist to create a proper environment, one that supports the teacher's vision for a smooth-running and effective class and inspires the students to actively engage with theatrical art. The teacher's philosophy towards teaching, acting, and theatre is instrumental for making decisions about the workspace and the kinds of learning events that will take place there. Having considered the setup for the classroom, the teacher must also decide what types of materials the student will work on, how much leeway will be given to the students to pick scripts and partners, the thinking behind play choices, and the reasons for casting the students in particular roles. These and other topics concerning scene selection will be the subject of the next chapter.

Notes

1 See Chapter 4.
2 See Chapter 12.
3 See later in this chapter for a discussion about how to involve the student audience in the scene work.
4 Francis Hodge, *Play Directing: Analysis, Communication, and Style* (Englewood Cliffs, NJ: Prentice-Hall Inc., 1971), 175.
5 Kazan, *Kazan on Directing*, 240.
6 Kazan, *Kazan on Directing*, 240.
7 This need not be a regimented practice – although there are teachers who have been known to ask a gathering group of younger students to enter single-file.
8 Hugh O'Gorman, *Acting Action: A Primer for Actors* (New York: Rowman & Littlefield, 2021), 3.
9 O'Gorman, Notes from the Continuing Teacher Development Program, June 16, 2021.
10 O'Gorman, Notes from the Continuing Teacher Development Program, June 16, 2021.
11 Michael Chekhov, quoted by Hugh O'Gorman, Continuing Teacher Development Program, June 16, 2021.
12 See exercises in O'Gorman, *Acting Action*, particularly 36–45.
13 Kahoot is an app which can be used to create quizzes, polls, and discussions in game form; students receive instant feedback for their responses. Quizlet is a digital learning tool for creating study materials such as flashcards and games and quizzes. These are but two of the many electronic tools available online or for downloading.
14 See Stanislavski, *An Actor's Work*, for a fictional representation of this approach.
15 Brandon Stanton, *Humans of New York: Stories* (New York: St. Martin's Press, 2015). The website is https://www.humansofnewyork.com/.
16 See Chapter 11 on Feedback and Notes.
17 See Chapter 12.
18 See "Challenges for Acting Class" later in this chapter.
19 Toporkov, *Stanislavski in Rehearsal*, 65.
20 Toporkov, *Stanislavski in Rehearsal*, 65.
21 Davis, *On Acting . . . and Life*, 109.
22 See Chapter 5 for discussions of types of feedback.
23 See Chapter 6.
24 Schreiber, *Acting*, 36.
25 Schreiber, *Acting*, 36.
26 Michael Woolson, *The Work of an Actor: Michael Woolson on Technique* (Hollywood, CA: Drama Publishers, 2010), 8.
27 See the discussion on expectation failure in Chapter 1. This must be very carefully done so as not to embarrass the student but to allow them to embrace or dismiss the ways they are working.
28 Michael Chekhov, *Michael Chekhov's Lessons for Teachers*, Expanded Edition, ed. Jessica Cerullo (Ottawa, Canada: Dovehouse Editions Inc., 2000), 185.
29 Chekhov, *Lessons for Teachers*, 184.
30 That is, it is also important that the teacher not be the "know-it-all."
31 See Chapter 4, "Picking Materials for Scene Study."

4 Picking Materials for Scene Study

Before wading through the bookcase for scenes that students can work on, a number of factors need to be considered. First of all, how will the material for scene study be chosen? It depends upon the credo for your acting class and how much say the students will have in the choice. The scene could be:

1. Based on possible growth for each student.
2. Chosen by the teacher.
3. Chosen by the student.
4. Chosen by the student in consultation with the teacher.
5. One of a group of scenes from one play to be studied by all students (either a play of their choice or the teacher's).
6. Made up of scenes from one author's collected works.
7. From a scene book containing excerpts from plays by various authors.
8. Address a particular challenge that the whole group has as actors.
9. Based on a character the actor has always wanted to play.
10. A pairing of actors who have always wanted to work together.

Advantages to Students Picking Material

Letting the students choose their own material and explaining the reasoning behind their choices gives the coach an idea of how the actors see themselves, what characters they think they can play, their likes and dislikes, the kind of material they fear or that triggers negative responses, whether they are honest with themselves about what they should play, whether they see each other as particular types, what their previous acting experience has been.

Students may read contemporary plays with which the teacher is unfamiliar. The teacher has the opportunity to learn, to examine work that puts its finger on the pulse of the times. The instructor will also have new material to draw from in the future during scene selection, contemporary material that is more familiar or accessible to current students.

If the students choose scenes and use the same material they've studied elsewhere, this can have advantages and disadvantages. An advantage is that the student builds on the work they have already done, continuing to explore the scene in depth. On the other hand, they may be simply recreating a performance and avoiding the hard work necessary to rethink the scene and the role. Encouraging them to use fresh material and having them begin at ground zero gives everyone more to work on. It removes the possibility that the part has been set in other situations – such as in full productions in which they have already appeared, or in scenes they have performed for other classes. In the latter case, the teacher is avoiding making statements and diagnoses about particular scenes that might contradict their colleagues, who have already responded to them in their own way. The student will not draw upon work they have already done on a role, and the teacher will not have to correct what they see as misguided approaches or interpretations by the actor – or imply that other instructors are mistaken.

Students may still be in the process of discovery: their sense of self may be in flux. They may lack perspective as to their current ability to play certain roles. The teacher may be unfamiliar with the play. This means playing catch-up, either before the session or as the session begins.[1]

Students may choose to play roles outside of their perceived range – in different ages or mindsets, with large technical challenges, involving material outside the student's experience.

It is important to encourage growth, but not to the point of discouraging the student if they find the role beyond their capabilities. There is some value in allowing them to work on characters they may not have the opportunity to play elsewhere, at least until some time has passed in their professional careers. That is to say, such roles can help them to develop and grow, but not if they begin to question their own abilities based solely on the difficulty of the material.

Also, if the choices are wide open, the teacher may be dealing with far more challenges than they have time for in the course. For example, heightened-language plays will require further work with the text and its parameters and more time spent on making connections between classic plays and the students' own experience.[2] Beginning with contemporary plays by American writers, where students can deal with realistic issues set in an environment with which they are familiar, allows the teacher to concentrate on fewer, but very specific, tools.

The students may pick sketches or self-contained scenes which are harder both to play and to analyze. The ability to work in depth is limited. Sometimes, the characters behave illogically for the sake of a plot-driven piece that is low on character development. Sketches can be distinguished by the fact that they are idea-driven: the author is motivated by a novel situation and asks, "Wouldn't it be interesting if this happened?" Maybe it would and maybe it wouldn't, but such material often doesn't provide a character arc. If none of the characters in the play change in any way but simply serve as devices to drive the narrative, the actor doesn't learn about not only how to develop a character, but also how an effective play is constructed.

The students may want to use scene books that, although they contain material from well-written plays, present this material in isolation. The students then have a limited idea of the context from which the piece is taken.[3] They may head in unproductive directions without a full idea of the given circumstances, including the character's backstory. They are then operating at a disadvantage, and they don't learn how a thorough study of the text can aid them. Students should be encouraged to read the whole play, and time must be taken to verify they have done so. This is practice for the future – the basic homework an actor will be expected to do in professional situations.

Advantages to the Teacher Picking Material

The teacher can use material with which they are intimately familiar. They may have even made a thorough study of the author's oeuvre and biography and use both as a way of pointing students towards interpretation. In the first case, if the teacher has read all of the author's plays, they may identify recurring themes in the author's work and how these are manifested in the characters and their decision-making. For example, an author may continually return to the same concerns, but explore them in different ways. Tennessee Williams's view of human connection and the possibility of success for his characters is so often pessimistic that tragic circumstances seem to imbue the material. These circumstances are great obstacles for the characters to fight against. In the latter case, the author's life may suggest ways in which they were motivated to write, for example, to redress a wrong they experienced in their own lives, or as a confession or release from their own perceived shortcomings or actions. Tennessee Williams drew heavily from his own life for his work, while the father/son dynamic in Sam Shepard's plays is based on his relationship with his alcoholic and abusive father.[4]

Based on the teacher's knowledge of the student, they can suggest work that will aim students towards particular parts of craft; they can work on the student problems they have identified by having them study certain types of material. For example, a student may have trouble connecting with situations they have not personally experienced. This is an opportunity for them to develop their imagination in order to live in those circumstances. Teachers may have a desire to encourage students to take on particular roles that they could see the student playing. Konstantin Stanislavsky remarked: "Compare each role with the qualities of the actor who will portray it. Your demands on an actor must be guided exclusively by the material in the role."[5] The teacher asks the actor to compare themselves to the character, finding those similarities and differences that further define who the person is: "Develop the inner qualities of the actor necessary for the character and fight all his personal characteristics that are contrary to it."[6] This may require the teacher to offer the students more than one scene to consider. When the teacher chooses material, they will also pair students together or, with an uneven class size, cast them in three-person scenes. The teacher must have multi-person scenes at their fingertips for this purpose, since the class will vary in size.

The teacher must read widely and on a regular basis to update the material from which they choose scenes. When the teacher chooses scenes from an established canon of plays because of their familiarity with them, these scenes may not speak to students today and may even be insensitive to students' backgrounds and experience.

Student Requests

Teachers are not flying blind, because they can also ask the students in advance what they would like to do and what they want to work on. Considerations can include: what excites the student but scares them a bit at the same time; what level of status – in the Johnstone sense – they would like to embody;[7] how they would like to stretch as an actor; what they would like to work on in themselves; and what genre they would like to explore – for example, comedy versus drama. They may also be curious as to how the teacher sees them as actors or what roles the teacher would cast them in.

Students have the option of suggesting specific scenes they would like to do, which the teacher can consider and green-light. Especially when working with students new to the art of acting, the teacher's knowledge of many plays will allow them to more carefully select pieces that accomplish both the teacher's and the students' goals. The students can write a note or email the teacher with their ideas. This is a way to share their thoughts privately, especially in relation to partnering with others or to make the teacher aware of possible triggers in certain types of material. If the teacher asks for student suggestions, concerns, and desires early in the process, the students will have time to reflect on the questions posed by the teacher; they may also add to their initial suggestions with follow-up messages as they develop as actors during the course.

Disadvantages

If the teacher is unfamiliar with the students or their backgrounds, the choice of material is at first partly guesswork. If the teacher is unaware of previous events in the students' lives, they may inadvertently pick material that triggers negative reactions in the student. The material may remind a student of traumatic events they have experienced themselves, or even trigger a student who watches the scene. If the students have not previously indicated any issues, but the choice of materials brings such an issue to the surface, the teacher may offer a new scene to the former and allow the student to step out in the latter. It is also helpful for the teacher and student actors to introduce a scene by telling the class what it contains. This is where using student suggestions to make scene choices is helpful.

Finally, no matter how careful the teacher is in picking exciting and appropriate material for each student, the student may not respond to it. This is another reason to pick more than one scene in cases where the teacher wants to further sound out what is appropriate and will motivate the student. This is more work for the teacher, but it gives students options within the parameters they have requested.

If the students have certain conflicts unrelated to the class, partnering some students together may be a mistake. This is easily solved through soliciting information from the students for casting purposes as part of their private feedback during the selection process. This means not prying into their personal lives, but prompting them to express any reservations about their casting.

Great Moments

What kind of moments can students discover and aim for that embrace the theatricality of the playwright's vision? The teacher asks her students to think of theatrical moments that changed the way they thought about the world and that inspired them to become theatre artists, then helps the students to find the theatrical elements that make up those moments. An exercise in *Moment Work* by Moises Kaufman asks the actors to search their memories for exciting moments they have experienced as audience members. "Say your name and describe a moment of theatre you loved. Proceed around the circle until every person has spoken. Think of the most exciting, moving, breathtaking moment you've seen onstage."[8] The students can narrate any way they wish. The teacher can ask for more specific details afterwards. What was it about the moment that affected the student? How was the moment created? What did the actors do? How did the design elements contribute? How was silence used? Did the moment contain a surprise or use of magic as an element? This sets a bar for impressions the actors can make on their audience in individual moments and help them to construct their own moments in the future.

For example, in the play *War Horse*, based on the novel by Michael Morpurgo, Albert's horse Joey has been commandeered for the war effort. Albert goes looking for Joey on the battlefield, and at one point Albert has been wounded and his eyes are bandaged. Because he can't see, he doesn't realize his beloved horse is a few feet away and about to be executed. As the soldier brings up the pistol to end Joey's life, the audience gasps. But Joey was designed by Handspring Puppet Co., whose members can clearly be seen operating him. The pause before the soldier fires creates suspense. The belief by the actors in the environment, including the manufactured animals, must be strong enough that the audience shares that belief. The puppet is so well manipulated, and the actor playing Albert has made such a strong connection with Joey throughout the play, that the severing of that connection would be painful to both the actor and the observer. Such is the power of the story, and the commitment of everyone on the production to the events, that theatrical means suspend belief, and we are left with the possible death of an animal we care deeply about, a truly great moment.

One Formulation for Choosing Scenes

Ideal scenes for coaching would include:

Cuttings that start as new moments begin
Cuttings that end as a moment ends
Equal opportunities for all actors
Lengths of about five to seven minutes
An attempt by the characters to change each other
A change or turning point in at least one of the characters that affects both of them

Previous circumstances referred to in the scene or elsewhere in the play
High stakes or stakes that grow as the scene progresses
Material the student will be excited to explore or motivated to realize
Interesting relationships between characters
Hidden motives
News that at least one character is hearing for the first time – in a group of two or more
Events that provide work for the actors on character development, acting tools, connection, analysis or any number of agendas of the teacher or students
Memorable epiphanies
Actions that lead to evaluations[9]

Example of Casting

In an advanced class studying the pedagogy of acting, the coach was able to choose an eclectic group of scenes. Each of the actors wanted to move away from typecasting what they had been forced to play in the past.

The actors offered the following feedback on possible casting:

Linda wants to play a male-identifying character in a Shakespeare scene.

Agatha often plays the "funny best friend" and/or in light comedy. She would like to play someone with greater depth. She wants to know how the instructor sees her and in what roles.

Caleb wants to play a light scene that doesn't require deep personal exploration since he has had a number of classroom experiences "baring his soul." At this point he would like to work in a different way.

Iris wants to play someone who has "done bad things for good reasons," not a shallow female role such as a supportive sister.

Jules wants to play something according "to type." He loves the play *Angels in America* and has played Louis in a production of the play.

Bernice wants to play someone other than an old woman, wife, or mother – her standard casting in the last few years. And she doesn't want to play someone in a romantic relationship. She is otherwise open to the teacher's suggestions.

Suzanne usually plays "straight-laced" characters or "goofy sidekicks." She wants to play something different, perhaps more conflicted. She has worked a lot with several members of the class and would like a new partner if possible.

Patrick is open to playing any type of role except for a father type. He has done far too many of these. He wants to play an antagonist. He is open to any genre.

Rachel has been attracted lately to the plays of Ibsen, Chekhov, and Strindberg. She has played many mother types and would like something that takes advantage of her range.

Aretha wants to play an odd character whose choices aren't always obvious. She likes the idea of unpredictability as a character trait.

The following casting decisions were made, based on the actors' suggestions:

Linda and Patrick will do the famous Tent Scene from Shakespeare's *Julius Caesar*, Act Four, Scene 3, with Linda as Brutus and Patrick as Cassius. Patrick has the opportunity to defend himself against accusations of corruption; he has also killed Caesar for personal reasons rather than for the good of the state, and this currently is manifested in anger based on shame for his behavior, especially when Brutus subtly points to his motives; as requested, Linda gets to play a complex and noble character from Shakespeare with an excellent obstacle in the other character. The connection between the two roles is deep: they ultimately rely on each other, as they are bound by the decision to assassinate Caesar and the consequences that come with that action.[10]

Rachel and Iris will do a scene from *Hedda Gabler* by Henrick Ibsen, with Rachel as Hedda and Iris as Thea. Thea has left her husband and hasn't told anyone. Hedda wants to know what Thea's relationship is to her former lover, Krogstad. She uses the strategy of their previous relationship as fellow students to establish a rapport, even though the two were never more than acquaintances. Both have secret agendas.

Caleb and Bernice will do Scene One from *The Trestle at Pope Lick Creek* by Naomi Wallace as Dalton Chance and Pace Creagan, respectively. The play is set in 1936, during the Great Depression. The actors both play much younger than their own ages, Pace being 17 and Dalton 15. Pace is the leader of these two and provokes the younger Dalton to act out. Bernice and Caleb have this relationship in real life and can draw on it. For Caleb, the scene is full of humor. He can delve into the behavior of a younger self without feeling that the teacher will intrude on his private concerns. The deeper tragedy of the play is not apparent in this early scene, nor have their feelings yet deepened for each other, although there should be hints that their relationship has potential for growth.

Aretha and Suzanne will do Act III, Scene 1 from *A Lie of the Mind*, playing Lorraine and Sally, respectively. Sam Shepard writes characters who have their own kind of logic. As Lorraine, Aretha will have to make sense of her attitude towards her children; as Sally, Suzanne will play a character who is conflicted about what she should do in the current situation. Having dealt with her mother for so long, she gives Lorraine a taste of her own medicine. These actors have the maturity to take on these roles.

Jules and Agatha will do Scene 7 from *Angels in America, Part One* by Tony Kushner, with Jules as Prior and Agatha as Harper. Though Agatha is playing someone who is currently off-kilter, her character has depth and isn't a stereotype. Her issues and previous circumstances will be worth exploring. Jules, though he has worked on the play before, has not played Prior and sees this as a natural progression from his earlier work. Prior's backstory infuses the scene with certain feelings and behaviors.

In this particular case, the actors were very happy with their roles. This made working on them a pleasure rather than a chore: the instructor already had created enthusiasm in the students, who were motivated to work hard on the scenes.

The students are encouraged to work outside of class above and beyond the sessions they attend with the teacher. Each session of a scene should show progress, so they have plenty to occupy their time.

58 *Picking Materials for Scene Study*

Rehearsal Rules for Scene Study Students Working Outside of Class

1. Give each other your contact information.
2. Bring a pencil and your script to every rehearsal for noting blocking, business, ideas, concepts, etc.
3. Work on an analysis of the script and then "play" your discoveries at rehearsals to test them.[11]
4. Go over all notes after each in-class session and after each rehearsal so that you will not be going backwards at the next session or going over old ground.
5. Try not to use your rehearsals for line memorization. This will happen naturally within the course of rehearsal, but you should also be working on your lines at home once you have an idea of the character and the character's wants.[12]
6. Since acting is all about choices, use rehearsal to try different choices using the exercises from class. Establishing a connection between your characters by carefully listening to each other is the real work you will do on a play or scene. Bring new ideas to try.
7. Be on time and present for every rehearsal. Your partner relies on you to be there. Show the type of professionalism that will be expected beyond class.
8. Do not direct each other. Your part is your own and belongs to you. Encourage each other, but do not give each other "line readings" or interpretation. This will be resented by the other actor and is not proper theatre etiquette.
9. Spend at least an hour rehearsing for every minute of your script, and twice as much if you can fit it in. That means around 12 hours minimum of rehearsal. This means careful planning to create a workable schedule.
10. As you work, identify props and set pieces that you may have to ask for from the instructor or that you can look for yourselves. Avoid miming objects.
11. Look forward to sharing your outside work with the class.

The students are looking for moments that impress and excite them, serving as models to reach for in their own work. By creating a safe environment that inspires the work; sharing a philosophy of teaching, theatre, and acting; setting the ground rules for the class; and seeking input for student selection of material, the teacher has laid the foundation for a successful course. For students who use written play texts as the material for scene study – as opposed to devising – the next chapter will consider how the plays and scenes may be analyzed to aid the actor in realizing the written word through performance as embodied in characters. Whether the study of the playtext will involve outside preparation, both by the teacher and student, or exercises and discussions within the classroom, thought should be given to how scripts will be analyzed as aids to creative experiencing.

Notes

1 This becomes an advantage for the teacher, who has the opportunity to explore an unfamiliar work.
2 See Chapters 13 and 14 for advice on coaching period styles scenes.

3 Some scene book editors will offer a brief synopsis or other contextual clues as a preface to each scene in the collection.
4 "The adult Shepard's primary goal in life has been to avoid becoming his father," writes John J. Winters in *Sam Shepard: A Life* (Berkley: Counterpoint, 2017), loc. 283, published shortly before the playwright's death.
5 Nikolai M. Gorchakov, *Stanislavsky Directs*, trans. Miriam Goldina (New York: Funk & Wagnalls Company, 1954), 156.
6 Gorchakov, *Stanislavsky Directs*, 156.
7 See the discussion on Keith Johnstone's status in Chapter 10.
8 Moisés Kaufman, and Barbara Pitts McAdams, *Moment Work: Tectonic Theatre Project's Process of Devising Theatre* (New York: Vintage Books, 2018), 35.
9 See the discussion on Evaluations in Chapter 7, "Coaching: Categories."
10 Some directors have identified Act Four, Scene 3 as a kind of love scene. See Greg Doran, *My Shakespeare: A Director's Journey Through the First Folio* (London: Methuen, 2023), 219. I normally reserve classical work for styles classes. As this was a class for teachers, I didn't mind looking at different types of material.
11 See Chapter 5 on script analysis.
12 This depends on the time constraints as well as the teacher's philosophy towards line memorization.

5 Script Analysis

If realizing the text is important to the teacher's process, script analysis – for the student and the teacher – is vital. It's probably the one area requiring more attention than is usually stressed in scene study classes. Both the coach and the student should do prep work before the sessions begin. If the teacher is modeling how the students should study a play, their prep will guide the actors towards close examination of assigned texts – whether for class or for productions.

This does not mean, of course, that just because the teacher understands the script and helps the students to understand it, the scene will be realized. Analysis can become an intellectual exercise, the students falling into the rabbit hole of seeking background information for its own sake; the emphasis on script analysis may keep them there. Consideration needs to be made in terms of what the analysis can inspire, both the kind of tools that can be used for analysis as well as the value it has for encouraging the actor's engagement in mind and body.

Student actors, directors, or coaches can be at an immediate disadvantage if they don't understand the scene on more than a surface level: a poor analysis can lead to a misinterpretation of the events, a lack of depth in terms of the parameters of the role, a misunderstanding of the author's intent, or a failure to discern the effect on the characters of the given circumstances. Finally, the students may fail to realize the impact the scene can make in the playing.

Dramaturgy Workshop

One important goal for the teacher is to encourage lifelong learning in the student. Looking at the dramaturgical elements of the script involves methodical study. It engages critical thinking skills. It reminds the student that the play is a work of art, "a machine, one that manufactures meaning,"[1] with a set of principles that leads to a theatrical experience lived through the actor and shared with the audience. It is an exercise the students and instructor can practice together.

Reading the whole play, not just the scene selected from it, is essential; information such as previous circumstances and character relationships may be missed by studying the scene in isolation. The student should think of this as a standard practice whenever they approach a new role. The play should be read a number of

DOI: 10.4324/9781003498520-6

times, with different agendas each time.² The teacher, too, should read the play again regardless of their familiarity with it. The great plays always offer new information with each reading.

Have the students think of work on a script as solving a puzzle. Not only will they benefit from doing this exercise, but they can have fun in the process. Like the hidden pictures for children, items buried in a mosaic of images, important clues are hiding in plain sight, discovered by a careful focus on the overall piece.

When the British director Katie Mitchell begins to study the script for a new production, she divides her initial discoveries into those irrefutable facts – i.e., specifically mentioned in the play by author or characters, the main or "non-negotiable elements of the text" – and questions about those areas of the text which are unclear.³ She lists the characters' environment and biographies; the immediate previous circumstances – that is, during the last 24 hours before the play starts; the year, season, hour of the action; the intentions – which she calls "the pictures of the future that drive the present action of the characters";⁴ the events; and the relationships that "calibrate" the characters' behavior.⁵ Here, the instructor might seek references to past events, motivations for unexplained behavior, what societal forces are at play, relationships to offstage characters, and the true or false claims made during the course of a narrative,⁶ but these should not be inferred. Mitchell avoids giving inferences the weight of facts. For example, though she reads in Anton Chekhov's *The Seagull* that Arkadina quotes from *Hamlet*, she can't automatically assume the actress has appeared in the play or in the particular character of Gertrude.⁷ A second stage is to imagine the answers to those unresolved questions, including timelines for the lives of each role going as far back as birth. In this way, the entire cast is familiar with the forces at work, the constraints and stimuli of the past and present. If the students are all working on scenes from the same play, this can also be a classroom exercise.⁸

In connecting this analysis to the performance, Ron Van Lieu notes: "The actor is not coming in to show [their written work] but to build within themselves a belief system which is not their own so that they can more definitely inhabit it."⁹ What the playwright has given the actor is a gift to the creative state of believing in the character's circumstances: "You use it as a way to reach yourself, meaning believing that as you step into the shoes of this other person's life you are willing to take on the facts, wants, desires of this person."¹⁰ A deeper connection can be established between actor and character, leading to identification, sympathy, or empathy, while new imagery may arise that places the actor within the play's contexts.

Separating the Plot from the Story

Students may see story and plot as synonyms. In fact, being able to distinguish between them is important for analysis.

Sharon M. Carnicke reminds us, "The story (or 'backstory,' if you prefer the word used in cinema circles) refers broadly to everything that happens and has happened to the characters in their fictional world."¹¹ This includes the events that have led to what we see onstage. The story of Hamlet includes the death of Hamlet's father two months prior to the action of the play; Hamlet's relationship to the king's jester, Yorick, now dead; the marriage of Hamlet's mother to his uncle; Hamlet's studies in Wittenberg.

"By contrast, the plot refers only to what happens in the play itself." For example, *Hamlet* begins not with the murder of the King, but with the guards on patrol, asking a scholar to tell them if they imagine the ghost of Hamlet's father and, more importantly, if he exists, whether he is an evil spirit.[12] It is important to note that the plot is constructed; the author chooses what incidents to include from the story that create "particularly vivid and examinable form[s]."[13] The author may begin in media res, i.e., at the inciting incident upon which everything else depends. The author can also play with time and space, for example, arranging the events in a different order or having the events occur simultaneously, either on different sides of the stage, or in different settings where the events are considered to be happening at the same time but in different geographic locations.

This distinction is important when considering where to put one's focus. On the one hand, the actor may find clues to the current situation in the past, in events that are suggested but do not appear in the play. In that case, the actor is considering the overall story. On the other hand, if the actor is primarily concerned with the people or environments operating on her in the present, she will concentrate on the plot. There is no reason the actor can't do both, but this is one way to separate the search – by breaking it into parts. The facts, in the main, come from the plot, while the questions come from the story. In the same way, an actor will look for the things they say about themselves versus the things that are said about them. The actor must also consider whether the other characters are reliable narrators. If each view is wildly different, the actor has to determine who is telling the truth, if anyone.

Teacher Homework

The teacher must make the time to know the scenes' plays as thoroughly as possible, rather than relying on an initial run-through by the students to bring him up to speed. The following prompts are suggested as an incomplete list for the teacher's script analysis:

1. What kind of preparation do you do in advance? A study of the author's background might involve family life, profession, life experiences, locale, and sociological/political/religious background. All these aspects of the author's world influence the work, a reading of the author's entire oeuvre in a search for recurring themes, concerns, types of character.
2. What don't you understand about the text? What words or phrases are unfamiliar to you or the actors? How are foreign or unfamiliar words, places, and names pronounced? What references are assumed by the author but unknown by you? If a character is singing a song, even in a straight play, can you find the tune? What is the importance of those references? What do they say about the characters? For example, incomplete song lyrics may have a deeper meaning in the context of the entire song.

3. How do you gather information from the text? What are the facts that the text provides? What is the event of the scene? What is the story being told? Why is the scene essential to the story?
4. What are the steps that lead to the event of the scene? How do the characters end up having that experience, and what happens afterwards? Has the author planted foreshadowing, a hint of what is to come? Does the character reminisce about past events elsewhere in the play? Is that narrative clouded by a need by the character to rewrite events?
5. What do you highlight for your work with the actors? What is the news in the scene? How do you divide the scene into units? Where are the beat changes, and how are they embodied? How do the actors work towards emotional connection? Why is each character important to the script? What is their function? Do you use actioning – find the active verbs you believe may be helpful to reaching objectives – even if you, the instructor, keep these ideas to yourself?[14]
6. What discoveries do you make as you read and work on the script? What is different for the characters living in that moment in time? What surprises you – something a character does, or an unusual event?
7. How do you approach the scene in relation to the rest of the play? What do the actors need to know from the rest of the play that will affect their scene? Is there another character – not in the scene or the play – who affects the characters or the action?[15]
8. Why did you pick the scene? What interested you about the material? Why did you feel the material would connect to your actors? After a fresh reading, does your view change?
9. Character work: What are the relationships? What are some ways the author creates character connections? Why are these characters in the play? Who drives the scene? What are the characters really thinking? Who supports whom? What are the characters' attachments? What is each character's status? How does the character change from the beginning of the scene or play to the end?
10. What are the emotional and physical requirements of the scene? What emotional connections are the actors working towards? What special techniques are suggested by the playwright for realizing a character – dialects, styles, conditioning forces such as drunkenness, impairments?

Student Homework

Ideally, the teacher shares their homework with the students, i.e., models the kinds of questions actors should ask themselves when excavating a text. Primarily, the analysis is focused on realizing the scene rather than the whole play, but the teacher encourages the student to take a closer look at events outside the chosen scene. Preliminary work for the scene might include answering Lloyd Richards's six questions about the character: "What experience am I coming from? Where or what experience am I coming to? What have I come here to do? Why? Why now? What do I expect to gain from it?"[16] The following topics can serve as categories for study.

Determining the Events

An avenue worth pursuing before scene work begins is an important question Mike Nichols asked his actors: "What happens?"[17] By this he meant, "Name the moment. This is the moment they fall in love. This is the moment she sees him as a fool for the first time. This is the moment she feels her lowest."[18] What are the moments that take place in the scene, and how do they affect the character? At the same time, what is the major moment or event of the scene, the reason the scene takes place? Who is affected the most by it? If the actor and the coach can agree on these basic premises, they have formed a contract about the journey the character takes and the scene's trajectory. They are working in concert and creating the same events together. In particular, all parties should look for those events that are not named, and then not only the progressive steps within the scene, but also the steps leading towards the scene and away from it.

Character Actions:

1. What actions does your character take to move their life forward?
2. How far is your character willing to go to get what they want? Would they commit crimes or sins to achieve their goals?
3. What are the major obstacles keeping your character from getting what they want? Is one of them a moral compass?
4. How do these obstacles affect the scene, or do more specific obstacles arise as the scene progresses?
5. How does your character justify their actions?

Character History:

1. What history (previous circumstances) does your character carry around with them that affects what they do during the play?
2. What world is your character living in, and how does your character "fit" into that world?
3. What are your character's attachments?[19]
4. What happens before the scene begins that explains the behavior of the characters in the scene?

Relationships:

1. How are the characters in the scene related to each other, and how do they feel about each other?
2. Who is the most important character to you and why?

Given Circumstances for the Scene:

1. Where are you?
2. What time is it?

3. What is the weather like?
4. What day is it?
5. What surrounds you?
6. Are you in a place belonging to you or to someone else? How does this affect how you behave?
7. What has just happened before the scene begins?

Stephen McKinley Henderson, a onetime student of Richards, reiterated this list in an interview, but also Richards's alternative prompts:

> What was just said to you? Where or what experience are you coming from? What caused you to start talking here? And what do you want to change about the other person, the person you are talking to, when this speech is over?[20]

This focused the actor's attention on how they would attempt to affect the other character and when that decision was made.[21]

David Ball uses a similar approach to Nichols, but in reverse. Reading backwards from effect to cause, as in Ball's *Backwards and Forwards*: reveals "the triggers and heaps" of the play.[22]

> If I do anything that leads you to do anything, together we have an action. If I fire a gun at you and you fall over in a dead heap, we have an action. Your first task when reading a play is to find the first action: find each action's first event (its trigger), then its second event (its heap).[23]

What were those actions? The last moment of one play is the death of the lead character. What happened just before that led to the culmination of the character's life? Using the metaphor of dominos, Ball reminds us a trigger doesn't inevitably lead to a particular heap. In order to study the play's sequence, one should go in reverse order starting with the heap and going backwards to the trigger, effect back to cause.

Ball also makes an interesting point about the endings and beginnings of plays: if a play begins in stasis and returns to stasis by the end, according to Ball, "The ending of every play (the moments between climax and final curtain) could be the beginning of a new play," while "the beginning of every play could be the ending of another."[24]

A Study of the Author

This study includes the author's biography, complete works, and the environment in which they lived. This also suggests how important the background of the play is to the current circumstances. The author may never mention the earth-shaking events happening during the writing of the play because they are so much a part of the zeitgeist of the period. Any factor, whether place, period in history, or social mores, may be a given for the playwright but a necessary study for the actor and coach. Identifying varying historical behaviors also avoids the tendency towards what Sam Wineburg refers to as Presentism,[25] the view of the past through a lens of the present.

Larry Moss has the actors seek out the playwright's impetus for writing: "It also means you have to try to understand the ideas that inspired the writer to write the story; the ideas are emotional because they have the writer's passion behind them."[26]

Misunderstanding what the author is giving the actor causes confusion or, worse, a separation from the character or scene. The solution involves taking time to seek the answers, knowing the playwright is not being arbitrary, so the actor will be able to more easily express themselves as the character. At a first rehearsal, perhaps the teacher simply wants to hear the scene and the students' initial choices; in this case, the student can simply say whatever the word or phrase is without worrying at that point what it signifies.

Events

Georgy Aleksandrovich Tovstonogov, who directed and taught at the Bolshoi Dramatic Theatre from 1956 to 1989, used five steps for analyzing plays: (1) the "inciting" incident before the play begins that effects all of the characters; (2) the "fundamental" event that sets off the play's major conflict; (3) the "central" event, or the event which is the play's climax; (4) the "final" event or resolution of the conflict; and (5) the "main" event that explains why the author wrote the play and how the director perceives the author's intent.[27] The inciting event allows the actors to imagine how the characters have arrived at the play's first moments. The fundamental event sets the plot in motion. The central event is what all of the other events are leading to, the apex of the conflict. The final event resolves the conflict one way or another. The main event, what the author was saying about life or society or human behavior, is revealed in the final moments.[28]

An event may be implied but not clearly stated. Without certain information, the persons of the scene seem to act out of character. Their actions are confusing. The audience attempts to discern their mysterious motives. The actors must make decisions based on their extensive knowledge of their roles through their analysis.

Relationships in Essence

Some relationships are not as clear as they seem on the surface. Characters may take on other roles than those implied by a traditional relationship. William Esper gives an excellent example of how labels are not helpful: Torvald and Nora are husband and wife, but the essence of their relationship is of parent and child. Without this dynamic, their behavior doesn't make as much sense, especially at the end of the play when Nora, tired of Torvald's infantilizing of her, leaves him and the children.

Relationships as Related to Previous Circumstances

Relationships may be formed long before the story begins, and these may not be mentioned within the dialogue of the play, since the characters take them for granted. The feelings one character has for another may be ingrained based on interactions over a long period. A close couple may now be estranged. A loving family may now be at odds. A character added to a family unit may unravel the ties among siblings. When Andrei marries Natasha in *The Three Sisters*, she disrupts the household and makes her in-laws miserable.

Antigone contains a dark secret familiar to those who have read another of the Theban plays.[29] In Sophocles's play, Antigone has defied Creon in burying her brother, who is a traitor to the state. Creon is the ruler of Thebes, and Antigone is a subject. Underlying all of this is the family dynamic of Oedipus and Jocasta. Jocasta is both Oedipus's mother and his wife. She is also Creon's sister. The stain of incest affects the whole family, including her brother Creon. When Creon looks at Antigone, she is not just a rebel, but a niece – a product of a son and a mother – who reminds him of the shame of his sister's actions.

Who Is the Protagonist?

Sam Smiley explains, "For most dramatists, it means the character receiving the most attention from the playwright, the other characters, and eventually the audience."[30] They drive the action of the play because "they usually make the major discoveries and decisions."[31] Titles can be deceiving in this regard. Shakespeare's *Cymbeline* does not concentrate on that king, but on his subjects. The titular character in *Antigone* would seem to be the protagonist in Sophocles's play. Based on a definition of the protagonist as the character who is most changed by the events, Creon is actually the focus of the playwright's attention. His decisions lead to the suicide of his son. Antigone never changes her position, even when threatened with death. Though she loses her life, she believes the gods support her, and her death as a martyr will suggest the wrongness of Creon's actions. She accepts her fate, as she has been destined since her birth to be an outsider, to go her own way. As Chemers notes in his book on dramaturgy, "Note that the change from 'alive' to 'dead' is usually not very significant: a character that dies for what he or she believes in (like Antigone) hasn't really undergone any significant character change."[32]

Where Does the Problem Come From?

One avenue of exploration is the origin of a problem: where did the issue driving the scene come from? The director Mike Nichols referred to this as "the secret cause."[33] During his scene study sessions at the New Actors Workshop, Nichols would ask, " 'What's the dead whale?' Meaning, what's the thing under this scene that's stinking up the whole room that no one is talking about?' "[34] The coach helps the actors understand that the real conflict can involve something the characters can't even express because it's too painful, has been buried for a long time, has long affected the family dynamic, would destroy relationships protected by denial of its existence.

Conditioning Forces

Uta Hagen defines conditioning forces as those factors which influence behavior and are realized through sense memory, such as the weather, the urgency of the situation, an illness, the temperature, and so on.[35]

Conditioning forces may or may not be played depending on how they affect the behavior of the characters. Drunkenness is often a device playwrights use to turn off a character's filters: they begin to tell the truth, to act on their impulses rather than tamping them down. The heat or climate may affect characters; for example, in *Romeo and Juliet*, where the hot days lead to "the mad blood stirring."[36] Characters are more on edge, grumpy, quick to anger.

Conditioning forces can also consist of a character's mood based on recent experience. Though acting teachers such as Larry Moss suggest actors should not play a mood, Les Chantery believes this philosophy refers to an actor playing an "emotional wash or indulgence,"[37] which is used throughout a scene, which he agrees is ineffective. On the other hand, a mood may be a previous circumstance that still affects the actor even though she has other goals and is entering a new environment. In this case, "Mood is a starting point to understanding a person's temperament,"[38] and a character's as well. This character state can be used as a "launching-off point"[39] and then combined with current circumstances: the new ways the character is affected by current events.

Character Secrets

One character may have secrets few other characters have. A friction is created between characters who have contradictory information. The audience may or may not know these secrets as well. In the first instance, the situation is ironic. In the latter instance, the reveal is a surprise, pleasant or unpleasant.

Juliet's secret marriage to Romeo affects Act II.5 because, without that information, her behavior finally makes no sense to her parents. At first, they believe her tears are for her cousin, who has been murdered by Romeo, rather than because Romeo, her husband, has been banished. She is the apple of her father's eye, an obedient daughter who has done whatever he asked. When she becomes defiant, she seems a completely different person. The shock of her personality change brings out his temper. This anger management problem explains, in some ways, why the feud between the Capulets and Montagues lasted so long.[40] This secret also affects Juliet's relationship with the Nurse, who knows the truth. Because she still counsels Juliet to marry Paris, she is suggesting Juliet commit bigamy and damn herself in the eyes of God. And the Nurse actually encouraged the relationship in the first place. She has thrown Juliet under the bus to avoid her own culpability. This betrayal can never be forgiven. It also leaves Juliet without help, save for the Friar, and all of the subsequent decisions are based on her feeling abandoned by everyone she loves.

Character Attachments

Characters are driven by their deep beliefs, their views of the world, and their sense of self.

Ron Van Lieu asks his students to consider the characters' attachments. He defines this concept and gives a formula for discovering them: "Attachments can be objects, philosophy of life, a view of self, a position, politics, religion, a substance, a thing, a memory, people, a circumstance, a feeling, etc. – things which announce what [the character] is."[41] These aren't necessarily going to announce themselves: "The characters might never reveal them. They could be unconscious."[42] More specifically, their importance comes from the struggle the character has to maintain to live a life based on that attachment: "Who or what does the character care most about? What would the character fight to keep?"[43] The loss of an attachment can be devasting if it is the key to the character's identity.[44] When any of these are in danger of being disproved, the character is in crisis and must do everything possible to course correct. If they can't, they might not be able to survive.

These severe effects on a major character are the source of great drama. In *Next to Normal*, Diana is a bipolar woman in the suburbs who is waiting for her son Gabe to come home, as he is out past his curfew. It is only in the second act that the audience realizes Gabe died as a baby 16 years before, but he is haunting Diana, who can't let go of him. One question for the actor playing the mother is, what kind of son would she want to conjure? In a realistic portrayal of a teenager, he might act out in rebellious behavior, have angst, take many things over seriously. As a figment of her imagination, it makes sense for her to imagine he has grown into the best possible version of himself, the one she wants to remember, rather than how he might be in real life. This is also a clue to the audience, although not so obvious that it will give away the secret too early. It contrasts with Gabe's later persona, a malevolent figment who will never leave his mother even when she realizes he doesn't exist.

Society's Influence

Social conditions influence characters in each period of history, although the playwright may take them for granted, being immersed as he is in the social fabric of the time. Actions that seem offensive or abhorrent to a modern actor may be acceptable behaviors for people living in the past. For example, homophobia may be nonexistent in the Classical Greek period, pervasive in the United States in the 20th century, and complicated in contemporary society.

As enlightened as the 21st century is on many issues, people still operate from a mindset of biases and engrained behaviors. For example, in Johnna Adams's *Sans Merci*, Tracy's mother Elizabeth visits Kelly to ask her how her daughter died. Her suspicion may be motivated by the fact that Tracy and Kelly were lovers, a situation she has trouble accepting.[45]

In *Antigone*, it is clear Creon's beliefs are rooted in the patriarchy. He can't allow his niece to break the laws of Thebes; this will not only lead to anarchy and further rebellion but will emasculate him. As a male, he cannot countenance a woman defying him.

Presentism

Presentism involves applying contemporary thinking to characters and situations affected by society at an earlier period in history. Sam Wineburg uses this term to identify scholars who study history but fail to "achieve mature historical understanding."[46] Characters might be more naïve because they don't have access to the kind of information we have. Characters may display chauvinistic, racist, colonial attitudes based on their upbringing. Those who are marginalized are encouraged to see the world as a natural consequence of the development of humankind. For actors to operate differently from their historical counterparts – to be offended by historical behavior – is to ignore the possibility of showing the audience how society has changed or remained the same. For example, if the actors in the television program *Mad Men* had played enlightened men of the 21st century, this would ring false to the patriarchal, chauvinistic attitude such men had in the 1960s. Paul Mann and Lloyd Richards both encourage this approach: "[A] performer could use personal memories to inform the role, but also had to interact with the cast in a way truthful to the time and place of the play."[47]

Alternative Sources

The play's origin may lie in other texts. The teacher and student can find helpful information by comparing the different sources. Many contemporary plays are adaptations of earlier works, whether plays, novels, short stories, or true accounts. Why did the author revisit them? What are the differences between the older and newer versions? Does the original text provide useful information either through comparison or contrast? If the play is based on a novel or short story, does the latter provide environmental or character descriptions and inner character thoughts that might be useful?

How to Begin: The First Reading

Carol Rosenfeld, in her workbook *Acting and Living in Discovery*, stresses how important the first reading of the play can be: "Reading a play for the first time is an exciting event. It is also a sacred event. Give yourself a chance to experience that event."[48] It should be a special time for the actor: one requiring a quiet mindset, a specific place to read – whether at home, outside, or in a coffee shop, setting aside enough time to read the play in one sitting, and noting first impressions. As hard as it may be, she enjoins the student to turn off all electronic devices during the reading. She also believes it is helpful to have a dictionary nearby for an early glance at the definitions for unfamiliar words, for the actor to take time after the reading for reflection. Also, if the actor often reads plays for class or for work, she suggests creating a ritual for this activity. Of course, the student should do their best to forget the particular scene they are working on, but to experience the whole play as a unit.[49]

Students will sometimes put off reading the entire play or use a synopsis they have found online. This is a rudimentary and sketchy form of research which may have served a function in the past but should be discouraged. The coach must inspire the students to find the deeper work interesting and worthwhile. Fundamentally, the teacher must know the play inside and out.

Some prompts for encouraging reading of the entire play might include:

- What secret is your character keeping to themselves? Why do they keep it secret? How is the secret finally revealed?[50]
- What would happen if your character were removed from the play? This gives the actor a sense of their role in the events.
- How many scenes is your character in? Could you have selected another scene for working on this character? What would it be? This encourages the actor to carefully read other scenes besides their own and to make critical decisions about the scene they are doing.
- What do other characters say about your character? Are these assessments accurate? These other characters can lend the actor perspective or an objective assessment. Another consideration, when you disagree with their opinions, is that what other people say about you can say more about them.
- Who is in your corner and who is an obstacle to your needs? Do you have a support system, or are you on your own? Obstacles are found in other people or within oneself. Who or what is stopping you, and why? The actor can begin to consider strategies for dealing with these external and internal obstacles.
- What do the previous circumstances – either in earlier scenes or before the play begins – tell you about your character? The key to the character's behavior may lie in the past: their rejections, hurts, successes, losses, failures, the changes in their relationships with others. How are these affecting the characters now?
- What is the most important relationship your character has, and why is it so important? The relationship can even be with a person who doesn't appear in the play but still has influence over the other characters. For example, in *Twelfth Night*, the deaths of Olivia's father and brother create chaos, since Olivia, in her grief, rejects her role as head of the household and gives those duties to Malvolio, "a kind of Puritan."[51]
- What is your character's arc? How does their mindset change from the beginning to the end of the play? Francis Hodge, who taught directing for many years at the University of Texas at Austin, elaborated this idea in his directing textbook:

In the course of a play a principal character *does not change* as a character, but *his attitudes towards the environmental world of the play change* under pressure from sources outside his control – the other characters who serve as instruments to his change.[52]

He referred to the mindsets of protagonists as polar attitudes: "Every character in a play, as in real life, is conditioned by the special world he is caught in, and he will hold specific attitudes, or points of view toward that world."[53] It is these attitudes, "his prejudices, his tolerances, and his assumptions about his special world, where he is forced to have relationships with others and is forced to take actions affecting both himself and others."[54] A change in this attitude helped to identify who the play was about: only the main characters have polar attitudes;

secondary characters may influence these changes but not change themselves.[55] By noting the difference in attitudes, the actor can map the character's journey through the play. It is the distance between the poles that reveals how far the characters travel based on the given circumstances.[56] The play's shape is driven by the character's arc.

The student should choose a mission for the character – even if, in the long run, they change it – to have a starting point and something for the coach to respond to.[57]

This chapter presupposes that the teacher wants to explore the play text in greater detail with the students. There are teachers who feel this is a dramaturgical practice that keeps actors operating on an intellectual plane. Using the analogy of the train that stops at each station, Sharon Marie Carnicke notes that "too many stops on the train can try the patience of the passengers."[58] By this she means the students can become overloaded with information but, "Unless such research illuminates what actually happens in the play, it can waste precious time."[59] And she quotes Stanislavsky, who warned of actors "coming onto the stage with 'a stuffed head and an empty heart.'"[60] Ultimately, the actors must let go of their homework and respond to what is in front of them, their current environment and partners.

A deep understanding of the play by itself does not create the conditions under which the character is embodied, their needs pursued and realized, their feelings manifested in behavior. At the same time, whatever can help the actor both to connect with their character and to delve into the events that have affected her in the present circumstances – including coming to conclusions about the character's psychology – can be tied to action. Actioning as a tool can be an important basis for initial interpretation by the coach,[61] or the teacher may apply such concepts as tempo-rhythm.[62] Whatever is stressed, this homework will reap benefits for both student and teacher as applied in the scene study class.

While this chapter has concentrated on preparation and homework – dramaturgical and literary – to give the student one foundation for proceeding, the next chapter will deal with the way in which a teacher begins work on a particular scene with the actors – including the first reading in class – which may, in part, be informed by analysis. Now begins the delicate process of coaching.

Notes

1. Michael Mark Chemers, *Ghost Light: An Introductory Handbook for Dramaturgy* (Carbondale: Southern Illinois University Press, 2010), 69.
2. In his autobiography, Patrick Stewart reads the script at least eight times: (1) for the narrative, (2) for the subject of the play, (3) for what the character says about himself, (4) for what other characters say about his character when he is present, (5) for what they say about him when he is absent, (6) for what is true in the play, (7) for what is false, and (8) for what the character does. Patrick Stewart, *Making It So: A Memoir* (New York: Gallery Books, 2023), 122–123.
3. Katie Mitchell, *The Director's Craft: A Handbook for the Theatre* (London: Routledge, 2009), 11.
4. Mitchell, *The Director's Craft*, 10, which includes the entire list of initial factors.
5. Mitchell, *The Director's Craft*, 10.

6 These are author suggestions.
7 Mitchell, *The Director's Craft*, 12.
8 Sharon Marie Carnicke calls these bits of information that require further investigation "open clues" which "invite the actor to collaborate with the author." See Sharon Marie Carnicke, *Dynamic Acting Through Active Analysis: Konstantin Stanislavsky, Maria Knebel, and Their Legacy* (London: Methuen Drama, 2023), 205.
9 Van Lieu, Teacher Development Notes, June 2013.
10 Van Lieu, Teacher Development Notes, June 2013.
11 Carnicke, *Dynamic Acting Through Active Analysis*, 306.
12 The guards rely on Horatio's knowledge of Latin to repel such an entity.
13 Carnicke, *Dynamic Acting Through Active Analysis*, 314, quoting Robert L. Belknap, *Plots* (New York: Columbia University Press, 2016), 17.
14 They are available as a basis for the characters' intent, although the actors should ultimately choose what to do.
15 For example, as Chekhov's *Three Sisters* begins, the characters feel the loss of their father the year before. His absence leads to the decisions that his family makes – without his guidance and presence, they may not have chosen the actions that led to their unhappiness.
16 Stephen McKinley Henderson, quoted in Dixon, *Lloyd Richards in Rehearsal*, 161–162.
17 Diane Paulus, quoted in Ash Carter and Sam Kashner, *Life Isn't Everything: Mike Nichols, as Remembered by 150 of His Closest Friends* (New York: Henry Holt and Company, 2019), 311.
18 Natalie Portman, quoted in Carter and Kashner, *Life Isn't Everything*, 298.
19 See the discussion on attachments later in this chapter.
20 Stephen McKinley Henderson, quoting Lloyd Richards in Francis, "Preparing Birds to Fly," 111.
21 William B. Davis asks himself, "Why Do I say that? Why do I say that now? Why do I say it that way?" See Davis, *On Acting . . . and Life*, 111.
22 David Ball, *Backwards and Forwards: A Technical Manual for Reading Plays* (Carbondale: Southern Illinois University Press).
23 Ball, *Backwards and Forwards*, 10.
24 Ball, *Backwards and Forwards*, 93.
25 See a discussion of Presentism later in this chapter.
26 Larry Moss, *The Intent to Live: Achieving Your True Potential as an Actor* (New York: Bantam Books, 2005), 93.
27 Carnicke, *Dynamic Acting Through Active Analysis*, 316–317.
28 Vyacheslav (Slava) Dolgachev, a former artistic director of the Moscow Art Theatre and artistic director of the Moscow New Drama Theatre since 2001, has shown how Anton Chekhov's plays are masterful in many ways, but particularly in realizing this form. I was introduced to Slava's work in the Teacher Development Program in June 2012.
29 *Oedipus Rex* by Sophocles. The third is *Oedipus at Colonus*.
30 Sam Smiley and Norman A. Bert, *Playwriting: The Structure of Action*, revised and expanded edition (New Haven, CT: Yale University Press, 2005), 142.
31 Smiley and Bert, *Playwriting*, 142.
32 Chemers, *Ghost Light*, 77.
33 Harris, *Mike Nichols*, 435.
34 Diane Paulus, quoted in Harris, *Mike Nichols*, 435.
35 See Uta Hagen, *Respect for Acting*, 2nd edition (Hoboken: John Wiley & Sons Inc., 1973), Chapter 18, "Conditioning Forces," 129–133.
36 *Romeo and Juliet*, Act III, Scene 1.
37 Chantery, *Life in a Mid-Shot*, 120.
38 Chantery, *Life in a Mid-Shot*, 120.
39 Chantery, *Life in a Mid-Shot*, 120. For a thorough discussion of this tool, see Chantery's Chapter 4, "Find the Human in the Character," in subsection #2, "The Human Is in a Mood."

40 As far as the parents are concerned, the feud has ended by the second scene of the play.
41 Van Lieu from Teacher Development Program Notes, June 2012.
42 Van Lieu from Teacher Development Program Notes, June 2012.
43 Van Lieu from Teacher Development Program Notes, June 2012. He suggests that if the teacher ever wants to analyze themselves in this way, it can be quite interesting.
44 When Joe Keller in Arthur Miller's *All My Sons* loses his attachment, the respect he believes everyone has for him – especially his family – he also loses the means of avoiding his own culpability in a crime that has led to the death of his son Larry and the dishonor he has brought to his son Chris, and he commits suicide. Arthur Miller, *All My Sons: A Drama in Three Acts* (New York: Dramatists Play Service, 1974).
45 Their relationship did change Tracy, but it gave her a voice. Kelly's survival guilt is partly based on Tracy's defiance of the soldiers who then killed her. Johnna Adams, *Sans Merci* (Los Angeles: Original Works Publishing, 2013).
46 Sam Wineburg, *Historical Thinking and Other Unnatural Acts: Charting the Future of Teaching the Past* (Philadelphia: Temple University Press, 2001), 90.
47 blackchild, "Lloyd Richards in the Classroom," 119.
48 Carol Rosenfeld, *Acting and Living in Discovery: A Workbook for the Actor* (Indianapolis, IN: Focus, 2014), 4–5.
49 Rosenfeld, *Acting and Living in Discovery*, 4–5.
50 For example, one of the characters in Shakespeare's *Titus Andronicus* has a secret that isn't revealed until late in the play. Can you find it? Answer: Tamora is pregnant with Aaron's child, though she is married to the emperor of Rome. Her relationship with Aaron would destroy her status as empress.
51 The character of Maria from William Shakespeare, *Twelfth Night*, Act II. 3, in Stanley Wells and Gary Taylor, eds., *The Oxford Shakespeare*, 2nd Edition (Oxford: Clarendon Press, 2005).
52 Hodge, *Play Directing*, 25, emphasis Hodge's.
53 Hodge, *Play Directing*, 25.
54 Hodge, *Play Directing*, 25.
55 Hodge, *Play Directing*, 25.
56 Hodge, *Play Directing*, 25–26.
57 Hugh O'Gorman makes the brilliant suggestion that actors "should really highlight the other actor's lines, as they are the genesis of your behavior." O'Gorman, *Acting the Action*, 28.
58 Carnicke, *Dynamic Acting Through Active Character Analysis*, 314.
59 Carnicke, *Dynamic Acting Through Active Character Analysis*, 314.
60 Carnicke, *Dynamic Acting Through Active Character Analysis*, 314.
61 See Chapter 8, particularly the discussion on Active Analysis.
62 See the discussion of tempo-rhythm in Chapter 7, "Coaching: Categories."

6 Coaching

Beginning

Once the instructor has shared their teaching philosophy with the students, once the scenes are chosen, once the student partners and teacher have decided on an order for scene work rehearsals and presentations – finally, the day arrives to begin coaching. The students may have been asked to do preliminary work outside of class, such as to answer Lloyd Richards's six questions,[1] but now they will begin to share the work with each other and the coach.

Beginning

One of the hardest journeys the actors will ever make is from the safety of their chairs to the front of the class. The teacher must make this transition as comfortable as possible. Without some attention to creating a calm and relaxed atmosphere, everyone – teacher and student alike – is already at a disadvantage. The student performers will be full of tension, they may hold their breath, they may be unable to think of answers to simple questions, or they may assume an adversarial or vulnerable attitude. Their bodies will inhibit them from appropriate character behavior. As the teacher asks them to sit in the space, they may display "covering" behavior, crossing their legs away from each other and the teacher, crossing their arms as a shield, or avoiding eye contact. Just as mammals feel each other's breathing change when there is danger, the teacher may find himself mirroring this conditioned response in the student. Sometimes the class itself will hold their breath in empathy. Tension is also contagious; the students become uncomfortable, and everyone may find they tense up in a sympathetic but subconscious reaction to those feelings. Often it is enough to point out these behaviors to the student, asking them to breathe and uncover, but the teacher may also release the students from the pressure of performing by first engaging in a dialogue with the performers as a means of bypassing some of the sources of discomfort.

If the teacher uses this approach, she must consider the first thing to say to open that conversation. For the initial session, the teacher is treading lightly, taking the temperature of the actors to see how they are responding to being the focus of attention and reassuring them they are under no pressure to deliver quick results.

DOI: 10.4324/9781003498520-7

The teacher may also ask students how they would like to proceed. They can have a read-through, they can put a small section on its feet for examination, and they can discuss goals they have for today's work. The teacher's aim is to move the actors towards a mindset that focuses on the present rather than on a recent past full of distractions, disappointments, elations, and other circumstances that still occupy their attention. Sometimes the actors will let the teacher know why they are a bit unfocused or less energetic; and sometimes when the teacher asks them to think about the future, this reminds them of where they are heading – the performance – which may lead them right back to nervousness. When the students do put scenes on their feet, the teacher can encourage the actors to speak and move as themselves – the onus is off them to create a character, but instead to see where the material takes them: their initial impulses and responses to each other.

If the teacher gives the students the homework assignment of reading the entire play, the teacher can ease them into the scene by asking for their initial impressions: what they thought of the overall work – its characters, its plot, any interesting features – and what questions came up while they were reading, what valuable discoveries they made about their characters, what was confusing to them, what themes suggested themselves – simple questions that require the opinion of the actor rather than serving as a test to prove they have done their homework. The teacher may also ask the actors to share the plot of the play and what the character relationships are with the whole class, so everyone will have a common understanding of the background and basic details. The actors may be asked to talk about their familiarity with the author's work – whether they have seen or read the play before and under what conditions, whether they have had encounters with other plays in the author's complete works, or even if they have appeared in the play or in other plays by the author. There is no pressure to create a performance; instead, the student is introduced officially to a process-oriented approach – to begin with, by answering the kinds of questions the teacher asks.

Sometimes, a student who is reluctant to begin will attempt to prolong the initial conversation. This is also true of those students who rely on an intellectual approach to their roles over a visceral one. This may indicate fear and a desire to delay the inevitable: they know they must eventually approach the character by interacting with their partners, by embodying the thoughts and feelings of the character, and by exploring the connection between their personal lives and the life the author has given them to play. And they must do so in front of their peers. Talking is a tactic to avoid the difficult work of plunging into the unknown, making themselves open to affect, and embracing discomfort. Their intelligence here is a disadvantage, as it short-circuits the path from outer stimuli to inner response.

The Initial Read-Through

A common practice is to begin with a simple read-through of the material so the whole class is introduced to the scene and initial actor choices are made. The teacher will use this first read-through to learn how carefully the actor has studied the script; if the actor chooses a particular strategy or mood not in keeping with what the author has written, the teacher can later ask questions that lead the students back to the text. If it is clear the students have done their homework, the teacher can also encourage the student's industry – the care they have taken to begin the exploration of the given circumstances, the character's motivations, and other ideas they have picked up from a private analysis of the script. Every early choice the actor makes can suggest means for later diagnoses.

An exercise that allows actors to connect with each other from the very first read of a scene works as follows: when giving the actors their scripts, the teacher asks them not to look at the words right away, but to wait until they are given a prompt to begin reading with their partners. The teacher places the members of each group in chairs facing each other with a small space between them. At a signal, the students turn over their scripts and note who has the first words of the scene. Instead of glibly reading through the script, they begin by lifting the words from the page and offering them as simply as possible to each other. The rules are: both actors must look at each other whether they are speaking or listening. In other words, the actors are not to glance down as they utter the lines or look ahead for their next cue or line as their partner is speaking.

This is not a memorization exercise. If an actor has more than a sentence or phrase to speak, they can break up the dialogue into small sections and then look up and deliver them; they can then look down and memorize the next small section – but again, only when it is their turn to speak, not when their partner is speaking. The actors are encouraged to take their time, to allow for silence as they capture each bit of dialogue. In a sense, this is not a reading, but a chance to commune with the other actor in a personal interchange that is otherwise disrupted by concentration on smoothly delivering the lines in the mistaken belief that glibness is a desirable goal and will impress others. An actor can't help but try to read ahead, returning to the page as they speak or when the other actor is speaking to them: this is the force a text can exert on the actors through habit and the need to make sense of what they are reading. The connection with the partner is paramount, not the ability to rattle off paragraphs of dialogue. The teacher discourages this tendency to push the dialogue forward and asks the actors to stay on point, to share their characters' words with each other in a more complete form of connection, using direct eye contact during the colloquy.

The first-reading technique takes the actors further than a simple recitation of the text. As the words are shared between them, the actors must imagine the words come from themselves: if they just talk to each other, in a sense they will bypass the need to act. Harold Guskin refers to this operation as "taking it off the page."[2] In his coaching, the actor takes the time "to let the phrase into his head,"[3] inhaling and exhaling as he reads. If the actor can avoid censoring the thoughts that arise as suggested by the passage, they can go wherever the text takes them with a freedom that allows them not only to explore their impressions, but to respond spontaneously and honestly.[4]

Sam Kogan believes that, in an ideal situation, the actors who are looking into each other's eyes are actually looking through them, into the brain to see the thinking.[5] The actor receives impressions from the other actor in order to know what to do. In a first read-through, whether in a play rehearsal or in a scene class, students attempt to show their facility for reading their scripts cold. Cold reading, or reading the script with no advance perusal, is a skill that can be useful in auditions, but it is not the point here.[6] The point is to connect directly with the other actor as early as possible, using one's own voice to convey the character's initial thoughts. Unless the actors do so, they can't affect each other with their first impulses as they are glued to the page. They miss their partners' subtle reactions, which may appear spontaneously and never resurface. They begin to understand the character's thinking based on their spoken responses to each other, their respective facial expressions, and other stimuli they can use as they react to their partners.

Strasberg seems to agree with this type of first reading when he says:

> Actors need not even make an effort to read the lines well. . . . If they make a simple effort to read the lines and respond to them naturally and sympathetically as in conversation, you are amazed at the extent to which they come alive.[7]

Of course, the coach is watching carefully as this process unfolds. They can remind the actors what choices they made during the scene, what was effective at this early stage: "At the first reading actors can give you such wonderful results that the problem becomes, 'How do you keep this?'"[8] In both cases, the teacher is there to remind the actors what they did intuitively.

Another advantage to this approach is that, until the students look down at the script, they don't know whose turn it is. Before they consult the script again, they may have a natural response and are then surprised the character is given no words to say at that moment. The teacher can point out the nature of the inner monologue, the thoughts characters have regardless of whether they are speaking or not.[9] As in life, we don't stop thinking but have a never-ending dialogue with ourselves, actively listening and looking at what our partner says or does to determine whether or not it is useful to us. As Ron Van Lieu notes, we ask ourselves, "Is this good for us, or bad for us?,"[10] i.e., does what is said or done to us move our agenda forward, or is it an obstacle to our plans and desires? Characters are no different. This is subjective listening: it is paramount that the characters, while attempting to achieve their goals, search for positive and negative partner responses.

There is a major difference between hearing and listening: the latter has to do with letting the other actor's words penetrate or affect you. As Larry Moss suggests to the actors when they first encounter a script and respond to their partners, "As you read the script, keep asking yourself, *Who are they to me now emotionally?*"[11] And this works both ways: when the actor is saying something to another actor, what part of them are they trying to penetrate?

Having gone through the text once, the actors can try to repeat the scene without looking at the pages at all, playing what they remember of the dialogue while also considering what the initial reading inspired in their playing. They will be surprised how much they will have grasped even in this early stage – and how many of the actual words come to mind.

This avoids the return to a standard procedure that involves a reliance on the script pages. The actors no longer worry about exact language at this stage; they have more freedom to experiment. The work is useful as the actors are playing together from the very beginning; they take from each other the clues they need; they make choices by instinct, spontaneously. The actors avoid "text tyranny" – the need to impress the director or class with their reading ability – as well as the constant urge to use the script as a safety blanket, a familiar prop they can grab onto. A side benefit is that the lines come surprisingly quickly.[12]

William Esper, the famous teacher of the Meisner technique, used a similar approach, a way of establishing early connection between actors: "If you work like this, from unanticipated moment to unanticipated moment, small things, real things, can start to happen between you."[13] It is not just a reading: "It will be a real conversation." This supports his overall principle of working off the other person, "slowly allowing your responses to each other to bring you to an authentic life."[14] This spontaneity is a key goal of the Meisner approach.

Methods of Coaching

After the first reading, or perhaps eschewing the first reading altogether, the teacher begins to coach the actors in the scene. Robert Benedetti offers six considerations for communicating with students in a coaching session: Simplicity, Clarity, Specificity, Directness, Playability, and Brevity.[15] By simplicity, Benedetti is enjoining the coach to offer the "well-chosen note," while allowing some notes to work themselves out in the course of the class sessions. Clarity is self-defined, but here he emphasizes the need for the teacher to consider whether what is about to be said will be clearly stated or requires more thought. Concurrently, the teacher should be willing to admit when they themselves don't have an answer, and he gives the teacher permission to delay a response for the sake of further consideration and/or research or so the actor can discover her own solution. The coach uses specificity when they narrow their feedback to particular instances and examples, the latter of which are helpful to the entire class when stating general principles. When a coach is direct, they are sharing the work straight from their personal feelings and instincts about what they are seeing.

If the notes are to be played, the teacher encourages active behavior rather than a concentration on emotions or moods.[16] Students will then play verbs rather than adjectives, character strategies for success rather than traits. The emphasis is on doing rather than being.

Finally, long discussions or teacher discourses can become lectures or – worse – keep actors in their heads, isolating them in intellectuality rather than provoking physical embodiment and instinct, or derail the work altogether.[17] Sometimes the students will encourage the teacher to expand on their thoughts; the teacher may be tempted to expound but should keep such remarks brief. The student may offer intellectual points in line with the teacher's thinking. Though this can be impressive, this strategy delays a commitment to making choices and trying them – to getting on one's feet and plunging in.

Stumbling Blocks

If the teacher has established a scene order – who will work each day – the class may be disrupted by an absent partner. If each student has also been working on a monologue, then the instructor can concentrate on those instead of on the scheduled scene. However, for a first rehearsal, the teacher can concentrate on one character rather than two, working with the single actor who is present, modeling the process of rehearsal. The teacher can ask questions based on the student's goals for the day and suggest ways to continue the process outside of class. The key is not to waste the time available. The teacher may ask to work with another group instead. Dismissing the class is never the answer.

The Students' Attitude

The key for any session is the students' promise to commit fully to whatever work they do – to make strong choices and to trust their instincts. Their initial work is a first offering to the teacher and sets up an important situation: regardless of how the work goes, the teacher has something to examine. This situation is similar to advice for young writers: if they put something on the page, the material can be massaged into a better form; absence of words on a blank page leaves the writer nothing to edit and revise. The students must not think of their first drafts as a mistake: "[T]he important thing is to make the mistake, in glorious detail, so there is something serious to correct."[18]

Early Thoughts

As the students do an initial reading of the play, the coach listens intently for intimations that suggest a way forward. What do the characters want from each other? What motivates them to choose the language they use? Is the line straightforward, or does it contain subtext? The teacher may ask the actors dramaturgical questions about the given circumstances to determine how much they understand about what they are embodying. These questions can be asked without providing the answers if the teacher wants the actors to return to the text to find them, and if the point is to model the asking of particular kinds of questions – those the actors may use on future texts. An early topic of discussion may involve making an agreement with the actors about the main event of the scene so everyone is operating from the same starting point.

Each coach decides how they will proffer their diagnoses to the students.[19] Some teachers will want to plunge in, seeking to cover all of the mistakes, triumphs, missteps, and good instincts the actors have had. In short, they want to offer all of their possible constructive criticism and ideas at once. Based on the enthusiasm to share knowledge and to demonstrate expertise, the teacher can cloud the issue, bombarding the students with notes. This can shut the students down altogether by overloading them with too much to consider; they can't accomplish every note at once. The teacher must select which area to concentrate on.

When to Offer Notes

During the actor's scene work, the teacher may have a desire to address a problem as it arises. This may lead to the teacher interrupting the students. How can this be avoided? The coach may write the note down and refer to it later. The coach may ask the actors if they would like to work on the scene section by section and stop for comments on each section. They may ask if the students would like feedback wherever the coach notices an issue. Side-coaching may be one less intrusive way to do this.[20] Sometimes the students want to run the whole scene without interruption to establish an overall arc and see what they have.

Interrupting halts the flow of the actor's work. It can cause great frustration in the actors. "A director who interrupts on a habitual basis is essentially badgering the actor, and that badgering will be retaliated in some form of revenge."[21] Interruptions can also disrupt the creative state, cutting off the actor's access to their own impulses and cease the flow of spontaneity. For this reason, even when the actors have agreed to work on one section of the text, they may continue beyond it, and the teacher should allow them to do so.

How to Know When to Say What

The coach should consider how much time is spent watching and how much time critiquing. If the coach has limited time to respond, they should consider what two or three key points to offer. The suggestion here is the coach can choose from a variety of possible categories.[22] These categories can also be used to narrow the possibilities and to take mental rather than written notes.[23] The teacher should also concentrate on the actor's stated goals and either apply the categories to them or respond intuitively in the moment. The coach who is worried about saying the wrong thing or accidentally making an error in judgment should remember that mistakes are a natural consequence of the process approach. Sometimes it is enough for the teacher to stop themselves and proffer the comment, "I said too much there," or to offer an alternative when the suggestion is obviously not working, or to ask the student to consider their options.

What if a student has a meltdown or a breakthrough? A breakthrough, no matter how labeled, may be a positive or negative experience – not in relation to the success of the scene, but in terms of how it affected the actor personally. If the revelation was useful and not psychologically damaging, then a solution was found to a particular acting challenge. As a scene goes into dangerous territory, the teacher may want to shut the scene down and address it later. The teacher is usually not certified to handle the fallout from a negative experience.

Teacher Goals

One of the teacher's primary goals is to tell an actor what they see the actor doing, what impression their work is making on the audience. This third eye is essential as a measure of how effective or ineffective the acting is at that point in the process.

The actor may not realize what they have done. Working intuitively, they "behaved" without concentrating on how this was accomplished. When a teacher tells the student what they noticed, it isn't a judgment but a simple recounting of what the actors did as far as the teacher could understand it and verifying that this effect is what the actors were striving for. One example might be whether the feelings were actor- or character-driven. For example, "I saw you getting frustrated." This can be followed by questions such as: "Were you doing this because you yourself were frustrated, or because the character was?" This is a point too where habits can be discussed, especially if the teacher isn't sure whether the seeming habit is actually a character choice. If this is the first time the actor has done something that seems not to serve them, the teacher needs to discern whether the choice was made deliberately or unconsciously. Does this action make the actor more comfortable onstage while failing to accomplish what the actor had in mind? Does it seem antithetical to the teacher's understanding of the character?

Student Goals

In his acting classes at Yale, Lloyd Richards would ask the students to predetermine goals for the work they were presenting. They would perform the scene, and then Richards would ask what they had planned for the work and whether or not they felt that plan had been successful.[24] "Whenever you finished the scene, inevitably at some point in the discussion, Lloyd was going to say, 'What were you working on and how did it go?' And you knew that you had to have actually thought about that."[25] This was particularly important to the actors because in posing this question, he "made you understand the degree of self-responsibility that you had as an actor. That you actually have had to study the play, to have gotten inside the character, understood the situation of the scene you were in."[26] This allowed Richards to take on the role of an objective observer: "He could then serve as an arbiter of this answer: he was an outside observer who could note whether certain goals were reached or not. In the long run, the audience can serve as one as well."[27]

Lee Strasberg wanted his actors to be self-observant: "The essential part of the actor's training tries to make him aware of what he is doing at the time a thing is happening. Otherwise, he doesn't know whether to do it more or to do it less."[28] To be inside and outside of the character is a delicate process:

> This split awareness, which Stanislavski calls "the feeling of truth," must develop as a kind of sixth sense, and yet it cannot do so at the expense of the actor's belief, his concentration, his involvement in what he is doing.[29]

To do otherwise is to become so absorbed in the role that the person performing loses control: "One of the most serious misunderstandings of an actor is to assume that to act truly and believably means to forget what you are doing. But that's hysteria – in life as well as in acting."[30] The actor is purposefully performing in service to the character and repeating that performance in the same basic fashion for each audience: "Yet in order to repeat, which is the ordinary professional requirement of the actor, there must be some element of awareness working."[31] This does not mean, however, that the actor, in their awareness of creating the character, can't continue to live spontaneously. This awareness does not keep the actor from "fusing" with the character: "On the contrary, the awareness is essential if he is to accomplish that fusion and involvement."[32]

Nikolai Demidov calls this a Doubled Consciousness: for the actor, "part of his consciousness works normally – he cognizes that he is acting onstage, that he sees and feels the public; the other part lives the life of the play and character."[33] Attending to both, the actor resembles the child who plays an imaginary character but can always step out of it with no difficulty. Without both processes in play, the sense of reality onstage would be lost by both actor and audience, or the actor would lose themselves in a part to the point of psychosis.[34]

The students may want to clarify the events of the scene. They may want to establish the relationships suggested by the author. They may want to understand why they say certain lines or why they make certain choices.[35] The teacher can also ask the actors for their goals before each session. In this way, the teacher can form ideas about how to proceed and know what to comment on in the notes. The teacher may have their own ideas about work to be done, but inevitably, these can be woven into the students' goals. Any number of goals are possible, as long as they are specific. "I want to perform like a professional" is an admirable goal, but it requires simpler steps in a long process of work.

Be aware of the choices the actors have made. Is the behavior voluntary or involuntary? What is the thinking behind the choice? Will this choice be worth developing, or should an alternative be substituted in the long run? How can the choice be improved? Has the coach acknowledged a useful choice?[36]

The Actors' First Moments

When the character first enters a new situation – this might include a known space but a change in the conditions of the relationship with persons in that space – do they read the room? Do they take their bearings before they begin pursuing their objectives? Stanislavsky saw this as a natural response to entering a space: "If you don't find your bearings first, the organic living process is destroyed."[37] This is something that happens in the real world but is often subconscious: even if a character already has a goal in mind, the actor wants to know what the character is confronting before choosing how to proceed. This is a helpful technique to put the actor in the scene: "How to select very clearly where they are living within themselves when the scene begins so that you are not distracted by the conditions of the rehearsal room."[38] The false conditions of theatre are countered by the actor's inner preparations.

Encouraging Discomfort

Unlike other subjects which use the classroom as a laboratory, an acting class encourages the students to experiment with themselves, to use their personal experiences and reveal themselves in ways other disciplines don't require. What blocks the actor from connecting easily to what the character is feeling is a fear of being vulnerable or that others will mistake the actor for the character and therefore judge them. Ron Van Lieu uses the phrase "Tolerate your discomfort" because of the reluctance by actors to play the character's situation.[39] Acting can be uncomfortable and lead to self-consciousness because the author places the character in dramatic situations; what a person tries to avoid in life – unpredictability and difficulty – is embraced by the actor to advance the narrative.

Plays are rarely about happy-go-lucky people who lead enjoyable lives. Wonderful conditions for real life don't make for exciting or captivating theatre. Playwrights put their characters through terrible ordeals, placing them in nearly impossible situations, so the audience can watch how they will escape from them (comedy) or be destroyed by them (tragedy). Such situations make the character vulnerable emotionally. "The best kind of acting I like and is the most effective is the degree to which it illuminates the human condition; you do that by embracing the degree of vulnerability that the character doesn't have any choice but to deal with."[40] The audience comes to the theatre to see characters experience high-stakes situations in the comfortable knowledge that they themselves are merely spectators to the characters' ordeals.

When actors are blocked, it may be because they can't embrace the struggle the character must go through. Patrick Garland noted that shields go up because the actors respond as themselves with their own social conditioning, while the story requires the characters to live unprotected: "All human beings surround themselves with layers of protection to prevent exposure, and yet actors are in part required and impelled to reveal themselves all the time."[41] This is one of the challenges separating the dilettante from the true actor:

> One of the hardest things for an actor to learn is the mechanism for allowing his vulnerabilities to breathe, and to break down his emotional rigidities. These rigidities are like flags, which the actor holds up as if to say, "this isn't me."[42]

Larry Moss, agreeing with this principle, created the "I Can Be Hurt by You Exercise" to address this challenge.[43] The exercise helps the actor to answer the question, "Are you willing to work through your discomfort and your fear of other people's judgments and find out what it's like to have increased emotional access as an actor?"[44]

Lee Strasberg spent years with actors to free them from tension, which included the way they fought their impulses due to social conditioning: "Thus the manners and needs and customs of society create a hindrance that in later years interferes with the actor's freedom of expression or freedom of response."[45] Not that he felt this was a complete deterrent: "There is nothing terrible about this process of social conditioning. The actor still has to be a human being, which means a social being in part."[46] Blockage can continue with the wrong kind of training:

> But when at eighteen he wants to train himself as an actor, he too often finds only a kind of training which is a continuation of the social process of telling

the child how to behave. The training does not free the instrument for the process of creation in acting.[47]

The training imposes the very conditioning that actor is trying to fight.

The teacher does her best to create the conditions under which the students can feel secure and supported as they go through what is ultimately an intimate process.

Timing

The notes may land and be used effectively by the actor. When someone suddenly responds naturally after being given a note, remind them to use that response and tell them to trust their instincts. Sometimes the lines the actor says don't seem natural, and the teacher tries to help them rethink what is happening in those moments, but it only makes it worse. This is because the actor has already memorized their line reading. Even telling them to stress another word can mean they stress the new word *and* the old one. Stay away from line readings, but also note how an actor may themselves be stuck on a line reading. Ask them to paraphrase the line and then use that rhythm to say the real line or ask them to throw a portion of the line away that isn't as important as the material they should be stressing. And sometimes the words the character has to say are difficult to get out: the character may be breaking bad news and want to do so gently. The character may have something to say that they have taken a long time to build up to. The character may reveal a secret, and the response from the other character could just as easily go wrong as right. In this case, it takes more time to build up the courage to speak those words and to find the right words to say. Take the time.[48]

When the coach recognizes a wisp of an impulse on the part of the actor, they should mention it, with a phrase such as "I felt you wanted to do X here." Many times the coach is right, and the actor agrees to repeat the scene by giving in to the impulse. Demidov calls this injunction "green-lighting" the impulse, identifying and then giving into it. Side-coaching may be used in this way as the actor is going through an etude, so the moment isn't missed.[49]

Beginning the process of working on scenes in class offers so many opportunities for success or failure. It is important to remember as a coach that both are valuable in learning. As the teacher continues to coach scene study courses, they will find their own workable approaches and be able to eliminate many attempts that were ineffective. The key is to continually reflect on the class whenever possible – to consider the types of questions and suggestions proposed in this chapter – and to invent one's own approach.

In the next chapter, the means for improving the work and giving students tools for self-assessment – based on the previous experiences of both teacher and student – are discussed in greater detail. The assumption is that the teacher has at their disposal categories to guide the discussion and suggest the means for diagnoses and remediation. The nature of these categories, and how they are organized in the teacher's mind, are the keys to appropriate and timely feedback for the benefit of each actor.

Notes

1. See Chapter 5 the "Student Homework" section.
2. Harold Guskin, *How to Stop Acting: A Renowned Acting Coach Shares His Revolutionary Approach to Landing Roles, Developing Them and Keeping Them Alive* (New York: Farrar, Straus and Giroux, 2003), 21.
3. Guskin, *How to Stop Acting*, 21.
4. Guskin, *How to Stop Acting*, 27.
5. Sam Kogan and Helen Kogan, *The Science of Acting* (London: Routledge, 2009), 141.
6. And it can be counterproductive.
7. Hethmon, *Strasberg at the Actors Studio*, 283.
8. Hethmon, *Strasberg at the Actors Studio*, 283.
9. See the discussion on inner monologue in Chapter 7.
10. Van Lieu from The Teacher Development Program Notes, June 2012.
11. Moss, *The Intent to Live*, 107, emphasis Moss's.
12. This is also a useful technique when auditioning, as the auditors are ultimately more interested in the connection between the actor and partner.
13. See William Esper and Damon DiMarco, *The Actor's Guide to Creating a Character: William Esper Teaches the Meisner Technique* (New York: Anchor Books, 2014), 97, for the steps to the exercise.
14. Esper and DiMarco, *The Actor's Guide to Creating a Character*, 98.
15. Benedetti, "On Acting," 101–102.
16. See the discussion on Active Analysis in Chapter 8.
17. Benedetti, "On Acting," 101–102.
18. Daniel C. Dennett, *Intuition Pumps and Other Tools for Thinking* (New York: W. W. Norton & Company, 2013), 24.
19. The way in which the feedback is offered may consist of three different approaches: appreciation, coaching, or evaluation. See the discussion on types of feedback in Chapter 11.
20. See the discussion on side-coaching in Chapter 7.
21. William Ball, *A Sense of Direction: Some Observations on the Art of Directing* (New York: Drama Publishers, 1984), 62.
22. The next few chapters will contain examples of these categories for diagnoses.
23. See the discussion on categories as a means of dispensing with writing notes in Chapter 11.
24. Van Lieu, quoted in cfrancis blackchild, "Lloyd Richards in the Classroom," in *The Great North American Stage Directors: Kazan, Robbins, Richards*, ed. Harvey Young (London: Bloomsbury Methuen, 2021), 130.
25. blackchild, "Lloyd Richards in the Classroom," 130.
26. blackchild, "Lloyd Richards in the Classroom," 130.
27. blackchild, "Lloyd Richards in the Classroom," 130.
28. Hethmon, *Strasberg at the Actors Studio*, 165.
29. Hethmon, *Strasberg at the Actors Studio*, 165.
30. Hethmon, *Strasberg at the Actors Studio*, 165.
31. Hethmon, *Strasberg at the Actors Studio*, 165.
32. Hethmon, *Strasberg at the Actors Studio*, 166.
33. Nikolai Demidov, *Becoming an Actor-Creator*, eds. Andrei Malaev-Babel and Margarita Laskina, trans. Andrei Malaev-Babel, Alexander Rojavin, and Sarah Lillibridge (London: Routledge, 2016), 621.
34. My introductory students bring up the case of Heath Ledger, who they claim died because he was lost in the character of the Joker in the film *The Dark Knight*. This is an urban legend based on the idea that Ledger was not able to separate the actor who observed from the character whom he embodied. Ledger, however, was a professional actor who could make this distinction. He died of cardiac arrest due to an accidental overdose of prescription drugs. At the time, he was playing a new role in *The Imaginarium*

of *Doctor Parnassus* and suffering from a bad cold and insomnia. He was 28. See Brian J. Robb, *Starstruck: Heath Ledger* (Edinburgh: Glencairn Press, 2020), 170–194.
35 In heightened language, the students may want to find ways to connect to the material without losing their familiar approaches to acting. Ultimately, they want to grow more comfortable speaking in verse and/or making it sound more natural to their own ears. See Chapter 14.
36 Francis Ford Coppola, when he directed for the stage, would stress what worked for him and encourage the actors to continue in that direction: "where you came in and approached her, I *liked* what happened there. More of that!" See Ball, *A Sense of Direction*, 64, emphasis Ball's.
37 Toporkov, *Stanislavski in Rehearsal*, 145.
38 Van Lieu from The Teacher Development Program Notes, June 2012.
39 Van Lieu from The Teacher Development Program Notes, June 2012.
40 Van Lieu from The Teacher Development Program Notes, June 2013.
41 Patrick Garland, quoted in Robert Cohen, *Acting Power: The 21st Century Edition* (London: Routledge, 2013), 43.
42 Cohen, *Acting Power: The 21st Century Edition*, 44–45.
43 Moss, *The Intent to Live*, 272.
44 Moss, *The Intent to Live*, 272.
45 Hethmon, *Strasberg at the Actors Studio*, 80.
46 Hethmon, *Strasberg at the Actors Studio*, 80.
47 Hethmon, *Strasberg at the Actors Studio*, 80.
48 This phenomenon is also a reason to suggest other ways to memorize lines: for example, through the process of rehearsal.
49 See Demidov, *Becoming an Actor-Creator*, Chapter 23 "Free Reaction ("Green-Lighting"), 279–297.

7 Coaching
Categories

When teachers diagnose student work, they take what they know – their expertise – and from it pluck the particular advice that will help someone improve onstage or even off. Of the well of experiences and propositions available, the expert in any field must decide what to share at any given moment. Some will have organized their knowledge into categories in their heads – that may connect to or overlap other categories – so the necessary instruments/tools/ideas can be easily retrieved from the mind. "As experts in our fields, we create and maintain, often unconsciously, a complex network that connects the important facts, concepts, procedures, and other elements within our domain."[1] This section of the book suggests making and using such a network, grouping the different parts of the web of entangled thoughts so as to access them in memory.

If there is one way to distinguish between the novice and the expert, it is the speed with which the expert can find the solution among the myriad possibilities, continually narrowing down their options until the obvious answer appears. The nature of the knowledge itself is connected in the brain differently for the beginning and seasoned practitioner: "Novice and expert knowledge organizations tend to differ in two key ways: the degree to which knowledge is sparsely versus richly connected, and the extent to which those connections are superficial versus meaningful."[2] It's not only what experts know, but how they organize and connect that expertise to previous and related knowledge: "Organizing knowledge in a sophisticated, interconnected structure – as experts tend to do – can radically increase one's ability to access that information when one needs it."[3] Experts each have their own mental models consisting of categories that lead towards the smooth operation of their skills. Whether they are pilots or surgeons, they have learned to absorb a large amount of information and create connections for quick access. They have codified this information into mental constructs or even physical checklists to which they can refer.

Like the doctor who has to make split-second decisions concerning a patient in distress, the scene coach must identify, among many different possible avenues, the proper course of treatment for the actors in a scene in the heat of the moment – i.e., with the actors waiting patiently for feedback. Just as the physician can separate the body into its parts and their functions – and how these functions may be disrupted – so a teacher can consider the elements that make up a successful scene and performance. Sometimes the famous teachers will share such categories. Milton

Katselas would give his students what they came to call "The Checklist, "a series of tools any actor can use to help approach their work on a scene."[4] Larry Moss lists his "Essential Questions for Working on a Part."[5] Michael Shurtleff has his goalposts; though his book speaks specifically to the audition process, he breaks his ideas into categories that aid actors in approaching a scene or play.[6] These lists can be used as coaching diagnostic tools, if the teacher's familiarity with a list can suggest ways for improving a scene, or if the student or teacher uses any item on the list as a focus for that day's work.

For example, if one category is labeled "Previous Circumstances" – the immediate past is sometimes called "The Moment Before" – both teacher and student may examine the character's past as a way to effect the immediate present. How well the student succeeds in letting the character's past inform his behavior can be observed and commented on.

The following categories were selected as a kind of checklist, but also as a means of grouping topics for analysis: rather than the clues in medicine that indicate what is happening in the circulatory system or what illness is causing blotching on the skin, these are dramatic prompts for examining a scene when the teacher is presented with a number of symptoms that she sees in a student that prevents them from thoroughly grasping what a scene is about and how it might be truly experienced. These categories are not, of course, all inclusive, and many overlap. If they inspire the invention of further categories, that is a goal here too.

Each category begins with questions that aim the teacher towards a missing or weak element in a performance that can be corrected – or the successful recognition and use of an element the actor has discovered and used properly, i.e., in service of the scene.

Category: Previous Circumstances

Did the actor take on the life of the character through taking on the character's past? How do we know? How do past circumstances live within the actor/character? First of all, the previous circumstances generally affect what is happening now. Whether just before its initial action or long before the scene began, an event in the past created the behavior the audience is seeing now; previous problems still have to be dealt with, such as ruptures in a relationship; serious challenges of the character's identity, desires, and hopes for the future were not confronted at the time; physical and psychological wounds live on in the body of a character, affecting their continued struggles.[7] Depending on the strength of these past experiences, they may rise again to affect a character who is put under stress or whose psychological buttons are pushed. Besides their present circumstances, the characters are a bundle of conditioned responses based on past traumas, childhood experiences, family dynamics, previous relationships with other characters, important decisions they have made, and survival modes. No matter how subtle, either this behavior is present or it is not. Beginning a scene by considering the Moment Before establishes a foundation for what is to come in the work as it progresses. As Lloyd Richards said to his actors, "'You've got to start right to stay right.'"[8]

A character's feelings may not be based in the present circumstances. They may lash out at the character who shares the stage, but the source of that anger may be deeply rooted in experiences residing in the psyche. A behavior unrelated to the current conflict can serve as an obstacle to the other character who is surprised by the vehemence with which they are attacked or dismissed. One button may ignite the character's belief that their competence is being questioned. The character may feel embarrassment or shame or hurt from actions that evoke memories of those feelings, and this manifests itself in unreasonable rage or other emotions that, in other circumstances, would be held in check. The other character, not to blame for those feelings, is hurt or outraged at this insensitive and startling onslaught. The actor's familiarity with the true source of their feelings will allow them to play based on specific – if subconscious – character stimuli. For example, the relationship between Catherine and her sister Claire in *Proof* is a fraught one, since Claire has been serving as a surrogate to their mother and treats Catherine as a child who needs to be guided rather than being allowed to make her own decisions. This is never clearly stated, but all of their interactions suggest Claire's overprotective attitude to her sister and Catherine's resentment.

What Can the Coach Do About It?

The actors may not be dealing with the immediate past; they may not have studied the previous scene and the events that led to the one they are working on. A thorough analysis of the text will reveal secrets and unspoken thoughts the character carries inside them. The coach should know the text backwards and forwards and read it again just before the first coaching session takes place. Even if the coach is familiar with the play – may have even acted in it – they will discover new information to aid in an interpretation of the scene.

One strategy is to work on the first moment of the play. If the coach can establish a basic foundation to start with, they will be modeling the idea that time can be taken in moment-to-moment work and the actors will have a better idea of how to begin. The coach concentrates on how the scene begins, to determine when and why it went "off track." If the opening of a scene can be properly diagnosed for its challenges, using imagined recreations of the Moment Before, the actor will have a place to start from, a previous life they are living as they enter the scene. Trying more than one option for an entrance reminds the actor that their first choice may not be the best one, and that it is worth exploring further. Uta Hagen's Three Entrances exercise is a tool to practice this.[9] One effect it has is to establish the residue of whatever has happened just offstage in the life of the character. This work can serve as a catalyst. The "Where am I coming from?" influences "What am I there to do?"

Playing versions of the Moment Before is an example of using an etude, an improvisation to affect current behaviors.[10] A discussion with the actors about the influence of the past on the present can be useful, but ultimately, the actor must live in the circumstance physically rather than intellectually.

As a reminder, the coach can ask the actors to consider the baggage they bring with them to class. Every day has a different Moment Before for each student: sometimes they are running late; they have had a nice breakfast, or they have gone hungry; it is extremely cold or hot outside; they have just had a breakup; they have received good or bad news. They need not share with the teacher the personal events that affect them, but they can see how, when living their own lives, their current states of mind are not just about what they encounter in the classroom, but about the outside events that continue to influence their current, in-class behavior.[11]

One offshoot to the idea of the past as affecting the present is that the character's day may begin normally, but, because this is rarely interesting to an audience for very long, the routine is disrupted by new information or events. If the play begins with a disruption, the actor should imagine what a normal day looks like, so they can compare this type of day, based on previous circumstances, to the present unusual circumstances. The specific question to ask the actors is, "What's different about today?"

Sometimes the writer will show the characters going through their daily lives and then create an inciting incident for the events to come that throws everything into disorder.[12] One answer may involve the coach and the actors establishing an average day with its concomitant activities – who cooks, what book is a character reading comfortably in his study, what does the character usually do at work – in keeping with the author's intentions.[13] For example, on any other day the characters will not be interrupted by new situations, such as visitors they haven't seen in ages, or news that changes how they see their present circumstances. In Miller's *All My Sons*, Joe Keller is sitting in the backyard reading his newspaper and chatting with Tommy, the neighborhood boy, who regularly gives him reports on the neighborhood. Near Joe is a tree planted in his son Larry's honor which a storm uprooted the night before. Larry, who disappeared during a mission as a pilot in World War II, is memorialized, and though his mother refuses to give up hope, the sudden falling of the tree symbolizes to the audience he is dead.

Two characters return to town after a long absence. Each of them has a specific agenda that will affect the status quo: though Ann has been Larry's girl, she comes to town hoping to marry his brother Chris. Though George's father was jailed for supervising the installation of flawed engine parts at the factory where Joe works, George, having finally visited his father in prison, now believes his father is innocent and wants to interrogate Joe about the incident.

It cannot be overemphasized that script analysis is a key tool in the coach's toolbox. A thorough familiarity with the scene and the play from which the scene is taken is essential to discovering the clues that will open the script up to interpretation. This is one reason standalone scenes, such as those created in scene books, are less effective; they offer far fewer clues to the reasons behind the scene's events.

The references to previous circumstances can be subtle. If a scene is lifelike, the character is unlikely to spout exposition about their past. The playwright may use the characters' dialogue but also their actions towards each other. Characters who have been fighting may resort to passive-aggressive behavior when they meet again – be aloof to or dismissive of each other. If the problem is one all of the characters are avoiding, it is the "stinking whale," as Mike Nichols would call it, whose smell will continue to pervade the air even if no one refers to it lying in the room. Such will be the stench – or repercussions of previous circumstances – that, finally, none of the characters will be able to ignore it.

The concept of previous circumstances – information that may or may not be directly referred to by the characters – is such an important factor in their present behavior, it is a category that may be applied in a first session for the benefit of the entire scene.

Category: Character Mission

The word "mission" is a strong term suggesting high stakes that may serve as a substitute for motivation, objective, intention, action, or tactic.[14] The character's mission, one that can be divided into various strategies, creates behavior the audience can observe in order to assign motives to the characters, as we do in real life. Without recourse to the character's thoughts, the audience can still infer why he is performing certain activities, making specific choices, reacting to his environment and other characters. Actors are working backwards: they must use the dialogue and stage directions to determine behavior that is then read by the audience; in real life, the observer sees behavior and then comes to conclusions about why someone acts this way. This is a useful idea for the actor to consider. She uses the mission as a means for determining behavior that creates physical and vocal signs for the audience to decode.

As Richard H. Felnagle notes, "Because we assume that all human behavior is purposeful, we assume that purpose is always reflected in human behavior."[15] He points out, however, that human beings do not have to consider what they are doing: their motives dictate their behavior, while the actors, who are not the characters they play, do not have an automatic response to conditions imagined by the playwright: "Actors must consciously make their characters' behavior appear purposeful in the same way that they must consciously create the proper responses to the situation and the relationships."[16] Essentially, the audience can tell the difference if the actor hasn't bothered to take this important step.

The reason for having a character mission is the effect it has on the actor: they must constantly respond to the circumstances as they unfold. The characters must pay close attention to the signals they are receiving from the other characters to see if their mission is succeeding or failing. This also involves active listening in the actor, a subjective viewpoint of the character in which all input is useful or detrimental. Any clues that will tell the character how their strategies are serving their mission come from what they see and hear in others. Since characters are at cross purposes to each other – that is, have opposing missions – the likelihood is that they will serve as obstacles to each other; while pursuing their own goals, they prevent their partners from doing likewise.

Is the actor listening subjectively? This involves active listening in which the character continues to try to achieve their goal or complete their mission. However, the actor may not be pursuing their intentions as strongly as the conditions indicate. Sometimes, the teacher will note physical or vocal signs that signify the character has given up too early. Sometimes the mission isn't clear. Two characters may even want the same things; however, what differentiates their missions is that they don't want those things in the same way. For example, they both want to be in a relationship, but they have different ideas about how that relationship should unfold, what the rules will be for continued engagement.

What to Do About It

The actor should ask whether what the other character is doing is helping or hurting their mission, or as Ron Van Lieu would ask, "Is this good for you or bad for you?" The coach encourages an inner monologue that unspools in the actor's mind. The actor continuously notes every clue the other actor gives them. As in life, human beings never stop assessing a situation for the benefits it may provide.

One exercise is to ask the actors to express their thoughts out loud as they listen to and watch each other, to give voice to their inner monologues. Another is to create vivid images depicting the success or failure of the mission for the character and to imagine them throughout the scene: a pleasant image as the other character aids the mission, an unpleasant one if the character continues to serve as an obstacle to the mission.

Active Listening and the Inner Monologue

Is the actor's mind full of images the audience can see? Is the character present in a scene regardless of how many lines they have? What is the film going through their minds as they observe the events onstage?

Active Listening

Is the actor focused completely on the forces operating on the character, or is he waiting to say his next line? Is the actor affected by the stimuli from others, or is she thinking of her homework and how to apply it without considering whether her proposed actions have a chance of being effective? In *Acting on Film*, Michael Caine told of advice he learned while rehearsing *The Long, the Short, and the Tall* by Willis Hall. Though he had no lines to say, the director asked him, "What are you doing in the scene, Michael?" When Caine replied he had nothing to do because he had nothing to say, the director surprised him with, "'Of course you have something to say. You've got wonderful things to say. But you sit there and listen, thinking of wonderful things to say, and then, *you decide not to say them*.'"[17]

The actor hangs on every word and closely examines every move the other actors make to determine if he is succeeding in his mission, or whether he must change his strategy or upgrade his tactics or actions in order to succeed. It is only by constantly appraising others that the actor can determine what he should do under the circumstances. He can adapt spontaneously to new conditions if he has paid attention.

Konstantin Stanislavsky instructed young actors on "The Inner Monologue," as he worked with them on *The Battle of Life*, a play adapted from the 1846 novel by Charles Dickens.[18] He took the following steps: while the two actors in the roles of Grace – Sophia Nikolaevna – and Marion – Angelina Osipovna – played a scene, Nikolaevna spoke the dialogue as written. While Osipovna continued to speak Marion's lines, she also expressed her thoughts aloud, reacting to Grace's lines. Stanislavsky asked Osipovna to speak in two different tones to differentiate between her dialogue and her inner monologue. "Very likely the second tone will be much lower and more expressive. But I want to hear both clearly."[19] He noted, "This second text, made up of your thoughts, may sometimes coincide with Grace's words. You may both speak simultaneously."[20] Meanwhile, Nikolaevna was to pay no attention to Marion's inner monologue, while Osipovna had to speak clearly enough so Stanislavsky could observe and critique her inner monologue choices. This step in the exercise encouraged Osipovna to observe her acting partner carefully. It gave new life to her acting, and her movements were full of intention.

Stanislavsky asked the actors not to lose the state they were in, but to begin again. In the second step, Stanislavsky asked Osipovna to whisper her lines. He told her she could offer new thoughts if they seemed appropriate. For the third step, Stanislavsky asked Osipovna to convey her inner monologue silently but through her eyes. In this way, he told her, "The text which the play gives you will be filled now with all that you are not allowed to say."[21] The director no longer had to remind the actors to use active listening or to suggest their reactions to each other's words. "Remember that to know how to listen to your partner means to know how to conduct the inner dialogue with him instead of waiting for your cues."[22] The character's true feelings were now easily detected even in silence.

Side-Coaching

How can the teacher serve as a coach in the heat of the moment, as the scene unfolds, to encourage active listening? The teacher can use side-coaching for any number of categories: "the insertion of brief comments into the flow of the scene without interruption."[23]

Side-coaching can be used with the teacher serving as a partner to the character's thinking, agreeing with the character's assessment of the situation and encouraging them to consider certain reactions. Olympia Dukakis would side-coach in this way, serving as an advocate for the character and offering further comments in support of their attitudes towards each other and the situation, including reactions to what the other character was doing. For example, the coach might say, "Can you believe how ungrateful they are? You've gone to so much trouble, and they just take you for granted."[24]

Konstantin Stanislavsky used side-coaching during his work on Alexander Griboyedov's *Much Woe from Wisdom*.[25] "He prompted the direction of [the character's thought]" when she was speaking dialogue, inciting her disapproval of the other character.[26]

The teacher may prompt the actor to ask, "If I wanted the other character to say or do something that would move my life forward, what would it be?" In an interview with Peter Rinaldi for *Filmmaker Magazine*, Jason Isaacs, when asked about learning lines, pointed out:

> For everything that's written down, there's the hundred things you're not saying. There's all the things that you think you'd like to say and stop yourself saying. . . . There's the things you're hoping the other person is going to say when they're speaking.[27]

For example, if the character wants an apology, what would that apology consist of? What would satisfy the character if they heard it?

As the scene unfolds, the teacher's notes can come quietly to the actor from the teacher. In this way, the teacher is responding in the moment to what they are seeing and guiding the actors as they proceed, in particular encouraging them "to release a suppressed impulse."[28] This occurs when the teacher intuits that an actor wants to move or react in a specific way but avoids doing so. A prompt gives the performer a license to trust their instincts.

Category: Evaluations

What happens in the character's mind when they receive new signals/information? Is there an immediate response, or do they need more time to comprehend what is happening? Do they require further signs in order to understand what they are hearing or seeing? Are they avoiding a response to outside stimuli for their mental security? Are they hearing the same dialogue that they have heard many times and begin speaking again before the other character is finished? Are they thinking about what they want to say so that they ignore the other character's argument?

"Stanislavski referred to 'reflective delay' as a technique calling the actor's attention to the time needed for a character to process information."[29] The actor must determine how much they comprehend in the moment and how much time they need to work out what they don't yet understand, including how much they will be changed by the revelation. A character may hear that a death has occurred, but their mind isn't ready to take it in – the delay acts as a defense mechanism, avoiding the pain a realization will cause. For example, in *This Is Us*, a television series about a family in various points of their lives, Rebecca Pearson is in the hospital waiting for her husband to be released. He has just rescued his family from a house fire. She goes to the vending machine to get a candy bar. The doctor comes out and tells her Jack has died from a heart attack due to smoke inhalation. Rather than react to this tragic news, she is still holding on to the impression of him just moments before when he was alive; she takes a bite of her candy bar. The evaluation is longer because her mind can't grasp the magnitude of the doctor's words; they seem unrelated to her own experience.

Category: Acting Versus Living

Are the actors demonstrating their homework, or are they thinking as people in specific situations? Are you thinking like the person, or are you imagining how your acting is perceived by the audience? This also connects to active listening: the actor is thinking the character's thoughts as they evaluate what they are hearing, paying strict attention to the positive and negative implications of what is being said as it relates to their mission.

One sign of living is the actor should ask a question as if they really want to know the answer to it. As obvious as this sounds, merely noting a question mark at the end of the sentence will suggest a reading of the line whether filled with intent or not. An actor can give a perfectly intelligent reading, but it is one that comes from the intellect recognizing what is needed vocally – anger, sadness, happiness, nervousness, delight. Meanwhile, the actor is disengaged from the recreation of the character's feelings.

One important tool is to ask the actor to use as much of themselves as possible, in order to find the truth of the character: using their own voice, their own body. As Philip Seymour Hoffman said to Ron Cephas Jones during a rehearsal of the play *Jesus Hopped the A-Train* by Stephen Adly Guirgis, "You are enough."[30] According to Cephas Jones, this "shifted" his thinking. What Hoffman meant was, "[w]e as humans have the ability to do everything that is humanly possible that has been done in the history of mankind."[31] This took the pressure off of Cephas Jones to look outside himself: he could use as much of himself as he wanted rather than relying on externals to connect him to an imagined character. "It took me away from acting and brought me into what my abilities are as a human being to do, the things I am capable of doing which is also love and also hate."[32] If the side effect is an actor is forced to look at themselves more closely, the teacher should be prepared to deal with this byproduct. "How deep and horrible you want to delve into your own psyche is up to you."[33] If any one human being has perpetrated an unconscionable act, all of us – being human – are capable of doing the same, given the right circumstances. This can be a difficult concept to embrace: "It's not acting but revealing what's in you. And that's really scary."[34] David Hyde Pierce learned the same lesson from Mike Nichols: "The underlying message of his direction is: You are enough. I don't need more than you. I don't need less than you. You're enough."[35] The actor avoids creating a false persona so removed from themselves that it seems false.

The coach can suggest analogous situations that might occur in the actors' lives, giving them insight into these more dramatic or unfamiliar circumstances or helping them to identify with the characters' feelings. It is not unusual for a teacher to share stories from their own life, though the same teacher is not insistent on prying into the actor's private thoughts. It is only important in the long run that the actor remember their own parallel experiences and that they are useful. Mike Nichols would "share everything about his life, his history, the way he thought about directing drama," in order to inspire his actors.[36] At the same time, "He would often tell humiliating, embarrassing" ones "as a way of letting actors know in a rehearsal situation that there was nothing they could do that was worse than what Mike had done, and it would free them up."[37]

Personalization or substitution is a tool that connects the actor to their own experience. The actor imagines a personal situation and substitutes it in their own minds for the author's. Or the actor uses someone they have feelings for and substitutes them for the actor they are dealing with onstage.³⁸ The same can be done with objects. A coffee cup may have been made by one's child, or a briefcase they use for work may have belonged to someone's parent.

Category: News

News consists of any information that at least one character doesn't know until that moment in the scene. News is a powerful stimulant for a character's reactions: revelations can lead to deep evaluation, to epiphanies, and to a change in the character's overall view of the world. What does a character discover during the course of a scene? Is any new information revealed? Is that news a secret, and is the secret unearthed or confessed? How does this news change the characters? Does it destroy their relationship? Was this news suspected and then confirmed, or was it a complete surprise? Can the news be used by either character as a weapon against the other?

Michael Shurtleff, in his seminal book *Audition*, uses news as one of his Guideposts – his own version of diagnostic categories – and labels it a discovery that a character is encountering for the first time. "The discoveries may be about the other character, or about oneself, or about someone who is offstage, or about the situation now or the situation as it existed ten years ago and how that affects the now."³⁹ It is important that the actors acknowledge discoveries, not only because it helps the audience to follow the story but also because of the effects the discoveries might have on one or more of them. As Shurtleff points out, "The more important you make a discovery, the more it becomes an event."⁴⁰ When a character realizes they have made a terrible mistake, this discovery is life-altering. If the audience is aware of a secret, they will be fascinated to see how a character will react when he realizes or discovers it.

In Henrick Ibsen's *Hedda Gabler*, when Hedda learns from Thea that Hedda's former lover Eilert Lovborg has returned to town, is sober, and seeing another woman – Thea herself – she determines to destroy him. She now has something to occupy her time besides her tedious marriage, and she can punish Lovborg for attaching himself to a woman whom Hedda considers her inferior.

Category: Openness

Openness is that state that allows an actor to be affected by external stimuli and to the point that the body reacts instinctively. Those habits that close the actor down have to be addressed. Does the actor have access to or holding their breath? Do they have access to their own body? Are they allowing each moment to live in their bodies? What's getting in the way? Does the teacher see/feel tension in the actor? Where?

Keith Johnstone offers an interesting tip:

> If you get tense, there's an old actor's trick; you push your forefinger and thumb together. As you talk you are trying to separate the thumb and the forefinger. Finally, they are going to come apart. And as they relax your body begins to relax.⁴¹

He attributes tension in an actor to such experiences as those they received in school: "You do not want to be uptight as an actor. If you are badly trained, you are always uptight as an actor."[42]

A primary source of tension is an actor's tendency to stop breathing because of the pressure to perform. Not only does this shut the actor down, but the audience subconsciously begins to tense or hold their breath as well. If the coach begins to realize this, then they can recognize it as coming from the actor.

The teacher can begin by calling the actors' attention to their breathing, whether shallow, quick or nonexistent – sometimes the actors hold their breath. When an actor holds his breath, he is using an internal censor to edit what he will share with the class. To stop breathing is to resort to a defense mechanism, to avoid vulnerability. It shuts down the instinct to go with their impulses, a kind of editing of their own performance. The solution is to ask them to take in some breath and to ready themselves to be affected by their partners.

The very act of appearing in front of other people, especially one's peers, can lead to substantial bodily tension. Muscle tension is caused by the autonomic nervous system, so telling the body to relax may not help. Teachers may use a series of exercises to identify where tension lives in the body and help the actors to deal with each spot. A number of books on the subject use the Alexander Technique as the foundation for this work. Developed by Frederick Matthias Alexander (1865–1955), the process allows the actor to realign the body, remove habits that lead to tension, and perform with only the required effort. According to Jean-Louis Rodrigue and Scott Weintraub, its benefits include: "Awareness; Buoyancy; Weightlessness and freedom; Centering; Release of tension; Organic breathing; and connectedness to oneself, the story, the environment, and others."[43]

Sending the student to a good Alexander Teacher or taking a certification in the technique will address many of these concerns. Ron Van Lieu spoke of an instructor he had in Alexander: "Drew Matthews . . . had a deep definition of what 'poise' was: 'to help the actor do the most difficult thing without engaging one unnecessary muscle.'"[44]

Michael Schulman suggests using affective memory as a way to deal with the phenomenon of tension caused by fear: The Confidence Stimulus Exercise.[45] It is a sequential process which begins when Schulman asks his students to sit in a semicircle and "think of some object, place, or person in whose presence they feel strong and confident."[46] He reminds them to remember with all five senses. He then asks them to make noise coming from that confident feeling. This can take some time, as the students return to self-consciousness and lose concentration; they must recapture the memory through images and senses, and Schulman encourages them to be specific and commit further to the exercise. The students then picture themselves with the stimulus before making the sound, which leads to a deeper connection to that sound and to their private selves. This exercise can be used both for the self and for the character.[47]

Categories: Activities

Bill Wilson, the founder of Alcoholics Anonymous, offers a thought from recovering alcoholics to those still dealing with the disease, that an awareness of what to do is not the same as taking action: "It is easier to act your way into a new way of thinking than to think yourself into a new way of acting."[48] This precept can be applied to acting as well. In this book, much discussion centers around thinking – analysis of the script, thoughts about the character, and so on – but ultimately, the book stresses *doing* as a primary method. What if the actor feels aimless? What can they do to ground them in a scene? What activities can they perform that are appropriate in the context of the script?[49]

An example of how a playwright can use this idea throughout a play is the one-act *Laundry and Bourbon* by James McClure. The scene is not about the activity of folding clothes and drinking alcohol, but about a wife who is worried about the disappearance of her husband and the feelings of the characters about being married. The folding and drinking gives the characters an alternate task to use as they pursue their goals.[50]

Category: Groundplan and Blocking

Where do the characters need to be to fulfill their missions? Would it be more helpful to be here or over there? Sitting or standing? Blocking is really based on where the character needs to be at any given time to fulfill their mission. By the same token, the actor shouldn't move unless the character is motivated to do so. Young actors tend to move for the sake of having something to do. Too much movement will dissipate the effects of an important or revealing move.

Categories: Tempo-Rhythm

How does the actor's speed of movement affect their behavior? How can the teacher tell that the actor is somehow moving at the wrong pace either inwardly or outwardly?

Konstantin Stanislavsky was fascinated by the combination of tempo and rhythm, two elements that affected the actor and also created a certain tone for a scene: "All human beings are affected by the speed, or pace, of their environments, called Tempo. In addition an individual has his own Rhythm, or beat."[51] Each character has a tempo-rhythm that arises in each circumstance. The definition continues:

> Work in Tempo-Rhythm coordinates and exercises the actor's external and internal processes, so that stage activities (like a worker going to a factory in the morning or coming home at night) add a specific and different physical component to the acting.[52]

Tempo-Rhythm has an added benefit, the prompting of emotion: "Although Tempo-Rhythm would seem to belong solely to the actor's physical preparations, in fact, it is as important a stimulus for the actor's feelings and inner state."[53] The inner tempo-rhythm comes from the character's thoughts and feelings.

Sam Kogan refers to tempo as "the speed of thinking."[54] The students should learn that tempo is an inner process, while rhythm is the external manifestation of that process. "Tempo doesn't necessarily have anything to do with any physical movement."[55]

The thinking Kogan refers to consists of images or pictures that are in the person's head appearing at a certain rate. Tempo is "just the speed of mental pictures."[56] An awareness of tempo allows human beings to determine whether a situation is unfolding in its usual fashion, or whether something is off about it. As Kogan notes, this is because we have experienced everyday situations many times in our lives, whereas "when the impression of this particular situation doesn't match, it sticks out."[57] We notice tempo – our mental pictures – because it is manifested in a rhythm that is observable in a person's gestures and movements, as well as their tone of voice, and attitude. Since tempo leads to rhythm, the two words are united as tempo-rhythm.[58]

Bella Martin, in *The Complete Stanislavsky Toolkit*, in her discussion of tempo-rhythm, defines tempo as "the speed at which you carry out an action, and "rhythm is the intensity with which you carry it out."[59] She also refers to the notion of inner and outer tempo-rhythms.[60] They may not be the same, the physicality of the character belying the mental pictures of the character; for example, the ability to stand physically still in a line for a train ticket as the train is about to leave the station. The outer tempo-rhythm seems slower than the inner one – the character forced to maintain their dignity as they panic about the possibility of missing their train. Whatever the outward tempo-rhythm seems to be, the inner mental pictures tell us the true story.

What the actor must avoid is using their own inner tempo-rhythm when it contradicts the character's, for example, when they have a high state of tension because of opening night nerves versus a character's lower state of tension based on the play's circumstances.[61] Stanislavsky also saw tempo-rhythm as a key tool in his Method of Physical Actions.[62]

Where the idea of tempo-rhythm is misused is in rehearsal and performance, applied as jargon without its concomitant meaning: "We don't need tempo-rhythm for its own sake. It must be related to the inner meaning that Tempo-Rhythm always hides within it."[63] A fast inner tempo can lead to anxiety, heavy breathing, sweating, and fast heartbeat. Unfortunately, some directors confuse rhythm with tempo and use it to refer to speeding up a performance. This use of rhythm can be harmful, as it is an external request unrelated to what the actor has been discovering. It disrupts the inner creative state.[64]

Norris Houghton, in *Moscow Rehearsals*, writes that Stanislavsky divided the types of tempo-rhythms into ten parts.

> In rehearsal every movement was marked. The normal rhythm was 5. Rhythm 1 was that of a man almost dead, 2 that of a man weak with illness, and so on progressively to rhythm 9 which might be that of a person seeing a burning house, and to 10 when he is on the point of jumping out of the window.[65]

The same idea is used by John Wright as a list of States of Tension.

States of Tension

John Wright uses the States of Tension he learned from Simon McBurney, who studied with Jacques Lecoq. Wright chooses which states to apply to which genres because "different tension states dominate different theatrical forms."[66] Though his primary focus is on comedy, his discussion applies to many different forms. The eight categories allow the actor to capture "different states of physical intensity."[67] An important note is, "These tension states have no meaning in themselves; meaning is conveyed by the context."[68]

Wright points out that the tension builds from one state to another, but finally the outward indication of either 1 or 8 is the same: though the first is a lack of all tension and the last is the apex of tension, both cause inertia.[69] The eight types of tension are: (1) Exhausted, (2) Laid Back, (3) One Movement at a Time, (4) Neutral, (5) Is There a Bomb in the Room?, (6) There Is a Bomb in the Room!, (7) The Bomb is About to Go Off!, and (8) Rigor Mortis.[70] Wright explains each state of tension in some detail and creates games for practicing them. "Is There a Bomb in the Room?" is the first suspicion of danger in the environment which causes a certain level of tension. The tension grows at the realization of an actual danger and even further when the danger is imminent. "Rigor Mortis" is that state of such great tension a person is no longer able to move, so frozen are they by fear or stress.

When an actor uses a tempo-rhythm or a state of tension which seems to contradict the situation of a scene – and Kogan has already suggested that, based on a knowledge of various situations, observers will notice this – the teacher can work with him on these two concepts, allowing him to physically feel the gradations as a nuanced means of manifesting the appropriate physicality based on the student's mental pictures.

Using categories allows the teacher to organize their thoughts in smaller containers and choose between them, since a scene may suggest many different ways of responding. One particular category, which deserves its own chapter, concerns the way actors succeed or fail in accessing their feelings and finding emotional connections with a character. Chapter 8 discusses how the coach may identify or suggest ways an actor reaches a creative state that places her viscerally inside the character.

Notes

1 Ambrose et al., *How Learning Works*, 43.
2 Ambrose et al., *How Learning Works*, 44.
3 Ambrose et al., *How Learning Works*, 52.
4 Milton Katselas, *Acting Class: Take a Seat* (Beverly Hills, CA: Phoenix Books Inc., 2008), 29–87.
5 Moss, *The Intent to Live*, 303–304.
6 Michael Shurtleff, *Audition: Everything an Actor Needs to Know to Get the Part* (New York: Walker and Company, 1978).
7 Susan Batson's excellent book, *Truth: Personas, Needs, and Flaws in Building Actors and Creating Characters* (New York: Stone vs. Stone Inc., 2006), proposes ways to create the past of the character based on the public persona that masks their inner child and its needs. Her work is in part based on another work. See Alice Miller, *The Drama of the Gifted Child: The Search for the True Self*, trans. Ruth Ward (New York: Basic Books, 1997).
8 Stephen Henderson quoting Lloyd Richards in Francis, "Preparing Birds to Fly," 121.
9 Hagen, *Respect for Acting*, 95–100. Hagen also insists on establishing what the character is there to do and why.
10 See the discussion on etudes in Chapter 12.
11 These are also conditions that may affect their work.

12 At other times, the writer will begin with the inciting incident, and the audience will have to infer what has been disrupted.
13 Another example of an etude. See Chapter 12.
14 See Chapter 8 for a discussion of these terms and the ideas behind them.
15 Richard H. Felnagle, *Beginning Acting: The Illusion of Natural Behavior* (Englewood Cliffs, NJ: Prentice-Hall Inc., 1987), 89.
16 Felnagle, *Beginning Acting*, 89.
17 Michael Caine, quoting Lindsay Anderson in *Acting on Film: An Actor's Take on Movie Making* (New York: Applause Theatre Book Publishers, 1990), 68–69, emphasis Caine's.
18 Gorchakov, *Stanislavsky Directs*, 49–57.
19 Gorchakov, *Stanislavsky Directs*, 51.
20 Gorchakov, *Stanislavsky Directs*, 51.
21 Gorchakov, *Stanislavsky Directs*, 55.
22 Gorchakov, *Stanislavsky Directs*, 109.
23 Benedetti, "On Acting," 102.
24 Van Lieu from Teacher Development Program Notes, June 2012: "When I went to NYU I had no interest in Chekhov until I had Olympia. She just understood them as people. It wasn't directorial: she would say, 'You know she's . . .' and then she would *do* something. And I would see that. It was a way of expressing the essence of somebody in some way that helped you to do that."
25 Gorchakov, *Stanislavsky Directs*, 190–191.
26 Gorchakov, *Stanislavsky Directs*, 190.
27 Jason Isaacs on Episode 176 of *Back to One* hosted by Peter Rinaldi, https://filmmakermagazine.com/112512-back-to-one-episode-176-jason-isaacs/#.ZEPZt-zMJBY
28 Benedetti, "On Acting," 102.
29 Allen Barton, *The Oasis of Sanity: The Study and Pursuit of Acting at the Beverly Hills Playhouse* (Beverly Hills, CA: Beverly Hills Playhouse, 2017), 142.
30 Ron Cephas Jones on Episode 116 of *Back to One*, hosted by Peter Rinaldi, https://filmmakermagazine.com/109981-back-to-one-episode-116-ron-cephas-jones/#.ZEPY5ezMJBY
31 Cephas Jones on Episode 116 of *Back to One*.
32 Cephas Jones on Episode 116 of *Back to One*.
33 Cephas Jones on Episode 116 of *Back to One*.
34 Cephas Jones on Episode 116 of *Back to One*.
35 David Hyde Pierce, quoted in Harris, *Mike Nichols*, 301.
36 Harris, *Mike Nichols*, 435.
37 Harris, *Mike Nichols*, ix.
38 The actor should still connect strongly with the partner onstage. The danger of this approach is the actor will still be imagining the other person while dealing with the live person in front of them.
39 See the discussion on Goalpost 6: Discoveries in Shurtleff, *Audition*, 58.
40 Shurtleff, *Audition*, 61.
41 Johnstone, "Ten Days with Keith," July 11, 2017.
42 Johnstone, "Ten Days with Keith," July 11, 2017.
43 See Jean-Louis Rodrigue and Scott Weintraub, *Back to the Body: Infusing Physical Life into Characters in Theatre and Film* (Alexander Techworks, 2023), 25.
44 Van Lieu, Teacher Development Program Notes, June 2013.
45 Michael Schulman in Eva Mekler, *The New Generation of Acting Teachers: More Than 20 Revealing Interviews with Today's Master Teachers on the Art and Craft of Acting* (New York: Penguin Books, 1987), 38–40.
46 Mekler, *The New Generation of Acting Teachers*, 38.
47 For a more complete discussion, see Meckler, *The New Generation of Acting Teachers*, 38–40.

48 Alcoholics Anonymous, *Alcoholics Anonymous: The Story of How Many Thousands of Men and Women Have Recovered from Alcoholism*, 4th Edition (New York: Alcoholics Anonymous World Services Inc., 2001), 192.
49 For a larger discussion about activities, see the Method of Physical Actions in Chapter 8.
50 James McClure, *Laundry and Bourbon: A Comedy in One Act* (New York: Dramatists Play Service, 1981).
51 Definition of Tempo-Rhythm in the "Glossary of Terms" in Mel Gordon, *The Stanislavsky Technique: Russia: A Workshop for Actors* (New York: Applause Theatre Book Publishers, 1987), 243.
52 Gordon, *The Stanislavsky Technique: Russia*, 243.
53 Gordon, *The Stanislavsky Technique: Russia*, 243.
54 Kogan and Kogan, *The Science of Acting*, 138.
55 Kogan and Kogan, *The Science of Acting*, 137–138.
56 Kogan and Kogan, *The Science of Acting*, 138.
57 Kogan and Kogan, *The Science of Acting*, 139.
58 Kogan and Kogan, *The Science of Acting*, 138–139.
59 Bella Martin, *The Complete Stanislavsky Toolkit* (Hollywood: Drama Publishers, 2007), 139.
60 Martin, *The Complete Stanislavsky Toolkit*, 140.
61 Martin, *The Complete Stanislavsky Toolkit*, 141.
62 Martin, *The Complete Stanislavsky Toolkit*, 141.
63 Stanislavski, *An Actor's Work*, 473.
64 See Demidov, *Becoming an Actor-Creator*, 311.
65 Norris Houghton, *Moscow Rehearsals: An Account of Methods of Production in the Soviet Theatre* (New York: Harcourt, Brace, and Company, 1936), 6. Even as Houghton was writing the book, he noted that "the fractional system is no longer in use at the MXAT," although the use of rhythm was still explored with the actors. (61)
66 John Wright, *Why Is That So Funny? A Practical Exploration of Physical Comedy* (New York: Limelight Editions, 2007), 122.
67 Wright, *Why Is That So Funny?* 122.
68 Wright, *Why Is That So Funny?* 103.
69 Wright, *Why Is That So Funny?* 103.
70 Wright, *Why Is That So Funny?* 103–122.

8   Coaching to Inspire Emotions

This chapter concerns the process by which an actor finds within themselves a place where emotion lies and expresses those sentiments, so an audience may know what lives within a character's heart. No one methodology can be said to encompass the definitive process since, like feelings themselves, the ways circumstances touch a character are as many and varied as they are to us in real life.

Admittedly, a portion of the methods described in this chapter have a basis in Stanislavsky's System – that is, Konstantin Stanislavsky's attempts to codify the kinds of practices he observed in the inspired geniuses of his own lifetime. He realized each great artist has his or her own approach to onstage life, even if many of them cannot describe it other than through demonstration on the stage – that no one can rely on inspiration to strike every time they step into the spotlight, but the truly brilliant thespians are able to catch that lightning more than anyone else. After a lifetime of on-the-job training, these preeminent masters had laid the groundwork that made it possible for them to reach the very heights of art.

As Stanislavsky was struck by the virtuosity of Tommaso Salvini, he began to observe how that actor was able to play Shakespeare's Othello so completely, riveting the spectators with his otherworldly skill. He discovered Salvini would come to the theatre hours in advance, to prepare not his makeup, but his soul. He had complete concentration on the stage, and perhaps the most important element in the art, the imagination to believe completely in the given circumstances of the play. Stanislavsky spent many years experimenting with ways to prepare the actor to reach for the high standards his idols had set in the acting art. His examination of the great led him to feel that actors needed to carry on those practices "passed down to us as traditions, created by the genius of our predecessors through the ages."[1]

Today's acting teacher or coach has her own standards, based on prior experience and observation, for preparing for a role and instilling in themselves the means for producing feelings. They may also find their students also connect to an emotional life in more or less successful ways. It is most likely that these actors have been inspired on at least one occasion to reach higher than they believed possible, but they do not know how this was accomplished. It is the teacher's aim, then, to offer a process for inspiration and to discover how the actor in front of her accomplishes, in their own view, an emotional state which may or may not be repeatable.

The teacher should keep in mind that specific acting training may also be offered in other courses, or the student's prior experience may include training in a particular technique. The teacher should identify what that method is. Rather than stepping on their colleagues' toes, the teacher can acknowledge other practices to which the students are being introduced, while relating that work to new work they are offering as another form of training. Alternatively, all of the teachers of a program may combine their efforts, speaking to their students with a knowledge of each other's definitions or vocabulary in order to communicate with the students they share.

Some means that the student actor may already find effective for inducing emotion in themselves include empathy, personal emotions or Affective Memory, imagination, or actions. None of these should be dismissed offhand if they produce results. Even Lee Strasberg, father of the Method, lamented during a session at the Actors Studio that various approaches were compared to each other, as if one was better than another: "I wish we could stop this senseless opposing of one approach to another and begin to seek real values within each possible approach."[2] In particular, he was referring to the dismissal of the external as opposed to the internal approach of creating a character. In his view, "Every approach has such values so long as it is not mechanically but artistically followed." Is acting about the external or internal? About physical and vocal technique or identifying and connecting to a character's inner feelings? Or is it both?

Here is where Stanislavsky's early and late work are contrasted, especially as his various books were published at different times – sometimes years apart – and the later work was altered by Soviet censors. Both in his early experiments and towards the end of his life, he was still searching for answers, testing, rejecting, and trying again. At first, he promoted the idea of Affective Memory.

Emotional Recall or Affective Memory is an exploration of the actor's past to mine it for an analogous feeling to the character's, one he can invoke repeatedly for use onstage. The actor identifies specific triggers that bring the original feeling back. At best, the actor relives the memory completely in her entire body. At worst, the memory will be so powerful as to render the actor overwrought and incapable of performing. In Affective Memory, the actor is asked to recall all five senses from the original incident, so as to find the specific detail that inspires the return of overall emotion. A factual reminder of what happened, even stated out loud, is an intellectual understanding only, and can separate the actor from their feelings. It is a defense mechanism, an objective statement of the facts. One can say, "I was in an accident," but to recall the texture of the seatbelt cutting into the chest, or to smell gasoline leaking from the tank, or to see the amount of blood on the car seat, or to hear the sound of the approaching ambulance, or to imagine again the coppery taste of blood in the mouth, is much more likely to trigger the feelings from that time: disorientation, fear, horror, or panic. Any one of these senses can serve as a trigger, and simply recalling that trigger can bring the entire incident back, a much more powerful recollection from the past. As Lee Strasberg, a proponent of Affective Memory, told his students,

Affective memory is not mere memory. It is a memory that involves the actor personally, so that deeply rooted emotional experiences begin to respond. His instrument awakens and he becomes capable of the kind of living on the stage which is essentially reliving.[3]

On the other hand, some actors reject Affective Memory – just as Stanislavsky eventually did – and find it ineffective, problematic, or even traumatic. Strasberg was aware that the conditions for practicing this exercise had to be ideal, and even then the result might be disappointing or unanticipated: "Sometimes nothing happens; although the actor remembers the experience, it did not actually make the impression he thought it did."[4] The original memory, despite its promise of emotional connection, can weaken over time, the actor having a different perspective years later: the traumas of youth seeming trivial in adulthood, for example. The actor may also be unprepared to deal with emotions he has repressed and which come flooding back in an overwhelming torrent: "Sometimes when the actor thinks that not much is going to happen, a lot happens."[5] Another issue is that the emotion the actor may be looking for is different from the one that actually arises in recollection: "Emotional response induced by affective memory cannot be determined in advance."[6]

"If"

Though Stanislavsky's system is sometimes equated with Strasberg's method – which stresses the access of emotional memories – eventually, as noted by Sharon Marie Carnicke, he came to believe "that empathy can be a more powerful prompt to creativity than personal emotion."[7] Carnicke also pointed out that Stanislavsky's findings were confirmed decades later by the discovery of mirror neurons in the brain: the audience member could have the same feelings as the actor they were watching onstage.

Empathy was created in the actor through what Stanislavsky called the "Magic If," a tool used by the actor to imagine themselves in the character's given circumstances. The famous formula is as follows: when the actor asks, "If I were in this situation, what would I do, 'if the circumstances were real,'"[8] leads the actor to respond naturally in a way, "which is well-founded, apt, and productive."[9] For example, though a student may not have dealt with an escaped criminal at the door to her home, "if" she imagined there was one, how would she behave in those circumstances? What kind of reactions would she have? What kind of steps would she take to defend herself? In *An Actor's Work*, Stanislavsky, in the guise of the teacher Tortsov, gives great emphasis to the importance of the "if" to the actor's creative state: "For actors, 'if' is the lever which lifts us out of the world of reality into the only world where we can be creative."[10]

The Magic If can lead to strong feelings, the actor's imagination allowing him to feel they are experiencing the fictional event. However, it can be a bit more complicated than that. Howard Fine, founder of the Howard Fine Acting Studio, writes that "What would I do?" is a dead-end question, since the answer could simply be, "I would never do this."[11] Instead, Fine poses the question as, "What would make me do this?"[12] or more elaborately, "What would make me do what the character is doing?"[13] And Eugene Vakhtangov's formulation makes a distinction between an actor and a character choice to emphasize the character's agency in the process: "What would I have to do in order to do what the *character* does in this situation?"[14]

This is because, as Fine suggests, the actor might not personally feel like doing what the character does, depending on how far apart the two are in sensibilities. The question "What would I do if . . .?" may best be applied after a study of the character's similarities and differences from the actor's own.

Complexes

If the actor is open to the stimuli of the environment and other characters, these lead the actor to feeling. The actor doesn't have to rely on any one impetus. Sam Kogan was fascinated by "the very basic processes that take place inside our skulls when we are faced with what is going on outside them."[15] He pointed out that one is affected not by a single stimulant, but by all of the other thoughts that come with it. He calls this collection a complex, "a circle of thoughts where when one is activated, then so are the others to different degrees."[16] The other, ancillary thoughts, are called affinities, "every activated thought in the complex other than the main one."[17] These are "pictures and impressions" that evolve as the main idea penetrates the actor and is under examination.

This is good news for the teacher who wants to inspire creative imagination in the student. Each actor has more than one impulse per stimulus: he has all of the connected stimuli suggested by the first impulse – a complex of them. For example, being handed a cup of coffee at a coffee shop may lead to the thought that the caffeine is especially important today because of all the work you have ahead. This work comes into focus as a list of duties. One of the duties may be to pick up a suit at the cleaners. This suggests what the suit means to you: you have a gala to attend and want to look your best. The gala makes you think of the people you will see there. One particular person comes to mind whom you don't want to see. This reminds you of how you parted on bad terms. And so on. Or the writing on a coffee cup from a coffee shop may misspell your name. This may remind you that your name is often mispronounced and misspelled, an irritant that then reminds you of a particular incident that demoralized you because your employer never knew or cared enough to remember your name. This reminds you of the other terrible conditions at work. This reminds you that you have been job searching, which reminds you that you need to check your emails. And so on.

Substitution

The actor may bring his or her own experience and background to those of the character through the practice of Substitution. Alice Spivak offers a two-part definition: "The use by the actor of events, objects, people, or places from his or her own life, analogous to those things as experienced by the character," and "A conscious replacement of the fictitious objects in the play with remembered objects from the actor's own experience."[18] In the first instance, the actor uses their memories to replace the onstage persons and objects, imposed on them by casting and design, with material that is much more familiar. This can lead to natural reactions that otherwise might not arise, such as contempt for the partner in front of them through imagining that actor is someone else, an acquaintance the actor finds contemptible in real life. In the second instance, instead of relating to the prop onstage, the actor might imagine it was a specific object with many memories attached to it, such as an old toy that reminds them of their childhood.[19]

Larry Moss warns about one possible side effect to this approach: "[I]f you think about something personal and it takes you out of the story, it's not helpful."[20] The actor must still connect strongly with the partner onstage. The danger of substitution is that the actor will still be imagining the other person while ignoring the live person in front of him, overlaying an image on the face and body of his partner and paying more attention to that figment than to the reality.

Imagery

Imagery has already been introduced as necessary for creating complexes and as a significant ability of the successful actor. It is a foundation for living onstage and an alternative to Affective Memory. As Larry Moss explains, "In acting, it doesn't matter whether you *actually* lived it or you imagine it fully, because if you imagine it in detail in your imagination, and you commit to believing it, it is *as if* you've lived it."[21]

William Esper asks the actor to imagine a character's frame of mind and let it guide the actor as they enter a scene. To prepare this state, Esper asks the actors to use daydreams to activate their imaginations. He insists on separating the idea of a dream from a daydream because "the content of daydreams is not disguised."[22] Dreams are subconscious and appear as symbols or substitutes for the worries the dreamer may be having. Daydreams are deliberative and dredged from the unconscious life of an actor to become conscious thoughts.

Daydreams are a simple and useful tool because they are natural responses to desires. To conjure a daydream doesn't require training. "[T]hey often arise in response to some event in life that's unacceptable to our egos[.]"[23] If someone upsets us, we are not likely to physically attack them, due to social norms; however, we can imagine perpetrating violence by dreaming about it. In this way, "Daydreams often act as emotional ventilators, meaning that our unconscious minds almost always introduce a daydream whenever they want to re-create reality into something more satisfying."[24] When using an imaginary situation, the actor must determine "which emotional life will be most appropriate for the circumstances,"[25] and then consider why. Esper asks the actor to consider that they are in a particular state "because."[26] This magic word spurs the actor to feel the past that has led to this moment and why it is happening now. The actor may say, "I've been belittled and emasculated for years by my boss. I can imagine telling her off, basking in the warm feeling of turning the tables on this bully." These daydreams come from instinct; in life, we wouldn't or couldn't share them, but in art, we can use them.

Embodying or Physicalizing the Feeling

Larry Moss offers the key: "[F]or something to be an emotional trigger, the image or the memory or whatever choice you make must not stay in your head; it should urge you to be physical."[27] The elements that create a reaction in the body can be suppressed or acted on; either way the audience will notice it. The stimulus is there to use or not as seems appropriate: "You may not act on the physical impulse, but it should cause one."[28]

An emotional trigger may come from many sources: "An emotional trigger can be a sensorial memory from your life, it can be an "as if," it can be completely about your imagination, it can be a physical gesture . . . It can be anything at all as long as it will ignite the emotion you need to make the script work."[29] In fact, Stanislavsky moved from an emphasis on the mind to the significance of physicality on the mind.

The Method of Physical Actions

In his last work with members of his studio, Stanislavsky had rejected his work on Affective Memory, the reliving of personal moments on the stage. Instead, "Stanislavski considered action to be the sole, the indisputable basis of acting."[30] First of all, he tied behavior to the goal or objective the character pursued within the scene and the play. In the latter instance it was the "through-action," an overall goal for the character's life. He continually asked his actors, "Why are you doing that? What does it contribute to the through-action?"[31] Stanislavsky joined the emotions to the actions the actor discovered for the character, based on the given circumstances and used as means to accomplish their goal, objective, and through-action.

As Sharon Marie Carnicke explains, "The actor first examines the 'given circumstances' in order to describe the character's situation. The situation poses a 'problem' . . . which the character must solve through the choice of an 'action.'"[32] This is what leads to feeling: "During the performance, the actor places his or her full attention on carrying out the required action, with the character's emotions arising as a natural result of the action."[33] This is because, "by focusing solely on action, the actor experiences something akin to the role's emotional life as a subsidiary effect."[34] The actor can concentrate fully on what they are doing, and the feelings will take care of themselves.

This discovery of Stanislavsky is still an important part of the acting process, stressed by many well-known acting teachers. Larry Moss believes,

> The superobjective, the dream, tells you how you feel about everything in the play or film, including the other characters, and in every scene it drives you to actions that you believe will help you to get what you want.[35]

The lines of dialogue were yet another way to do this: "Every physical action must be dynamic, and lead to the accomplishment of some goal or other, and that includes every line you speak on stage."[36] Studying the dialogue, he was able to use words to suggest operating in two ways, "One was to follow the external line, to study the logical construction of the sentence; the other was to follow the inner line, to make the actor develop the right mental images and pictures behind the dialogue."[37] That external line was the through-action, also known as the superobjective.

His definition of "action" in The Method of Physical actions still used the objective as a spur for the actor's behavior; however, rather than the mental tactics – which Stanislavsky refers to above as the "inner line" and will be discussed further when explaining his other late experiments in Active Analysis[38] – an action had to do with an activity. Stanislavsky created activities for actors to launch them into a character: "a rehearsal technique with which Stanislavsky experimented in the last part of his life, by means of which the actor develops a logical sequence of physical actions (activities) for his or her role in improvisation."[39]

The actor imagines everything they do to accomplish their activity. This can be as specific as finding the objects the character needs in a drawer and placing them on the desk. Sometimes the author will give the character activities normally finished in the Moment Before. The teacher can suggest they be used as activities during a scene instead. By performing every part of the preparation for a major activity in the play, such as performing an office job as part of the play's action, the actor also prepares an inner connection to the occupation, especially if it is one the character has been doing for a long time. Warming up for a major tennis match, making last-minute notes for a presentation, putting on the proper clothes to deal with a grimy job, eating breakfast, and finding all of the papers needed for work or class: each of these puts the actor into the circumstances that lead to the actor's onstage life. If the actor is not given the time to go through these steps, they may create a series of images that, sequentially, take their imagination through those procedures.

The purpose is to occupy the actor's mind with activities the character would perform in order to lead them away from self-consciousness and towards instinctual behavior: "If [actors] could turn their attention away from big emotional delvings, leaving the SUBCONSCIOUS alone and focusing instead on small, manageable, everyday, physical tasks, then the SUBCONSCIOUS had the chance to spring to life and fuel the actors' creative impulses."[40] The actor identified an objective that gave purpose to her actions. She then created a score, a list of actable tasks, in order to achieve her objective while at the same time giving her an inner justification for those tasks. Finally, she tested the score by enacting those simple steps during a silent etude, an improvisation in which she performed all of the steps for an overall goal. In the process, she could note whether the steps were in the proper order and natural or needed to be rearranged or changed.[41] In an ideal etude, those steps would "stimulate complex psychological experiences in the actors if they carried them out with precision and commitment."[42]

For example, when Stanislavsky directed Vasili Toporkov as Vanechka in Valentin Kataev's *The Embezzlers*, he asked the actor to go through the motions of a bank cashier preparing for the day. "You see, you don't know what's essential about your character, his daily work."[43] The way Vanechka organized his office revealed the seriousness with which he took his job as the most important part of his life. Without this, said Stanislavsky, Toporkov "didn't put down the roots through which to feed [his] role."[44] Therefore, the actor dusted his desk, sharpened his pencils with his penknife, looked for the necessary forms to fill out, and counted his money before his customers arrived and the scene began. By doing the things the character would do, Toporkov was also feeling his way into the character. The Method of Physical Actions is able to "stimulate an experiencing of the role's human spirit in us as a natural reflex."[45]

At the Moscow Art Theatre, Vasili Toporkov wrote about his training with the great teacher and how he did not understand the principles right away:

> At the time I still had not grasped the full significance of this type of work. I didn't know the meaning of Stanislavski's secret, that by truthfully performing physical actions and following their logic and sequence you can achieve the most complex feelings and experiences, those qualities which we had tried unsuccessfully to achieve in this first period of work.[46]

Toporkov came to believe, "The shift from the search for inner feelings to the fulfilment of tasks is one of Stanislavski's greatest discoveries, and solves one of the major problems actors have."[47]

The Method of Physical Actions was used to follow the external line of the character. Stanislavsky's second method was to use Active Analysis, a psychological approach used to inspire actions, versus actions as literal tasks the character does step-by-step, connecting the actor to the role through "material reality" to realize their objective.[48] In the latter case, the actions are related to chosen verbs that suggest the how and why of the behavior.

Active Analysis

When Stanislavsky died, his work was taken up by his assistant Mikhail Kedrov, who championed Stanislavsky's Method of Physical Actions as the politically correct means of training, while Maria Knebel, whom Stanislavsky made an Assistant Pedagogue who taught at the Opera-Dramatic Studio, promoted his Active Analysis. Kedrov, as head of the Moscow Art Theatre, made the first method a standard for the System in the USSR with an emphasis on behaviorism, while Knebel was fired from the Moscow Art Theatre for insisting on the inclusion of the psychological approach to the role, which the Soviets rejected. Instead, she taught Active Analysis at the Central Children's Theatre in Moscow and later at the State Institute of Theatrical Arts. Her students went on to become notable actors and directors, including Oleg Efremov, who eventually took over the artistic directorship of the Moscow Art Theatre in 1970.[49] As a disciple of Stanislavsky's final work, she was able to keep these principles alive.[50]

Human beings want things, and they have to figure out how to get them. They have to take particular forms of action with particular people who have what they want. An actor can perform tasks to get what she wants, including moving the other character from his intractable position to one that supports her wants. If an audience doesn't follow that line of action, the actor hasn't responsibly told the story of this event. The character looks for a strategy, one they try on other characters. This strategy is embodied in a transitive action verb chosen by the actor and pursued as hard as possible. His verb must inspire the actor to literally do and say things in a particular way. William Ball separates the various types of verbs to identify those that are most helpful – are actable. The coach "should be prepared to accept only those that an ordinary person could get behind with his shoulder and push for at least ten minutes."[51]

Intellectual verbs: "no ordinary human being ever spent two seconds, much less ten minutes, pursuing them." He gives the examples of "to cogitate," "to figure out," and "to reciprocate."[52]

Behavior or Condition verbs: "These verbs describe a state of being or an action that does not require a strong commitment of intent. They are usual reflexive or subconscious activities that can be accomplished without effort." He includes "sleep, laugh, sneeze, cry, eat, wait, or stand."[53]

Existential verbs: "These verbs include those vast activities that go on without our volition. They are too vague to be endeavored in." He includes, "to be, to exist, to die, to become, to live, to use, to try, to think."[54]

Adjectival verbs: "Does the choice of the verb sound dangerously close to indicating – or playing the adjective?" He gives the example of "to argue," which can too easily be translated as to be "argumentative." Or "imagine because it leads to imaginative." He considers this up to the particular director/coach.[55] For example, "to deceive," though it can lead directly to being deceptive, can be a strong, actable verb.

Trigger verbs: "depict actions that occur so quickly the doer could not pursue them for ten minutes: shoot, kick, kiss, touch, quit."[56]

None of those types of verbs fit Ball's criteria. They are not actable. According to Ball, "seven-eighths of the verbs in spoken English are of absolutely no use to the actor."[57] His examples of actable verbs include, "convince, excite, tease, encourage, destroy, prove, entice, intimidate."[58]

Ultimately, the objective must pass from an intellectual idea to a visceral response. The character's desire must be embodied in the actor, stimulating him and leading to behavior the audience can see. To know what the desire is can't be just a thought. Elia Kazan obviously agreed with this when he wrote, "I put terrific stress on what the person wants and why he wants it. What makes it meaningful for him. I don't start on how he goes about getting it until I get him wanting it."[59]

It would seem that activities are easy for the audience to see rather than the inward thoughts the actor may have as tactics to use with another character. However, "[i]ntentions are *active doings* aimed at overcoming obstacles and achieving your objectives. They are *how* you go about getting what you want." The intention is clear in the commitment the actor has to acting on that intention: "The degree to which you overcome an obstacle with your intention is the degree to which you're successful in achieving your want."[60]

Like the physical tasks in the Method of Physical Actions, the inner actions of the character produce emotion in the actor based on her success or failure in moving her character's life in a positive direction. The partner's responses operate on the actor as a physical force. Success and failure have to be equally important so the other character raises the stakes through their obstruction of the actor's goals.

Seeking the right action verb can sometimes become an intellectual exercise that separates the actor from their partner. The actor is demonstrating and therefore concentrating on their homework rather than the other actor. If an actor's actions are so pre-planned that they ignore the character in front of them, then the actor is not acting spontaneously. After all, the other character has their own actions to pursue. Robert Benedetti noted that Active Analysis can leave the actor thinking "'This is the scene... where I get her to run away with me by appealing to her vanity; I'll do this, and this, and this.'"[61] Instead, in the spirit of spontaneity, the actor may think, "'I want her to run away with me; what do I see in her that will give me a clue about how to proceed?'"[62] It is fine to have an initial strategy, but the actor must be prepared to abandon it in the heat of the moment based on the reactions of their partner. "This approach to acting can help actors to focus on sources outside themselves."[63]

Counteraction

Sharon Marie Carnicke, who teaches Active Analysis and was a student of Maria Knebel, who learned and adapted Active Analysis from Stanislavsky, proposes, "First the scene starts with an impelling action – a force, a drive, a desire that is described by an active verb."[64] These verbs are transitive; that is, they have a direct object. For example, "I must open their eyes to what their spouse is doing to them." "Second, the scene develops because this action meets resistance from a counteraction – a force, drive, or desire that is also described by an active verb."[65] "I must convince my friend that my spouse has good reasons for what he does." The counteraction is both an action for one character and an obstacle to the other. "Third, the counteraction operates simultaneously with the action and continuously resists the forward motion of the scene until such time as one force overcomes the other."[66] When this happens, an event occurs. For example, while actor A tries to open B's eyes, B rejects A's belief and tries to convince A that they are wrong. Ultimately, A is able to offer enough proof that B's belief in the spouse is destroyed. An entire play is the chain of such events: action, then counteraction, and so on. The actor learns they have an action, but they also serve as a counteraction to the other character, a contravening force that can raise the stakes for the other actor or force them to change strategies to accomplish their mission.

Carnicke also notes how the counteraction is the key to both the length of the scene and the reason a scene happens in the first place. A scene cannot take place without a counteraction: "[T]he resistance from the counteraction conditions how long the scene takes to get to the event."[67] Eventually, someone must change, i.e., one character's goal must be thwarted, creating change in that character. If one character doesn't work hard enough to counteract the other's action, the partner soon succeeds. A story takes place only if each side works hard to achieve their goals. At the same time, if both characters will not give in, they reach a stalemate: "If there is no counteraction, or if the action and counteraction are of equal force, such that no event can occur, the story cannot unfold."[68] In the example, A and B may never convince each other and leave the conversation hanging; they agree to disagree, and the situation is in stasis because B may be in too much denial to listen to A.

Carnicke prefers the word "counteraction" to "reaction" because she sees the latter as passive. The character has to wait for an action to react to, whereas a counteraction "names a force that exists independently."[69] In this way, "Counteractions have agency. You don't have to wait for something to happen to initiate a counteraction."[70] At the same time, counteractions are useful when a scene doesn't seem to contain conflict or when conflict suggests "forced anger."[71] The idea of counteraction "helps actors to avoid the trap of angry fighting and encourages them instead to deal confidently with interactive nuance."[72] In an etude for discovering actions, the improvisations will break down when, because of the direct counteractions no one gives in, i.e., is willing to be changed.

The character can also use what Carnicke calls the "oblique counteraction." The character who is being acted upon "sidesteps" the other character by changing the subject or ignoring what the other character has said or done. Anton Chekhov's characters use this strategy to avoid uncomfortable conversations or to delay decisions. Harold Pinter's characters continually use oblique counteraction by pretending to ignore what has been said or implied by someone else. This is a way of shielding themselves and at the same time remaining invulnerable to others. They then use counteractions to attack the other characters in subtle ways through mockery or denigration but covered by a mask of courtesy or politeness or the façade created by their choice of language. Pinter uses indirect counteractions as a weapon in his plays, a character deflecting the other character's attempts to use action against them.

If there are more than two characters in the scene, the actors should determine who is using an action and who is the counteraction; the remaining characters will form alliances with one or the other, "thus assisting or resisting the scene's forward momentum."[73] This gives the supporting players a role in the struggle between the two characters.

The Gister Method

Earle Gister taught a variation of Active Analysis using a different target for the action: "Action in this approach is the act of *committing yourself, as the Who am I?, to making another person, image or object feel something.*"[74] This simple adjustment is a personal approach creating a greater connection between the characters, because each actor "is committing herself to making him feel whatever she chooses."[75] For example, it is harder to play "to chastise" than it is to evoke of feeling of chastisement. According to Gister, the actor has a choice of where to aim the action: the emotions, the senses, or the psyche.[76] The actions can also be positive or negative, using a kind of carrot-and-stick approach.[77]

Hugh O'Gorman, writing of his work with Earle Gister at the Actor's Center, explained how this tiny adjustment – from making someone do something to making them feel something – "changed everything for me."[78] For O'Gorman, Gister's focus on "the exchange of energy" established a greater connection between the two actors in communion with each other, "to pay more attention to my partner, forget about myself, and focus on one thing: changing the emotional life of the other actor in the scene." O'Gorman also noted that the ancillary effect was the same as if he had used the original approach: "If we accomplished this, then the other person would eventually do or think what we wanted them to."

Gister, and his former student Joe Alberti, stress that the actor must decide *how* to accomplish this action, using any number of adverbs or adverbial phrases. Alberti provides an entire "lexicon" of words to use for the "how."[79] The character is defined by the way in which they make someone feel a certain experience. Characters may have the same motives which lead to the same actions, but the manner in which each of them attempt to accomplish their goals can be strikingly different. For example, "I want him to feel incompetent in a heartless way" is very different from "I want him to feel incompetent in a helpful way."

Other teachers suggest that the how is actually the part of the equation that occurs when one actor is confronted with the other actor's action or obstacle. It is then a spontaneous rather than a planned action. The actor can't choose how to proceed until they have seen how their action has worked or not worked. The actor must wait for their partner to give them the stimuli to react, which means that, to a great extent, they can't predict what the other character will do. This reliance on spontaneity can be unnerving. The actor must have the confidence to proceed, counting on the other actor to help them. Fear of making a mistake can block what is really important – living a spontaneous life. It is up to the teacher to encourage the actor to try the various options without worrying about the results. Learning will occur either way.

However an actor approaches the idea of actions, the concept prompts a behavior that drives the actor and clarifies the motivations of the character. In the long run, the actor will use this idea instinctively rather than in a more ordered and analytic way.

Cybernetic Analysis

Robert Cohen, in his book *Acting Power*, discusses the work of Gregory Bateson and Paul Watzlawick on cybernetic analysis: "A cybernetic approach focuses on feedback from the future rather than causes from the past."[80] Cohen suggests that, rather than thinking of running from a bear, a man is running towards the safety of his cabin. He is pushed by the past and pulled by the future. To reorient the actor from using the past as the focus and cause for character actions, Cohen suggests the following reminders: (1) Seek the purposes rather than the causes of your character's behavior. (2) Do not ask "Why?" – ask "What for?" (3) "Look to your character's future; do not obsess about her past."[81]

The actor must seek the right question to answer: "What for?" instead of "Why?" because the second allows the character to base their actions on causes outside of themselves. "Why?" relates to the past and to determinism, while "What for?" considers the character's purpose for her actions, "and the actor will always be better off by exploring, with frankness, the intentional and purposeful nature of her character's acts – even the most unconscious and seemingly innocent characters."[82] Cybernetic thinking, then, is the key to not only understanding the character, but playing them.

Also, "One of the great advantages of seeing action as being pulled rather than pushed is that pulling is a far more accurate process."[83] Or, as Lloyd Richards noted, "You don't go to the corner to wait for the bus. You go to the corner to catch the bus."[84] To be pushed also means to be forced to do something, while to be pulled is to be drawn towards something. The latter is purposeful.

Relacom

Robert Cohen has invented a term for the interactions between two or more persons: Relacom – short for relationship communication – has two levels: "On the first level we transmit content," and on the second "we proffer a relationship between ourselves and with whomever we are communicating, suggesting how the receiver of the content should process it."[85] Relacom is "future oriented"[86] and "largely unconscious,"[87] "a *continuous feedback loop* between communicators."[88]

The director Katie Mitchell too experiments with physicality that leads to emotion. She notes in William James's essay, "What Is an Emotion," that, "Bodies respond to stimuli before brains become conscious of the reaction."[89] She refers to Darwin's six universally recognized primary emotions: "happiness, sadness, fear, anger, surprise, and disgust."[90] Mitchell's etudes with actors showed how they can produce emotions when reacting physically to stimuli.

Look for the True Feelings Under the Behavior

In these various processes, including a thorough analysis of the script, the actor may actually discover the character's true feelings are different from what they supposed, that the real feeling that the character is having is hidden at first, while the actor is deceived by the play's focus on the character's surface responses, such as in the author's stage directions. The teacher can remind the actor that, as their character curses their former lover's name and angrily attacks them, they may still secretly be in love with them. The opposite of love is not hate, it's indifference, and a character may love and hate someone at the same time. A character may be angry, but the true reason for this anger may be a different feeling: embarrassment can lead to anger, shame to rage, and anger may also come from being hurt.

Whatever the process used, the actor is finally creating an emotional landscape for the character. If they can do that in class, the teacher is seeing progress. If the actor is still having trouble accessing feeling or pursuing actions, one reason may be that their ingrained habits, subconscious or conscious, are blocking them. Identifying and changing or adapting habits is the subject of the next chapter.

Notes

1 Konstantin Stanislavsky, quoted in Carnicke, *Dynamic Acting Through Active Analysis*, 30.
2 Hethmon, *Strasberg at the Actors Studio*, 281.
3 Hethmon, *Strasberg at the Actors Studio*, 109.
4 Hethmon, *Strasberg at the Actors Studio*, 109.
5 Hethmon, *Strasberg at the Actors Studio*, 109. To combat this possibility, Strasberg insisted that any memories be at least seven years old.

6 Hethmon, *Strasberg at the Actors Studio*, 109.
7 Carnicke, *Stanislavsky in Focus, 2nd Edition*, 2.
8 "If" defined in the Glossary to Stanislavski, *An Actors Work*, 684.
9 Stanislavski, *An Actor's Work*, 42.
10 Stanislavski, *An Actor's Work*, 48.
11 Howard Fine and Chris Freeman, *Fine on Acting: A Vision of the Craft* (Los Angeles: Havenhurst Books, 2009), 90.
12 Fine and Freeman, *Fine on Acting*, 90.
13 Fine and Freeman, *Fine on Acting*, 90.
14 Hethmon, *Strasberg at the Actors Studio*, 120, emphasis Hethmon's.
15 Kogan and Kogan, *The Science of Acting*, 17.
16 Kogan and Kogan, *The Science of Acting*, 19.
17 Kogan and Kogan, *The Science of Acting*, 18.
18 Alice Spivak and Robert Blumenfeld, *How to Rehearse When There Is No Rehearsal: Acting and the Media* (New York: Limelight Editions, 2007), 268.
19 Spivak was a student of Uta Hagen's at HB Studio. Hagen devotes a chapter to this process in Hagen, *Respect for Acting*, 34–44. She calls the latter example a "Personalization."
20 Moss, *The Intent to Live*, 64, emphasis Moss's.
21 Moss, *The Intent to Live*, 61, emphasis Moss's.
22 Esper and DiMarco, *The Actor's Art and Craft*, 199.
23 Esper and DiMarco, *The Actor's Art and Craft*, 201.
24 Esper and DiMarco, *The Actor's Art and Craft*, 202.
25 Esper and DiMarco, *The Actor's Art and Craft*, 204.
26 Esper and DiMarco, *The Actor's Art and Craft*, 204.
27 Moss, *The Intent to Live*, 85.
28 Moss, *The Intent to Live*, 85.
29 Moss, *The Intent to Live*, 79–80.
30 Toporkov, *Stanislavski in Rehearsal*, 28.
31 Toporkov, *Stanislavski in Rehearsal*, 54.
32 Carnicke, *Stanislavsky in Focus, 2nd Edition*, 87.
33 Carnicke, *Stanislavsky in Focus, 2nd Edition*, 87.
34 Carnicke, *Stanislavsky in Focus, 2nd Edition*, 87.
35 Moss, *The Intent to Live*, 28.
36 Toporkov, quoting Stanislavsky in *Stanislavski in Rehearsal*, 54.
37 Toporkov, *Stanislavski in Rehearsal*, 55.
38 See the next section.
39 Carnicke, *Stanislavsky in Focus, 2nd Edition*, 221.
40 Martin, *The Complete Stanislavsky Toolkit*, 187, emphasis Martin's. Action will take on another meaning in the Active Analysis section.
41 The outline to the Method of Physical Actions process was suggested to Bella Martin by Sharon Marie Carnicke. See Martin, *The Complete Stanislavsky Toolkit*, 188.
42 Martin, *The Complete Stanislavsky Toolkit*, 187.
43 Toporkov, *Stanislavski in Rehearsal*, 16.
44 Toporkov, *Stanislavski in Rehearsal*, 18.
45 Carnicke, *Stanislavsky in Focus, 2nd Edition*, 190.
46 Toporkov, *Stanislavski in Rehearsal*, 52.
47 Toporkov, *Stanislavski in Rehearsal*, 28.
48 Carnicke, *Stanislavsky in Focus, 2nd Edition*, 190.
49 Carnicke, *Stanislavsky in Focus, 2nd Edition*, 191.
50 Even in the 21st century, according to Bella Martin, "There's some disagreement among scholars and practitioners as to whether there is actually a difference between ACTIVE ANALYSIS and THE METHOD OF PHYSICAL ACTIONS." See Martin, *The Complete Stanislavsky Toolkit*, 196, emphasis Martin's.
51 Ball, *A Sense of Direction*, 85.
52 Ball, *A Sense of Direction*, 85.

53 Ball, *A Sense of Direction*, 85.
54 Ball, *A Sense of Direction*, 86.
55 Ball, *A Sense of Direction*, 86.
56 Ball, *A Sense of Direction*, 86.
57 Ball, *A Sense of Direction*, 88.
58 Ball, *A Sense of Direction*, 86.
59 Kazan, *Kazan on Directing*, 275.
60 Moss, *The Intent to Live*, 32, emphasis Moss's.
61 Robert Benedetti, "Zen in the Art of Acting Training," in Hobgood, *Master Teachers of Acting*, 98.
62 Benedetti, "Zen in the Art of Acting Training," 98.
63 Joe Alberti, *Acting: The Gister Method*, 2nd Edition (New York: Joy Press, 2015), 72.
64 Carnicke, *Dynamic Acting Through Active Analysis*, 154.
65 Carnicke, *Dynamic Acting Through Active Analysis*, 154.
66 Carnicke, *Dynamic Acting Through Active Analysis*, 154.
67 Carnicke, *Dynamic Acting Through Active Analysis*, 162.
68 Carnicke, *Dynamic Acting Through Active Analysis*, 164.
69 Carnicke, *Dynamic Acting Through Active Analysis*, 164.
70 Carnicke, *Dynamic Acting Through Active Analysis*, 164.
71 Carnicke, *Dynamic Acting Through Active Analysis*, 176.
72 Carnicke, *Dynamic Acting Through Active Analysis*, 184.
73 Carnicke, *Dynamic Acting Through Active Analysis*, 170.
74 Alberti, *Acting*, 64. Emphasis Alberti's.
75 Alberti, *Acting*, 64.
76 Alberti, *Acting*, 65.
77 Alberti, *Acting*, 65–66.
78 O'Gorman, *Acting Action*, 12.
79 Alberti, *Acting*, Appendix B, 140–143.
80 Cohen, *Acting Power: The 21st Century Edition*, 32.
81 Cohen, *Acting Power: The 21st Century Edition*, 33.
82 Cohen, *Acting Power: The 21st Century Edition*, 33.
83 Cohen, *Acting Power: The 21st Century Edition*, 34–35.
84 Stephen McKinley Henderson quoting Lloyd Richards in Francis, "Preparing Birds to Fly," 128.
85 Cohen, *Acting Power: The 21st Century Edition*, 61.
86 Cohen, *Acting Power: The 21st Century Edition*, 61.
87 Cohen, *Acting Power: The 21st Century Edition*, 61.
88 Cohen, *Acting Power: The 21st Century Edition*, 61, emphasis Cohen's.
89 Benjamin Fowler, *Katie Mitchell, Beautiful Illogical Acts* (London: Routledge, 2021), 114.
90 Fowler, *Katie Mitchell*, 116.

9 Coaching Habits That Don't Serve

Just as comfort food can assuage the strain of a difficult day, so a habit – good or bad – can ease the playing of a difficult moment. The actor can come to rely on such a behavior whether they are aware of it or not. This seems a minor matter unless the habit itself has either outlived its usefulness or has been a substitute for a behavior that would have better served the actor. As Laurence Olivier notes in an interview with Kenneth Tynan, "Mannerisms are cushions of protection which an actor develops against his own self-consciousness."[1]

Pedagogically, when students continue to use habits that have worked for them in the past – that is, behaviors that made them more comfortable onstage or served as outlets to release tension in incremental or unmotivated movements, such as swaying in place, pacing, or using small, ineffective gestures – they bring to a new scene study course those learned behaviors that were not corrected by a teacher or director – that may have even been encouraged or ignored – but ultimately will not serve them in the present. This is the kind of prior knowledge that is insidious and difficult to correct. The behavior may be unconscious, a tool for relaxation that over time has become automatically triggered as a survival mechanism against stage fright. To correct the habit is to take away a safety net, throwing the actor into a tense or even alarmed state of mind. Sometimes the knowledge is simply used in the wrong context. For example, a student creates a fast inner tempo appropriate to a nervous character in one performance that he continues to exhibit in another: playing a calmer, more confident persona with the same inner impetus,[2] with the mistaken idea that any increase in tempo equals energy, a way for the student to invigorate himself every time he appears onstage.

Susan Ambrose and her colleagues explain that prior knowledge is always at play when students begin a new course. They explain how to distinguish between the kinds of knowledge which are useful and those that prevent the student from grasping new concepts or learning new behaviors. They compare inappropriate knowledge to a more functional form, "accurate prior knowledge," information the students have already acquired that is still germane to the subject and may be connected to material introduced in class.[3] This kind of knowledge may come from previous courses or even lessons taught earlier in the current course; the teacher may use analogies from the students' everyday lives and experiences; or the teacher may ask the students to explain how their prior knowledge may be effective in predicting how new problems and challenges may be solved.[4] Which kind of questions can you ask a student to determine the habit's origin without offending them? How can one behavior be replaced with another?

One corrective for a habit created by an actor's nervousness is to present tools that will accomplish relaxation of the body and mind through concentration on an objective, or by using warmups that ease tension prior to rehearsal and performance. These new techniques replace the old. By reminding the student when she is at her most confident, the teacher can focus attention on what that state feels like and where it comes from – previous knowledge of what confidence feels like is appropriate to the task at hand and can be connected to new procedures.

According to Ambrose, teachers can use a number of strategies based on the principle that prior knowledge affects present learning.[5] Using a diagnostic to determine students' prior knowledge, and planning the course based on what the students already know, can lead to both remediation and new learning. The teacher identifies what each student does, then asks the students to question their assumptions and how those ideas became a part of their thinking. If the student can articulate the reasons for their choices, the teacher can address the processes at work and correct or modify them. Sometimes the reasons are based on false assumptions, such as what constitutes an effective performance.

For example, an actor may feel that they cease to be interesting if they remain in the same place for too long. However, stillness can be a powerful tool to draw focus onstage, whereas constant movement can dissipate the actor's effectiveness. When students receive laughter onstage it may not be the appropriate kind – i.e., a bit of schtick or overacting produces a response that has more to do with laughing at business that is out of place rather than truthful behavior that comes from the given circumstances.

The teacher should consider actor habits to be one of her main objects of attention: those behaviors acquired over time that either still have some value for the actor or distract him from a complete embodiment of the character. Not all habits are bad; those habits that serve the actor can be left alone. On the other hand, the teacher must address those habits that counteract the impressions the actor is trying to make.

The coach may sometimes solve the problem by observing, "I notice you do this. Is it something you feel the character does?" Some actors become self-conscious, and it may take time for them to readjust. If this is the case, the teacher can replace the habit with a better habit or add to the current habit so that it is more effective – for example, the actor may be asked to use the whole arm to express a thought rather than small and barely readable gestures with the hands. Or the actor may be asked to find a motive for staying in one place, since they may agree that it makes no sense to execute a motiveless cross to somewhere else.[6]

As the actors rehearse, the teacher can ask each actor to explain why they are using specific habits, what their reasoning is for those choices. Within bad habits are contradictions that lead to ineffective performance. The actor's inappropriate knowledge has skewed their thinking. For example, if an actor moves to another part of the space during the scene, he may say it is because he is tired of standing in one place. Is this true of the character? Where is the character going? Do we ourselves make arbitrary movements? If so, when? What are they based on? Why do we move from one place to another? What is wrong with stillness? Is it really boring, or is the actor predicting how the audience will feel? Can they think of examples they have seen of scenes which are exciting or full of tension but where no movement happens at all?

In *How Learning Works*, the authors suggest correcting inappropriate knowledge by asking the student to predict what will happen under specific conditions when they apply what they already know. Given sufficient time and multiple rehearsals, the students will have opportunities to identify how certain of their mental models fall apart, to practice better habits, and to apply accurate knowledge that replaces inappropriate knowledge.[7]

One habit an actor may have will be based on their understanding of what realistic acting or truth is. They may believe theatrical acting is somehow different in size from film acting. This is certainly true when it comes to reaching an audience in a large theatre, where technique will be needed to vocally fill the space, and it is less so in an intimate space, where the actors are feet away from the spectators. What is meant here, however, is the mistaken sense that only the oversized performance is suitable for the stage, that if the audience can't see the technique, they are not watching acting. This ignores a basic principle that the actor's occupation is to experience the circumstances and feelings of the character, to reveal the behavior of particular people in specific situations, and to do so without at the same time displaying their technique. A heuristic here might be, if the actor can be caught "acting," they aren't living the part. Stanislavsky's cry of "I don't believe you," however irritating it may be during rehearsal, is a mental yardstick for the actor in performance. This is not to say that certain styles of presentation, including direct address to the audience, cannot be based in intention and an honest effort to motivate a character who breaks the fourth wall. Or a character on film cannot resort to histrionics, as we do in real life. In these instances, at heart the actor is still embodying a role.

The phrase "louder, faster, funnier," according to a neophyte director/teacher, will cure all ills. However, it is a cliché, the introduction of mechanical ideas, layered over the real work that must take place. To work deeply on a scene may lead to a certain pace, and the study of the text may suggest the irony or humor of certain situations, but speeding up or chasing laughs and mugging are imposed without determining if an increase in speed and an underlining of humor are appropriate. Some actors equate projection with loudness. If the student predicts everyone will be able to hear them – they will be both easy to understand and will seem to be living onstage while yelling – they will discover how false this is. This is the contradiction that disproves the belief. Instead, projection is based on resonance in the body.[8]

What follows in this chapter are further examples of habits that don't serve the actor.

Pushing or Indicating

When an actor is forcing results, this can give the teacher a clue to what the actor is trying to accomplish. If the actor is pushing for a result, they may know what should be done but not know how to do it. Something is holding them back that the teacher can try to identify and bypass. But mentioning the idea of "pushing" to the actor is self-defeating, since it is the last thing they want to hear about their own work. Pushing is equated with overacting. It is a misplaced energy which drives the actor to shut down any instinct to respond to stimuli, to become self-conscious, to hold their breath. The actor will be full of tension, frustrated with their inability to express the character's feelings.

Indicating, or mugging, involves the external expression of emotion while nothing is happening inside. It means the work hasn't been done to connect with the feelings of the character. It isn't believable to an audience. Actors will indicate that something is humorous, for example, while the experience they are having is not lived through. Ball defined indicating as a state in which "You are allowing yourself to represent a picture of the experience and avoiding a personal commitment to the want of the character."[9]

When an actor is pushing too hard, it may be they lack technique, have tension in the body, aren't breathing properly, or any number of issues the coach can address in order to release the understanding, feeling, and physicality necessary. In particular, the teacher can suggest a sense of mission for the character that will give the actor something specific to aim for. They will no longer be acting in general.

Improper Use of Breath

One of the most basic habits, a mechanism that is acquired in life under many conditions, actor or not, is the holding of breath every time someone gets close to a strong feeling. This is a subconscious reaction to stress, an attempt to hold in those feelings, but it has a number of unfortunate side effects. The actor, unlike the average person, needs to be able to release a feeling; therefore, they have to breathe into it rather than stifle it.

The students may stop breathing when they begin a scene or when the coach seems to be putting them on the spot by asking them a question. The coach and the audience can sense this, sometimes even responding in kind without realizing it. When actors stop breathing, they don't get enough oxygen. It's harder to think. Sometimes the student, while rehearsing, will run out of breath before the ends of sentences, which will drop off and be unintelligible. Sometimes actors take in too much breath and don't know what to do with it; they may use this extra breath to sigh out, suggesting a defeatist attitude in the character.[10] They may become breathy and less resonant.

Actors need breath support. They should begin with relaxation exercises. In particular, they should locate the area from which they naturally breathe. They can do this by lying on their backs on the floor, bending their knees and sliding their feet towards their bottoms so the lower back is flat against the floor. By breathing all the air out of their lungs and waiting for a natural inhale – rather than holding the breath – they will realize the natural intake of air comes from the diaphragm rather than the chest. This mechanism kicks in, and exhalation happens. Actors will learn freeing and placing the voice, recentering, flexibility, control, and breath capacity with a good teacher and vocal coach.[11] They will stop breathing from the chest. They will begin to express themselves with ease rather than based on physical constraints created out of habit.

The brain determines how much air is needed to express the thought – the exact length of an inhalation required to complete the thought without strain – and does so automatically. When speaking someone else's text, since the author's words are unnatural – i.e., not initially created by the actor's brain – the actor can make a breath score of their roles, marking places to breathe throughout the text. They will then be doing what the brain would have done in an offstage conversation.

Speaking Up Without Shouting

Volume is not about pushing and being louder, but using the voice properly. Volume without strain comes from resonance, the body as a chamber for vibration: the more the vibration, the greater the resonance. A number of exercises, practiced on a daily basis and in warmups before a performance, will improve the body's ability to vibrate. These include accessing the mask of the face, the area of the mouth and nose. Closing the mouth and making an "m" sound concentrates attention forward; the actor should hum the "m" until the lips vibrate. When the student relaxes and opens the lips and makes an open "ah" sound, they will notice the increase in volume. Concentrating on the nose, using an "n" sound until the nose feels as if it is being tickled, will add to the vibrations in the mask. Pounding the chest lightly while producing an "ah" also opens up the torso. Ideally, the student will be taking other classes in vocal technique.

One means of placing your voice involves pitching it towards the front of the face. Sir Derek Jacobi describes a technique he learned from the voice teacher Clyde Vinson: "Take your thumb, push your thumb against the roof of your mouth for about twenty seconds, take it away: you can feel where your thumb has been. Now just hit that with your breath."[12] Jacobi found that "it stopped my voice getting caught on the way up. Even if I was suffering a bit of a cold or something else, I could speak above the cold, because I was really thinking about the resonance in my head."[13] Vinson "put a sort of microphone in my voice instantly,"[14] and "the breath went from the diaphragm to the mouth,"[15] instead of getting caught in the throat. Jacobi felt that Vinson was one of the best vocal coaches he had ever worked with.[16]

As noted earlier, an actor's use of resonance increases the volume of their lines, and he can be trained to improve. However, sometimes it is enough to say, "Make sure you include the room in your work," or "I can't understand the words at the end of the line." In the latter case, the actor often runs out of breath before the end of a line and needs to be reminded to take in enough air to complete the thought. Meryl Streep quotes one of her teachers at Yale, Marge Philips, who worked with the students on heightened text such as sonnets: "A thought is a breath and a breath is a thought, the same thing. You have to make the breath last through the entire thought."[17]

Faster Is Pace

Actors can be obsessed with getting the rhythm or tempo of the scene too early, as if that will solve all their problems. A play may have a longer running time than was expected, but this is not a reason to speed up the delivery of the lines. When a young actor talks about the pace of a scene, they may be talking about speed. Pace comes from the amount of time the evaluation takes, when the inner monologue leads to a response, based on the stakes. It also pays to take time at first to understand why the words are being said, how they relate to the actor's overall mission. As William B. Davis notes: "Pace is the illusion of speed. It's not speed itself."[18]

Pace is built into scripts by the author, such as when the Greeks use stichomythia, the alternating of single lines of verse between characters. Such a form discourages the pauses between lines and heightens the intensity of a scene. Shakespeare creates shared lines within the verse, where a ten-syllable line is broken up between two characters. Twentieth- and 21st-century authors will include forward slashes to indicate where one character's line will overlap another's, or overlapping dialogue will be printed in two columns on a page.

Rushing through the dialogue, the actors may miss some important clues as to how to behave. For example, an actor's line may be based on something the other actor has already done. For example, if one character says, "I see I've embarrassed you," does the actor need the partner to react – regardless of the playwright's direction – in a manner that leads to that line? Or is the character projecting his feelings onto the other actor and responding accordingly? Either is possible.

When such evidence is not implanted by the playwright in contemporary prose, the actor must conclude whether a character will have a quick or slow evaluation to what they have been given by another character. One character may also know the other so well, they begin to respond before the other character has even finished; they have had habitual conversations like this in the past. Pace is ultimately imposed from the outside: it is an external imposition unrelated to the internal psychological feelings of the character. On the other hand, actors can sometimes pause longer than is necessary or fail to pick up their cues. Taking the air out between lines of dialogue – i.e., responding more quickly but without rushing the words themselves – can enliven a conversation.

The Stakes Aren't High Enough

The actor either hasn't fully committed to pursuing the objective, or the strategy they have suggested, the action, isn't something they can get behind, or doesn't thrill them to play, or doesn't prompt them to push hard to accomplish. To raise the stakes in a scene, if the students are using Active Analysis,[19] William Ball suggested upgrading the verbs the actor has chosen. Because the actor can be going through the motions to pick a verb that will work for the time being, or is, for whatever reason, avoiding the strong push needed to achieve the objective, "a verb may be weak, frail, or thin."[20] Dipping into a thesaurus will give the actors many synonyms with gradations of intensity, or slight variations in meaning, that may work better than the word first chosen.

Strangely, a mechanical instruction such as "increase the level of your reaction five times" will sometimes be the green light the actor needs to commit more fully. Polly Findlay will ask her actors in rehearsal to "resist the condition" as hard as they can.[21] And Declan Donnellan reminds the actor of what he calls "the double rule": "1) At every living moment there is something to be lost and something to be won" and "2) The thing that may be won is precisely the same size as the thing that may be lost."[22] What the character pursues has as large an effect on the character whether the character succeeds or fails, and considering both possibilities at the same time helps the actor to raise the cost of the result.

Bigger Versus Stakes

"Bigger" is used in the mistaken assumption that it equals the note, "Raise the stakes." Instead, movements become larger, voices become louder, much is exaggerated in the pursuit of a larger demonstration of what is asked for by the director, teacher, or coach. This also puts the actor's attention on the self rather than on the other actor, the place where actors should concentrate their attention. "Be bigger" is a dangerous phrase encouraging the actor to push. Instead, each actor is working generously and in tandem to give those stimuli that will lead to affect.

Defeatist Attitude Leading to Weak Actor Choices

Sometimes the actor will have the character give up before they should. Instead, the character should pursue the mission – the objective – as long as possible. Think of Wile E. Coyote, who never gives up despite tremendous setbacks. Characters work hard to overcome obstacles and to achieve their life-and-death goals.

If an actor chooses negative actions or behaviors, they may already be defeating their mission. If the actor is an advocate for their character, they will justify or sympathize with their choices, no matter how they personally feel. They will choose the action most likely to accomplish their mission: "to mock" may be a strong choice, but if the character is trying to win someone back, this action will backfire.[23] Actors will sometimes pick the objective "to leave." This can be a weak choice for several reasons: (1) the author does not have the character exit until later in the scene, but (2) the character will not leave until they do everything they can to succeed. Robert Cohen's analogy is, "The actor who shows a character not trying to win in a life situation will be as successful with the public as a boxer who throws fights."[24]

Though the actor has an option to choose what is most interesting, some actors will default to an easier choice. The teacher shouldn't allow the actors to avoid difficult realizations that occur during the scene or act as if they already know information that another character reveals in the present. By making less interesting choices about happenings, they avoid having to evaluate new data and to have epiphanies about it. They avoid change, i.e., they don't allow themselves to be vulnerable. Instead, the teacher can ask the actor why the author has placed a revelation at this point in the play, rather than in previous scenes. Ron Van Lieu asks the actor to "try to make anything that happens in the scene to be *a first event*. Even when it is a familiar argument, there is always something in it that makes it different from last time."[25]

A teacher might be disconcerted if an actor told her that they didn't care about the consequences of their actions. Howard Fine calls this situation making a "brush-off" choice, choosing the easy route rather than one that leaves the actor vulnerable, the "I don't care" choice.[26] This strategy is counterproductive, both because it takes the stakes out of the scene, and it doesn't leave the actor, and therefore the character, open to affect. For example, when the playwright doesn't reveal certain aspects of the previous circumstances, the actor may choose a background that doesn't drive her character. If the actor is indifferent to his family, then on the day he leaves for college and says goodbye to them, he will have no regrets. Human behavior suggests this isn't what happens: if the family has been a loving and a nurturing one, he will miss that support deeply; if they have been awful and abusive to him, what sibling has he left behind to deal with that terrible environment when he is not there to help them? This is a much more interesting scene to play, and one the audience will pay to see.

Mechanical or Pre-Prepared Gestures

When an actor prepares gestures in advance as a score for a monologue or scene, their plans have destroyed spontaneity. Their staging may not be necessary in the heat of the moment or be in the wrong place or simply be movement for the sake of moving. This tendency is in the same category as unnecessary movement across the stage, the tendency on the young actor's part to gesture for the sake of doing so, without an impulse that arises from the words, the given circumstances, or the feelings of the character. Attention to those details will aid in creating conflict and tension within the actor, which is fascinating to observe.

Using Incomplete or Further Unnecessary Movements and Gestures

Actors will sometimes make a gesture half-heartedly, beginning the movement but not completing it. They may use small parts of their bodies to express themselves. "The Penguin" moves her hands, but the arms are still at the actor's side. The actor may also use parallel gestures, punctuating the rhythm of a speech with the tempo of their hand movements. Since the actors are apologizing for their choices, give them permission to experiment, and remind them that failure is necessary for growth. When the actor is really nervous, he may sway from side to side as if rocking on a boat. Teach him how to plant himself and the power that can bring.

Anticipating

The student reacts before the impulse has occurred in their body or the response has been elicited by the other character. They don't give themselves time to be stimulated by impulses outside of themselves. They fail to give the character time to evaluate the situation before speaking. When actors live in anticipation – always ready to do the next thing before they've taken in the present circumstances – they live in fear.

> The *fear* actors have of doing something wrong is why they anticipate: They want to be ready and they want to do it right when the time comes. So maybe the most basic thing is to encourage them to find the lives of the characters more compelling than the fact that they are acting.[27]

This is because the actor has not returned to zero: to the point of not knowing just as the character does not know. "He tends to act the result rather than to make the result happen."[28] Also, if the play is about that character, and the character must change by the end of the play, then they can't if the actor plays the end of the scene or play earlier.[29] The character must go through a number of scenes, of experiences, in order to change. Lee Strasberg asks his actors to consider the question, "What would be going on here if the scene never happened? What would I really be doing?"[30]

Milking

When an actor dwells on a pause or silence, or luxuriates in an emotional diatribe, or adds extra business to chase more laughs, they are said to be milking – drawing unnecessary focus or adding too much time to a performance through self-indulgence. They fall in love with certain moments they can't let go of. This can be pointed out directly, but lightly, although it is not always appreciated because the teacher seems to be suggesting the student is overacting. They never want to seem to be doing that. Also, in the past, students may have received kudos for their comic invention or extra applause at the curtain call because of their antics. This is what a director means when they return to the long run of a show and find they must "take out the improvements."

Seeking Approval

Sometimes, during a scene, the student actor will glance ever so slightly at the audience. This is an unconscious habit of looking to the teacher for confirmation that what they are doing is "right." This could mean that at some point in their early training, they continually received feedback from the teacher/coach as they acted, and they continue to expect it. It's also a reminder to the coach to avoid interrupting the work as it precedes, as it may lead to this behavior.

Putting the Attention in the Wrong Place

There are actors who have trouble looking at their partners during a scene and will focus on a point just off to the side of the other actor's face. Pointing this out can help, but the root of the problem is also important to identify. Is it a way to avoid vulnerability? Is it an ingrained habit the actor isn't even aware of doing? Is fear a factor? Are the two actors not connecting because of some personal issue? The teacher should investigate – carefully. The opposite of avoiding eye contact is to never take the eyes off of the partner. Actors who seek to connect in this way are under the mistaken belief this is natural human behavior.[31] They have also substituted one unnatural habit for another.

Creative Hiding

Milton Katselas points out that characters don't always stare into each other's eyes for an entire scene; just as in real life, people don't either. Sometimes, for whatever reason, they can't face each other. They resort to Creative Hiding. The actor can use Creative Hiding in two ways: "1) by covering the emotion – hiding it . . . and 2) by playing away from your partner . . . you create behavior which is the major thrust of the actor's work."[32] People will avoid looking at each other when they need to admit something they are ashamed of, or the content of their speech will hurt the other person, or the stakes for succeeding or failing are extremely high, and they can't bear to look at the reaction to their words for fear of being rejected. "Creative Hiding during moments of high emotion can allow the actor to release and express feelings more deeply, because by hiding they deflect those feelings, as people do."[33]

Self-Consciousness in General

Students become self-conscious in the very act of being "onstage." This leads to nervousness or even paralysis. Besides giving the actors activities that focus their concentration on objects outside of themselves, as Stanislavsky does in the Method of Physical Actions, the teacher may give the actors mantras to tell themselves to take the onus off of performing. Keith Johnstone, using a technique by Joanna Field in her book *A Life of One's Own*, suggested his students say "I want nothing" as a mantra to open up the actor to the creative spirit despite their knowledge of how to do something – in this case, how to act.[34] They are giving themselves permission to start from zero without expectations. "It alters your attitude to the world."[35] Positive phrases build confidence: "A strong one is "I love you, I hate you.' It gives you more courage, I think."[36] According to Johnstone, the actor begins to breathe better.

Ineffective Action Verbs

Not all verbs are action verbs in the sense of being active, i.e., moving partners to respond. Verbs can have no relation to the other actor, may apply to the future rather than the present, or may be so vanilla as to lower the stakes. An actor should never "try" but do. An actor should never "think of" or "like to," but act on a desire. The actor should use the words for a specific purpose other than to simply give information. They should apply actions that affect others and heighten the experience the character is having. Words such as "tell," "would like to," or "try" keep the actor in his head; they distance the actor from the material and keep them from raising the stakes. Also, words are often unnecessary. If the actor embodies the character, what they are thinking and feeling can be inferred by the audience. The doing is silent.

Playing Mood, Quality, State of Being

Does the actor seem to have a personal connection to the character, i.e., are the feelings natural and honest, or is the actor struggling to realize them? How will the teacher know? The actor may choose the obvious and play the emotion rather than the doing that caused the emotion. If the actor is purposeless, they will fall back on a state of being. They will be charming or angry or happy. To play one mood throughout a scene is boring for actor and audience member alike. The audience loses sight of the importance of the events and therefore may lose the narrative. To play a quality is to show a surface understanding of what the character is going through and has nothing to do with their desire to move forward with their lives. Most of all, "mood spelled backward is *doom*! You *can't* and should never try to act a mood."[37] The actors should be reminded to seek behavior based on the overall objectives and actions of the scene and play. "Remember, you can't *play* an emotional condition; you *have* an emotional condition and because of that condition, *you try to overcome it with active* doings (intentions)."[38] The actor should be responding to what the other actor gives them to achieve their objective. Unless this is a presentational work, the focus is on the other actor.

Underplaying

Student actors are worried about overacting. The fact is, because they don't want to be seen as hamming it up, they rarely go far enough. Underplaying can also be a means of taking focus because it can be such a contrast to the stakes of the scene. If the other actor is pursuing their objective as hard as possible, the underplayed reaction calls attention to itself and not in an appropriate way.

One way to solve this is, surprisingly, to give the actors permission to go too far, to overact. They are encouraged to play melodramatically or in a heightened way. Stanislavsky believed overacting could be a useful tool. He encouraged the actors of the Moscow Art Theatre to do this as a way to either rid them of their shyness or allow them to see how far the outlines of the part actually were. When he was working on a new production of Alexander Griboyedov's *Much Woe from Wisdom*, in which he played the role of Famusov, Stanislavsky asked the actors he was working with to join him in going quite far and noted the following results:

> "Well," he said, "we all over-acted to the hilt. In order to keep in line with you, I was forced to shout. But now we've learned how far our character would go if they were not restrained by the conditions of the time, by the surroundings, by the line within which the character grows, by an artistic sense of proportion."[39]

In this way, he encouraged the actors who "'are shy of living their role on the stage.'"[40] He noted that in life, people sometimes go quite far: "'Most likely you have observed in life the most insignificant person has a strength of emotion that is quite unexpected, when he comes up against difficult circumstances.'"[41] At such times, the emotion, though large, seems appropriate. Young people are afraid of looking foolish or being ridiculed by their peers, which prevents them from seeking the outer limits of a role.

Muting the Lines

Barring the use of a stage to hold class in, that is, without a setup approximating the actor/audience relationship of a medium to large theatre, students will be rehearsing in an intimate space with the concurrent advantages and disadvantages. The advantage of being able to hold a natural conversation that can be easily heard by classmates is offset by the disadvantage of acting that can't be received at a distance for a large audience. Coupled with no need to project in the space is the feeling that intimacy leads to muted speech: as in real life, the actors may lower their volume when having an intimate conversation, such as a love scene or when sharing a secret. As Nikolai Demidov reminds us in a collection of his works, the actors have the habit "of speaking quietly in life."[42] Certain expressions are not meant for prying ears – in this case, the audience's. This tendency may come from the actor's upbringing: "Actors who come from such families of 'whisperers,' needless to say, begin whispering in etudes."[43] Also, when the student is trying so hard to experience the given circumstances, the pressure can lead to tension and lower volume. "This tension is not immediately visible to the untrained eye – the actor is seemingly free, yet tension exists, and it chiefly affects the laryngeal and respiratory muscles."[44] Under such conditions, the actors can't be heard even in a small space.

The simplest answer is to avoid entering the psychological state completely and to concentrate on vocal production. However, if the teacher has created an environment in which the actor is encouraged to do as they feel at any given moment, this is anathema to the spontaneity the teacher seeks at an early stage in the actor's development, which is disrupted by the requirements of technique. Demidov, who creates etudes with dialogue of his own devising, and wants the actors to respond without self-consciousness to the feelings and actions such words invoke, offers two solutions: (1) "[A]dvise these whisperers to radically change their habits and get used to *speaking loudly in everyday life*,"[45] and (2) being on alert, at the second or third rehearsal, to the moment when, despite the student's instinct to speak up, "the student reined himself in and said a line more quietly than it was coming."[46] The student still needs to be complimented after an initial etude if they have not censored themselves in any way. The teacher gives the student "the green-light" to speak up, based on the student's own instincts. One last method Demidov offers: "[W]hen the students repeat the text to remember it, a teacher must ask them to *speak it loudly enough*."[47] Volume can be added during memorization as well.

Paraphrasing

The student may have the impression that an approximation of the words will be enough as long as they fulfill the emotional and physical requirements of the role. In their minds, the words get in the way. The teacher may agree and dismiss the need for word-perfect accuracy if the student is working on an exercise about the physicality of the role, such as a Silent Scene.[48] However, the teacher needs to inculcate in the student the habit of respecting the language, from whatever source. The prime example is the use of heightened text: the teacher might joke that the actor is not a better writer than the Bard of Avon. The actor also misses clues to the meaning and embodiment of events when the proper words or not said in the proper order, such as when a soloist sings the wrong notes in a piece of music. There is a pride to be found in the ability to be word perfect and to honor the playwright's work.

This list of habits is not an all-inclusive one, and teachers and coaches will adapt this list based on their own experiences in the classroom, onstage, or in an audience. In the next chapter, specific coaching techniques will be discussed concerning the creation of characters. There too, actors have certain habits and mindsets that may not work to their best advantage. Characters themselves will have habits that speak to who they are, and these must be separated from the actor's own.

Notes

1 Laurence Olivier, quoted in Hal Burton, ed., *Great Acting* (New York: Bonanza Books, 1967), 25.
2 See the discussion on tempo-rhythm in Chapter 7.
3 Ambrose et al., *How Learning Works*, 32–33.
4 Ambrose et al., *How Learning Works*, 32–33.
5 See Ambrose et al., *How Learning Works*, 27–39, for many examples of implementing this principle.
6 A fascinating way to reveal physical habits is to use the neutral mask: since facial expression is no longer available, the movements that the actor makes will stand out. See Rick Kemp's discussion of Jacques Lecoq's work in *Embodied Acting: What Neuroscience Tells Us About Performance* (New York: Routledge, 2012), 84.
7 See Ambrose et al., *How Learning Works*, 36–37.
8 See "Speaking Up Without Shouting" later in this chapter.
9 Ball, *A Sense of Direction*, 84–85.
10 See the discussion on the defeatist attitude later in this chapter.
11 Many great teachers and the students that have trained to carry on their work offer expert advice and training. They have also written books on their methods, although these are not a substitute for the direct experience. A partial list includes Patsy Rodenburg, *The Right to Speak* (London: Routledge, 1992); Kristin Linklater, *Freeing the Natural Voice* (New York: Drama Publishers, 1976); Arthur Lessac, *The Use and Training of the Human Voice: A Bio-Mechanic Approach to Vocal Life*, 3rd Edition (Mountain View, CA: Mayfield Publishing Company, 1996); Cicely Berry, *Voice and the Actor* (New York: Wiley Publishing Inc., 1973); J. Clifford Turner, *Voice and Speech in the Theatre*, 5th Edition (London: Routledge, 2000).
12 Derek Jacobi, *As Luck Would Have It: My Seven Ages as Told to Garry O'Connor* (London: HarperCollins Publishers, 2013), 236–237.
13 Jacobi, *As Luck Would Have It*, 237.

14 Derek Jacobi, quoted in Ron Destro, ed., *The Shakespeare Masterclasses* (London: Routledge, 2020), 11.
15 Destro, *The Shakespeare Masterclasses*, 11.
16 Clive Vinson, a Texan, coached voice for over 30 years in various universities and in his own private studio in New York. When the Royal Shakespeare Company appeared on Broadway, he served as a vocal coach for their productions of *Les Liaisons Dangereuses*, *Cyrano de Bergerac*, and *Much Ado About Nothing*. The Voice and Speech Trainers Association (VASTA) offers a scholarship in his name.
17 Meryl Streep, quoted in Rosemarie Tichler and Barry Jay Kaplan, *Actors at Work* (New York: Faber and Faber Inc., 2007), 291.
18 Davis, *On Acting . . . and Life*, 86.
19 See the discussion on Active Analysis in Chapter 8.
20 Ball, *A Sense of Direction*, 86.
21 See the discussion on Resisting the Condition in Chapter 10: Coaching: Character.
22 Donnellan, *The Actor and the Target*, 43.
23 It's amazing how often this basic principle is forgotten in the heat of acting.
24 Cohen, *Acting Power: The 21st Century Edition*, 22.
25 Van Lieu, Teacher Development Program Notes, June 2013, emphasis mine.
26 See the discussion on Brush-off Choices, in Fine and Freeman, *Fine on Acting*, 123–124.
27 Ron Van Lieu, quoted in an interview with Orenstein, "Shaping the Independent Actor." Emphasis Van Lieu's.
28 Hethmon, *Strasberg at the Actors Studio*, 180.
29 This does not apply to information that has always been present but hasn't been referred to until later in the script, such as Oedipus's limp, which is not addressed until some time has passed in the text.
30 Hethmon, *Strasberg at the Actors Studio*, 181.
31 As acting coach Miranda Harcourt points out, the only people who stare constantly at someone are psychopaths, the hearing-impaired, and actors.
32 Katselas, *Acting Class*, 47.
33 Katselas, *Acting Class*, 47.
34 Johnstone, "Ten Days with Keith," July 19, 2017.
35 Johnstone, "Ten Days with Keith," July 19, 2017.
36 Johnstone, "Ten Days with Keith," July 19, 2017.
37 Moss, *The Intent to Live*, 44, emphasis Moss's.
38 Moss, *The Intent to Live*, 44–45, emphasis Moss's.
39 Gorchakov, *Stanislavsky Directs*, 186.
40 Gorchakov, *Stanislavsky Directs*, 188.
41 Gorchakov, *Stanislavsky Directs*, 188.
42 Nikolai Demidov, *Becoming an Actor-Creator*, 208.
43 Demidov, *Becoming an Actor-Creator*, 208. See the discussion on etudes in Chapter 12 of this book.
44 Demidov, *Becoming an Actor-Creator*, 209.
45 Demidov, *Becoming an Actor-Creator*, 209, emphasis Demidov's.
46 Demidov, Becoming an Actor-Creator, 209.
47 Demidov, *Becoming an Actor-Creator*, 209, emphasis Demidov's.
48 See Chapter 12.

10 Coaching

Character

To approach the process of creating a character, the teacher must avoid the idea that each student will bring the same set of previous experiences to the work or will even be at a common place in their growth as people. At this point in their careers, students may still be exploring their own sense of self – and individually: "Students differ from each other on multiple dimensions – for example, in their identities, stages of development, and personal histories – and these differences influence how they experience the world and, in turn, their learning and performance."[1] Students will have varying responses to the characters they encounter. One student will embrace the opportunity to play an antihero, an amoral individual, or an oppressor. Another student will take offense at the very idea of either playing such a character or even experiencing this role as an observer. One student will have the maturity to deal with certain situations that another will still be grappling with. One student will be able to find those parts of self that lead to a deeper connection with a role. Another will reject the idea they could ever act and think as a disparate persona.

One strategy is to discuss with the students the types of scenes they would like to do, gaining a perspective on where each student is on a learning or identity continuum.[2] Another is to encourage students to work outside their own comfort zones in order to stretch their acting muscles – to take on roles entirely at variance with either their own thinking or current environment as a means to develop further empathy or sympathy – or at least understanding – for another. This still requires that the students agree to whatever material is suggested.

As a student begins a college career while still processing who he is as a person, the training he encounters often involves an exclusive focus on the self and the ways in which that self can connect directly to the internal impulses provided by external exercises, play texts, or improvisations. Meanwhile, character work – with its suggestion of external layers as a means for realizing an outward, and sometimes even unrecognizable, physical form, with different walks, eccentric behaviors, pronounced changes in physiognomy, varying centers of gravity, and so on – is reserved for another, later, course. This is one philosophy. Another is the belief that all acting is character acting – the actor does her best to find common ground with the character she is playing, perhaps through analogous experiences she herself has had and uses to stimulate the necessary feelings – a sympathetic or even empathetic bond with the role.

DOI: 10.4324/9781003498520-11

Regardless of where teachers place this process in the curriculum and how they approach it, ultimately actors must use what they have to tell the story – their bodies and minds at the service of the events and persons of the drama. Uta Hagen wrote,

> The expression "to lose yourself" in the part or in the performance, which has so often been used by great artists in the theater, has always confused me. I find it much more stimulating to say that I want "to find myself" in the part.[3]

This is a reminder that the work on the self continues during the work on a character. The very idea of playing a character is sometimes rejected by acting teachers because it encourages the actor to put on a false veneer. Instead, they stress what the person in the scene is doing: "Do what the character does, and you will be the character."[4] In either case, the teacher has a number of avenues to introduce this side of acting.

In line with self-exploration and the basics that lead to a creative life onstage as a foundation for character work, Nikolai Demidov suggested, based on his experiments with the Stanislavsky System, that after the students show signs of mastering the art of living onstage, "At such a time, it would be easy to *lead them to any role by carefully tossing at them certain thoughts about the play's circumstances*."[5] This is because the actor begins to perceive these new elements as a means to create new impulses inside herself. Demidov believed that "*our perception should be considered the primary cause, both of our actions and of our emotional* state."[6] The more an actor perceives, the more they have to work with. They gather material and study the role to conceive images the character would use and that would guide their perceptions.

One approach is dramaturgical: a close examination of the text will give the teacher and the students indications as to who the character is. William Esper promoted this fact-finding mission. He wrote, "You should approach every character you play like a detective approaching a crime scene."[7] What does the character say about herself? What do other characters say about her? What kinds of choices does the character make? What are the characters' relationships? What are the important events of the time period that influence the society of which the character is a part? Actors look for ways they resemble and distinguish themselves from their characters: they find common ground with a character's backstory; they imagine parallel relationships; they identify with the character's feelings; they have philosophical differences; they have different tastes; they imagine making alternative choices. This is the kind of homework that can happen outside of the classroom or rehearsal but can also be part of what is called table work, where the entire company studies the play together before putting it on its feet.

The actors are also looking at the variations in temperament the character conceals beneath the façade of manners required of civilized people. The character may conduct themselves with magnanimity under the best conditions, and they may be polite and caring to people they want to impress or cherish, but what about the people they don't have to be nice to? Dating advice includes noting how a potential partner treats the wait staff, or how they operate under pressure. They are more agreeable when everything goes their way. But what if their needs are frustrated? A more complete picture reveals itself.

Self-Based Training Versus Character Training

The downside of a concentration on the self is that the actor can come to rely on personality acting – a persona develops to which the audience responds in a positive manner. There is then no further need to play anything else, but simply to look for plays or films that will showcase this persona to its best advantage. An actor, after great success playing again and again the role the audience expects of her, begins to long for portrayals that stretch her. Imagining all parts as character parts can readjust the actor's thinking. Character actors are not simply supporting players; they play many different roles, including the protagonist, from a variety of viewpoints. If the students are introduced to leading roles that are outlandish or antiheroic, or if they are cast against type, they may begin to see how, even though they may not see themselves this way, they are impelled to bring their uniqueness to whatever the part requires.

Obstacles as Stimuli

One of the best ways an actor can serve their partner is to be a major obstacle to the other character's goals. In life, obstacles irritate us at best and utterly defeat us at worst. Actors, on the other hand, hope for strong obstacles. They work harder to achieve what they want and raise the stakes of the scene or play. Are the characters serving as strong obstacles to each other? This is one of the best gifts – together with their complete attention – that one actor can give to another. In life, we will avoid like the plague anything that makes us uncomfortable unless, by tackling it, we will receive great benefit. Onstage, this benefit is to be found in the spur it gives us to work harder to achieve our objectives. Fortunately, in a fictive situation, failure is far more consequential for the character than for the actor.

There are two sources for obstacles, the internal and the external. An internal obstacle is a thought in the character itself which constrains the actor from achieving an objective. Internal obstacles can be based on attachments; on secrets the character must keep hidden; on the character's sense of self; on an attitude conditioned by the past, including a hidden bias towards the other; on fear of rejection or failure – all are grounded in the feelings, conscious or subconscious, that originate in the self. External obstacles come from outside of the character, in the surrounding environment and the other characters. However, Declan Donnellan suggests that the objects of attention, whether internal or external, lie outside of the actor as the actor's targets. Even when an internal thought takes place, when an actor, and character, seeks a memory, the image is located in a specific place in front of her, not in the back of her mind. "The target always exists outside, and at a measurable distance."[8]

Attention Paid to the Other

Terry Gross, on the radio program *Fresh Air*, played an excerpt from the television series *Justified* for its star, Timothy Olyphant. She asked Olyphant what he was doing when he acted in a scene. Olyphant replied, "If I'm really aware of what I'm doing it's not good. I more or less try to make the other person do all the work."[9] This allows the actor to take in the other actor, which in turn allows the actor simply to react to situations as they arise, rather than display their homework. If the actor's sense of mission is in place, they note whether the other actor is responding to it and how. But this only happens if the actors allow themselves to be affected by each other. As Olyphant remarks, "Whatever you're doing, you are doing for them, because of them."[10] Good actors support each other by providing what is necessary for interaction. This leads to a state in which the actor has done their preparation but then lets it go so as to be open to their partner: "When someone calls, 'Cut,' if I can remember everything the other person did, I'm fine. If I'm aware of everything I did, I'm not very good at my job."[11] A constant interchange is lively and spontaneous, like life. It produces honest reactions, often unpremeditated. "Acting as reacting" is an important, if commonly held, precept that still rings true.

Stanislavsky identified this important principle as well: "Remember, if, after a scene, you can recall all the barely perceptible finer points of your partner's behavior, it means you played the scene well, and you have the most important quality an actor needs – concentration."[12] This is a game that an actor plays with her partner: "You are playing chess with [the other character]. You don't know what his moves will be, but take account of the essentials – his voice, inflexions [sic], eyes, every movement of his muscles."[13] The other actor gives his partner direction: "Your partner should tell you which way to go. This then becomes genuine action."[14] For example, each actor imagines their character's experiences using what Stanislavsky calls inner images which, when specific and vivid, are more likely to be shared with their partners: "You have to convey your inner images, you have to make him see things through your eyes."[15]

A discouraging alternative is when the other actor plays by himself. Stanislavsky notes the way this destroys the idea of ensemble and becomes showboating: "Sometimes they may be accused of not listening, but the truth is, they don't need to listen. They don't need the other actors except to know when to speak."[16] This actor has planned the effects he will make and will stick to that plan regardless of what else is happening onstage.

Is the actor allowing the other actor's words and deeds to penetrate him? That is, can the actor let her partner in? Is each actor open to affect? Sanford Meisner called this "The Pinch and the Ouch." The attempt to impact the other actor is like a physical pinch; the ouch is the response to that impulse, like the pain one feels on the skin, that leads to a spontaneous, truthful reaction.[17] William Esper, who studied with Sanford Meisner, also trained his actors to use their partners to create spontaneity in the performance: "Acting comes alive only when you invest in contact between you and your partner, then work from unanticipated moment to unanticipated moment."[18]

In Earle Gister's view, seeking to make the other character feel something takes the onus off of the actor:

> You do not need to manufacture feelings or emotions: let your scene partner create it in you; if you are sending action, you are helping your scene partner live and be alive; if you receive action, you'll feel. This is what playing actions is.[19]

Each actor provides actions that induce their scene partners to *feel* in a way that also encourages them to *do*; if both are open enough to being changed, they will receive all they need from outside of themselves.

One of the exercises which helps to make a deeper connection between actors is "Seeing-Seeing." That is, when the actors look at each other, they are really seeing each other – and really being seen – in a deeper sense, in a form that creates communion between them. The glazed eyes that can appear when actors are concentrating on their homework suggest they aren't really attending to the individual before them.[20] The actors may be using soft focus, an awareness of other bodies or objects in space without concentrating on them. Seeing-Seeing reminds the actors to be open to affect, not only being completely seen for who and what they are but truly seeing each other in a powerful form that is a stimulus to their honest reactions as characters. A disadvantage is that actors may read Seeing-Seeing as an instruction to glue their eyes to each other. First of all, the actor will not be living in the space with an awareness of the whole environment, whether they refer to it or not. Second, people don't always put a laser focus on each other. They avoid eye contact, they look away to think, they hide their feelings.

Being an Advocate for the Character

Judgment versus Understanding versus Defending the Character's Actions

The actor should be the best possible advocate for the character and their actions that they can be. A lawyer, regardless of her own feelings, must defend her client to the best of her ability. Also, people who are guilty of misconduct or perpetrate reprehensible acts do not think of themselves as scoundrels or reprobates; they can always justify what they have done. The actor should look for these justifications. Even if, in the long run, the reasons do not excuse the behavior of the character, they may explain the character's motives and give the actor an idea of the mindset of the character they are playing.

Some actors will refuse to play villains or perform evil deeds. If this were true of all actors, the narrative wouldn't contain the necessary antagonist, there would be fewer or an absence of obstacles to fight against, dramatic conflicts would weaken and become one-sided, and fights would be over before they started.

Taking on the worldview of the character helps the actor to make a personal connection and to realize that the character is not so different from himself in many ways. Howard Fine notes actors have everything within themselves to play any character. Human beings tend to defend their own actions on the basis of their intentions and ignore the consequences. The actor must allow the character, no matter how reprehensible, to have the same mindset. Fine suggests, "When you look at a character and say that's not me, there's a part of you that you don't see."[21] The actor hasn't done the homework on themselves to discover those things that are less flattering – but being human, they must have these facets of character that would be useful in performance.

Judging a character closes off the possibility that the actor will play within the structure of the scene without commenting on the character. They play on a surface level, as a caricature, or refuse to play the character as written at all. The actor contains within him the whole range of possible actions; in extreme cases, where acting on impulses would lead to real injury or fatalities or jail time, he doesn't follow through. A key principle here is the ability of the actor to identify with the character. It is understood some actors may be reluctant to take on certain roles for deeper reasons, such as personal traumas, and the teacher should consider each case individually without pressuring the student to take on these difficult personas. Though the practice helps to stretch the actor and to open up a larger range of acting opportunities, the teacher must not do so if there is a risk of intruding on issues the student is still dealing with. The teacher should be open to student behavior and in private have an honest dialogue about constraints that shut the student down without delving too far into personal areas that are outside of the teacher's purview.[22] As Jacques Lecoq notes, actors "have learned not to play themselves but to play *using* themselves."[23]

If the actor is having difficulty embodying a character with which they disagree, the coach can suggest that an understanding of the character's motives is possible without sympathizing with them. In Susan Batson's excellent book *Truth*, she asks the actor to create a painstaking backstory for any role they are playing – or auditioning for – that provides images for the actor to use as character memories in the present. She emphasizes the character's public persona as a mask for their inner child and its needs. Dealing with a character's past may lead the actor to the origins of certain behaviors, with a journey as far back as childhood. Childhood trauma has a powerful impact, whether the person finds himself repeating the behavior inflicted on him, or the trauma has shut him off from certain feelings, or he has fought to avoid perpetrating trauma on others.

People become menacing societal figures – bullies, abusers, and murderers – through nature or nurture. Some congenital defect may affect their relationships to others. For example, if the amygdala in the brain is smaller than the average size, a person – or a character – does not register other people's feelings. A common characteristic of the sociopath or psychopath is an abnormally sized amygdala; this prevents them for recognizing signs of fear or pain on the faces of their victims. On the other hand, a sadistic character may be a victim of abuse and repeat that cycle on others. To take on such a role means to imagine what that background would be like and create images for it. The actor can understand the character without agreeing with his or her choices. It is a difficult path to tread and should be handled delicately.

Michael Woolson suggested the actor should ask herself, "What event could happen in my life that would connect me to the emotional life of the character?"[24] The actor's ability to imagine circumstances, particularly to create images for them, is an important skill which the teacher can train them to do. Esper refers to the daydreams we all have when we imagine getting even with someone who has wronged us, or even causing them pain in our minds, although we would never act on such an impulse. The important point is that the thoughts are there and based on wrongs perpetrated on us that cause strong feelings.

Analogous situations may involve Stanislavsky's "magic if," imagining an environment, a relationship, or a situation that would lead the actor to consider desperate measures. The actor is asked to identify within his personal biography a situation in which the actor has had similar feelings or impulses. A classic example is the murderer. "What if someone maimed or killed one of my loved ones – one of my children?" The actor has not participated in a homicide and yet may have been angered to the point the fantasy was there, with the understanding that such a desire, when acted on, would have led to serious consequences. The actor, and her victim, is safe in a theatrical environment of controlled conditions.

Empathy and Identification

If the teacher wants to make a case for the study of acting, she can point out one of the most desired results of a theatre performance: the ability to create empathy in the audience. William Esper felt this was the most important reason for doing theatre: the display of empathy as a model for behavior in a contemporary society that was losing sight of its shared humanity, for example, through the marginalization of groups of people. He defined empathy as "the ability to so identify with what another person is experiencing that you literally feel what the other person feels."[25] It is much harder to dismiss strangers when their experience is shared from the stage.

According to the neurophysiologist Vittorio Gallese, a connection with others' feelings and actions already exists in the brain. The simulation theory is based on neurons, particularly mirror neurons, "which are neurons in an observer's brain that fire in a similar pattern when an action is observed as when that action is actually activated."[26] Gallese, in studying this phenomenon in the brain activity of monkeys, posited that human beings have a similar mirror neuron system, i.e., "the human behaves in a similar way – the motor strip is activated not only when we act, but when we see other individuals acting."[27] At its best, the events on the stage are mirrored, i.e., stimulated in the audience, in a communion of identification.

Identifying means the actor takes on the character's feelings, beliefs, and concerns, in a double-consciousness of being the role and monitoring herself in relation to the audience. While the actor responds emotionally, physically, and intellectually as the character, at the same time she is verifying the audience can hear and see her, that she adjusts her performance if unpredictable events occur, such as a prop breaking, a spectator coughing during an important line of dialogue, or another actor arriving late for his entrance or forgetting a cue. The audience is more likely to invest in the story and follow the character's travails with empathy if the actor creates a life for the stage based on identification. At the same time, without an internal monitor, the actor may not be in a position to control the conditions of an artificial environment or to keep impulses within reasonable bounds.

Part of this discussion concerns how deeply the actor will identify with the role he is playing, how deeply the actor will disappear into the life of another. Do actors lose themselves in the character? This is a myth, sometimes used to denigrate the business of acting, or the actor and his process. The exception is a psychologically troubled person who has no business being on the stage but should be seeking help from a mental health professional. However, how an actor feels in his real life may affect a performance. Since the actor is a human being, she can't help but contain the residue of whatever experiences have occurred earlier in the day. This is one of the reasons an actor may arrive at the theatre earlier than the scheduled call – to prepare for the part mentally as well as physically. Or the actor may use these feelings as a means of living truthfully onstage.

Michael Schulman's Possession Exercise moves deeply into identification through an act of abandon. The exercise is based on observation: the student chooses someone he knows who might resemble the character he wants to play. He allows that character to "possess" him: "Imagine that character moving right inside you, taking over the rhythm in your body, taking over the distribution of your weight, taking over your legs," and so on.[28] Once the actor has imagined relinquishing control to this outside being, the teacher then coaches the new entity through the suggestion, "You are now seeing through that actor's eyes and hearing with his ears."[29] Then the teacher asks him to do activities as the actor's character might, "to walk around as that person: feel that person take over your stride, take over your temperament."[30] Then this persona is encouraged to speak or even sing as the character, then to perform simple tasks such as sweeping the floor. In each case, it is the possessor, the alternative personality, rather than the actor, who performs these actions.

One variation for this exercise is to ask the character who has inhabited the actor to remain seated for an interview. The actor may not know every single fact about the person they have chosen, but the teacher may give her an escape clause, to use such phrases as, "I'd rather not say," or "none of your business" – depending on the character's attitude – to avoid stepping out of the exercise.[31] With an interview situation, the coach offers the conceit that the character has been invited to the class as one of many who will serve as examples of types of people; the character is doing the students a favor, demonstrating alternative behaviors they can study. Once she is comfortable talking about herself, she is asked to carry out tasks at the request of the teacher, activities the theatrical character will be performing. The actors can repeat this experience much more simply when using the same character in performance, with the awareness that they have identified those characteristics that make it possible to connect with the role physically and mentally. An actor can rehearse in this new role by performing their everyday activities, but as the character rather than themselves; simple actions such as morning ablutions – brushing their teeth, showering, fixing their hair, and so on.

William Esper used a similar approach he called Imitations. He asked his students to choose a person and "fully re-create that person's behavior and bring the person into the room."[32] It is important the actor imitate someone whom they have had many opportunities to observe. However, it shouldn't be anyone the class can identify. "Imitations help us access hidden parts of ourselves that fit the characters we play. They help us to turn up the volume on the different aspects of our personality."[33] The ideal result is that the imitation leads to impulses in the actor that lead to new behavior, so they are no longer simply depicting a character unlike themselves, but living as one.

Relationships

What are the basic relationships between people in the scene or play? A character's objective, by necessity, attaches him to another character, as only through that interaction will a character's mission be accomplished. As anyone who has a complicated relationship with their loved ones knows, the depth of a relation doesn't necessarily improve the chances of success. Quite the contrary: the person who is an acquaintance rather than a close friend or relative may not have a personal investment in the outcome. A shared history of some length, on the other hand, may create stronger barriers to the accomplishment of important goals.

A relationship may be the main obstacle to an actor's mission. The characters may have an unspoken relationship, such as exists in a family unit. The structure of the family, with assigned roles for each member, is a deeper dive into a character's previous circumstances. In a dysfunctional family, these roles tend to be played in adulthood when the members reunite, even many years later. Playwrights set up such situations for the conflicts they promise.[34]

John and Linda Friel have identified roles children take in a dysfunctional family, usually one role per child, but some overlap. Because this person isn't one of the adults, the role is unhealthy and leads to many psychological problems. The roles include:

- The Do-er: the person responsible for making the family run smoothly.
- The Enabler/Helper/Lover: the person who wants to keep the family together as a family; the behavior to accomplish this can take many positive and negative forms.[35] This person can also be a do-er, but not always.
- The Lost Child/Loner: the child who deals with the dysfunction by escaping into isolation and separation.
- The Hero: the person who, through their success, gives the family its value.
- The Mascot: the one who provides comic relief, often a younger child.
- The Scapegoat: the person who acts out and is therefore blamed for the family's dysfunction.
- Dad's Little Princess/Mom's Little Man: This troubling role provides the needs that an unresponsive spouse can't or won't. It has been labeled "emotional or covert incest," because of psychological implications this relationship creates between parent and child.[36]
- The Saint/Priest/Nun/Rabbi: the person expected to serve as the spiritual model for the family.[37]

One of the interesting aspects of this family dynamic is that, even when a child escapes the family role – for example, has been the scapegoat but is now a successful entrepreneur – other children, now grown adults, may try to place that adult in the original, inferior role so that they, the siblings, can benefit from reestablishing their superior roles. For example, the sister in the Hero role may now continue to treat the brother as the Scapegoat or Mascot, because the sister still wants the Hero role, regardless of her brother's personal success as an adult.[38] If the adult children meet again in the course of a play, the behavior they exhibit may not make sense – may be unreasonable – without a knowledge of the original childhood roles. However, the actors can infer from previous circumstances and current behaviors what still affects the characters in the present.[39]

The External Rather Than Internal Approach

To take on another persona is to return to the childhood game of being other people: our parents, the characters we admire in films, the heroes we read about in books. Children can move smoothly and swiftly between roles without effort, using their fertile imaginations. Simple costumes and set props can turn a bedroom into a castle or a broomstick into a broadsword. Adult actors still enjoy dressing up and playing imaginary characters, this time with more extensive trappings: the clothes; the makeup; the masks; the wigs; the facial hair; the nose putty; the historical artifacts such as canes, fans, and snuffboxes; the occupational tools of the trade; all are simply more sophisticated aids to personification. Famous actors, such as Laurence Olivier and Alec Guinness, based their portrayals on a walk; a pair of shoes or spectacles; a different nose or voice; a habit, such as smoking or drinking alcohol; a uniform or a bald piece – anything that would stimulate their imaginations to become another. They played different races,[40] used different accents as "vocal costumes,"[41] assumed different ranks and social standings, lived the biographies of historical figures. They delighted in being unrecognizable from one role to the next, in an act of complete transformation. They were incredible, highly regarded technicians, but some audiences were unmoved by their depictions of, rather than their identifications with, their roles. This was because, at worst, the external forms were an imposition from the outside without a direct connection to feelings from the inside.

Just as Denis Diderot, in his essay "Paradox of the Actor,"[42] argued against identification with a role, actors argue over how much they are supposed to feel the emotions of the character. If the audience can't tell the difference because the technique is so developed, does it matter? According to Diderot, an external approach is more effective. Feeling the emotions of the character or "sensibility" is a deterrent to great acting: "Extreme sensibility makes middling actors; middling sensibility makes the ruck of bad actors; a complete absence of sensibility paves the way for the sublime actor."[43] His ideal was the actor who had worked out every gesture and vocal tone, every effect, in advance: "He who comes upon the stage without having his whole action marked out will be a beginner all his life."[44] A prototype for Diderot's master actor was Constantin Coquelin, who remarked, "The actor does not live, but 'play.' He remains cold towards the object of his acting, but his art must be perfect."[45] One night Coquelin, after crying real tears, gathered the whole company together after the performance, and he apologized for his feelings. He wanted the audience to cry rather than himself. It was, in his mind, a loss of control and bad technique.

Joseph Jefferson's philosophy – "the actor should have a cold head and a warm heart"[46] – was one that kept him from being carried away by his own feelings, but he did believe in both the external and internal facets of the part, both experiencing and monitoring, rejecting the absence of identification.

The emphasis on external training – to reach the back gallery of the audience – mirrors that of the apprentice system for actors in earlier periods: the young proteges were expected to learn through example: how to get laughs; how to make an effect; how to focus the audience's attention; how to comport themselves properly in various styles.

Categories: Character Arcs

What is the journey the character is taking? Though the actors can't play a character's knowledge of the future, sometimes later scenes will reveal what a character is capable of or confirm the actor's thoughts about the character's mindset based on their future decisions. The actor must know if the character has within them the will to perform certain actions. This may include actions that were not suggested by earlier behaviors in the play but appear because of the experiences that character has gone through that make those actions inevitable.[47]

Category: Character Language

Many clues to the character are to be found in what they say in the course of the play. Their means of expression can indicate their backgrounds, their level of education, their personality as taciturn or voluble, their motivations, their attitude towards others, what they know and don't know about a situation, and so on. Teachers can ask:

Does the actor always understand what the character is saying?
Are they using the text to reach one another? Are they using the language to get what they want?
Are they highlighting the important information?
Are there any "headlines," new information they must emphasize?

In steering the actor towards connecting the character's words with their thoughts, the coach can ask, "What's the thought that prompts you to say that?"

A Character's Intelligence

A situation may arise when the student is using intention, committing completely to their pursuit of objectives, embodying previous circumstances – all of the techniques they have learned in the course – but still missing something in the portrayal of the role. Students will play characters outside of their realms of experience, but no more so than someone who hasn't the sophistication of the highly educated, the perception of the distinctly intelligent – in short, someone who hasn't successfully navigated the world of higher education programs and its challenges. A character's responses, their forms of expression, the speed of their evaluations – but not necessarily their economic or social backgrounds – suggest their ability to grasp what they are hearing and to express what they are thinking and feeling. If the actor is at a loss as to how to connect with the dialogic and physical clues of the script, it may lie in the fact that the student is simply more self-aware, capable of deeper and more complex thinking, more in touch with their feelings, than the character she is playing.

The teacher can help the actor to connect with a character who cannot – as the expression goes – "read the room." The character may have difficulties handling the environment or situation appropriately or with acumen. They may be self-conscious about their feelings of incomprehension. They may apply simplistic thinking to complicated ideas. It takes more effort for them to grasp a situation, or to make appropriate decisions. They may be initially confused by the information they are receiving. They may quickly take offense when none is intended through a misunderstanding of what is being said or done to them. They may have to apply greater concentration to a problem. The difficulty they have with other characters may stem from the difference between their own and their interlocutors' patterns of perception. Their thinking, based on habitual reactions to unusual or perplexing situations, may serve as a major obstacle to successful completion of objectives by other characters.[48]

Traits Versus Situations

Having read a study in social psychology by Edward Jones and Richard Nisbett, Robert Cohen noted, "The professors concluded that the human being is peculiarly egocentric in this regard: that human beings believe that 'personality traits are things *other* people have.'"[49] Instead, they consider their own behavior "'depends on the situation.' Other people are the 'characters' in our lives. We, on the other hand, behave according to the situations in which we find ourselves."[50] In other words, no one trait will define the character the actor is playing. Instead, the character will respond to each situation uniquely. The students themselves interact differently with parents, siblings, peers, romantic partners, coworkers, strangers – and later, with children, employers or employees, and their own students or proteges. During those interchanges, the character's concentration will be on the particular circumstances – one of which is the nature of the current relationship – leading to varying behaviors.

Remind the actors they are playing two sides: the person underneath the current persona who is in a dramatic situation versus their character "at rest." As Di Trevis notes, "Once you have the ordinary life of characters, you can explore the changes that the dramatic event and unexpected catastrophe impose upon them, how their physical responses change under the force of circumstances."[51]

Animal Work

Picking, observing, and embodying an animal's physical behavior can be a means for creating a new character. It is essential to observe the animal directly, ideally by visiting a zoo. If the actor doesn't live near this resource, they can watch nature films, or study their own domesticated animals in the household. Teachers such as Jacques Lecoq could tell the difference between direct observation and imagining because "the first [students] act, the others demonstrate."[52]

The students are asked to learn everything they can about the creature they choose. In Larry Moss's Animal Exercise, he asks his students to study their animal's breathing, the way they use their muscles, eat food, defecate, and procreate.[53] He reminds them to enlarge their choices by considering not only mammals but insects, snakes, and birds.[54] Lecoq gives his students a starting point: "Research on animal bodies begins with their purchase on the ground: how do they stand? What is their contact with the ground and how does it differ from ours?"[55] Other factors may have to do with an animal's reactions to each other and the environment: "Next we investigate animal attitudes."[56] The speed with which animals move can also be used as a character trait: "Some animals provide cases of slow motion."[57] Movement in general can be applied to gestures and progress from place to place: "Locomotion is an important aspect to be observed in animal movement."[58] Reactions can also vary in speed from animal to animal and from human to human: "The movement from relaxation to being on the alert is a special element in animal dynamics."[59]

Lying

The character's facility with lying will be tested by the other characters but is also a consideration when it comes to the audience. Should the audience suspect the character is lying or not? The playwright may choose the ironic position that the spectator is aware of the lie, while the other characters are not, through earlier situations that suggest this – the character having done a previous activity which she denies in the present, or the actor exposing the lie to the audience through his inability to lie as well as he should. Finding the balance is difficult, especially if the characters onstage are fooled. Rarely is the playwright suggesting the other characters are easily deceived or stupid.

Endowment of the Other

Uta Hagen's Endowment Exercise replaces the dangerous or distracting property of an onstage object so that the actor can use her imagination rather than reality, to avoid harm; for example, she can imagine the cup of coffee she is holding is hot and treat it as if it is, rather than worrying about whether she will be burned by the scalding liquid.[60] Alice Spivak created a variation on Uta Hagen called Endowing the Other, that involves the actor's partner instead. Without telling the other actor, each actor applies "a secret investment in the partner to create more vulnerability in the relationship."[61] So Actor B doesn't realize Actor A has made them an escaped prisoner and Actor A doesn't know Actor B has given them an imaginary flu bug, either a "physical secret or a judgment" each actor is then responding to.⁶² This attitude affects both actors because they each notice they are being treated in an unusual manner. These endowments do not have to be negative: the actor can become just as vulnerable if they give the other actor a loveable or romantic attribute that leads to desire. Spivak uses this approach as a step towards substitution, when the actors will each imagine interacting with a completely different person from the one in front of them – for example, someone they are attracted to or are repulsed by.

Status

Keith Johnstone's status transactions are an effective shorthand for creating character attitudes, with an emphasis on the interaction between at least two characters, or even a character and her environment. By taking particular physical positions and using different vocal forms, the actor produces a specific attitude, a mien, a type of comportment. Status here is unrelated to the rank or position of a person in society. Instead, it is the means by which each person negotiates the minefield of interactions between various persons whom they either dominate or submit to. "It is not your social status, it's what you do to someone else."⁶³ The key to this behavior is that it is played, and therefore a person's – and a character's – attitude can be adjusted to each new situation.

Johnstone discovered this principle when working with playwrights to identify realistic dialogue. His first suggestion: " 'Just try to be just a tiny bit more important than the other person or a tiny bit less important,' and suddenly they were human."⁶⁴ It is a subtle adjustment, often subconscious, but it can be the key to interaction: "It's a huge motive – life or death – but it's unconscious. It governs all human behavior. So after six years of trying to find the secret I found it by accident."⁶⁵ He was reading about the behavior of jackdaws and applied it to people: "Human beings are a status animal, a herd animal."⁶⁶ This discovery changed the teaching of acting in many academies: "Every decent acting school teaches the actor to change their level of dominance. Hugh Cruttwell from the Central School would cast against type. If you were a working-class guy, he'd make you play Hamlet."⁶⁷ This avoided the use of typecasting and led to a wider breadth of character work: "The normal thing in drama school, is that you see a Hamlet arrive and have him play Hamlet all through school. The status would do that; someone who only played high status would play low."⁶⁸

Johnstone taught status through external means that could be immediately observed and either accepted or corrected. The high-status actor could be trained to play low: "You make [high-] status people go 'Huh-huh-huh,' a goofy laugh, and they could play comedy."⁶⁹ This behavior has always been present in the human animal, but to point it out is to suggest people have selfish motives for their actions: "[It seems so obvious.] Only I know how painful it was to discover. It was not obvious at all."⁷⁰

Actors should begin by adjusting their behavior in relation to each other: "Learn to balance the status between you and other people. It's a great way to start. You are more likely to get work."[71] Status in Johnstone's thinking is not about rank or economic position; indeed, someone of lower rank may play low in order not to be demoted or discharged but otherwise display many high-status behaviors. In basic training, soldiers are placed in high-status postures at attention, and then the drill sergeant does anything they can to try to lower that status. In the long run, if a leader falls in battle, others must be willing and able to immediately take the officer's place. Charlie Chaplin was famous for being the lowest on the economic scale as the Little Tramp, but he could lower others through his high attitude towards himself. This was a great source of comedy.

Johnstone encouraged the actors to see status as flexible and an opportunity to explore many options: "There are many ways to do it: you can do it with what you say, how you sound, how the body works. You can play contradictory stages at the same time. If you have bad posture, you can still play number 1 [high] if they let you."[72] For practice, Johnstone played etudes using three numbers: 1 as highest, 3 as lowest, and 2 adjusting to either side. Max Stafford Clark, in his etudes with actors who participate in new play development, uses numbers 1–10, with 10 being the highest in status.[73] The nuances to be found between, for example, a 4 and a 5 are instructive. The 4 exhibits a few high-status behaviors – as opposed to a 1 – while the 5 is equipoised between low and high. An 8 will exhibit a few low-status behaviors preventing them from being recognized as a 10, and so on. The numbers are a means for actor and audience alike to identify statuses distinguished by subtle changes in movement and speech. A 9 is high, but a small waver in eye contact can prevent the actor from being read as a 10. A groveling number 1 would physically lower themselves to distinguish themselves from a nervous and excitable 2.

There are two strategies for playing status: if an actor wants to play high status, she can raise herself or lower the other person. This means promoting one's own abilities and mocking, denigrating, or dismissing another's. If an actor wants to play lower status, he can lower himself or raise the other person. This involves self-deprecation for self and admiration for the other.

The idea of changes in status accords with Eric Berne's observation that "from time to time people show noticeable changes in posture, viewpoint, voice, vocabulary, and other aspects of behavior."[74] To Berne these changes, which include changes in feelings, are based on states of mind. In turn, these states of mind are connected to ego states. These states include parental ego states, based on patterns of behavior inculcated by specific parental figures; an adult ego state that is "capable of processing objective data";[75] and a child ego state, that Berne calls "a fixated relic from earlier years which will be activated under certain circumstances."[76] The changes in behavior are here based on the idea that "at any given moment each individual in a social aggregation will exhibit a Parental, Adult, or Child ego state."[77] Certain triggers will activate one of the three states at different moments.

The Offstage Character

If all of the characters discuss a person who doesn't appear in the play, they should each have a strong impression of that character, imagining what he looks like, what his attitude is, how they feel about him, how he affects the scene, how the character brings them together or separates them. Their ideas of the offstage figures do not have to match, because the actors may be stimulated by different mental images and may have different attitudes towards the unseen characters. For example, in Chekhov's *The Three Sisters*, their father the general had a huge influence on their lives, but he has died the year before. Each character must imagine a relationship with the general, and each will vary. Each must picture a real man they can see in the mind's eye.

Music

Music is a useful tool for stimulating a connection between the actor and the character, or serving as a soundtrack for the actor's performance. The music may help the actor to move in a way that embodies the character. As they prepare a role, the actor can also prepare a playlist which tracks their character's journey through a scene or an entire play. They can use this music as an inspirational warmup or imagine it running through their heads in certain moments to elevate the feelings their characters have. Music is a powerful trigger for sense memories and for ego states.

Laban Movement Efforts

Rudolf Laban, in his study of movement and its identification and recreation, *The Mastery of Movement*, suggested the importance of movement to human beings, and thus to actors: "When moving we create changing relationships with something. This something can be an object, a person or even parts of our body, and physical contact can be established in any of these."[78] Movement has the capacity to work as a connection between characters and the way that their interaction creates change.

One of Laban's most popular concepts is a set of categories for types of movement based on time, space, and weight.[79] These three elements are divided into dichotomous forms: Time is a matter of Quick or Sustained movement; either "sudden" or continuous – "a feel of endlessness"; Space involves movement in a straight line or in curves, "a pliant or lineal attitude," that is, Direct or Indirect; and Weight involves "a relaxed or forceful attitude,"[80] either Heavy or Light. With these three elements and two variations, Laban created eight combinations:[81] (1) Quick, Direct, Heavy or "Punching"; (2) Quick, Direct, and Light or "Dabbing"; (3) Quick, Indirect, and Heavy or "Slashing"; (4) Quick, Indirect, and Light or "Flicking"; (5) Sustained, Direct, and Heavy or "Pressing"; (6) Sustained, Indirect, and Light or "Floating"; (7) Sustained, Direct, and Light or "Gliding"; and (8) Sustained, Indirect, and Heavy or "Wringing."[82]

The same combinations can be used with the voice: a character can punch out their words, dab their suggestions, and use wringing as if squeezing the words out of their mouths. These vocal characteristics do not have to match the physical elements of the character's bodily movements, and the number of possible combinations rises when the choices of bodily and vocal movements are combined.

The actor, in her observation of the movements of others, can note which elements are at play and duplicate them. If the actor uses various combinations as they move their bodies and speak dialogue, they can create interesting and varied characters. For example, a character who is noble, upright, and smooth may glide across the space because his is a sustained movement in a linear direction and lightly executed. If spoken dialogue is broken up into light, quickly tossed-out bits of information, the voice might be said to be flicking.

Resisting the Condition

The characters who strongly pursue their objectives are also dealing with emotional and physical conditions that serve as powerful obstacles to fight against, to resist. Polly Findlay learned from Conor McPherson "the only note you need to give any actor is to resist the condition, and what that means is whatever condition your character is in, you should work really hard to push very hard against it."[83] She considers his advice, "just the best acting note of all time."[84] Findlay gives a classic example, the condition of being drunk. In that instance, "You put all your energy into working really hard to look sober."[85] If an actor is having trouble producing tears onstage, "It's more moving to watch somebody try not to cry,"[86] and if the actor believes the character should be angry at a certain moment, Findlay asks him to "[w]ork hard not to lose your temper."[87] This is an excellent diagnostic tool as well, since the actor can be monitored for the committed energy they apply to the resistance: "'Resist that a bit more' is a quick note."[88]

Switching Roles

This technique is not one used in every classroom. The teacher may consider switching the actors' roles in a scene as a rehearsal exercise, but only if she creates an atmosphere that encourages and explains the reasoning for this process, and the actors are comfortable doing so. If egos are in play, an actor may resent the suggestion that the other actor is telling them how to play the role. Under the proper conditions, the actors will get an outside perspective on their roles which encourages them to consider further facets of personality, actions, physicality, or mindsets. This is a perspective they may have lost the moment they read a script, knowing which role they would be playing. At that point, it is difficult to imagine the character in a larger context and concentrate on the overall narrative and the character's participation in it. They are not imitating each other in the roles but bringing their own perspective to their enactments.

Moral Stance and Will

The values of the character are defined by her moral code: sense of moral responsibility, integrity, and fair treatment of others.[89] Eric and Ann Maisal, in writing about the creation of characters in a novel, call this Moral Valence: if the character is basically a good or bad character and where they might lean in either column.[90] Of course, good and bad actions may depend upon the society in which they are enacted.

The will of the role is "a character's relative strength for attaining his desires."[91] Does the character give up too easily, or before they should? Does the character never give up, even when defeat seems complete? Does the character's will overpower his moral stance, so that no action is off limits to the success of his enterprise?

Acquired Frames of Reference

Our consciousness is affected by what Sam Kogan calls our Natural Frames of Reference, "points of reference in the mental world."[92] These are powerful influences over all of our thoughts and actions: "These are innate in all of us as human beings and if we have swayed from them, every one of us is capable of returning to them."[93] Combined with outside influences, Acquired Frames of Reference are created. These influences include the Prenatal, Persons in Control of Our Lives, Awareness and Self-Conditioning, the Non-Biological, Emerging Awarenesses, and the Somatic.[94] Kogan believes the prenatal influence occurs when the unborn child can respond not only to the vibrations of music, "but to the vibrations of what the mother is thinking and feeling."[95] Persons in Control, or People in Charge (PiCs), may have frames of reference that either reflect conflict or agreement between them – for example, the thoughts of two parents may accord or not.[96] Awareness is a way of examining one's own thoughts, while self-conditioning occurs "[w]hen we successfully impose thoughts on ourselves."[97] Non- Biological influences include "society, language, environments, climate."[98] Emerging Awareness refers to the first thoughts we have that stay with us, early moments that create thought patterns.[99]

The word "somatic" refers to how our consciousness is influenced by the body. For example, how does the character's lifestyle alter that body and therefore its consciousness? When the character is a clerk, sitting at his desk all day, this will prescribe the nature of their feelings about the body. Or if the character is a manual laborer, either the character will be suffering from hard work or will have a strong body which has adapted to the conditions of their occupation. How often does the character bathe or shower? How often and what does the character eat? Perhaps the character's gums, although never referred to, throb with pain, or the character has dentures instead of teeth, or they obsessively brush and floss.[100]

These tools and many more of the teacher's devising lead the students towards a realization of character. In the final analysis, it is the teacher's philosophy of what defines a character that will determine what kinds of tools are selected.

Before turning to the next chapter, a discussion of what feedback is and how and why it is used, the following prompts, suggested by previous chapters, are offered for determining how sessions with the students are progressing:

1. What kind of categories did you identify and highlight as topics for coaching based on the particular students you had in the scene?
2. How can you involve the whole class when you are working with small groups such as a duet? Did you do this on this particular occasion and if so, how?

3. How did you know whether what you were offering yielded some changes in the nature of the scene?
4. How did you begin? (What were your first steps as the coaching started?)
5. Did you work on early goals (easing into the process), or did you also tackle more essential goals that were necessary for realizing the scene in its ultimate form?
6. How much coaching did you do during the session, and how much directing? Identify examples of each.
7. Would you describe your coaching as primarily guiding, questioning, leading, experimenting, motivating, playing, or any combination of these?
8. How did you approach the actor in terms of developing the character or dealing with emotion?
9. Did you find yourself second-guessing the results or your prep, or did you feel comfortable in the space with your actors? What led to either of these feelings?
10. What habits did you discover, and did you replace or develop them further?
11. How was your time management? Did you have enough work for the full class period? Did you feel rushed at all? Did you run out of time? If so, how would you avoid this in the future?
12. What did you feel was your most successful moment during the coaching session?

Work on character, as I have mentioned, can be a full course or courses. The material for this chapter is concentrated in order to offer certain initial ideas for additional diagnostic or analytical tools depending on how far the character is from the actor who is playing them. It is, for this reason, brief, with overarching topics worth much more exploration.

This and previous chapters on coaching have suggested means for diagnosing the work the teacher sees in rehearsal. The next chapter concerns the thinking behind giving feedback or acting notes, including ways to deal not only with the individuals performing in front of the class, but the other students watching – what tasks the latter might have, when the teacher should address the entire class and when she should attend exclusively to the scene partners, how the class will know who is being addressed, and what the comments to the audience of peers will consist of. Waiting to receive feedback from a teacher or peer can be nerve-wracking, and any opportunity to use a professional approach to criticism is to be encouraged.

Notes

1 Lovett, et al., *How Learning Works*, 13.
2 See Chapter 4.
3 Hagen, *Respect for Acting*, 34.
4 Davis, *On Acting . . . and Life*, 107.
5 Demidov, *Becoming an Actor-Creator*, 245, emphasis Demidov's.
6 Demidov, *Becoming an Actor-Creator*, 267, emphasis Demidov's.
7 Esper and DiMarco, *The Actor's Guide to Creating a Character*, 119.
8 Donnellan, *The Actor and the Target*, 20.

9 *Fresh Air*, https://www.npr.org/2011/03/28/134629395/timothy-olyphant-justified-in-laying-down-the-law
10 *Fresh Air*.
11 *Fresh Air*.
12 Toporkov, *Stanislavski in Rehearsal*, 75.
13 Toporkov, *Stanislavski in Rehearsal*, 142.
14 Toporkov, *Stanislavski in Rehearsal*, 142.
15 Toporkov, *Stanislavski in Rehearsal*, 142.
16 Davis, *On Acting . . . and Life*, 103.
17 Sanford Meisner and Dennis Longwell, *Sanford Meisner on Acting* (New York: Vintage Books, 1987), 35.
18 Esper and DiMarco, *The Actor's Guide to Creating a Character*, 95–96.
19 Earle Gister, Teacher Development Program Notes, June 2003.
20 The reading exercise in Chapter 6 is one way to introduce this idea at the beginning of scene work.
21 Fine and Freeman, *Fine on Acting*, 91.
22 One recent development in teacher training and rehearsal protocols is the introduction of intimacy work, the careful collaboration with actors whose vulnerability, consent, and personal boundaries must be considered when staging moments in a play that involve physical contact of an intimate nature. See Chelsea Pace and Laura Rikard, *Staging Sex: Best Practices, Tools, and Techniques for Theatrical Intimacy* (Abingdon, Oxon: Routledge, 2020).
23 Jacques Lecoq, *The Moving Body (Le Corps Poétique): Teaching Creative Theater*, 3rd Edition, trans. David Bradby (London: Methuen Drama, 2020), 98. Emphasis Lecoq's.
24 Woolson, *The Work of an Actor*, 136.
25 Esper and DiMarco, *The Actor's Guide to Creating a Character*, 89.
26 Kemp, *Embodied Acting*, 108.
27 Kemp, *Embodied Acting*, 108.
28 Schulman, quoted in Mekler, *The New Generation of Acting Teachers*, 60.
29 Schulman, quoted in Mekler, *The New Generation of Acting Teachers*, 60.
30 Schulman, quoted in Mekler, *The New Generation of Acting Teachers*, 60–61.
31 Having experimented with this exercise, I've noted some highly unusual changes in the actor. For example, one of the students had a bad cold, with coughing, sneezing, and sniffling, but insisted on performing. Once the alternative personality took over, all symptoms disappeared, only to reappear after the exercise was completed.
32 Esper and DiMarco, *The Actor's Guide to Creating a Character*, 74.
33 Esper and DiMarco, *The Actor's Guide to Creating a Character*, 85.
34 Read the play *August Osage Country* by Tracy Letts for an extreme example.
35 John Friel and Linda Friel, *Adult Children: The Secrets of Dysfunctional Families* (Deerfield Beach, FL: Health Communications Inc., 1988), 57.
36 Friel and Friel, *Adult Children*, 56.
37 Friel and Friel, *Adult Children*, 54–57.
38 Perhaps this is why Thomas Wolfe titled his novel, *You Can't Go Home Again*.
39 Interestingly, characters can insult or mock their family members as much as they want, but they don't necessary encourage this in non-family members – they may in fact resent it.
40 Much less likely today, and deemed offensive, are performances such as Alec Guinness's Professor Godbole in *Passage to India* or Olivier's *Othello*.
41 Woolson, *The Work of an Actor*, 140.
42 As quoted in William Archer, *Masks or Faces: A Study in the Psychology of Acting* (London: Longmans, Green, and Co., 1888).
43 Archer, *Masks or Faces*, 27.
44 Archer, *Masks or Faces*, 23–24.
45 David Allen, *Stanislavsky for Beginners* (Danbury, CT: For Beginners LLC, 1999), 116. Constantin Coquelin (1841–1909) was the first actor to play Cyrano de Bergerac.

46 Gamaliel Bradford, "Joseph Jefferson," *The Atlantic*, January 1922. Jefferson (1829–1905) was an American actor famous for comic roles.
47 The audience doesn't know that Quinn Carney, the protagonist of Jez Butterworth's *The Ferryman*, is capable of the shocking violence he perpetrates at the end of the play, but the actor must know that Quinn's feelings for Caitlan are strong enough to make this possible. Jez Butterworth, *The Ferryman* (London: Nick Hern Books, 2017).
48 Many of Neil LaBute's characters can be understood only if the actor is willing to play this type of person – whose mistaken actions are based on misunderstandings that lead to knee-jerk reactions such as anger and hurt.
49 Cohen, *Acting Power: The 21st Century Edition*, 18, quoting Edward E. Jones and Richard E. Nisbett, *The Actor and the Observer: Divergent Perceptions of the Causes of Behavior* (New York: General Learning Press, 1971), 2. Emphasis Jones and Nisbett.
50 Cohen, *Acting Power: The 21st Century Edition*, 18.
51 Di Trevis, *Being a Director: A Life in Theatre* (London: Routledge, 2012), 81.
52 Lecoq, *The Moving Body*, 127.
53 Moss, *The Intent to Live*, 142.
54 Moss, *The Intent to Live*, 142.
55 Lecoq, *The Moving Body*, 125.
56 Lecoq, *The Moving Body*, 125.
57 Lecoq, *The Moving Body*, 125.
58 Lecoq, *The Moving Body*, 127.
59 Lecoq, *The Moving Body*, 125.
60 For a further discussion about the Endowment Exercise, see Chapter 11, which includes a means for grading the exercise objectively.
61 Mekler, *The New Generation of Acting Teachers*, 176.
62 Mekler, *The New Generation of Acting Teachers*, 177.
63 Keith Johnston, *Impro: Improvisation and the Theatre* (New York: Routledge, 1979).
64 Johnstone, Notes from "Ten Days with Keith," July 11, 2017.
65 Johnstone, Notes from "Ten Days with Keith," July 11, 2017.
66 Johnstone, Notes from "Ten Days with Keith," July 11, 2017.
67 Johnstone, Notes from "Ten Days with Keith," July 11, 2017.
68 Johnstone, Notes from "Ten Days with Keith," July 11, 2017.
69 Johnstone, Notes from "Ten Days with Keith," July 11, 2017.
70 Johnstone, Notes from "Ten Days with Keith," July 11, 2017.
71 Johnstone, Notes from "Ten Days with Keith," July 11, 2017.
72 Johnstone, Notes from "Ten Days with Keith," July 11, 2017.
73 Max Stafford-Clark, *Letters to George: The Account of a Rehearsal* (London: Nick Hern Books, 1989), 25–27.
74 Eric Berne, MD, *Games People Play: The Basic Book of Transactional Analysis* (New York: Tantor eBooks, 2011), 23.
75 Berne, *Games People Play*, 8.
76 Berne, *Games People Play*, 8.
77 Berne, *Games People Play*, 8. For further discussion about social transactions as games, see Chapter 12.
78 Rudolf Laban, *The Mastery of Movement*, 3rd Edition, rev. Lisa Ullmann (Boston: Plays Inc., 1971), 73.
79 Laban, *The Mastery of Movement*, 76–81.
80 Laban, *The Mastery of Movement*, 76.
81 Laban, *The Mastery of Movement*, 77. The two other factors are a "unhampered or 'free flow'" and a "hampered or 'bound flow.'" 21. For example, pressing requires a bound flow, "so that the movement can be stopped at any moment" (21), and slashing has a free flow so that "the movement is suddenly and energetically released." (21)

82 Laban, *The Mastery of Movement*, 77. Laban also includes "derivatives," for example, "shove, kick, poke" for punch and "flip, flap, jerk," for flick.
83 Polly Findlay, *National Theatre Talks*, podcast, Polly Findlay on *Rutherford and Son*, December 13, 2019.
84 Findlay, *National Theatre Talks*.
85 Findlay, *National Theatre Talks*.
86 Findlay, *National Theatre Talks*.
87 Findlay, *National Theatre Talks*.
88 Findlay, *National Theatre Talks*.
89 Hodge, *Play Directing*, 44.
90 Eric Maisel, PhD, and Ann Maisal, *What Would Your Character Do? Personality Quizzes for Analyzing Your Characters* (Cincinnati, OH: Writer's Digest Books, 2006), 19.
91 Hodge, *Play Directing*, 44.
92 Kogan and Kogan, *The Science of Acting*, 11.
93 Kogan and Kogan, *The Science of Acting*, 11.
94 Kogan and Kogan, *The Science of Acting*, 94.
95 Kogan and Kogan, *The Science of Acting*, 81.
96 See Kogan and Kogan, *The Science of Acting*, 81–85 for various examples.
97 Kogan and Kogan, *The Science of Acting*, 86. See the more thorough discussion on pages 86–90.
98 See Kogan and Kogan, *The Science of Acting*, 90.
99 See Kogan and Kogan, *The Science of Acting*, 93.
100 Kogan and Kogan, *The Science of Acting*, 93–94.

11 Feedback

The moment has arrived when the actors stop and look expectantly at the instructor for a response. Before the instructor begins to speak, she determines what kind of feedback to offer. Some students brace for a rash of negative comments. Some want tough love and to use the feedback as soon as possible, regardless of what type and how much – to go away and work on it. Some want to calculate if the feedback suggests the grade they will receive at the end of the semester. In general, they will want the teacher to offer specifics for improvement.

Imagine being a student who has just performed for the class. She is very proud of the work. Though she is unsure what the teacher is looking for, she has identified some goals for herself: she is off book, has followed all of the teacher's notes to the letter, related strongly to her partner, and acted with intent. Because the teacher consistently searches for the habits that hold the student back, he may skip the praise and instead move on to constructive criticism, devastating the student by concentrating on what still needs to be improved rather than what was accomplished. The teacher is offering feedback, but it is not the type the actor was expecting. Nor is it sometimes clear what the teacher was looking for in the first place, other than the general goal of doing the scene well, or professionally, or smoothly; in that instance, the teacher has not established the direction of the work for the session.

In studying what operations are at work in teaching and learning during practice and feedback, Susan Ambrose and her colleagues formulated this principle: "Goal-directed practice coupled with targeted feedback are critical to learning."[1] It is important that both are in play in a productive way. The course itself provides many practice opportunities for the students. Ideally, the practice "a) focuses on a specific goal or criterion for performance, b) targets an appropriate level of challenge relative to students' current performance, and c) is of sufficient quality and frequency to meet the performance criteria."[2] One tenet of this book is that the students themselves will determine their goals for the session, while the teacher considers both the student goals and their own to use in targeted feedback.[3]

One obstacle to learning that can make feedback difficult is the lack of specific goals defined by the teacher and aimed for by the students in that practice. Sometimes teachers mistakenly believe they have clearly defined the goals. Instead, they may be speaking in generalities, or operating from a mastery mindset, i.e., much of their initial learning has been absorbed into fewer steps or a singular precept they can draw on with little effort. This expert blindness seems clear to the instructor with their years of practice, but it is not transparent to the student at all. In that case, the feedback will consist of remediation in concepts that should have been clearly taught before any practice took place.

The teacher should concentrate on making the goals clear and observable. For example, "to understand" is not observable, unless one can read the student's mind. The same is true of "appreciate." However, "To use the previous circumstances to affect the scene" can be observed with a change in the students' behavior. Sometimes a goal will be qualified by the manner in which it will be accomplished, "To deeply engage in Stanislavsky's concept of the Inner Monologue," is important but needs further defining. What does "deeply engage" mean? Instead, to make the goal observable, the teacher may restate the learning objective as, "To speak an inner monologue out loud revealing the thoughts the character has when responding to the partner's verbal and physical stimuli."[4] Since the whole class will also be learning from the successful accomplishment of goals, those goals should be clear to the observers as well. In this last instance, since the students and teacher can hear what the student believes the character is thinking, they can compare that thinking to what the scene requires. A less spontaneous method, but also observable, would be to have the student put an inner monologue on paper and submit it to the teacher before performing.

The teacher should meet the students where they are in their development and choose student goals that will challenge but not discourage the actor. These should be achievable at the student's current level of skill. One way to introduce new material is to use scaffolding: like the use of training wheels for a child learning how to ride a bike, teachers use "instructional supports early in their learning, and then gradually remove the supports as students develop greater mastery and sophistication."[5] For example, students can practice subtext by performing open scenes: small portions of dialogue that do not suggest specific intentions. They can then apply various motivations to basic roles and simple dialogue without the need to do a thorough analysis of a scene before performing it.[6]

Establishing a foundation and adding processes on top of it with increasing complexity is another example of scaffolding. In the acting classroom, the teacher is encouraged to break down concepts into steps, providing guidance until the steps are integrated into larger practice; this means making the time for exercises of increasing complexity that are practiced separately from the study of particular scenes. For example, Alice Spivak's "Endowment of the Other" presupposes the student's familiarity with Hagen's "Endowment Object Exercise," while Spivak's "Endowment of the Other" exercise is introduced as a bridge to her next concept, "Substitution."[7] This is an example of sequential learning, where the student is not expected to do many different tasks at once but is encouraged to master one at a time. This is another reason the teacher should avoid overwhelming the student actors with advice and concentrate on one or two areas for improvement.

Philosophically, the teacher should try to remember what it was like to be a student learning something for the first time and recall the original steps they themselves took to master a concept, a process, or an exercise. This is because once they have truly mastered an activity, they have reached what is called "unconscious competence." This is the fourth and last stage in a learning process.[8] To be able to accomplish something automatically without thinking about it means they are no longer starting at zero. They are experts in that activity.

Students go through four phases to reach mastery, unconscious competence, or expertise, being the last. First, the student must grow through three other phases: "unconscious incompetence," "conscious incompetence," and "conscious competence."[9] With unconscious incompetence, the student does not yet know what they don't know. Knowledge of the steps is nonexistent. They then graduate to a conscious incompetence, where they realize what they don't know and which steps they must master. When they reach conscious competence, they know the steps of a process well enough to go through them carefully in order. Mastery means the student no longer has to concentrate on every step but does so without thinking about them. For example, a student can't really learn how to drive a car without going through particular steps, but if they are to reach mastery, when they are simply driving the car, they must be able to perform each step automatically and unconsciously. To continue to be conscious of all of the steps would be counterproductive, would slow them down, or would even disrupt their activity completely.

Because the last step is unconscious, the master develops an "expert blind spot,"[10] in which they "employ short cuts and skip steps that novices cannot."[11] Experts tend to combine their knowledge into "chunks,"[12] larger categories in which they gather specific knowledge for quicker access.[13] They may end up keeping this larger category intact when teaching rather than breaking it down into the specific parts that will explain what steps need to be taken.

At first, when an actor is learning basic skills to improve their own instruments, they can become self-conscious because they are in the conscious incompetence phase. Skills they thought they had mastered, such as talking and moving, are suddenly inadequate for performance and require further steps. Before they began courses in voice and movement, they were in a state of comfortable unconscious incompetence. Until the stage of conscious competence is reached, they are uncomfortable and self-conscious. Teachers must recognize this feeling and avoid discouraging the student by breaking down the items to be mastered into smaller and realizable steps. They must also give the students many chances to practice and master these smaller steps before moving on to the mastery of an entire operation, such as acting a role in a scene or a full-length play.

Another consideration at the higher education level is identifying the stage of the process that should be graded. A teacher will sometimes grade the students at the conscious incompetence level when they are not yet sure of the steps. These small grades, added together, can lower their overall grade for a course and discourage the student from seeking mastery.

Mastery of an art form means the student is able to use all they have been taught to finish the course with a performance or product. Ultimately, the only product that counts is the final one: they act a scene with competence, accomplishing the stated goals of the class. If someone is trying to learn how to build a cabinet, they will receive feedback as to how to proceed when they make mistakes, but they are really judged when, at the end of the course, they have built a cabinet to the teacher's specifications. With the smaller grades along the way – for improper plumbing of a baseboard or using too many hinges – their final grade could be lower than an A or even a B, even though they have finally mastered the skill and built a perfect cabinet.

The number of sessions for each scene should be enough that the students have more than one chance to meet a number of criteria or to improve on advice given at the end of a previous session. To have an answer to a problem but not be able to practice or solve it can be extremely frustrating. If nothing else, without application – a higher level of learning – the new concept doesn't impress itself into the actor's body and brain for use in future work. They don't reach a state of unconscious mastery. Throughout, they must receive feedback so they feel they are moving towards a larger goal.

In her "basic elements that must be considered in the design of an effective lesson," this feedback would come in the stage Madeline Hunter called "Guided Practice," that is, a check by the teacher on the student's progress, with remediation applied immediately so that the student is successful.[14] This step in the instruction model is not graded. The building of the final cabinet, or the performance of the final scene, will be done without the teacher's guidance and is called "Independent Practice."[15] This is graded, as the product is a sign of the student's fluency of learning.[16]

Principles of Feedback

According to the authors of *How Learning Works*, "[E]ffective feedback can tell students *what* they are or not understanding, *where* their performance is going well or poorly, and *how* they should direct their subsequent efforts."[17] This means, of course, the teacher must provide further opportunities for guidance and mastery of specific concepts. During the coach's early feedback, i.e., Guided Practice, they don't worry about the students mastering the scene on the first try. The early sessions give the coach a means of monitoring student work and guiding them towards improvement. Though no grades are necessary at this point, some teachers will give a participation grade for students' attendance at all scheduled rehearsals of their scenes.

"[F]eedback at the right time and of the right nature can promote students' learning not only in the present but also in the future."[18] If the feedback the student receives gives them an understanding of an overall concept, they may avoid the same mistake in future attempts. For example, if the student is studying the use of actions, and the verbs they choose only relate to their own characters, then every verb in the present instance, and any future verb, will be ineffective. "To stew," "to sulk," "to be angry," "to blush" by a strict definition will not be directed at the other character to change their feelings or make them do something that supports the actor's mission. The idea of action verbs must be given further criteria;[19] any full definition of a concept must contain all of the attributes that define it. Without a clear definition, including non-examples – or features that do not apply – the student can form an inaccurate idea of a concept. For example, if a definition of being "off book" does not include the feature "to be word perfect," the student can assume that a rough familiarity with the lines will be enough to master that skill.

Timing is relative depending on what the goals are. For example, offering frequent feedback over the course of the semester helps the student to track their progress and avoid making the same mistake over and over. Delayed feedback, on the other hand, may be necessary if the teacher wants to give the student an opportunity to discover their errors for themselves. In this instance, students would receive feedback "only when they a) showed sufficient signs of not having recognized their error or b) made multiple failed attempts at fixing their error."[20] At this point, the teacher is still guiding their efforts.

Kinds of Feedback

An important question to ask is: When an actor awaits feedback, what is it that the actor really wants to hear? According to Douglas Stone and Sheila Heen, it is important that the person giving the feedback understands there may be more than one way to give it.[21] They divide the possible feedback into three types: "appreciation (thanks), coaching (here's a better way to do it), and evaluation (here's where you stand)."[22] Using this principle, the teacher should be aware that, when students await feedback, though the nature of the course suggests that correction is the primary form, the students may in fact want one of the other types. They may want suggestions for improvement that are actable, but at this stage in their development, they may want validation, to feel what they are doing is worthwhile and acknowledged by the teacher. In a scene study course, they will want to know what grades they will receive for their work. Since they are being assessed, they can't help but compare their own work to others and will be gauging whether their feedback has the same quality as the responses the teacher gives to their peers. Evaluations are based on a set of standards; if those standards are clear to the student, laid out clearly in rubrics or a checklist,[23] then the feedback will seem consistent because it comes from a series of possible topics with which the class is familiar. The teacher will also note when the feedback applies to all of the students rather than just those who are the subjects of the session.

If the students are to remain motivated, some form of appreciation is necessary. This positive feedback is omitted when the coach is focused on finding all the things the student has done wrong rather than acknowledging what they've done right. "Appreciation is fundamentally about relationship and human connection. At a literal level it says, 'thanks.' But appreciation also conveys, 'I see you,' 'I know how hard you've been working,' and 'You matter to me.'"[24] This strengthens the teacher/student relationship. It satisfies, even if briefly, what many students need when they decide to pursue theatre beyond their initial experiences, whether in church, school, or in the community. They seek belonging, connection with individuals who appreciate and support them, forms of mentorship, or positive relationships with authority figures.

One form of validation the teacher can offer is to serve as an ideal audience and respond to the students' work vocally and physically – to laugh or nod appreciatively, or to groan sympathetically when the character has a terrible moment. Another form of positive feedback is a silent but respectful concentration on the scene; mentally picking categories for diagnoses makes this simpler, so the coach is not buried in written note-taking. To state the obvious: no matter what phase of the scene work the class is in, the teacher shouldn't let his mind wander but should give the current session his full attention. After the final session, the teacher can send the students a written form of feedback to sum up what they have accomplished.

"Coaching is aimed at trying to help someone learn, grow, or change."[25] If the coach prioritizes what they consider the essential challenges to cover, this is less likely to overwhelm the student and to be more beneficial. Sometimes categories overlap; this may be because they address previous challenges, either positively or negatively. With further practice, previous lessons that have led to successful behaviors should be acknowledged. Coaching itself involves "formative feedback," suggesting both criteria for success and means for reaching those goals.[26]

"Evaluation tells you where you stand. It's an assessment, ranking, or rating."[27] This is a summative judgment, a final assessment. The disadvantage of a grade is that it doesn't tell the student why they received it[28] and stresses product over process. This is based on the students' independent practice that occurs only when the teacher/coach believes the actor has mastered basic concepts while performing. The teacher should explain the grade so further learning can take place. If the student is given reasons for the grade based on a rubric, and the teacher lists specific criteria for success within it, the feedback should be clear.

However, "[i]t doesn't matter how much authority or power a feedback giver has; the receivers are in control of what they do and don't let in, how they make sense of what they're hearing, and whether they choose to change."[29] The actors may even resist the teacher's feedback, feeling their hard work on the scene is being dismissed. They may be unaware that what they understand or feel about the scene is not being embodied: cannot be read by the instructor or the rest of the class. The coach is the third eye the student needs for an objective assessment. When students are unaware what they planned isn't reaching the audience, they may resent that their hard work isn't acknowledged or may even wonder if the teacher believes they haven't been doing their homework at all. They experience a trigger.

Three triggers that can keep the students from responding well to the feedback are "Truth Triggers," "Relationship Triggers," and "Identity Triggers."[30] Students respond negatively to a Truth Trigger, because they disagree with the veracity of the feedback. It is not what they experienced; therefore, it is wrong. With Relationship Triggers, the student responds more to the person giving the feedback than the feedback itself. Is the peer giving the feedback someone who the actor trusts? Based on what they hear, does the actor lower their opinion of the person giving it? Has the teacher established a good relationship with her students? Does she give the impression she is asking them to do things she wouldn't do herself? Do they trust the teacher to give helpful feedback without judgment? Identity Triggers strike at the heart of who the student believes they are; their sense of identity is threatened to the point of disorientation, hurt, or shame.[31] The teacher should identify the students' triggers before beginning their feedback.

When students accept the same feedback from someone else, even though their teacher has been offering it over and over, what may have changed is that the Relationship Trigger may have been removed that blocked the feedback.[32] For whatever reason, the relationship between the student and teacher has prevented its reception. It is all right for the teacher to ask what kind of feedback the student would like above and beyond coaching. Or the teacher may begin with validation and move on to advice for improvement. Finally, the teacher, without taking it personally, may realize the student responds better to another teacher.

Perhaps the student was the lead actor in her high school plays or has won awards for their work. They have been given the impression they are already skilled at what they do because of constant positive feedback and are resistant to learning more because what they have done has worked in the past. The students may be so attached to a feeling about themselves that any threat to the attachment can be terrifying and debilitating.[33] They may have a "fixed," as opposed to a "growth" mindset.

Carol S. Dweck, in her book *Mindset*, asks an important question, "What are the consequences of thinking that your intelligence or personality is something you can develop, as opposed to something that is a fixed, deep-seated trait?"[34] The first is a growth mindset, "the belief that your basic qualities are things you can cultivate through your efforts, your strategies, and help from others."[35] With a fixed mindset, the student believes people are born with innate talent and skills that will not change over time, that such qualities are "carved in stone."[36] With a growth mindset, the student believes dedication and hard work will allow them to improve.

The implication here is that a student who sees their talent as something that can't be improved upon will consider the attempts at improvement a waste of their time or come to believe they are not superior after all because, with new challenges, they have not succeeded, despite their talent and innate ability. These students may feel like failures. Three strategies can result: they ask for less difficult work within their current wheelhouse, refuse to ask for help, or drop the class.[37]

The actors can also self-impose pressure because of competitiveness, the need to do better than others. These barriers can even be subconscious: the need for approval both from the teacher and from their peers, negative feedback in the past – any sense of making mistakes, an exaggerated impression of their own self-worth instilled by earlier teachers, or the belief by their loved ones they are wasting their time with acting courses unless they are immediately successful. These ideas are part of the fixed mindset, another relationship with the student which adds a layer for the teacher to work on.

The good news is that the growth mindset can be developed in any student. This is key to dealing with student recalcitrance; having a fixed mindset means they take any hint of failure personally: challenges to their work are challenges to their natural abilities and therefore their identities. Instead, the growth mindset "is the mindset that allows people to thrive during some of the most challenging times in their lives."[38]

In particular, teachers inculcate the growth mindset when they teach their students "to love challenges, be intrigued by mistakes, enjoy effort, seek new strategies, and keep on learning."[39] It turns out praise can backfire if it is focused on the student's personality, talents, or intelligence. Instead, the teacher should concentrate on their efforts and achievements. To say "This student will be the next Meryl Streep" will actually impede their progress. If they don't live up to this assessment – which they can't – they will become defensive or bitter of others' success. Instead, the teacher should use constructive criticism that is honest and specific about their efforts.

The mindset of coaching as opposed to directing can also be useful: "While identity is easily triggered by evaluation, it is far less threatened by coaching."[40] When coaching is considered evaluation and becomes personal to the receiver, "We snatch defensiveness from the jaws of learning."[41] The teacher should aim the students towards coaching as a means of learning something useful and embracing growth rather than a fixed identity.[42] The teacher can address the student in terms of the clarity of the narrative, serving as an impartial observer of what was offered, an appraiser who gives the actors an idea of how they were perceived by the audience rather than how they felt they were perceived. In this way, he aids them in accomplishing the tasks they have set themselves: the teacher and students are trying to reach the same destination. In keeping with the idea of coaching as opposed to directing, if the teacher frames their notes as questions rather than answers, the student is given the opportunity to consider further means for realizing the scene, including returning to the text. This may be a means of asking them not only to seek new answers, but to verify the work they have done so far.

Types of Questions

Dan Rothstein and Luz Santana offer a questioning technique involving two types: open and closed questions.[43] Distinguishing between these types is helpful for both the teacher and for the students as they begin to give feedback in the form of questions. A common closed-ended question involves "Yes" or "No" or a brief answer. It does not automatically prompt elaboration, whereas the open-ended question does. The open-ended question leads the student to higher-order thinking. Rather than simply restating facts, the students begin to consider the reasons behind that information. They may know Lee Strasberg was famous for his Method – a fact – but they may be unaware of how he developed his approach to acting. Students can learn to reframe their closed-ended questions as open-ended and practice distinguishing between them. "Open-ended questions start with *Why?* and *How?* Closed-ended questions start with *Is?*, *Do?*, and *Can?*"[44] In some cases, either can begin with "*What?*, *Who?*, *Where?*, and *When?*"[45]

The authors suggest a further test for dividing the types of questions into one or the other: "Because some questions can go into one or the other category, it is helpful to remind students that the key is to think about the limits and extent of information they can get from their questions."[46] The teacher gets deeper responses by examining how many of his own are open-ended and how many are closed and adjust accordingly. For example, "Do you have any questions?" can become "What questions do you have?" or "What questions do you have about_____?"[47] However, a closed-ended question can be followed by an open-ended one: "Did the actors accomplish their stated goals today?" leads to "What were those goals and how could you tell?"

"How did that feel?" is a popular closed-ended question teachers like to ask. If the teacher is asking the student to respond to how a prompt or exercise might have helped the scene, this may be the most direct way to find out. However, this question can be so closed-ended as to encourage general responses such as, "It felt good," an answer that doesn't address what the teacher wants to know. However, converting this question to a more open-ended one will avoid any confusion: "What did this do for your character?" "What differences did you notice?" "What changed about your perception of the scene?" "What discoveries did you make?"

Targeted Feedback

Targeted feedback can be highly effective in the heat of the moment, but even so, it should be connected to the students' overall goals. The teacher may ask the students to concentrate on a single section of the scene so that he does not interrupt their work but deals with specific moments, one at a time. Side-coaching allows the teacher to serve as a guide who partners with the student, much as a coach may talk into a quarterback's helmet to suggest the best possible plays for advancing the football. The teacher is able to green-light work that is showing promise, to encourage the student to raise the stakes, or to take the character's viewpoint in a kind of inner monologue she shares with the student as a character advocate.[48]

Making the Feedback Text-Based

Fewer arguments occur between the teacher and students, or the students with each other, when the primary focus is on the play itself and the needs of the scene. Though the way in which the students realize the scene during the session can vary, the parameters the author has given them remain the same. If the teacher and actors can agree on the event of the scene and moments that lead to and away from it, this is their concentration.

The character takes a series of steps that can be named. The steps will be correct if they lead inevitably to the event and away from it. The characters also respond to the event based on their wants, and these too are delineated by the playwright, if sometimes in subtle or subtextual form. If the students haven't yet read the full play, they must rely on the teacher to guide them. Ideally, they know all of the given circumstances for their characters, including their previous circumstances. Van Lieu describes these as "the steps that this character moved through that brought him to this state that we see."[49] Otherwise, the actor may mistake the motivations for the character's behavior in the scene. For example, if Character A attacks Character B for a seemingly trivial matter, B may feel that A is being hysterical or unreasonable, when A is in fact responding to a memory which B has unwittingly brought to their attention. B has inadvertently pushed a button that sets A off.[50]

Students as Independent Analyzers

The students should be able to both do the work and talk about it. In the final analysis, the teacher is modeling means for independent practice. Questions for them to ask as they continue to work on the scene may include: What progress have we made on the scene? Have we incorporated previous feedback from other sessions? Where do we want to go from here? What do we want to accomplish in subsequent sessions? How is my relationship with my partner(s)? Are we on the same page in terms of the events of the scene? Are we comfortable with working together? How might we improve our trust with each other? How do we relate as characters? How strong is the connection between us in the scene? Are we open to being affected by each other? What still doesn't make sense in terms of the narrative, the language, and/or the decisions made by the characters? Am I allowing the previous circumstances to have an effect on my behavior?

Once the students have been introduced to certain methods, how can they remember them, adapt them, and use them in the future? How do they achieve mastery? In *How Learning Works*, Susan Ambrose and her colleagues offer this principle: "To develop mastery, students must acquire component skills, practice integrating them, and know when to apply what they have learned."[51]

You will know your coaching has been successful when (1) there has been a notable change in the student's behavior, (2) that behavior works to improve the scene within the parameters the author has created, (3) the student can reflect on how the change occurred, and (4) the student can apply principles to new theatrical circumstances. If the student approaches each new situation without the ability to apply previous learning, one of the teacher's main goals has not been accomplished: to create independent learners and practitioners.

Student Engagement

What if the students are engaged only when their scene is being coached? How will the instructor encourage the other students to respond in a constructive manner? When should the students respond to each other's work, and what forms should this feedback take? If all of the students in class are to benefit from a scene session, they must have some stake in each other's success; the teacher must encourage them to apply the principles inherent in one scene to their own. However, a number of issues may arise if feedback is sought from the students in the early days of the course.

The students may not be ready to offer the kind of feedback the teacher thinks is fruitful. Until the students have become familiar with how the teacher responds to the work, they may offer surface readings of what they saw, general opinions about the scene's quality. They may be positive in their remarks but not yet be able to articulate what it was they felt was successful. They may even begin to direct the scene themselves. In the latter case, this may lead to resentment on the part of the actors, whom the teacher has been trying to lead towards their own solutions. The coach has instilled a sense of ownership of a role by the actor which is suddenly disrupted when others outside of the scene have opinions about that role. Instead, the use of student feedback has to be carefully mediated.

Feedback from students is a delicate process and should be instilled: they need to learn how to observe properly, to know what to look for. The teacher establishes principles to focus the students' attention on specific points of discussion. Students may gravitate towards evaluation, the idea of good or bad, that will be of little use at this point. They may also use coaching but concentrate on providing personal opinions about the student's problems. In their excitement to offer help, they are taking possession of the student's process, feeding them the answers instead of leading them towards their own solutions. Because of this, Lloyd Richards did not allow peer feedback in his early sessions. He was very clear to establish certain rules: "Later, after they were working at a certain level, Richards might invite them to contribute to the class discussion."

Richards proposed two specific questions as prompts for peer responses to a scene which led them towards proper coaching: "Do you have a question to ask that would help [the actors] if they answered in behavior?"[52] Students were also told, "Don't speak until you have really crafted a question, the answer to which, if they answer it, will bring their attention to the thing you saw missing in the work.'"[53] Both of these prompts lead the students watching a scene to be more specific about what they see and to be helpful without directing each other. "These restrictions minimize superfluous questions that did not bring the actor's attention to a text-based answer."[54]

By prescribing the specific responses the peers could give, he avoided the possibility of the observers speaking from the perspective of taking on the roles themselves. "Actors were not allowed to say what they would do if they were performing the scene."[55] If these rules are established early, the responses from the class are less likely to lead to ill feeling. If questions are proposed before a session begins, they focus an observer's attention.

Using a Rubric

One tool that serves as a map for the students and teacher is a rubric. A rubric is "a scoring tool that explicitly represents the performance expectations of a given assignment."[56] This instrument lists the criteria for success in a model product, performance, or written assignment. It also suggests non-examples, those actions or non-actions that will lower their grades. Students will therefore know in advance what behaviors and practices will lead to a grade of A, B, or even F.

The teacher creates the rubric by imagining an ideal performance and its constituent parts as well as an inadequate performance that misses most of the major points. These are the A and F grades. Between them are gradations of items that have been correctly and incorrectly realized. The criteria should be clearly stated and observable: students should be able to do what is asked of them in a way that can be measured. A rubric can be used throughout the course for creating journal assignments, play reports, scene performances, peer critiques, exercises, or etudes. A rubric makes each assignment easier to grade because it becomes a checklist: either all of the criteria have been met or they haven't. The student also has the option of aiming for a lower but still passing grade.

Here is an example of an exercise rubric for Hagen's Endowment Exercise. The students are using their imaginations to convince the audience that a particular object or activity contains an element of danger or distraction when, for safety's sake, it has actually been removed.[57] For example, dealing with any hot object would be dangerous since the heat of the object could burn the actor. First the student identifies what that property is that causes problems and makes a substitution: the student, in a sense, diffuses the possible bomb that might go off, so it will not disrupt or destroy the scene. Then the student treats the object or activity as if it still contains that property. If an actor is going to drink hot coffee, the dangerous property is the heat of the coffee. The student will substitute a lukewarm or cold liquid but treat the coffee as if it still might burn them, blowing on it, sipping slowly, handling the coffee cup carefully, adding creamer, stirring the contents of the cup. The audience then makes the inference that the coffee must be hot because of the way the actor responds to the heat.

RUBRIC FOR ENDOWMENT EXERCISE

Exceeds expectations In all or most of the following: A	Students completely embrace process in class: 1. Students explain in specific terms what was dangerous or distracting about the original object or activity. 2. Students "diffuse" the object while retaining the sense that the danger is still present. (Brown liquid such as cola is substituted for hot coffee instead of water.) 3. Students use at least four steps to endow the object so that the audience believes the dangerous property is still present. 4. Students describe in detail why it is important to endow the object rather than use it. 5. Students give deep thought to and describe carefully how well the exercise worked. 6. Students relate in detail what worked best about the performance of the exercise. 7. Students describe changes they would make or things that they thought could have been improved in the performance. 8. Students turn in the work on time.
Meets expectations In all or most of the following: B In some of the following: C	Students are ready to work and commit to process in class: 1. Students describe what was dangerous about the activity or object but do not go into much detail. 2. Students diffuse the object but in a nonrealistic way. It is not as believable as it might have been. 3. Students use three or fewer details to endow the object but leave out some specifics. 4. Students describe why the object or activity should be endowed but not in detail. 5. Students relate how the exercise went but not in great detail. 6. Students describe what worked best but don't explain why. 7. Students give some suggestions for changes they would make. 8. Students turn their work in on time.
Does not meet expectations D or F	Students are not ready to commit to process for any of the following reasons: 1. Students list few or no details concerning their object or activity. 2. Students do not diffuse the object in a way that is believable. 3. Students use one or two steps to endow the object but are not specific. 4. Students do not give reasons why it would be important to endow the object or activity. 5. Students fail to describe how the exercise went or don't seem to know. 6. Students do not relate what worked in the exercise or don't seem to know. 7. Students have few or no suggestions for changes they would make. 8. Students do not turn in their work on time.

Using a rubric offers the student a model answer, as well as an example of how the exercise may be incomplete or insufficient, whether for a paper, an exercise, or a performance. A performance example may be a checklist, which the teacher can use to score the performance quickly for immediate feedback. The rubric is not just for the teacher to use as a grading instrument. It should be given to the students at the beginning of the learning process to remind them of what criteria you are aiming for and the kind of feedback they might receive: what they have accomplished, as well as what they should continue to work on. Whether the teacher offers the instrument directly or uses it to define clear goals to the class, the student will be confident in what is required.

A teacher may have a mental model of the rubric in her head based on the available criteria she has established for herself for responses to student work.[58] She can mentally check what she wants to work on and what she feels constitutes effective feedback without using written notes. This gives the teacher the opportunity to concentrate fully on the work going on in front of them.

The teacher should also tell the students what is not required or is incorrect. He will give them non-examples and non-criterial examples. Non-examples are included in the D/F criteria. If the student fails to do any items, including being specific and detailed in listing the steps to rehearsing the exercise, their grade goes down. Non-criterial examples are important because they head off potential missteps caused by an incomplete list of criteria. The teacher discovers the list of criteria is incomplete when a student gives an answer that fits the listed criteria but is still incorrect. In the future, the teacher will adjust the original list and add a criterion that covers this mistake.

One aspect of this exercise is believability. If a student mimes a microwave or substitutes another object for it, this is a diffusion of the property that isn't believable, even if the rest of the exercise, dealing with a hot pocket or baked potato, may be done properly. This is why the second criterion now reads, "Students 'diffuse' the object while retaining the sense that the danger is still present. (Brown liquid such as cola is substituted for hot coffee instead of water.)" The original item was the non-criterial example: "The student will diffuse the object using a substitute." The believability factor became important when students began to make inadequate substitutions that destroyed the suspension of disbelief.

Another non-criterial example the teacher can offer the students is the idea of miming. This is a separate discipline, and any means for simplifying the exercise – for example, asking the students to bring all of the necessary materials – will avoid dealing with a separate issue when critiquing. This means the students must pick an activity that can be performed within the constraints of the classroom or the availability of personal resources. This is also an important criterion that addresses the believability issue.

Finally, a rubric can be used as a guide for teaching. By identifying criteria for success, the teacher can concentrate on these areas when introducing the topic for the first time. They already know what they will be evaluating, so they can teach with the end in mind: the meeting of all criteria.

Concentrating on the forms of feedback and the possible repercussions that can result will avoid misunderstandings, confusion, and sometimes resentment. The students will become better judges of their work and the work of others. The students will be encouraged to embrace a growth mindset. This delicate operation deserves constant attention, as ultimately it is an important product the students expect from the teacher.

Exercises are used to both guide and remediate, both as initial instruction and feedback. They clarify steps in a larger process. In the following chapter, exercises, etudes, and games are used as a means of motivating the students through enjoyable activities that increase their skills in play form, create ensembles, and encourage students to support each other in a growth mindset.

Notes

1 Ambrose et al., *How Learning Works*, 125.
2 Ambrose et al., *How Learning Works*, 127.
3 See Chapters 7 and 8 for examples of teacher and student goals.
4 See the discussion on the Inner Monologue in Chapter 7. The inner monologue is spoken aloud.
5 Ambrose et al., *How Learning Works*, 146.
6 See Appendix 2 for examples of simple open scenes.
7 See Mekler, *The New Generation of Acting Teachers*, 176–179.
8 See a discussion on expertise in Ambrose et al., *How Learning Works*, 95–99.
9 Ambrose et al., *How Learning Works*, 96–97.
10 Ambrose et al., *How Learning Works*, 99.
11 Ambrose et al., *How Learning Works*, 98.
12 Ambrose et al., *How Learning Works*, 98.
13 This concept was used to create the idea of categories for diagnoses. See Chapter 7.
14 Madeline Hunter, *Enhanced Teaching* (New York: Macmillan College Publishing Company, 1994), 3.
15 Hunter, *Enhanced Teaching*, 3.
16 This is one approach to evaluating student work. See, for example, Maryellen Weimer, PhD, ed., *Grading Strategies for the College Classroom: A Collection of Faculty Articles* (Madison, WI: Magna Publications, 2013).
17 Ambrose et al., *How Learning Works*, 137, emphasis the authors'.
18 Ambrose et al., *How Learning Works*, 138.
19 For a list of criteria, consider Melissa Bruder, Lee Michael Cohn, Madeleine Olnek, Nathaniel Pollack, Robert Previto, and Scott Zigler, *A Practical Handbook for the Actor* (New York: Vintage Books, 1986). The criteria and explanations for them make up the majority of the text.
20 Ambrose et al., *How Learning Works*, 143.
21 Douglas Stone and Sheila Heen, *Thanks for the Feedback: The Science and Art of Receiving Feedback Well* (New York: Penguin Books, 2014).
22 Stone and Heen, *Thanks for the Feedback*, 18.
23 See the discussion on rubrics later in this chapter.
24 Stone and Heen, *Thanks for the Feedback*, 30.
25 Stone and Heen, *Thanks for the Feedback*, 32.
26 Ambrose et al., *How Learning Works*, 139.
27 Stone and Heen, *Thanks for the Feedback*, 33.
28 Ambrose et al., *How Learning Works*, 139.
29 Stone and Heen, *Thanks for the Feedback*, 5.
30 Stone and Heen, *Thanks for the Feedback*, 15.
31 Stone and Heen, *Thanks for the Feedback*, 15–17.

32 Stone and Heen, *Thanks for the Feedback*, 108–109.
33 See the discussion on Attachments by Ron Van Lieu in Chapter 5.
34 Carol S. Dweck, *Mindset: The New Psychology of Success*, Updated Edition (New York: Random House, 2016), 3.
35 Dweck, *Mindset*, 6.
36 Dweck, *Mindset*, 4.
37 Dweck, *Mindset*, 6–8.
38 Dweck, *Mindset*, 6. For strategies in developing a growth mindset in students, see Dweck, *Mindset*, Chapter 8.
39 Dweck, *Mindset*, 179. Students are substituted for children, but the principle is the same.
40 Stone and Heen, *Thanks for the Feedback*, 198.
41 Stone and Heen, *Thanks for the Feedback*, 198.
42 Stone and Heen, *Thanks for the Feedback*, 204.
43 For a thorough discussion of this topic, see Chapter 5 of Rothstein and Santana, *Make Just One Change*.
44 Rothstein and Santana, *Make Just One Change*, 96, emphasis the authors'.
45 Rothstein and Santana, *Make Just One Change*, 96, emphasis the authors'.
46 Rothstein and Santana, *Make Just One Change*, 96.
47 Rothstein and Santana, *Make Just One Change*, 96.
48 See the discussion on side-coaching in Chapter 7.
49 Van Lieu from Teacher Development Program Notes, June 2013.
50 For a shocking example of this as a dramatic device, see the first season of *The Sinner*.
51 Ambrose et al., *How Learning Works*, 94.
52 blackchild, "Lloyd Richards in the Classroom," 129.
53 blackchild, "Lloyd Richards in the Classroom," 129–130.
54 blackchild, "Lloyd Richards in the Classroom," 130.
55 blackchild, "Lloyd Richards in the Classroom," 129.
56 Ambrose et al., *How Learning Works*, 146.
57 Hagen, *Respect for Acting*, Chapter 15: Endowment, 112–117.
58 See Categories in Chapter 7.

12 Exercises, Etudes, and Games

The students are finding value in the diagnoses of class scenes. They are implementing the teacher's feedback and asking themselves the questions that help them to monitor and improve their work. One day, a different, more complex problem arises, one that is shared by several students exhibiting the same behavior, and any correction will take at least an entire class period to address. Is it worth disrupting the flow of the course to concentrate on this particular issue? Ideally, days have been built into the curriculum for just this purpose – to deal with special topics as they arise, or to reteach concepts where necessary. Regardless, the teacher ignores a missing facet of the students' education to the detriment of the overall progress of the group. By determining new goals and implementing them through exercises, etudes, or games, individually or in combination, the teacher introduces further tools and experiences for student growth.

Limiting the number of scenes may be necessary for this reason, to allow time for concentration on one element of craft. Sometimes the activity applies to a new concept or serves as a further example from a predetermined category; at others, it may aid in the realization of a particular scene, one that can add to an actor's experience of the character's circumstances. The teacher may want to begin the course with preparatory exercises to be applied to the scene study work, to give them an overall approach to the course, or provide them with mutual points of reference.

Needless to say, the following discussion on exercises, games, and etudes contains only a partial listing of the various activities that might be introduced, not only as enrichment, but as a corrective for challenges raised by diagnoses of student scenes. The idea here is to consider the value of activities that supplement the process of scene study but are essential to student growth. The teacher should participate in the games with the students. It is especially important that the teacher be willing to lose the game, a good faith gesture reminding the students that failure is an acceptable outcome.

Exercises

Terry Schreiber reminds us that the introduction of exercises is a delicate business. The teacher must be aware of how the exercise is affecting the student in a negative or positive way and when the teacher should stop the exercise because not only is it ineffective, but it has reached the point of diminishing returns – or does more harm than good. He uses visual clues – "the actor's breathing, her body language, and the words that come up within the exercise,"[1] and sometimes, he uses "a gut feeling that 'this exercise must be stopped.'"[2] When an actor is not responding well, the teacher shouldn't force them to continue. A better idea is to consider the reason why the student is finding the endeavor such a struggle. Tough love is not appropriate: "Never try to 'break down' an actor to tears by screaming at her or chastising her in front of others."[3] These so-called "breakthroughs" are dangerous. In such cases, the teacher may be trying to "use the exercises to exploit emotions that the actor is unwilling to share."[4] This is practicing therapy without a license.

Michael Chekhov wrote of exercises, "The teacher always must bring out quite clearly for the pupils what the *aim* of the exercise is."[5] Chekhov believes the timing of a stated goal should be sensitively considered: "As a teacher you must feel and discover when you can dictate to your pupils how a thing must be done or felt, and when you must suggest that perhaps they will feel this or that effect or result."[6] In other words, the teacher may use experiential learning – doing an activity before its explanation – as a powerful form of teaching, or she may teach the lesson before having the students apply it, guiding them towards mastery and then letting them work independently. The nature of the exercise will suggest to the teacher which method will be most effective. Fortunately, the resources for the instructor are vast.[7] Beginning teachers of acting have innumerable resources. A number of exercises have been introduced in previous chapters. What follows in this section is a small percentage of available books by teachers that reveal both the kinds of work they do and the reasoning behind their creation of certain exercises.

With exercises, the teacher separates the actor's study into digestible parts that, individually, require more attention, the teacher attending to both the steps of the exercise and their conceptual nature. One method for identifying an exercise which requires deeper exploration is the sense of whether it can be objectively graded. The results of a number of exercises can only be examined in the actor's mind and body. The external results may be noted and give a snapshot of the process in action; however, sometimes only the student will know whether the activity works on an internal level.[8]

Any supplementary material deals directly with craft, in the long run leading the student towards self-diagnosis through the new tools available to them. An exploration of previous circumstances, for example, can be addressed through one of Uta Hagen's Object Exercises. The Three Entrances Object Exercise deals with circumstances that occur just before an entrance, prompting the actor to embody the character's life before they step onto the stage. This gives the actor a starting point that launches them into a scene from offstage; just as a student would bring their emotional and physical baggage to the day's lesson, a never-ending panoply of experiences that lives in them regardless of their intentions for attending the class. Hagen's Endowment Exercise reminds students they need not suffer for their art but, through acting, replace dangerous or distracting situations with safe alternatives that still give the impression of reality to an audience.[9]

Larry Moss offers the reader of his book exercises for all manner of acting challenges. His Memories of Home exercise, for example, helps the actor to find triggers that might be useful in recreating an emotion based on personal experience.[10] Moss's My System of Wants Exercise focuses the student's attention on the desires they have throughout a day in their lives, a listing that includes the feelings that come up as well as the steps he takes to deal with them. Moss's Repeat Exercise resembles the Repetition Exercise of Sanford Meisner with the same goal, "You'll become hyperaware of your subjective response to the person sitting opposite you."[11]

Uta Hagen's *Respect for Acting* introduces basic concepts and means for realizing them that appeal to introductory students but also serve as reminders for those already in the field. Her object exercises build on each other as they offer means for practicing the craft on one's own between acting projects. Just as a member of an orchestra can continue to improve and maintain their musicianship, so the actor can develop an instrument in the service of any material offered to her. *The New Generation of Acting Teachers* by Eva Mekler covers a smorgasbord of exercises through her interviews with expert teachers on the East and West Coasts and in higher education. Teachers include Elinor Renfield, John Strasberg, Ron Van Lieu, William Esper, Alice Spivak, and Michael Schulman. In *The Actor and the Target*, Declan Donnellan shares his philosophy of acting and a series of diagnostics that identify the blocks that may prevent actors from realizing their full potential, along with means for overcoming those obstacles. *The Actor's Art and Craft* and *The Actor's Guide to Creating a Character* are lucid explorations of Sanford Meisner's methods by one of his pupils, the late William Esper. *The Method: How the Twentieth Century Learned to Act* by Isaac Butler is a review of Stanislavsky's system from its origins through its development for film actors, including Robert De Niro. In *The Warner Laughlin Technique*, the titular author shares her method of creating a past for the character that deepens the actor's experience and ability to realize the roles they are offered in auditions or which they play in performance.

Exercises that create greater connections between the actors as characters or help them to establish a sense of belief in the given circumstances, that stress the power of their imaginations and the flexibility required to respond spontaneously based on their initial impulses, are key, especially to beginning students.

Etudes

The teacher may also create etudes, improvisations that provide added experiences for the actor's character, situations outside of the script that introduce events the character has experienced in the past – or in offstage moments between scenes – that influence the character; for example, prompting feelings from relationships with people the audience never sees, or scenes that are referred to but not played onstage.

When teachers, coaches, and directors talk of etudes, they have different definitions of what etudes are and can accomplish. Sharon Marie Carnicke relates the etude directly to the play under study: she sees an etude as "a purposeful, improvisatory study of a scene that uncovers the motives, desires, and subtexts that prompt characters to speak and act as they do in the play."[12]

Nikolai Demidov has an important use for etudes. Although he admits his version is similar to those taught in drama schools, he sees that the primary difference "lies in the special method of application used by the teacher."[13] This involves assigning a text he has created himself, asking two actors to use this text as a means of responding in a "free and spontaneous reaction," as a means to instill a state of "creative experiencing and transformation."[14] First, he has each actor read their lines at least three times to see if the words are settling into place. These lines are not arbitrary but have a purpose: the teacher looks to see if any of the words are beginning to prompt spontaneous living behavior; such a response is recognizable in the student if the teacher pays strict attention.[15]

The words Demidov offers the actors, such as "(Do you want to say something to me?) required [the novice actor] to have beforehand seen [sic] something in the partner that would elicit such a question."[16] In other words, the partner also sees dialogue on the page, hears it articulated, and is affected by it enough to behave in such a way that it will automatically prompt a response in her partner. The partner may be nervous, fidgety, thinking hard about how to phrase something, unable to meet the other actor's eyes, or cold and distant when he is normally respectful or friendly. One of the points of his work is that Demidov can notice when students fall back on certain behaviors because they are uncomfortable with responding as themselves or are afraid they will not be able to assume the theatricality necessary to make the lines work – leading to forcing or pushing. Unless the students are in a certain state created by the dialogue, they can't say it.

The students have innumerable blocks that keep them from living a creative state, and Demidov uses these etudes as a way to diagnose and eliminate them. In particular he explores with his students all of the elements of the Stanislavsky System at once. This solved one of the main problems he discovered with the proposed course of study by Stanislavsky: when the elements were each studied separately, the actor did not make sufficient progress towards the creative state. Instead, this process "murdered the main thing: spontaneity and the involuntary nature of life onstage."[17] Demidov's etudes allowed him to teach the elements in a "synthesizing approach for acting training in contrast to the analytical one."[18] In this way he created a foundation for free expression at a very early stage in his work with students that could be applied to other considerations, such as a study of the script.

This spontaneity is introduced in early etudes by Sanford Meisner, who asks the actors involved to discover their lines by attention to each other. One begins the etude, the famous Repetition Exercise, by making a comment about the other actor; for example, "You are wearing a wrinkled shirt." The other actor repeats this line as "I'm wearing a wrinkled shirt." They then repeat the lines until one of them is sparked to use a new tone with the line, a variation on the repeated line, or the creation of a new line – in response to the impulse stimulated by the other actor. The repetition is partly used to reach the point of diminishing returns so one actor feels impelled to change a line or to invest it with meaning – until then, it has been a mechanical exercise. Some examples after "You are wearing a wrinkled shirt," might include, "I'm wearing a wrinkled shirt?" i.e., how dare you, or it's not that wrinkled; or "I'm not wearing a wrinkled shirt!"; or "That wasn't very nice." This new line is then repeated until one of the actors has the impulse to change the line once again. In this way, the actors don't respond unless they feel an inner need to do so. In the same way, when it comes to lines from the script, the actor has an intuitive or spontaneous response to reading the line on the page or in hearing a line spoken by another actor to them.[19]

Out-Scenes

The out-scene is an etude used as a means of creating a lived experience for an actor when that experience is not represented by events in the play but is an important factor in their behavior. Stanislavsky used a number of etudes to create an unfamiliar environment – particularly a historical one, to deal with past circumstances, or to launch an actor into a scene through activities that might be applied during a routine period in their lives before the inciting incident disrupted that routine.[20] For example, how characters normally prepare dinner rather than when they are laying out a meal after a memorial service for a loved one, or what the daily routine of the Orgon household was before Tartuffe arrived. Larry Moss's In-Character Improvisation exercise gives a step-by-step plan for playing such an etude.

Stanislavsky etudes are also exercises that introduce acting tools.[21] For example, shortly before he died, Stanislavsky worked with a group of actors on *Tartuffe*. His purpose was not to create a performance, but to share his working methods so they might be passed on to others. He had the actors create the groundplan for the Orgon household, determining where the characters were coming from and where the events of the play would logically take place. The actors could then imagine the entire environment and not just the rooms they would be acting in.[22]

In the classroom, the etude can create the experience of a backstory that may produce memories for the actual scenes. For example, if, according to the author, an argument has taken place between two characters offstage, but they now appear in a scene together, the actors can improvise the argument so as to refer back to feelings and actions that took place then. Even if the feelings are now unspoken, they exist in the reality of the etude, which the actors can draw on in the course of the scene. Ultimately, the teacher is using an etude to "inform a moment in the play," and/or "ground the actors in the given circumstances."[23] Rather than imagining an offstage past experience, the actors can live one and then recreate the experience internally for the sake of the play.

Strasberg also encouraged the actors to use out-scenes in this way: "Improvisation creates and conditions reflexes in the same way that we gain experience in life."[24] After one improvisation he noted, "Here today on the stage a reality has occurred, and in the future you can respond as a result of that reality in the same way that you would respond if you had had this character's actual experience and behavior."[25] This kind of activity replaces an imaginary conception of the given circumstances, particularly previous circumstances.

Etudes are created when the actors fail to bring the characters' previous lives into the scene. This missing element – a past – is a subtle one but can make the difference in relationships and the progress of the narrative itself. Observers can tell when actors are mere acquaintances rather than longtime friends or lovers without a word being spoken, and an actor can fail to realize the stakes of a scene if the obstacle in the other character is based on an event that affected both of them either years before or more recently. For example, in *Proof* by David Auburn, the effects of Catherine giving Hal her solution to a mathematical problem, and his subsequent suspicion she didn't write it, is complicated by their intimacy the night before, an intimacy that inspired her to share her proof and currently puts him in the delicate position of questioning her even though his feelings for her are warmer. This does not require the actors to improvise a sexual encounter – an inappropriate etude – but it may be helpful for their characters to have a private conversation using the feelings that arose subsequent to those moments.

An etude involving a change of location may be fruitful. For example, if the characters are having a private conversation in a restaurant, they may consider using that same dialogue in an actual eatery: the presence of other people, the ambience, the space between them at a particular table and sitting on specific types of chairs, may give the scene a new tone. They would perform this etude on their own and report back to the class the results of the exercise.

Games

In acting classes, games can be used for a number of purposes: ensemble building, warmups, focusing the class's attention, and so on. Games can be very simple and yet teach profound lessons. The principle here is to use a game in class that will solve a particular problem or challenge for the actors. It is important, at some point after the game has been played, to explain the "why" of it. That is, the teacher should include their reasoning behind the game, what the teacher wants the participants to experience while doing it or, upon reflection, what they should notice about the effect the game has on them. In this way, the game takes on deeper meaning and creates situations that encourage the students to raise the stakes, to invest as much of themselves in a scene as they do in a game.

It is possible to adapt a familiar game whose common use is ensemble building and use it to explain a particular concept; for example, Red Light/Green Light, in which one student at the far end of the room will try to catch the other students in movement as those students attempt to touch him/her/them. The game can be seen as a metaphor for the vulnerability or paranoia a character may feel as they try to maintain their position at the top of the hierarchy. Uneasy lies the head that wears the traffic light crown.

At the same time, students tend to take these games seriously, often with more investment than they initially demonstrate when taking on a new role in a play. Games are events in real time, with spontaneous reactions and high stakes. If the actors play a competitive game, then apply it to a scene, the stakes go up for the competitors. The actors will be trying to win, an example of pursuing an objective. As Cohen notes in *Acting Power*, "[I]n acting, as in sports, *situations become dynamic when a victory is sought*, when the actor pursues *winning*."[26] If the students imagine the games as little plays, with protagonists, antagonists, stories, and dramatic climaxes, they will begin to see the connections between games and theatre.

When students try to cheat at the game, the sense of injustice is highlighted. At the most stressful points in a game, the students might laugh to release tension or, as an audience, in appreciation of the invention of the participants. If the students can be persuaded to take the games seriously both as observers and participants, the actors seriously dedicate themselves to the characters' objectives, supported by the audience.

In a game, especially one that is competitive, the actors are dealing with high stakes, though the actual results will not lead to major changes in the students' lives. So why do they take games so seriously, when they cannot play with full commitment during a scene? The teacher can point out that, though the circumstances are imaginary or fictional, the feelings that arise during play, and the deadly seriousness with which players concentrate, can be transferred to a character's motivations, increasing the chance a character mission will be more important to the actor if they are willing to consider how important winning is in a scene's situation.

Declan Donnellan gives the example of the actor whose stakes went through the roof, not because of what they were playing, but because the actor forgot his line. "Such a moment is useful for it shows how much further we are from where we need to be."[27] Games reveal the same principle, that an actor's imagination can create heightened situations – filled with danger, for example – out of thin air, in a way that they fail to do when acting: "We fool ourselves that we are playing 'high stakes' when we are not even remotely near where the situation demands."[28]

Zombie

One game that particularly brings this out is Zombie. At first, the rules are complicated, so it is worth introducing the activity in steps. Students form a circle. One student points at another, who says the first student's name. The second student then points at another student, who says her name, and so on. After they practice this – and the teacher points out that the students tend to say their own names rather than the name of the pointer – once a name is called, the pointer switches places with the one who identified them. Once they have mastered this step, pointing and identifying each other, and moving to their new positions, the pointer, upon hearing their name, will become a zombie, a creature who shuffles towards the other student with the intent to touch her and thus kill her. When someone identifies a student by name, the student holds their arms out and walks in an even pace towards the person who has named them. The only way the namer can escape is by pointing at another student in the circle, who will say their name so they too may become a zombie and move towards the person who identified them so as to escape the approaching danger. If not, they are touched by the person they have identified and are eliminated from the game. It is important the students point at classmates across from them so the victim has time to move. If they point to someone next to them, there is little chance the identifier will survive because the distance from the zombie is so short. The students play the game until three people are left. The final three players are eliminated through other means, such as Rock, Paper, Scissors.

The game can be used early in the course to verify that the students know each other's names – if they don't, they "die." Though this game is fun to play, the students begin to worry about being touched and eliminated. A level of tension is created, and a feeling of dread is aroused. The teacher then points out that, despite the fact that the consequences are minimal – other than losing the game – the students fear each other as much as if this were a real-life situation. The seriousness in which they take the game can be transferred to work on scenes. If they can invest as much energy and feeling for mortality in a game, they can certainly do so as part of their acting training.

John Wright's book *Why Is That So Funny?* is full of wonderful games worth playing in the classroom. He gives thorough explanations of each: how they work and what they are for. Their primary purpose is to explore the nature of comedy. Keith Johnstone used games as a means to train actors in certain precepts. These were parallel activities to the skills required of a scene. For example, Johnstone's "Beep Beep Game" trains the actor to share their soliloquies with various members of the audience rather than concentrating on a single person.[29] This presentational skill enhances an actor's work on period styles. One important use of games is to help to create spontaneity in the actor, as they did for Ron Van Lieu when he was a student: "The games class was the central class because it forced me *to live an unplanned life in front of people.*"[30] Robert Cohen also believed games could lead to living onstage rather than performing: "Games are another means of removing the performance context from 'acting' behavior, since they involve the actor in situational interactions."[31]

A more thorough explanation of how games work to aid the actor is hard to imagine than Clive Barker's *Theatre Games.* Like Keith Johnstone, Barker developed and experimented with games throughout his teaching career. He stated five reasons for using game play:

1. "[T]o reveal something of the actor's movement problems and possibilities."[32] Games allowed Barker to deal with the actor's inhibitions when it came to physical self-consciousness by participating in nonthreatening activities that accomplished simple and then more difficult uses of the joints and muscles of the body. He called these "insurance policies,"[33] against the actor's tendency to avoid discomfort.
2. "[T]o lead actors to physical experiences and sensations that they could not find directly."[34] Play is an instrument for unusual but enjoyable activities that are nonthreatening.
3. "[T]o initiate in the actor a process of self-awareness and discovery."[35] The actor can learn more about himself through these new experiences than through technical exercises, and the games remind the actor of his past – his participation in games as a child – a source of comfort and joy.
4. "[T]o create a shared body of experience which one uses to build up relationships within the group and to develop an ensemble."[36] Students go through complex situations together, either each participating in a game, or working in groups

to solve puzzles, that bring them closer together in a communion of common circumstances.
5. "[T]o create a common vocabulary, based upon shared experience, with which to discuss the processes of human action and interaction and the work of the actor." A group that learns to work together with the teacher begins to think together, to respond to familiar cues, creating a shorthand for the work in class. This is also true of groups who participate in games during the rehearsal process.

Barker studied the work of Roger Caillois, who identifies "attitudes and impulses" which prompt the properties of various games that "are found in the unprotected realm of social life, where acts normally have consequences, no less than in the marginal and abstract world of play."[37] When actors claim they are unable to behave in ways that make them uncomfortable, games remind them that they have been doing so since childhood without emotional or physical repercussions. Drama itself can be seen as a game with rules that must be identified by the actor, and playing a situation as a game creates "expressive forms of human personal and social behavior."[38]

Barker's approach was a clever, indirect way of guiding actors towards mastery without fear. He used experiential learning, playing the games before ever explaining their purposes. In this way, students weren't aiming for a particular result.[39] One of his favorites was the "Fight in the Dark,"[40] adapted from the Peking Opera, where the characters dealt with the conditions of complete darkness, while the audience could examine them under bright stage lighting. Delineating a playing area with chairs turned away from the action, Barker asked two participants to play a thief of treasure and the treasure's guardian. Through a gap in the chairs, the thief enters and tries to steal the jewel without being caught or killed. Both students must act as if they cannot see each other or the jewel. The actors play the game twice: once in full light and the second time with blindfolds. The students discover how different their actions are in each case. An important effect, and one the teacher is aiming for, is that the blindfolded actors tend to become straighter rather than hunched over with "a marked improvement in balance."[41] This desired response is automatic and does not have to be instilled. "The main difference between the two versions is that, in the open-eyed version, the actor is concentrating on the *result*."[42] However, when blindfolded, "the actor does not reflect on the circumstances."[43] For example, the actor playing the thief connects with the "physical and imaginative centres [*sic*] of the brain."[44] At the same time, he acts with intention: searching for the jewel and avoiding the guard. As in cases where sight is impaired, his other senses seem to strengthen. The exercise allows actors to recreate truthful experiences as long as they have not planned the results in advance; they really play the game.

Barker encourages the reader to make up games as needed and keep the energy flowing from game to game. He groups his games by topic, including Simple Movement Games, Release of Physical Inhibitions, the Creative Imagination and the Use of Fantasy, Meetings and Encounters, and Space.[45] He also used games for style work and to fulfill the goals of playtexts. For an example of the former, the game Crossing the Ice requires the participants to use "quick, light, and direct movements,"

Exercises, Etudes, and Games   179

i.e., what Laban would call Dabbing.[46] In the latter case, Barker offers exercises for applying technical work to text.[47]

Viola Spolin, "The Originator of Theater Games," who inspired the American improvisation theatre movement – including her son Paul Sills's Compass Theatre – used exercises to create spontaneity onstage. Her classic book, *Improvisation for the Theater*,[48] stressed the utility of theatre games as preparation for invented and scripted performance. She stressed the process over results. The book outlines for the teacher how to create workshops in a sequence which leads towards mastery of problems of increasing complexity. Though she provides many acting challenges and matches them with activities, she asks teachers to "be constantly alerted to bring in fresh acting problems to solve any difficulties that come up."[49] She learned any age group could use games to create impressive performances onstage, even with non-actors.

Her sense of "creative group play" came from her studies with Neva L. Boyd at the Recreational Training School of Hull House in Chicago and as the director of the Young Actor's Company.[50] She got her students to strengthen their senses, to act with the whole body, to deal in conflict, to recognize and recreate nervous tics and habits, to develop their own material, and many other techniques essential to the actor's training.

In her book *Theater Games for Rehearsal*,[51] an expansion of later chapters in *Improvisation for the Theater*, Spolin concentrated on the director's role in the process of rehearsal. This included actor behavior during the first reading, listening and hearing games to concentrate the actors' attention on their partners, and reminders to the director of facets they should consider as they work with their performers. She believed in the technique of side-coaching for games and for scene work, and included a glossary of side-coaching phrases the director could use to prompt the actors.[52]

Finding the Game Within the Game

Meta-games, or games about games, are used by Robert Cohen to play with the idea of truthful behavior onstage. With "Game-fixing," Cohen has pairs of students compete against each other in one-on-one games, with one pair instructed to play full out to win and the other to predetermine how the game will go. "If they are to play a 'fixed' match, they pretend to play an honest match, but must reach the prearranged score as instructed by the group leader."[53] Either group can win if those watching think the game is honest – with a point for the fixers – or if the fixers are identified as dishonest – with a point for the observers. All participants should be given the opportunity to play honestly or dishonestly.[54]

Finding the Game Within a Scene

Another use of games is to identify a game taking place between the characters in a scene or play. One of Michael Shurtleff's goalposts, or acting tools, is to look for games to be played: "When we play games, it is for real; when we take on different roles, it is sincere conduct, for it is a way of dealing with reality not avoiding it."[55] This explains the tendency of characters to change given new circumstances: "For each situation we play a different role because it is a different game."[56] Scenes are full of invisible games which, once discovered, open up the scene to the actors, who then understand what they are playing. An example is *Otherwise Engaged* by Simon Gray. The protagonist, Simon Hench, has bought a new recording of Wagner's *Parsifal*, which he is looking forward to enjoying in his study. Once he has been initially thwarted, his game becomes to play the record before he is further interrupted. The other characters do their best to foil him by driving him to distraction. He maintains his outward appearance of calm until the end of the play, while the audience intuits his frustration is rising as he interacts with various characters who invade his space. Ultimately, his inner nature is revealed by someone who seems to not be playing the game at all, but accidentally causes an event that is the last straw, sending Simon into an unfortunate rage against his innocent victim. The victim wins the game.

One form of game worth discussing is any psychological game played socially or within the family. Psychological texts suggest ways in which our personas are developed through our experiences in childhood and sociological constructs in our adulthood and the reasons behind human behavior, whether isolated or in groups. Eric Berne's *Games People Play* is a classic text offering insights into the meanings behind social interactions. In particular he defines a transaction as "a unit of social intercourse," in which "two or more people encounter each other in a social aggregation."[57] The person who engages the others through acknowledgment has created a transactional stimulus. If a response is forthcoming, this is a transactional response. Berne has divided a person's ego states into Parent, Child, and Adult. Using these labels, "Simple transactional analysis is concerned with diagnosing which ego state implemented the transactional stimulus, and which one executed the transactional response."[58] In *I'm Okay – You're Okay*, Thomas A. Harris offers a jargon-free discussion of this tool for analysis for people who encounter these types of behaviors in their everyday lives.

Though this may seem like dabbling in the subject of psychology as layman with little understanding of the deeper implications, Harris asks the reader if this type of book under study – specifically Berne's *Games People Play* – "is a best seller because of a fad, or does it offer people some easily understood and authentic ideas about themselves as they reveal their past in the present games they play?"[59] His own book defends the latter position.

When the teacher is looking for entertaining but effective ways to coach her actors in the performance of scenes or plays, improvisations – in the form of games and etudes – are an effective means of immersing the players in their roles and the given circumstances. When the teacher wants to identify the essential core of a concept or focus on a facet of technique, they can use exercises from many resources or invent their own. Through implementation, they will know whether their training methods are effective or need to be retooled. The good news is that descriptions of all three tools – exercises, games, or etudes – are widely available, covering any imaginable topic, and can be practiced in a variety of spaces and with limited materials.

So far, this book has emphasized the coaching of contemporary material. The book concludes with a brief discussion on approaches to other material: to the study of scenes in the styles of different periods and genres. It includes a general philosophy, some notes about various playwrights, as well as a concentration on the most popular of the styles, work on the plays of William Shakespeare.

Notes

1. Schreiber, *Acting*, 36.
2. Schreiber, *Acting*, 36.
3. Schreiber, *Acting*, 36.
4. Schreiber, *Acting*, 36.
5. Chekhov, *Lessons for Teachers*, 32. Emphasis Chekhov's.
6. Chekhov, *Lessons for Teachers*, 32.
7. See the Bibliography.
8. Having the student journal about the experience is both gradable and a more accurate reflection of the experience.
9. Hagen, *Respect for Acting*, 95–100 and 112–117, respectively.
10. Moss, *The Intent to Live*, 82–84.
11. See Moss, *The Intent to Live*, 189–195 for a description as well as examples of moment-to-moment work. See also a brief description of the Meisner Repetition Exercise in this chapter.
12. Carnicke, *Dynamic Acting Through Active Analysis*, 16.
13. Demidov, *Becoming an Actor-Creator*, 219.
14. Demidov, *Becoming an Actor-Creator*, 219.
15. Examples of Demidov's etudes appear throughout his book, *Becoming an Actor-Creator*, including Book Two, Chapter 10, "On the Beginning," 191–202.
16. Demidov, *Becoming an Actor-Creator*, 366. Parentheses Demidov's.
17. Demidov, *Becoming an Actor-Creator*, 6.
18. Demidov, *Becoming an Actor-Creator*, 6.
19. For an initial discussion of the repetition exercise, see Chapters 2 and 3 in Meisner and Longwell, *Sanford Meisner on Acting*, 16–37.
20. See the discussion on the Method of Physical Actions in Chapter 8.
21. See his etude for introducing the inner monologue in Chapter 4, from Gorchakov, *Stanislavsky Directs*, 49–57.
22. After Stanislavsky's death, Mikhail Nikolayevich Kedrov, one of Stanislavsky's former assistants, completed the work, using the Method of Physical Actions, and *Tartuffe* premiered at the Moscow Art Theatre in 1939. See Carnicke, *Dynamic Acting Through Active Analysis*, 109.
23. Francis, "Preparing Birds to Fly," 111.
24. Hethmon, *Strasberg at the Actors Studio*, 304.
25. Hethmon, *Strasberg at the Actors Studio*, 304.
26. Robert Cohen, *Acting Power: An Introduction to Acting*, 1st Edition (Palo Alto, CA: Mayfield Publishing Company, 1978), 22, emphasis Cohen's.
27. Donnellan, *The Actor and the Target*, 55.
28. Donnellan, *The Actor and the Target*, 55.
29. Johnstone, *Impro for Storytellers*, 260–262.
30. Van Lieu Teacher Development Program Notes, June 2012, emphasis mine.
31. Cohen, *Acting Power*, 25.

32 Clive Barker, *Theatre Games: A New Approach to Drama Training* (New York: Drama Book Publishers, 1977), 65.
33 Barker, *Theatre Games*, 96.
34 Barker, *Theatre Games*, 66.
35 Barker, *Theatre Games*, 66.
36 Barker, *Theatre Games*, 66.
37 Barker, *Theatre Games*, 88.
38 Barker, *Theatre Games*, 88.
39 Though, over the years, Barker began to see repeated patterns, he continued to hope for new variations during game play.
40 Described in detail in Barker, *Theatre Games*, 57–61.
41 Barker, *Theatre Games*, 59.
42 Barker, *Theatre Games*, 60. Emphasis Barker's.
43 Barker, *Theatre Games*, 60.
44 Barker, *Theatre Games*, 61.
45 See Barker, *Theatre Games*, Chapters 6–11, respectively.
46 See the discussion on Laban movement efforts in Chapter 10. Quick, light movements must also be used for the game Grandmother's Footsteps. See Barker, *Theatre Games*, 81.
47 See Barker, *Theatre Games*, Chapters 12–14.
48 Viola Spolin, *Improvisation for the Theater: A Handbook of Teaching and Directing* (Evanston, IL: Northwestern University Press, 1983).
49 Spolin, *Improvisation for the Theater*, 21.
50 Spolin, *Improvisation for the Theater*, vii–ix.
51 Viola Spolin, *Theatre Games for Rehearsal: A Director's Handbook* (Evanston, IL: Northwestern University Press, 1985).
52 See Spolin, *Theater Games for Rehearsal*, 113–115.
53 Cohen, *Acting Power: An Introduction to Acting*, 28.
54 Cohen, *Acting Power: An Introduction to Acting*, 28.
55 Shurtleff, *Audition*, 85.
56 Shurtleff, *Audition*, 85.
57 Berne, *Games People Play*, 10.
58 Berne, *Games People Play*, 10.
59 Thomas A. Harris, *I'm Okay – You're Okay* (New York: HarperCollins, 2004), 17.

13 Styles

A study of the making of scenes would be incomplete without at least touching on material outside the range of the contemporary world. In this instance, I will speak to the type of plays within my own experience as a teacher and scholar with the knowledge that my limitations make me ill-equipped to speak of the masterworks of BIPOC authors or to directly engage in cultures I have not lived in or encounters I have not lived through. This is not to say I am a man with direct access to the classical Greek world, or a denizen of Elizabethan London, or a member of Davenant's company during the restoration of the monarchy in 17th-century England. It does mean I have approached these and other periods from dramaturgical, as well as personal, standpoints – as a teacher and researcher in period styles on the one hand, and as an actor in a variety of plays on the other.

The next two chapters do not presume to offer thorough instruction on the various styles of different periods or to claim a definitive approach to speaking verse or any other practice – this would be beyond the book's scope and the author's expertise. Rather, they serve to suggest some examples of how famous practitioners have come to conclusions about playing in different periods, and some of the methods I have found for helping my students to enjoy these studies. Given the breadth of the subject, this chapter will cover some general principles and tips about scenes the teacher may someday respond to, with comments on Comedy and Restoration and Religious Drama. The next chapter will be dedicated to the works of William Shakespeare and the way one might coach actors in scenes from his plays.

Style is defined in Merriam-Webster's dictionary as "a distinctive or characteristic mode of presentation, construction, or execution in any art, employment, or product."[1] Style is a slippery word in acting, since any character can themselves have a style outside the range of a larger societal view of what style is. Styles are therefore relative: within any given period, no one individual conforms exactly to the colors, the accoutrement, the wig sizes, the makeup, the shoes, the props, the postures, the sayings, the habits, the movements and gestures, the language, or the consumption practices of an exemplary person of the Restoration, the court of Louis XVI, or the Spanish Golden Age. This can be seen today in the myriad styles of 21st-century life, in different countries, states, cities, towns, hamlets, or neighborhoods. Even two people of the same gender in the same household won't imitate each other in their

DOI: 10.4324/9781003498520-14

choice of clothing or manner of speaking. Therefore, the resources available to us in our research give us some idea of the types of clothing worn and the attitudes of the people wearing it, the things they carried, their games and pastimes, vocabulary, economic pressures on their social class, and so on; they do not necessarily speak directly to the uniqueness any given character may bring to those matters.

Even within a particular period, the teacher may choose between comedic and tragic scenes or may ask the students to choose between these various genres. Ideally, the period is one with which the teacher is familiar, has studied its literary artifacts as well as the world of the author, has a deep interest in, and can model if necessary. When selecting scenes, the teacher will give some thought as to the number of roles to cast: classic plays contain duets but also large-group scenes worth exploring. The key will be to guarantee that all students have an equal amount of work to do. Sometimes this may mean double-casting a student in two medium-sized roles in two different scenes, or giving a student a major part in one scene and a small two-line part in another. Work on period scenes can give the teacher an opportunity to offer workshops in various techniques, including movement and comportment, the speaking of heightened language, and the use of period props. The teacher can also use the time as an opportunity to connect the studies of acting and theatre history. It is important to give enough rehearsal time for the teacher to cover a variety of challenges within each scene, whether language-, staging-, or character-related, and with an idea towards marrying the actors' previous training with these further approaches.

It is important that the teacher excite the students with the idea of learning about other times: how people thought about the world and the universe, what they ate, their living conditions, their ideas of romance, their contrivances, their sense of humor. Ultimately, this is a means for feeding the mind with the images required to play a part and the thinking that motivates the characters to make decisions and to act on their impulses. The actor is encouraged to consider plays not only from a psychological viewpoint, but also an anthropological and sociological one.

In his book *Acting Power,* Robert Cohen connects a style to its origins in real life: "Style is no adornment; at bottom, it is a social necessity. We have been performing it all our lives."[2] Cohen connects style to objectives; it is a means for the character to get what they want.[3] If the character seeks to climb the social ladder, he must be intimately familiar with the social graces: comportment, clothes, manners, and habits of his superiors. The actor must know the mores that have been inculcated in the character at a lower level of society in order to rise above them – just as, in Sheridan's *The School for Scandal*, Lady Teazle, though raised in a rustic community, easily moves in the society of the upper classes after marrying Sir Peter because she has longed for and studied the means for taking her place there. Someone of a higher social station must know how to properly treat those beneath her. They expect authority and the obeyance of certain rules and will be confused or even recalcitrant if these aren't followed.

An emphasis on period research and specifics is not just an intellectual exercise. The authors of *The Polite World* believe that to truly recreate a period "requires more than the outward show of period manners."[4] More germane to the actor is their belief that, "It needs such an understanding of the mind of the period that actors can penetrate it as deeply as they penetrate their roles."[5] Just as an actor of contemporary drama will seek to understand the character's given circumstances, actors will miss important clues about the mindsets of their characters without an idea of, say, the religious ideology of the Renaissance or the Restoration periods, woven into the very fabric of society.

Two approaches to period styles therefore suggest themselves. One is to return to the historical notions of how theatre was presented, with an eye to the developments they have led to and their influence on theatre practices ever since. Another is to work with the students on modern interpretations of classic texts. Students should be reminded that a director may decide not to set a play from the past in the time of the dramatist's writing or along the lines of that era's stage conventions; instead, they may approach classic plays in an infinite number of ways, for example, as a means of presenting theatre for social change, the work as an examination of the issues at play in the contemporary world, so original practices may not be a priority in the first place.

Adaptations of non-English works such as classical Greek plays have inspired rewritings and reinterpretations in each century, as they become adapted for an English-speaking audience. The plays of William Shakespeare have been set in various eras, many with an eye to contemporizing their impact on modern audiences, although the language, Early Modern English, is retained – with some cuts and edits.[6] Although Ralph Berry includes the Renaissance period as an option for directors,[7] he also suggests variations such as a modern milieu: a contemporary setting to create "illuminating analogues" with the past;[8] period analogue, using a historical period other than either a contemporary or Renaissance one; and an eclectic take, in which periods are mixed in costuming, props, and sets as a means of pushing the audience further towards identification and to clarify narrative.[9]

Berry, based on his experience of attending many plays of Shakespeare in many incarnations, notes that directors have recreated the original thrust staging and Elizabethan costuming; updated the plays to introduce objects and clothing familiar to a modern audience; used a period of history that, though not from the 16th or 17th centuries, offered parallels to the action and themes of the Bard; or mixed styles, with sets, costuming, and props from a variety of periods as a shorthand means of revealing a situation. As an example of Period Analogue, Trevor Nunn set *All's Well That Ends Well* during World War I. In this way, he highlighted Helena's subservient role in the household by equipping her with the chatelaine belt she wore at her waist;[10] while the courtiers to the King of France dressed as "leather helmeted aviators bearing dispatches," clarifying their roles in the court and in the military;[11] and Parolles, the cowardly hanger-on to Bertram, brought his set of golf clubs to the war in Italy.[12]

Style as Related to Plays and Playwrights

Style may be defined according to how it is described or assumed in plays. Francis Hodge defines styles for a director as "the collective use of those conventions in staging that each age developed and kept in use for a period of time to enable it to express its own plays in a specific way."[13] For performers, John Gielgud, the famous classical actor of the 20th century, wrote: "Style is knowing what kind of play you're in."[14]

Simon Callow points out that, even in plays of the same period, the style requirements will be different.

> [Y]ou need to ask questions about the world from which the play came, and the theatrical practice of the day. Once you've grasped these general characteristics of the period, the ways in which, as it were, plays from the same period resemble each other, then you can find out the ways in which the play you're dealing with is different from all the others, and try to discover the author's preoccupations, and to hear his special tone of voice.[15]

Familiarizing the students with the original performance space of a play can give them a sense of the player/audience relationship,[16] the need to fill a space as opposed to speaking intimately as if in one's own room, the props and scenery required of a specific theatre, and the use of stage machinery such as masking, special effects, and the presence or absence of curtains, backdrops, and flats. At the same time, teachers who have read a number of plays from the canon for each time period will be more likely to recognize not only similarities but the differences between authors and to compare and contrast the unique perspectives of, for example, Richard Brinsley Sheridan versus Oliver Goldsmith or Shakespeare versus Christopher Marlowe versus Thomas Middleton.

How the Actor Personalizes a Period Style

One of the complaints a student actor will have is their unfamiliarity with, and therefore fear of, another mode of speech and behavior. They feel unable to connect with material far removed from their own means of speaking, nor do they believe the play's circumstances are relevant to their own experience. These worries can be dispelled as the students discover the universality of the emotions at play, the excitement of the stories, and the range of acting required to realize the characters. They also become comfortable over time with heightened language, as they are exposed to many different scenes from the same era and handle the language within their mouths and bodies. As they imagine translations of the language into modern colloquialisms, they grow a new respect for the artistry of the playwright and the incredible power of expression offered to them by the text.

In a period play, not every character of the same station will behave the same, even if all of them know how to exist in that society – the audience wouldn't be able to distinguish between them onstage. But they do share a common knowledge of that society: "Characterization is a measure of how an individual character differs from other characters, while style is a measure of how much he or she resembles them."[17] While style is the "*shared behavioral characteristics* of its people,"[18] individuality comes from variations on a common theme.

The teacher should consider how many dramaturgical materials to bring to class. They may even decide on topics the students themselves can research and present to each other. Among many devices, Trevor Nunn used actor research as a directorial tool for the Royal Shakespeare Company's nine-hour production of Charles Dickens's novel *Nicholas Nickleby* with John Caird and Leon Rubin.[19] Individually, or in small groups, the company explored the world of the play: "Victorian theatre – London in the 1830s – music – government – sport – food – health – medicine – economics – the underworld – education – the opera – general politics – royalty – literature – class structure – work – wages – newspaper headlines – sexual habits and attitudes, and so on."[20] The directors created a hive mind that paid great dividends in terms of acting behavior, staging, design, and character work. For example: "Bob Peck spent two days relating to us a vast and rich account of pastimes and sports of the period," which "spilled over into a grim analysis of the whole underworld life of the time."[21] Meanwhile, Cathryn Harrison dived into health and safety issues – or lack thereof – and hygiene. She gave the company scientific explanations for the conditions of the Victorians, including "venereal disease, infant mortality and malnutrition-twisted limbs."[22] More than just delivering a historical lecture, Harrison shocked the group "with her details of the ignorance and neglect that caused premature death and illness in so many people of that time."[23] Such research, applied in a classroom setting, would raise the stakes for the students who work for their characters' survival and want to embody the physical plight of creatures who suffered from scoliosis, rickets, and lack of food. Research creates the pictures in their minds that inspire their use of the environment, their objects, and their fellow actors.

An example of research giving actors an in-depth historical context can be found in Max Stafford Clark's book, *Letters to George*, as he directed *The Recruiting Officer* by George Farquhar. Plume and Kite are soldiers in the British army who return to England and make their way to Shrewsbury as heroes of the Battle of Blenheim, fought the month before. As professional soldiers, they use the town as a place for rest and relaxation. Plume discovers he has fathered a child on his previous visit, and he asks Kite to serve as the father. Plume loves Melinda and his hopes are high for a liaison, as he is one of the heroes of the battle. At the same time, he is not particularly interested in talking about what happened when pressed by Melinda's father, Justice Balance.[24] The experiences that have taken Plume away from civilian life still affect his character; while in Bavaria during Worthy's wooing of Silvia, he has been unable to offer his friend counsel, and Worthy has failed to propose marriage to Silvia, an all but certain prospect before Plume went off to war.

An excellent book on the manners of figures in various eras is *The Polite World*. The authors wrote in great detail about salutations, including bows and curtsies; deportment and etiquette; entering and exiting a room; the use of gloves, pomanders, fans, tobacco, snuff, and parasols; managing the train of a gown; and other fascinating details that aid the actor in living the historical role. One example is the technical description of the 17th-century Bow, partially given here:

> Draw the left foot backwards, the leg and foot turned outwards slightly, the knee straight. Keep the heels of both feet on the ground, with the body and

head erect. Without pausing, bend both knees, simultaneously bowing the body forward from the waist. The head follows the line of the bowed body, without dropping the chin in towards the chest. As the knees bend, the weight of the body moves back partially on to the back foot, so that the weight is distributed evenly upon both feet.[25]

Tools for Practice

Exercises, etudes, and games can be introduced during scene and play rehearsals to focus on social attitudes within various periods. Clive Barker has created group games for period styles, for example, the Jacobean Street Scene and the Restoration Comedy Game.[26] A basic relationship game, Triangles, is by definition useful in establishing love triangles, common situations in Moliere's and Shakespeare's plays.[27] Trevor Nunn, when rehearsing *The Revenger's Tragedy* at the Royal Shakespeare Company, "making use of games and improvisation,"[28] created an etude in which the actors, as the courtiers, searched for the corpse of the Duke, while Nunn and the actor playing the Duke hid from them. "They then had to improvise the thrill of discovery and their disgust at the corpse's smell."[29] Nunn gave the players an experience they could then recreate in memory, leading up to the onstage scene where they discover the body.

Genres: Comedy

Many of the principles the teacher will use in other situations, for example coaching contemporary drama, will apply as well, while the subject of comedy gets its own passages here, as some of the most famous plays of the periods under discussion are comic in nature. One of the paradoxes of the form is the fact the characters don't know they are in a comedy. They are suffering horrible treatment or mired in terrible situations for the amusement of the audience. They are seriously fighting as hard as they can to avoid tragedy. Or, as Ovid maintained, "Comedy is tragedy narrowly averted." This means they are still pursuing objectives, and the stakes are very high for success or failure. Sometimes, the difference is that the level of intensity a character applies to the stakes isn't warranted by the actual situation. A character will overreact in a way that most wouldn't under normal conditions. Peter Barkworth, an actor who played a number of comedy parts, came to understand that "the only thing you are allowed to exaggerate in comedy is emotion, so that worry becomes frenzied anxiety, smugness becomes unbearable complacency and distaste becomes anguished indignation."[30] In general, however, the actor is safer if they play the reality of the situation rather than play the humor.

This brings up an important topic which the teacher needs to stress: is the play a comedy or a farce? A rule of thumb is that a comedy involves odd people placed in everyday situations, while a farce involves everyday people placed in abnormal situations. Since comedy concerns itself with odd people, these are the ones who will overreact to normal situations. In a farce, the stakes can be very high, requiring the characters to work very hard to overcome them – in this sense, overreactions are rare. Sometimes a play has a combination of these elements: odd people in odd situations.

The comedy character, an oddball, finds a common situation unbearable and impossible. Instead of solving the issue in a logical fashion, they will go out of their way to be their own worst enemy, to tie themselves in knots trying to escape the consequences of failure. The protagonist of a farce, an everyday person, will be forced to overcome obstacle after obstacle, the kind that becomes more and more difficult as the play progresses. The students should be given some modern examples, perhaps from situation comedies, so they may distinguish between the comic and farcical elements.

A master of comedy direction, Mike Nichols, gave the cast of *Spamalot* "Guiding Principles" for the musical he was directing as well as some basic rules about comedy "in [g]eneral."[31] These include the injunction to "Portray human beings in the course of their lives."[32] What is the reality behind the events? This is a tragic play as far as the actors should be concerned. He also warns them of a common trap: "Stop playing for the laughs"[33] – also referred to as "chasing the laughs" – the line has led to a laugh in the past, so the actor asks for the laugh instead of giving intention to the line. Nichols insists, "Don't get in the way of your own jokes."[34] An actor in a comedy who doesn't trust his material will feel that he must make the spectators understand that something is funny. Nichols tells this actor to "Stop mugging at the audience." He knew that by indicating or making faces, the actor telegraphed his personal view about the comedy in the script. The result was the audience was less inclined to agree with the actor's assessment, or the laughs would come cheaply, taking the audience out of the story.

Spamalot contains both farcical and comedic situations. Nichols wanted the actors to resemble actual people. Regardless of the unusual circumstances and the oddness of the roles, too often actors feel they must invent abnormal traits at the expense of connecting in some way to the audience's own experiences. Nichols enjoins them: "Pursue your task."[35] Their objectives will lead to justifiable actions, no matter how odd, i.e., farcical.

In Nichols's view this was the first rule of comedy: "It's the details that move us and remind us of life. Therefore, what you do can't be big – big isn't true."[36] He knew that the actors would consider tepid responses an injunction to force the comedy and offered, "When the response is low, instead of going higher you should concentrate more on each other and the truth."[37] He warned his actors, "It's easy to get a laugh. It's NOT easy to get a laugh when it's connected to an idea or the other people on stage. Stay connected to each other."[38] Feeding off of the other characters continues to hold true no matter the outlandishness of the situations.

Dame Edith Evans, the great British actress of the 20th century, explained her technique for speaking the complex language of a classic comedy: "Well I say everything as if it's dirty."[39] As she portrayed so many classical roles, including Lady Bracknell in *The Importance of Being Earnest*, this seemed a perfect place to apply the lesson, and she did in her famous delivery of "A hand-bag!"[40]

190 Styles

Religious Drama

In speaking of medieval plays, Peter Ackroyd wrote what could be a useful note for actors in any liturgical drama: "And it was in these plays, where private faith and public spectacle were one, that this vocabulary was wedded with rapture."[41] Actors understand ritual, whether it be private routines they use before going onstage, or their experience with acts of faith. Plays with characters who have religious fervor require the actors to believe deeply in the circumstances, including faith in a higher power. An excellent example of this approach can be found in *The Mystery Plays: The Nativity, Passion, Doomsday* adapted by Tony Harrison and directed by Bill Bryden for the National Theatre of Great Britain in 1985. The film of the production shows the British actors playing country people who absolutely believe in the stories they are enacting, making for simple but effective and cleverly told narratives. The *Abraham and Isaac* play is particularly affecting.

The Greek plays, too, are ritualistic in nature and were performed at the Festival of Dionysus in the 5th century BC. They were, in a sense, reboots of Homeric stories and stories of the gods and demigods. Some review of these legends will help the students to understand the context for the narratives, something the original audience would already know.

Masks were important for a number of reasons: men played all of the roles and could don the personas of women and gods using masks, and since all speaking roles were played by, at the most, three actors, very quick changes could occur with masks rather than elaborate makeup. This could also solve the issue of a character changing their own appearance, for example, when such violent acts as the blinding of Oedipus occurred offstage, an actor could merely change masks; or when Helen, the title character of Sophocles's play, cut her hair, a mask with the appropriate hairstyle could be worn.

Because of the three-actor rule, characters were killed offstage so other members of the cast would not have to remove their bodies – although dummies could be wheeled out on a rolling platform called the ekkeklema. This gave the actors playing messengers the opportunity to present aria-like speeches explaining what tragic events occurred that the audience wasn't privileged to see.

The Greek Chorus

The chorus, being such an important element of classical Greek theatre, can be studied as a separate performance piece. Since no scores for Greek musical pieces exist, the teacher can pick samples of music from various periods to stress the rhythmic nature of the chorus speeches. The teacher can divide a large class into groups of 12, or use an entire class of 12 or 15 and pick a choragus, or chorus leader, to choreograph a written text. They have several options for variety: the members speak in unison, the speeches are divided between members, or a combination is used. The scenes themselves can then be rehearsed in coaching sessions, with the audience of actors serving as chorus, retaining the presentational style.[42]

Plays from the period, especially those that don't often appear in drama anthologies, can be enjoyable to realize. *Helen* by Euripedes is a science fiction play about the gods creating a phantom of Helen to face the consequences of the Trojan war, while she herself is spirited away to Egypt, where she reunites with her husband Menelaus in the court of Theoclymenos, who wants Helen for himself and indulges in his favorite pastime, killing Greeks. *Women of Trachis*, by Sophocles, tells the tale of the jealousy Hercules's wife Deinaeira has for her husband, which leads to tragedy. Her discovery of Hercules's new lover Iole among the women who will serve in the household, and her attempts to hide her true feelings as well as her dialogue with Hercules's herald Lichus, are wonderful scenes to explore.

This brings up an important point: the students should learn how to pronounce the names of the characters and places of the dramas, and they should have some familiarity with the events of the Trojan War and the lives of the gods and demigods. They will have a deeper appreciation of the works and connect them to their classical origins.

The Restoration Period

The English Restoration began in Britain in 1666, when Charles II assumed the throne. During this period, the King granted William Davenant and Thomas Killigrew exclusive rights to produce theatre. At first, Shakespeare's plays were divided between the two companies, Davenant's Duke's Company and Killigrew's King's Company, at the Duke's Theatre and the Theatre Royal, respectively. When new comic and tragic plays were written for the stage, they were works by John Dryden; George Etheridge; Aphra Behn, the first successful female playwright; William Congreve; George Farquhar; William Wycherley; Thomas Otway; Thomas Shadwell; and John Vanbrugh. These were prose plays, with rhyming speeches relegated to prologues and epilogues. Unlike the practice of the Elizabethan and Jacobean theatres, the female characters were played by women. The plays were now indoors in a proscenium theatre and lit by candlelight. Sometimes playgoers sat on the stage, as many attended in order to be seen rather than to see a play. The comic plays appealed to the audience through narration and through plots concerned with the types of encounters the audience of the upper classes might have experienced.

Simon Callow writes: "A major component of behavior in Restoration society, and thus one that is reflected, celebrated, and ridiculed in the comedies, is the penchant for flaunting or displaying one's fine manners and clothing."[43] In the presentational play, the actor must not only acknowledge the audience, but conclude the audience is in love with her. Having the classroom audience applaud at the entrance of each character encourages the actor to enjoy being the center of attention and gives them the pleasant feeling of being desired. This is true even when the characters are talking to each other. Their wit is not only to score points, but to amuse those watching. The students are also taught to use the device of the aside, a brief speech to the audience.

When Donald Sinden began working on Lord Foppington in Vanbrugh's *The Relapse*, he asked an older actor, Baliol Holloway, to explain how asides worked. Holloway said the following:

> An aside must be directed to a given seat in the theatre – a different seat for each aside, some in the stalls, some in the circle. Never to the same seat twice – the rest of the audience will think you have a friend sitting there. If you are facing to the right immediately before the aside, then direct it to the left of the theatre, and vice versa. Your head must crack round in one clean movement, look straight at the occupant of the seat, deliver the line and crack your head back to exactly where it was before. The voice you use must be different from the one you are using in the play. If loud, then soft; if soft, then loud; if high, then low; if low, then high; if fast, then slow; if slow, then fast. During an aside, no other characters must move at all – the time you take does not exist for them.[44]

William Congreve describes why it is reasonable to see the aside as a necessary form of speech in that period. In his Epistle Dedicatory to *The Double Dealer*, he writes:

> We ought not to imagine that this man either talks to us, or to himself; he is only thinking, and thinking such matter as were inexcusable folly in him to speak. But because we are concealed spectators of the plot in agitation, and the poet finds it necessary to let us know the whole mystery of his contrivance, he is willing to inform us of this person's thoughts; and to that end is forced to make use of the expedient of speech, no other better way being yet invented for the communication of thought.[45]

According to Suzanne M. Ramczyk, the characters of Restoration drama can be divided into three types. The True Wits "are those gentlemen and ladies who are successful in presenting the socially prescribed, artful masks of the polite world."[46] They are successful in presenting the audience with the model for social elegance through their verbal wit and heightened mien. The False Wits are those who "have studied and honed the numerous details of social deportment and who can practice these with as much skill as the true wits, but who often go too far in the execution of their manners."[47] These are the fops of Restoration comedy. They think themselves far wittier than they actually are and, when given the challenge of wearing elaborate wigs, take this to an extreme. Lord Foppington, for example, is often sporting an enormous headpiece so heavy as to be carried in on a chair before being fixed in place. The Witless are the lower classes who do not have the social manners of the in crowd. One of the themes of both the Restoration and Georgian period shortly after involves an upper-class gentleman marrying a woman from the country without the manners of the elite in town. Wycherley's *The Country Wife* and Sheridan's *The School for Scandal* revolve around such female characters in Mrs. Pinchwife and Lady Teazle, respectively.

Simon Callow describes the attitude of the Restoration fop as feeling tipsy: "One of the things I have found useful is to imagine myself slightly drunk before I go onstage – no more than slightly."[48] This is because it creates in the fop the sense that they are the most witty and attractive fellow onstage. Being tipsy is "that lovely moment when the inner and outer selves merge, when self-consciousness disappears, and everything you say sounds rather marvelous – to you."[49]

Callow also speaks of the use of such props as the snuff box or the ladies fan. A complete listing of the Language of the Fan is available on the Sotheby's website.[50] The True and False Wits carry themselves upright and glide across the stage. One exercise for the students is to have them carry cups of water in each hand as they walk across the stage, trying not to spill them. They must place the arms in the proper position up at about torso height to show off the cuffs, with the elbows closer but not touching the body. When sitting, they give prominence to a well-toned calf with one leg forward.

Restoration scenes from *The Recruiting Officer*, *The Relapse*, *The Country Wife*, *The Beaux' Stratagem*, *The Double Dealer*, *Love for Love*, and *The Man of Mode* are all excellent material for students to explore with the teacher. They require great vocal facility with articulation and speed. Schemes or tropes are used by the speaker to catch the audience's attention in many of these periods. In fact, the prose of the Restoration and Georgian periods is clarified by the use of these figures of speech.

Eighteenth-Century Drama: The Georgian Period

The Restoration is a period of excess, the English having emerged from a period of Puritan severity under Oliver Cromwell. The Restoration ended when George I, great-grandson of James I, ascended the throne, and his son, grandson, and great-grandson ruled England until 1837. Hairstyles and costuming had changed, the enormous wigs of the Restoration by and large replaced with the periwig and the much smaller wigs such as those worn in the American colonies by George Washington. During the reigns of George I and George II, most plays of the period were written in reaction to the plays like those of Wycherley and Vanbrugh and had become more sentimental and less hedonistic. Wives, like Lady Teazle in *The School for Scandal*, considered being unfaithful, but did not follow through with the temptation.

Scenes from *She Stoops to Conquer*, *The School for Scandal*, and *The Rivals* are classics of the form, with rich characters from country and city, from the highest to the lowest ranks. The humor in these plays is still accessible to contemporary students. The classic screen scene from *The School for Scandal* is a model for comic execution,[51] and the character of Lady Teazle is delightful for a student to inhabit.

If the teacher is interested in looking at styles in the Restoration, Georgian, or Greek Classical periods, resources are endless, including books whose authors speak specifically to realizing those plays in performance. The next chapter will concentrate on Shakespeare, with some resources, techniques, and tools for approaching this challenging material.

194 Styles

Assigning a grade or giving feedback for scenes in period sounds subjective at best, but there are means for setting goals to be accomplished by the students.[52]

Notes

1 William Allan Neilson, Thomas A. Knott, and Paul W. Carhart, eds., *Webster's New International Dictionary of the English Language*, 2nd Edition (Springfield, MA: G.&C. Merriam Company Publishers, 1943), 2505.
2 Cohen, *Acting Power: The 21st Century Edition*, 147.
3 Cohen, *Acting Power: The 21st Century Edition*, 148.
4 Joan Wildeblood and Peter Brinson, *The Polite World: A Guide to English Manners and Deportment from the Thirteenth to the Nineteenth Century* (London: Oxford University Press, 1965), 2.
5 Wildeblood and Brinson, *The Polite World*, 2.
6 Projects such as *Play On!*, the Oregon Shakespeare Festival's adaptation festival headed by Lue Morgan Douthit, and such works as *A Tempest* by Aimé Césaire, rewrite or reimagine the plays completely.
7 Ralph Berry, *On Directing Shakespeare: Interviews with Contemporary Directors* (London: Hamish Hamilton Ltd., 1989), 14–23.
8 An example of the eclectic mode is Peter Brook's use of the 18th-century paintings of Watteau to costume the lead characters in *Love's Labour's Lost*, while dressing Constable Dull as a 20th-century London bobby, a figure so recognizable as to give the audience an immediate sense of his character.
9 Berry, *On Directing Shakespeare*, 20–22.
10 A chatelaine is an all-purpose accessory with various items to aid in the running of a household, a kind of Swiss army knife for a senior housemaid.
11 Martin White, "Trevor Nunn," in *The Routledge Companion to Directors' Shakespeare*, ed. John Russell Brown (London: Routledge, 2008), 296.
12 White, "Trevor Nunn," 295.
13 Hodge, *Play Directing*, 328–329.
14 Gerald Freedman, quoted in Rand and Scorcia, *Acting Teachers of America*, 215.
15 Simon Callow, *Acting in Restoration Comedy*, ed. Maria Aitken (New York: Applause Theatre Book Publishers, 1991), 6, emphasis Callow's.
16 This seems to be the primary finding of the experiment known as the New Globe Theatre in London. See Christie Carson and Farah Karim-Cooper, eds., *Shakespeare's Globe: A Theatrical Experiment* (Cambridge: Cambridge University Press, 2008). For example, Mark Rylance, first artistic director of the New Globe, realized in relation to the spectators, that it "became paramount to say to the actors, 'Don't speak *to* them, don't speak *for* them, speak *with* them, play *with* them.'" 107. Emphasis Rylance's.
17 Cohen, *Acting Power: The 21st Century Edition*, 147, emphasis Cohen's.
18 Cohen, *Acting Power: The 21st Century Edition*, 147, emphasis Cohen's.
19 Devised in early rehearsals, but ultimately written by the playwright David Edgar.
20 Leon Rubin, *The Nicholas Nickleby Story: The Making of the Historic Royal Shakespeare Company Production* (London: William Heinemann Ltd., 1981), 22. This was before the internet. The students can now use search tools to find anything, including walk-throughs of particular museums, filled with artifacts of all kinds.
21 Rubin, *The Nicholas Nickleby Story*, 22.
22 Rubin, *The Nicholas Nickleby Story*, 23. Arguably the most important character in Nicholas's life is Smike, whose treatment as a child has led to his deformed body.
23 Rubin, *The Nicholas Nickleby Story*, 23.
24 See Max Stafford-Clark's notes on the play in his book *Letters to George*, 56–57.
25 Wildeblood and Brinson, *The Polite World*, 261.

26 See Barker, *Theatre Games*, 125–131. First, Barker introduces basic games such as Touch Your Partner and the Coins. See Barker, *Theatre Games*, 125–128.
27 Barker, *Theatre Games*, 131–134.
28 The entry on Trevor Nunn in Samuel L. Leiter, *The Great Stage Directors: 100 Distinguished Careers of the Theatre* (New York: Facts on File Inc., 1994), 219.
29 Leiter, *The Great Stage Directors*, 219.
30 Peter Barkworth, *The Complete about Acting* (London: Methuen Drama, 1991), 264.
31 Harris, *Mike Nichols*, 552.
32 Harris, *Mike Nichols*, 551.
33 Harris, *Mike Nichols*, 552.
34 Harris, *Mike Nichols*, 552.
35 Harris, *Mike Nichols*, 551.
36 Harris, *Mike Nichols*, 552.
37 Harris, *Mike Nichols*, 551, emphasis Nichols's.
38 Harris, *Mike Nichols*, 551, emphasis Nichols's.
39 Jacobi, *As Luck Would Have It*, 138.
40 Oscar Wilde, *The Importance of Being Earnest and Other Plays* (New York: The Modern Library, 2010), 198.
41 Peter Ackroyd, *The English Actor: From Medieval to Modern* (London: Reaktion Books Ltd., 2023), 8.
42 Some excellent resource books for the period are Brian Kulick, *How Greek Tragedy Works: A Guide for Directors, Dramaturges, and Playwrights* (London: Routledge, 2021); Simon Goldhill, *How to Stage Greek Tragedy Today* (Chicago: University of Chicago Press, 2007); Garland Robert, *How to Survive in Ancient Greece* (Yorkshire: Pen and Sword History, 2020).
43 Suzanne M. Ramczyk, *Delicious Dissembling: A Complete Guide to Performing Restoration Comedy* (Portsmouth: Heinemann, 2002), 18.
44 Donald Sinden, *Laughter in the Second Act* (London: Hodder and Stoughton, 1985), 164.
45 J. L. Styan, *Restoration Comedy in Performance* (Cambridge: Cambridge University Press, 1994), 204.
46 Ramczyk, *Delicious Dissembling*, 15.
47 Ramczyk, *Delicious Dissembling*, 15.
48 Callow, *Acting in Restoration Comedy*, 35.
49 Callow, *Acting in Restoration Comedy*, 35.
50 https://www.sothebys.com/en/articles/the-secret-language-of-fans.
51 Richard Brinsley Sheridan, *The School for Scandal*, Act IV. 3.
52 See the grading rubric for period styles scenes in Appendix 3.

14 Styles

Shakespeare

Given the breadth of the subject, this chapter will cover some general principles and tips about scenes the teacher may someday respond to but will be primarily dedicated to coaching actors in scenes from William Shakespeare's plays. Ideally, work on Shakespeare would take place over an entire course or more, but students may want to dip their toes in the water with one scene in a scene study class dedicated to a variety of genres.

In particular, students are encouraged to explore Shakespeare scenes, as many professional jobs are on offer in Shakespeare festivals around the world. Many students have also read a few plays or performed them in secondary school or studied Shakespeare in an English literature class at the college level. Whether an entire semester or a portion is dedicated to his work, the teacher should consider what they want to accomplish. Professional actors devote their careers to grappling with the challenges raised by the Bard's plays, using certain roles to set the bar for personal growth and the kudos that come from a successful classical performance – tackling Hamlet onstage, for example, after they have achieved movie stardom or as a long-overdue return to the stage.

What follows in this chapter are suggestions of work that can be spread out over time along with some basic ideas that will help the teacher to diagnose a Shakespeare scene, whether the teacher offers a class devoted to his works or gives a special opportunity to students who desire it.

First of all, the good news is the teacher need not ignore the means whereby contemporary students create and connect with their characters and the scenes. Actors should operate as they have been with realistic and contemporary scripts: they must still create images in their minds of the given circumstances. They must still consider previous circumstances and embody them. They must still use intention. In the latter case, the difference is that, with Shakespearean scenes, the characters state their intentions clearly, and it is important to remember that, when characters speak in soliloquy, they are telling the audience the truth.

Preparation

When scenes are assigned, each student group is asked to obtain and read the full texts of the plays from which they are selected.[1] Annotated editions help them with unusual figures of speech or historical incidents either embodied or invoked in the work.[2] The Arden edition, which is now in its third incarnation, contains clear introductions to the plays and notes on any obscure passages or references, and most university libraries have copies for perusal. Such resources as Alexander Schmidt's *Shakespeare Lexicon and Quotation Dictionary* in two volumes and David Crystal's *Shakespeare's Words: A Glossary and Language Companion* should be made available in the classroom. If the course is an extensive one, the students may be asked to buy a copy of the complete works, many of which can be ordered online as eBooks.

The biography of Shakespeare, such as it may be gleaned from the records, may be studied insofar as it relates to certain plays. A moving bit of his life story is contained in two plays: when his father died, and he lost his son Hamnet to the plague, leaving behind his twin Judith, Shakespeare wrote *Hamlet* – a form of the name Hamnet – and *Twelfth Night*, with twins Viola and Sebastian, who are separated by a shipwreck. In *Hamlet*, the father who has been murdered reunites briefly with his son; in *Twelfth Night,* the twins are brought together again onstage, if not in life. These biographical details bring added emotional depth to the roles.

If one or two students are rehearsing a Shakespeare scene, their ability to speak the verse may be handled individually during their rehearsal sessions. However, if the entire class is working with Elizabethan or Jacobean material, if will be important to offer a review of the structure of the writing with the whole class.

Shakespeare's Verse

When diagnosing scenes, the teachers may find the students have a natural capacity for the language or have already been trained to speak it. On the other hand, when the rules are ignored, sometimes this can lead to misinterpretations or a muddied realization of the text. At that point, it will be worth the time to review scansion with the whole class in a verse workshop. Though Shakespeare uses other types of verse – for example, in songs – the attention here will be on his most basic tool for creating dialogue.

The following is a brief explanation for the rules of iambic pentameter and blank verse. The more examples the teacher can offer from the text, the more the rules are implanted. At bottom, the passages need to be read and acted by the students, and the rules need to be embodied in exercises. During this discussion, I will tie the rules to exercises both of my own making and by famous teachers of heightened language, such as Cicely Berry and Patsy Rodenburg.

It is helpful to remind the students that the actors of the Chamberlain's Men – and later the King's men – like other troupes of the time, had few days to mount the performance of each play, and even less time to revive one.[3] There were no "directors" to tell the actors where to move or how to perform the text. This is not to say the players were completely on their own. It was up to the playwright to provide these answers one way or another. Shakespeare could explain himself directly; being an actor as well as the house playwright and sharer of the theatre,[4] he attended rehearsals and performances.

In particular, Shakespeare's use of verse allowed him to tell the actors when to pick up their cues, when to slow down, when to speed up, when to pause, what to feel, and what business to perform. Stage directions between the lines of dialogue were limited, but not *within* the lines.[5] Certainly, he wrote for his company and their talents as well as for the specific stage space they used. But he could also plant pointers in the writing and make the words easier to memorize through a poetic form. In order to move quickly from scene to scene, set pieces were limited in the stage space, and Shakespeare also used spoken décor – actor dialogue that described the scene such as "Well, this is the forest of Arden."[6]

Basic Rules

Meaning of the Words

Students must always know what they are saying, but Shakespeare's words make this more difficult. For one, though his language is a form of our own English, it is an Early Modern one. This is why actors and audiences can still understand the simplest of phrases or work out the definitions through context, but it is also why, as the years pass, words and phrases become more and more obscure. It becomes the actor's job to know what they are saying and not to guess. It helps that Shakespeare invented words that are still used today, such as "submerge," "obscene," "pedant," "premeditated," "reliance," "dislocate," and "assassination."

However, Shakespeare's plays also include false cognates, words that are recognizable on the page but do not have the same meanings as they did in the Elizabethan and Jacobean periods.[7] For example, the word "cordial," a word that can mean "friendly," is actually also "a medicine to raise the spirits."[8] "Light," which has many of the same meanings today, also means, "frivolous, wanton, or loose."[9] It is also a verb, which means to "descend."[10] A "villain," can do evil, but a master can also refer to a servant with this word. "Recall" does not mean "remember," but "to call back in" or "revoke." A "fellow," someone with whom we are sympatico, can also be a term of contempt. "Merely" means totally, and "ecstasy" means madness.[11] A particularly tricky one is "doubt," which means "fear, suspect,"[12] as in *Hamlet*'s "I doubt some foul play";[13] as is "want," which does mean "need," but also means "to not have, to be without."[14] as in Richard of Gloucester's "I that am rudely stamped and want love's majesty/to strut before a wanton ambling nymph."[15] The word "clown" can refer to a comic character, but it primarily describes a country bumpkin, or "rustic,"[16] as in the Clown or Young Shepherd from *The Winter's Tale*. Actors may use the context to help them and still miss the meaning: "Anon," for example, means "right away," rather than "by and by."

Some words are used in a rude fashion now disguised by their common meaning today. Eric Partridge's *Shakespeare's Bawdy* contains an exhaustive list of words with ribald definitions as well as a ranking of the most pernicious examples in the plays.[17] Some are so obscure as to be unnoticed by the audience, although the actor may want to know the character's intent.

Shakespeare eases the audience into a play by using fewer obscure words to open it. Ralph Alan Cohen points out that only ten archaic words are used in the beginning passages of all of the plays.[18] When performing a full play, the actors should be aware that the audience needs time to acclimate themselves to the language and verse forms.

Some words are simply archaic, and it is not unusual for modern directors to replace them with words of the same syllables and stresses. If the passages are famous, the words are less likely to be replaced. These words that are off limits include "wherefore," meaning "why," and "fardels," meaning "burdens," which appear in speeches anyone can quote, in *Romeo and Juliet* as "wherefore art thou Romeo," and *Hamlet*'s "To be or not to be," respectively.[19]

The students may be reminded that the Early Modern poets took great license in shaping the verse form to their liking. Some words that seem archaic are merely shortened for the verse: Scott Kaiser calls this either front-clipping – the removal of the beginning of a word[20] – or end-clipping, cutting off the last syllable of a word.[21] Examples of the first include "plaining" for "explaining," "mongst" for amongst, "strain'd" for constrained, "gainst" for against, and "scape" for escape.[22] Examples of the second include "ha" for have, as in "Therefore ha' done with words,"[23] "ope" for open, and "morn" for morning.[24]

Myths and Legends

When characters make references to the heroes of yesteryear, such as the famous figures of legend in the Trojan War, the students should know these stories so they will understand the character is not just being poetic but using metaphor as a means of making their points. In *Twelfth Night*, when the Captain of the sunk vessel tries to comfort Viola by suggesting her twin brother may have survived, he reminds her of a famous legendary rescue:

> Captain: . . . I saw your brother
> Most provident in peril, bind himself –
> Courage and hope both teaching him the practice –
> To a strong mast that lived upon the sea,
> Where, like Arion on the dolphin's back,
> I saw him hold acquaintance with the waves
> So long as I could see.[25]

The Captain compares Sebastian to Arion – the mythological figure who, after being captured by pirates, is saved from drowning by dolphins – as a way of soothing Viola's fear her brother has been lost at sea. Such references are also used to show that a character's emotions are so heightened, only a legendary metaphor or analogy will do.[26]

Ultimately, the actor must serve as the translator, the medium between the dialogue and audience. The spectators may not understand every word, but they will get the overall gist if the actor is using the proper tone and gestures based on intention.

Iambic Pentameter, Blank Verse, Regular and Irregular Verse

Iambic pentameter verse was invented by the Earl of Surrey and was first used in a play called *Gorboduc* by Sackville and Norton around 1560. It is the verse form that most closely resembles natural English speech. Blank verse is verse that does not rhyme. Shakespeare uses rhyming couplets and iambic pentameter but also blank verse, which retains the ten-syllable line form and varying stresses.

An iamb is a small unit of two syllables in which the second syllable receives the stress; for example, "believe," or "to be." A pentameter is a line of five of these units. So, the basic iambic pentameter is ten syllables with stresses landing on the second syllable of each iamb. The regular iambic line has the following rhythm, described by John Barton as "de DUM, de DUM, de DUM, de DUM, de DUM," a rhythm that resembles a heartbeat.[27] Examples: "Your will be done. This must my comfort be."[28] This line is stressed naturally as "Your WILL be DONE. This MUST my COMfort BE." Viola's "I left no ring with her. What means this lady?" is "I [unstressed] LEFT no RING with HER. What MEANS this LA-dy." "You have prevailed. I will depart in quiet," is stressed as "You HAVE preVAILED. I [unstressed] WILL depart in QUIet." This last two examples include an extra unstressed syllable, another example of poetic license.[29]

Shakespeare bends the rules as far as pentameter is concerned. He may break the iambic form, he may add extra syllables to the ends of lines, he may squeeze words together to make a line work, he may expand words, and he may use short or shared lines.

Shakespeare relies on the audience to acclimate themselves to the natural rhythm of the verse lines. He then upsets their expectations through irregular rhythms, forms that give a new intent to the characters and extra dramatic weight to the words they speak. One way to explain this is to remind students that for each foot, Shakespeare has four choices rather than one: unstressed stressed, marked as U V; stressed unstressed, or V U; stressed stressed, or VV; and unstressed unstressed, or UU.

When the students try to say a line such as Richard III's exhortation to his troops, "Spur your proud horses hard, and ride in blood,"[30] as a regular pentameter – "Spur YOUR / proud-HOR / ses HARD/, and RIDE / in BLOOD, the pentameter rhythm overrides the sense. They must decide where the stresses belong in each foot. If they speak it for the sense, the stresses should reveal themselves. The troops, hearing the extra stresses in the line, would be more likely to follow their king: "SPUR your PROUD HORses HARD and RIDE in BLOOD."

In *Julius Caesar*, Antony begins his speech to the crowd with the famous phrase, "Friends, Romans, Countrymen, lend me your ears." As a regularly stressed line, it somehow doesn't sound right: "Friends, RO-mans, COUN-try MEN, lend ME your EARS."[31] But, if the stresses are used where they seem appropriate – on the nouns and verbs here – the line becomes "FRIENDS, RO-mans, COUN-try MEN, LEND me your EARS." Antony is stressing the lines by putting stresses in what Barton calls the "offbeat position," to get the crowd to listen to him.

When Shakespeare seems to be adding a syllable to the end of the pentameter, making an 11-syllable line, one of two things is happening: (1) the last syllable is not stressed, or (2) if the last syllable of an 11-syllable line must be stressed – i.e., is a single-syllable verb or noun or a multisyllable word that naturally gets a stress on the last syllable – then another word within the line is elided – i.e., contracted. In the first instance, the first four lines of "To be or not to be" contain feminine endings: "To BE or NOT to BE that IS the QUEST-ion. / WHETHer 'tis NOB-ler in the MIND to SUF-fer / The SLINGS and AR-rows of outRAGEous FOR-tune / Or to TAKE ARMS aGAINST a SEA of TROUB-les . . ."[32] In the second instance, the last syllable is stressed: "My MIStress' EYES are NOTH-ing LIKE the SUN."[33] "Sun" is a monosyllable noun that gets stressed, so "mistress's" is elided to "mistress.'"

Often feminine endings consist of two-syllable words and the second syllable is not pronounced, as is the case with Hamlet's famous soliloquy. With lines ending in monosyllables, personal pronouns, such as "I" and "me" are exceptions: "Away, my disposition and po-SSESS me."[34] Or "How all occasions do inform aGAINST me."[35] Unless a character is comparing themselves to someone else, they will tend not to stress "me" or "I." Stressing "me" here sounds odd because it is the feminine ending. An exception to the personal pronoun rule comes in *A Midsummer Night's Dream*, when Helena compares herself to Hermia: "Through Athens *I* am thought as fair as *she*."

Elision and Enlargement or Expansion

Elided words allow the writer to squeeze syllables together to make room for other syllables or give extra syllables to words in the same way he uses the feminine ending. Students will be familiar with contractions as, to this day, they use elision with "can't," "don't," and "it's." Shakespeare used common elided words such as "'Tis" instead of "it's" for "it is." Shakespeare treats some three-syllable words in this way: "hideous is pronounced as hid-yus – in "And see the brave day sunk in hideous night."[36] He will drop certain consonants such as the v in words like "even" – which becomes "e'en," as in Halloween or All Hallow's evening – or "never" shortened to "ne'er."

One common mistake a student will make is to pronounce certain letters without regard for the words from which they are elided: for example, Hamlet's "No offence i'th'world,"[37] contracts "in the world" to one syllable. Students will pronounce the "i" as "I" rather than the short vowel sound of "in." The same will happen with "o." In Antony's "A third o' th' world is yours,"[38] the o sound is pronounced as in "of," not as a long "o" as in "oval."

Shakespeare's use of foreign names allows him to elide them where necessary. Names like Romeo or Troilus can be pronounced in two or three syllables as TROY uh lus or TROY-lus and ROME-ee-oh or ROME-yo. If Romeo is not elided in Juliet's "O Romeo, Romeo, wherefore art thou Romeo,"[39] the line is 14 syllables long. And Shakespeare is not consistent – in the same play or even the same scene, he may use either strategy with the same character. Troilus is pronounced with two and three syllables in the same scene to make ten syllables out of two shared lines:[40]

Cressida: And is it true that I must go from Troy?
Troilus: A hateful truth.
Cressida: What, and from TROY-lus too? (two syllables)
Troilus: From Troy and Troy-uh-lus. (three syllables)
Cressida: Is't possible?[41]

The teacher can give students examples of elision from popular songs, where the meter requires a contraction of a word. For example, many of George and Ira Gershwin's songs – such as "S'Wonderful" – contain an elision in the title, which then appears in the song. In many hymns, the word "heaven" is pronounced as one syllable, as it often is in Shakespeare. Students have a harder time thinking of phrases such as "'i th' world," as one syllable. The coach can also play them a modern song where the lyrics are elided in this way.

Ultimately, each actor must decide how strict she will be. She can still pronounce the missing syllable quickly to retain the verse line because she feels the audience will better understand the word in its full form. Every rule is, as John Barton admits, a suggestion, "But if the verse actually helps you to phrase the line then that's the right answer."[42]

Just as with the three-syllable names and words, Shakespeare pronounces an ending syllable such as "ed" when the poet wants to expand a word in order to fit the pentameter. Queen Gertrude's line "And there I see such black and grained spots," is smoother when the "ed" is pronounced: And THERE I SEE such BLACK and GRAIN-ed SPOTS." It also gives further emphasis to the last word, which, as a monosyllabic noun, must be pronounced.

Oaths are also clipped to avoid using the name of God or the Virgin Mary: "S'blood" means "by the blood of Christ," Christ's blood shed on the cross "'Ods my little life,"[43] as in God's or "By God's."[44] These locutions allow the speaker to avoid breaking the third commandment – taking the Lord's name in vain.

Why should the teacher insist that the students worry about feminine endings, elision, and expansion? Because the line sounds right to the audience's ear; to ignore those changes creates a line that is more difficult to say or to hear. The teacher, over time, begins to notice these mistakes because of her familiarity with the iambic form, and eventually the students do too. As students work on the verse, they feel when it is smoothly spoken and when it seems to stop and start because elision or expansion has been ignored.

The students sometimes struggle with word order. Even when the sense is clear, they will unconsciously switch the words in rehearsal. For example, Petruchio says of Kate, "I know her father, though I know not her,"[45] instead of "I don't know her." The teacher can point out passages from the *King James Bible*, or KJV, that grammatically mirror Shakespeare's. James I commissioned this version in 1604, using poets of the period. It was published in 1611, during Shakespeare's lifetime.[46] In the book of Luke 23, Verse 34, the KJV verse reads, "Father, forgive them; for they know not what they do." In the New International Version or NIV, the same passage reads, "Father, forgive them; for they do not know what they are doing."

The King James version of the Bible is written in such a way the passages are easier to remember, as are the lines in Shakespeare.

New International Version of the Bible, Psalm 23:4:
The Lord is my shepherd, I lack nothing.
He makes me lie down in green pastures,
he leads me beside quiet waters

he refreshes my soul.
He guides me along the right paths
for his name's sake.
Even though I walk
through the darkest valley,
I will fear no evil,
for you are with me;
your rod and your staff,
they comfort me. . . .

The King James Bible Psalm 23:4

The Lord is my shepherd; I shall not want. (10 syllables)
He maketh me to lie down in green pastures: (10 syllables)
he leadeth me beside the still waters. (10 syllables)
He restoreth my soul: he leadeth me in the paths of righteousness for his name's sake.
Yea, though I walk through the valley of the shadow of death, I will fear no evil: for thou art with me; thy rod and thy staff they comfort me. . . .

Though the latter version is not in contemporary language, it is striking in its imagery and word placement.

Irregular Lines

The simplest way for a student to recognize an irregular line is to note when mono-syllabic words – two verbs, a verb and a noun, two nouns, and so on – are placed next to each other, or if a line of verse begins with a stress. Examples include: "**Grief fills** up the room of my absent child," "**Blow winds** and crack your cheeks. **Rage! Blow!**" "And "He was my **friend, faith**ful and just to me."[47] If the line has more than 11 syllables, the student looks for the words that may be elided. They can recognize such lines by using the regular pentameter beat to count the number of syllables either aloud or in their heads. Actors have been known to count the feet of a line using their fingers.

Shared Lines and Short Lines

In scenes between two or more characters, Shakespeare guides the actors to pick up their cues by creating a complete verse line whose parts are divided between them. Instead of 10 syllables, two or more characters may share 4 and 6 syllables or 6 and 4 syllables, respectively.

Short lines, that is, pentameter lines that contain far fewer than 10 syllables and are surrounded by complete, 10-syllable lines, suggest a pause, the other syllables being absent.

Examples of Shared Lines

All's Well That Ends Well

Helena:	. . . I put you to
	The use of your own virtues, for the which (10 syllables)
	I shall continue thankful. (7 syllables)
Gentleman:	What's your will? (3 syllables)
Helena:	That it will please you (5 syllables; a short line)
	To give this poor petition to the King, (10 syllables)
	And aid me with that store of power you have (10 syllables, power is elided)
	To come into his presence. (7 syllables; a short line.)
Gentleman:	The King's not here. (4 syllables)
Helena:	Not here, sir? (3 syllables)
Gentlemen:	Not indeed. (3 syllables)
	He hence removed last night, and with more haste (10 syllables)
	Than is his use. (4 syllables)
Helena:	Lord, how we lose our pains! (6 syllables)[48]

The Merchant of Venice

Portia:	Is your name Shylock? (5 syllables)
Shylock:	Shylock is my name. (5 syllables)

Richard II

Bolingbroke:	The shadow of your sorrow hath destroy'd (10 syllables)
	The shadow of your face. (6 syllables)
Richard:	Say that again. (4 syllables)
	When the Ghost beckons Hamlet to follow him, the shared lines show the way in which the pace quickens:
Hamlet:	It waves me still. Go on, I'll follow thee. (10 syllables)
Marcellus:	You shall not go, my lord. (6 syllables)
Hamlet:	Hold off your hands. (4 syllables)
Horatio:	Be rul'd, you shall not go. (6 syllables)
Hamlet:	My fate cries out (4 syllables)
	And makes each petty artery in this body
	As hardy as the Nemean lion's nerve. (Both artery and Nemean are elided to make 2 syllables each.)

Examples of Short Lines

A short line is used which allows the Ghost to exit in the first scene of *Hamlet*:

Marcellus:	Shall I strike it with my partisan? (There is a syllable missing at the beginning of the line. Perhaps Marcellus readies his weapon.)

Horatio:	Do if it will not stand. (6 syllables)
Barnardo:	'Tis here. (2 syllables)
Horatio:	'Tis here. (2 syllables making 10)
Marcellus:	(Short line of 2 syllables, for a pause during which the ghost "disappears." Then:) 'Tis gone.
	We do it wrong being so majestical . . . . (10 syllables with "being" elided to 1 syllable.)

In *All's Well That Ends Well*, when the King of France commands Bertram to marry Helena, he defies the King.

Bertram:	I cannot love her, nor will strive to do't. (10 syllables)
King:	Though wrong'st thyself. If thou shouldst strive to choose – (10 syllables)
Helena:	That you are well restored, my lord, I'm glad. (10 syllables)
	Let the rest go. (4 syllables)
King:	My honour's at the stake, which to defeat (10 syllables)
	I must produce my power. Here, take her hand. . . . (10 syllables, etc.)[49]

As "Let the rest go," a short line, is sandwiched between two 10-syllable lines, it creates a pause. But why? The actors and director must decide. If the pause comes after the line, perhaps the King is surprised that Helena suddenly changes her mind: she no longer wants what she specifically asked for, to have her choice of a husband. The King has to pull rank, despite her misgivings, and continues with "My honour's at the stake." Helena has created a situation; she can't go back on it now. She must be terribly embarrassed, as her plan has backfired: Bertram, who she loves, has rejected her. In her mind, there is no reason to draw this out.

After introducing the basic rules, students can be led through a guided practice to solidify the concepts in their minds. Ask them to break down the verse into smaller parts. Have the students first divide each line into two-syllable feet – separating the feet by drawing a vertical line between them: For example: "In sooth | I know | not why | I am | so sad," or "If mu|sic be | the food | of love | play on," or "O Rome | eo Rome | eo where | for art | thou Rome | eo." In the latter case the "eo" is elided to the sound "yo," and the last syllable is a feminine ending, making the line 11 syllables. This does not mean the student has to pronounce the name this way, but there is a sense that "Romeo" is shortened or the last two syllables are said more quickly.

Another example is a line with long, multisyllable words:

U V   V V U V U V V V
"So let | high-sight | ed tyr | anny | range on,"[50] or So LET | high-SIGHT | ed TYR | an-NY | RANGE ON.

Antithesis

Antithesis, the comparison of two words or phrases, often with opposite meanings, is used by Shakespeare on many occasions. By vocally delivering this argument of opposites, the actors are able to explain what is happening in the dialogue, especially in prose, where the verse is not available to suggest the stresses. The most famous example is from *Hamlet*: "*To **be** or **not** to **be** that is the question.*" In *All's Well That Ends Well,* Bertram uses antithesis to explain his refusal to marry Helena, despite the King's request:

King of France: Thou know'st she has *raised* me from my sickly bed?
Bertram: But follows it, my lord to *bring me* down
 Must answer for *your raising*?

"Raised" and "raising" are compared to "bring me down."

In prose speeches such devices help to guide the actor, as they do not have recourse to the clues that verse offers. Don Armado in *Love's Labour's Lost* uses antithesis throughout major passages to keep his argument clear. Here the speech is divided by thought and edited for space:

I do affect the very *ground*, which is base, where her *shoe*, which is baser, guided by her *foot*, which is basest, doth tread. . . .
 And how can that be *true* love which is *falsely* attempted? Love is a *familiar*; Love is a *devil*: there is no *evil angel* but Love.
 Yet was *Samson* so tempted, and he had an **excellent strength**; yet was *Solomon* so seduced, and he had a **very good wit**.[51]

Note in the last example, Armado uses four different antitheses in Samson and Solomon, tempted and seduced, excellent and very good, and strength and wit. It shows his love of words but also his pretentiousness and love of self.

In *The Merchant of Venice* Portia speaks in prose: "Portia: By my troth, Nerissa, my **little** body is a-weary of this **great** world."[52] "Little" is compared to "great," "body" to "world."[53] Shakespeare often uses antithesis in prose to make the argument clearer. Characters can also be wittier when they don't have to stick to a rhyme scheme or verse form.

Some antitheses have implied theses. The actor keeps the unspoken thesis in mind when considering the antithesis. For example, the Countess in *All's Well That Ends Well* has been told her ward Helena is in love with her son Bertram. When she sees Helena approaching, she prepares to interrogate her about her feelings. She has a soliloquy which begins, "Even so it was with me when I was young."[54] In this particular instance, she is comparing herself to Helena: she too has been in love in her youth. "I" and "me" may then be stressed with the implied antithesis of "her" and "she."[55] "Even" is elided as "e'en."

Punctuation Variations

One should point out that the actor has options as to how the speeches may be delivered based on the different punctuation used in the texts of plays that appear in Quartos or Folios. The Arden *Hamlet*, for example, was published in the First

Quarto of 1603, the Second Quarto of 1604, as well as the First Folio of 1623. In the Second Quarto and the First Folio, "To be or not to be" is placed at III.1.54, in the scene after the arrival of the players. In the First Quarto, he speaks the soliloquy before the arrival of the players, who offer him a solution to the mystery of whether his uncle is guilty. Further stage directions have been added to the First Quarto, including "Enter the ghost in his night gowne."[56] Perhaps most interestingly, the punctuation of some passages changes the meaning of a speech, for example in "What a piece of work is a man."[57]

HAMLET
First Folio:
What a piece of work is a man! how noble in reason! how infinite in faculty! in form and moving how express and admirable! in action how like an angel! in apprehension how like a god!

Or

Second Quarto
. . . in form and moving how express and admirable in action, how like an angel in apprehension, how like a god!

During his study of Malvolio in *Twelfth Night*, Tony Church noticed a change in punctuation in the First Folio: "It is not academic punctuation or reading punctuation – it is definitely *actor's pointing*."[58] His example: modern editors will often use a comma in place of a colon in the First Folio. In this way they remove a pointer: "The use of the colon as a *breathing punctuation*,"[59] an indication the actor may take a breath at that point in the text.

It is also helpful to create handouts around specific topics: The Basic Rules of Verse, the Use of Antithesis, the differences between You and Thou,[60] tests on Regular versus Irregular Lines – any subject that deserves a distinct and detailed study.[61]

A Verse Exercise[62]

How can these rules be embodied – that is, taken more deeply into the actor's system?

An exercise to put the various patterns into the brains and bodies of the students starts with the counting of numbers. Students stand in a circle in the space. One student is picked to start with the number one. In clockwise order each student says the next number until the number ten is reached, then the next student starts over. After a few rounds, the teacher points out that the word "seven" cannot be pronounced in the same way as the others: it must be elided to "se'en," omitting the "v" as in "ne'er" or "e'en" to make a single syllable number. The exercise is repeated, but this time, the students with odd numbers give them extra stress, so the exercise sounds like "one TWO three FOUR five SIX se'en EIGHT nine TEN." An alternative is to have the students raise their hands on the even syllables as they speak them. The students repeat several times, getting this iambic pattern into their bodies. Then the teacher asks them to add a feminine ending. The number added is eleven, but again, it must be pronounced as a monosyllable to fit the pattern. The student says, "Lev," ending the count. Ask the student not to stress the Lev and then have the next student pause, before beginning again. Repeat a number of times.

Next, divide the students into groups of two. Have each group practice saying all ten syllables with stresses on the even numbers, and then, once they are absolutely on rhythm, to add the 11. Then ask one of the pair to count to six: "one TWO three FOUR five SIX." The partner will continue in rhythm: "se'en EIGHT nine TEN." The two then switch and the partner will start. The two will add the "Lev." Then the two will start as follows: the one who starts will use four syllables – "one TWO three FOUR" – while the partner will continue with the final six: "five SIX se'en EIGHT nine TEN." Then they will switch. Then they will add the feminine ending.

Next, still in groups of two, the first student will say four numbers, "one TWO three FOUR," and then both students will silently count off the other six syllables. Then that student will count off ten more syllables: "one TWO, three FOUR five SIX se'en EIGHT nine TEN." Both students will practice this phase. Then they will use variations. One student will count to six and then pause, and the other student will repeat the entire pattern counting to 10.

In this way, the students have used the various forms the verse can take using a simple numbering system which they can translate to the actual words of a text: the ten-syllable line, the line with a feminine ending, the shared line, and the short line. Particularly with the shared line, the numbers require the students to stick with the iambic stresses. In this way, they can serve up the first part of the line in iambics so the other actor can reply in the same fashion, creating a full ten-syllable line.

Emotional Language

Poetic language can be very romantic. When a character uses analogous situations, or when only similes or metaphors will adequately describe the feelings they are having, the student should use the language as a clue to the emotional state of the character. In *The Merchant of Venice*, Portia, who has fallen in love with Bassanio, is afraid he will not find the right casket, a test that, if he fails, also means he may never marry. As he considers between the caskets of gold, silver, and lead, Portia commands for music to be played, but also uses a heightened language full of analogous situations from legend to express her feelings:

> Portia Now he goes,
> With no less presence but with much more love
> Than young Alcides when he did redeem
> The virgin tribute paid by howling Troy
> To the sea monster. I stand for sacrifice.
> The rest aloof are the Dardanian wives . . .
>   Go Hercules.
> Live thou, I live. With much much more dismay
> I view the fight than thou that maks't the fray.[63]

The O's of Shakespeare

Another indication that the feelings are heightened during a speech is the O. Shakespeare uses the one letter, capitalized, in many places, including Ophelia's "O what a mind is here o'erthrown,"[64] as a clue to the actor that they are working through strong emotions. Constance, believing her child Arthur to be dead, argues with Cardinal Pandulph, who sees her grief as madness. At one point in her speech she says, "O, if I could, what grief should I forget!"[65] When Susan Fleetwood performed the speech for the television series *Playing Shakespeare*, she remarked to John Barton that the O "is some indication of emotional release."[66]

The Soliloquy

Actors usually approach these monologues in two ways: as thinking out loud for their own benefit or directly to the audience. Actors at the Globe find that, playing in daylight with the audience so close to them, they must use more energy and include the audience in their thoughts. The character may be trying to get the audience to help them. Certainly, they don't need to say aloud things they have already thought. They wouldn't need to do that for themselves. One attitude I have used presupposes an audience's current thinking as the character imagines it. "I know what you're thinking. Why haven't I killed Claudius yet?" leading to "To be or not to be," or Helena explaining to the audience why she has been crying in Act I of *All's Well That Ends Well*, since Lafew has suggested an alternate reason – grief for her father:

Helena: O were that all! I think not on my father,
And these great tears grace his remembrance more
Than those I shed for him. My imagination
Carries no favour in't but Bertram's.[67]

Her tears are for Bertram, the man she loves – who is leaving Rosillion for Paris – rather than signs of mourning for the father she has lost.[68]

Verse and Prose

Three of Shakespeare's play are all in verse: *Richard II*, *King John*, and *King Edward III*. *All's Well That Ends Well*, *Henry IV Part Two*, *As You Like It*, *Twelfth Night*, *Much Ado About Nothing*, and *The Merry Wives of Windsor* all have more prose lines than verse lines, the latter being almost entirely in prose. The mixture of prose and verse is used to great effect by Shakespeare: to indicate the style of the different classes, but also to indicate a change in a character's emotional state. For example, Beatrice, who has speaking prose in a play that primarily consists of it, *Much Ado About Nothing*, suddenly begins speaking in verse when she discovers Benedick loves her: "What fire is in my ears? Can this be true?"[69]

In *Julius Caesar*, the reason Antony is so successful in turning the crowd on the conspirators who have killed Caesar is that, in speaking first, Brutus uses prose as a

means of reasoning, while Antony follows with a speech in verse to create emotion in his listeners. And in *Hamlet*, when Ophelia goes mad, she speaks in prose.[70]
Examples:

Brutus: Be patient till the last.
　　　　Romans, countrymen, and lovers, hear me for my cause, and be silent that you may hear. Believe me for mine honor, and have respect to mine honor that you may believe . . . .[71]

Notice the number of times antithesis is used. The speech is deliberately rhetorical, more of an oration.

Antony: Friends, Romans, countrymen, lend me your ears.
　　　　I come to bury Caesar, not to praise him.
　　　　The evil that men do lives after them;
　　　　The good is oft interrèd with their bones.
　　　　So let it be with Caesar. The noble Brutus
　　　　Hath told you Caesar was ambitious.
　　　　If it were so, it was a grievous fault,
　　　　And grievously hath Caesar answered it.
　　　　Here, under leave of Brutus and the rest
　　　　(For Brutus is an honorable man;
　　　　So are they all, all honorable men),
　　　　Come I to speak in Caesar's funeral.
　　　　He was my friend, faithful and just to me,
　　　　But Brutus says he was ambitious,
　　　　And Brutus is an honorable man . . .[72]

This verse speech, though poetic, can be delivered in a more natural way. This is not to say Antony is not a great orator, but his ability to persuade the crowd is more effective, and the verse helps him here. Notice the way in which he uses the refrain, "But Brutus says he was ambitious / And Brutus is an honorable man," implying just the opposite as he makes his counterarguments.

You and Thou in Shakespeare

In *Shakespeare's Words*, David and Ben Crystal show how Shakespeare very deliberately distinguishes between the use of the addresses "you" or "thou" as a character choice that tells us something about the changing nature of the relationship between the two people speaking.[73] Like the "vous" and "tu" in French or the "Sie" and "du" in German, this pair of words shows the speaker using formal or informal language, respectively. If the actors know the distinction, they will also realize how to interact with each other, whether with hostility, superiority, inferiority, or even love. "You" is used in the following ways: (1) inferiors to superiors; (2) children to their parents;

(3) servants to their masters; or (4) superiors to their equals – even when they are closely related. "Thou" is used when (1) superiors address inferiors; (2) parents speak to their children; (3) masters speak to their servants; (4) inferiors address each other; (5) superiors want to insult each other, or (6) the speaker wants to address someone they are close to, whether God or another character. This also applies to variations of words such as "your," "thine," "thy," or "thee."[74]

When Shakespeare has a character change from one to the other, the character has changed his or her mood or attitude towards the other person.

In the famous "closet scene" between Hamlet and his mother, Gertrude tries to establish her authority by speaking to her child. Queen Gertrude first addresses him as THOU.

Hamlet: Now, mother, what's the matter?
Gertrude: Hamlet, *thou* hast *thy* father much offended.

But Hamlet, being upset with her, replies as an equal in the less intimate form.

Hamlet: Mother, **you** have my father much offended.[75]

This sets the tone for the scene, in which Hamlet finally castigates his mother for her "o'er hasty marriage."

Twelfth Night

Throughout their first meeting, Olivia addresses Cesario (Viola) as "you." As a noble messenger of a Duke, she is addressed as befits her rank.

Olivia: Get *you* to *your* lord;
I cannot love him: let him send no more;
Unless, perchance, *you* come to me again,
To tell me how he takes it. Fare *you* well:
I thank *you* for *your* pains: spend this for me.

Viola addresses Olivia as "you," inferior to superior, or servant to master.

Viola: I am no fee'd post, lady; keep *your* purse:
My master, not myself, lacks recompense.
Love make his heart of flint that *you* shall love;
And let *your* fervor, like my master's, be
Placed in contempt! Farewell, fair cruelty.

Once Viola leaves, however, Olivia expresses different feelings about her to the audience; they are much more intimate. At first, she is recalling their conversation, which was kept at "you" and "your." But then her language becomes more romantic. The big clue is that she switches to "thou," "thy," and "thee."

Olivia: 'What is *your* parentage?'
       'Above my fortunes, yet my state is well:
       I am a gentleman.' I'll be sworn *thou* art;
       Thy tongue, *thy* face, *thy* limbs, actions and spirit,
       Do give *thee* five-fold blazon.[76]

When Henry V exposes the traitors, members of his own court who have been bribed by the French, he at first uses the required "you" as befits men of a noble rank:

King Henry V: The mercy that was quick in us but late,
       By *your* own counsel is suppress'd and kill'd:
       You must not dare, for shame, to talk of mercy;
       For *your* own reasons turn into *your* bosoms,
       As dogs upon their masters, worrying *you*.[77]

But when he turns on Lord Scroop, until now a close friend whom he trusted with his life, he finds the lord's betrayal so terrible, Henry switches to the insulting "thou," which is also more intimate.

King Henry V: But, O,
       What shall I say to *thee*, Lord Scroop? *thou* cruel,
       Ingrateful, savage and inhuman creature!
       Thou that didst bear the key of all my counsels,
       That knew'st the very bottom of my soul,
       That almost mightst have coin'd me into gold,
       Wouldst *thou* have practised on me for *thy* use:
       May it be possible, that foreign hire
       Could out of *thee* extract one spark of evil
       That might annoy my finger? . . .[78]

As these passages make clear, the changes between "you" and "thou" are deliberate and should be considered clues to changes in relationships.[79] Henry also indicates his emotional state with the "But O," which may require a pause as well, and he then follows with, "What shall I say to thee, Lord Scroop."

The Caesura and Completing the Thoughts

Shakespeare's lines can be end-stopped – that is, each pentameter line ends in a period and a thought is complete – or the full sentence can run over into further lines. When a Shakespeare character has a longer thought, it sometimes ends in the middle of the next line. This break in the middle of the next line is called a caesura. The actor must make the choice to ignore the ending of the pentameter line and continue on to the caesura, or to take a slight pause at the end of each pentameter line. For example:

Cassius: . . . Said Caesar to me 'Dar'st thou, Cassius, now
    Leap in with me into this angry flood,
    And swim to yonder point?' [caesura] Upon the word,
    Accoutred as I was I plunged in,
    And bade him follow. [caesura] So indeed he did.[80]

Greg Doran, former artistic director of the Royal Shakespeare Company, thinks of some run-on lines with caesuras as clues to turn-taking and offered cues. "I find it really useful to consider turn-taking opportunities, even when the character speaking has a very long speech."[81] When the speaker has a break at the caesura, the listener knows there is more to come. This is not true "if the sentence finishes at the end of the verse line."[82] Here the speaker may be giving the listener a chance to break in, especially during a long speech, that is, an offered cue. But the listener obviously doesn't – the speech continues. So either the speaker plunges on ahead before the listener can begin speaking, or the listener chooses not to speak. The speaker's offer makes the speech more dynamic for both parties.[83]

A portion of Tiffany Stern's discussion of Elizabethan rehearsals seems to support this idea – she suggests one of the ways Shakespeare uses a cue script – "called a 'part,' or 'parcell'. . . or it might be called 'scroll' or 'roll'" – as a means of false cueing.[84] The rolls are the sides, the scrolls of paper the actors are given with just their lines and a few words of their cues.[85] Within some speeches, a character repeats the cue line more than once so the other actor is not sure when to come in and may start to speak but be interrupted by the rest of the speech. Since actors were never given full scripts and studied their sides on their own, they wouldn't know what was coming – in fact, they wouldn't necessarily know who was speaking to them until their first rehearsal as a company. By this time, they were expected to know their lines by heart. In *The Merchant of Venice*, Solanio's cue is Shylock's "I'll have my bond." However, Shylock refuses to listen. He uses this cue five times before he exits:

Shylock: I'll have my bond; speak not against my bond:
    I have sworn an oath that I will have my bond.
    Thou call'st me dog before thou hadst a cause;
    But, since I am a dog, beware my fangs:
    The duke shall grant me justice. I do wonder,
    Thou naughty jailer, that thou art so fond
    To come abroad with him at his request.

At this point Antonio speaks after his cue "at his request":

Antonio: I pray thee, hear me speak.

214   Styles: Shakespeare

Shylock then goes on with more cue lines:

Shylock: I'll have my bond; I will not hear thee speak:
　　　　　I'll have my bond; and therefore speak no more.
　　　　　I'll not be made a soft and dull-eyed fool,
　　　　　To shake the head, relent, and sigh, and yield
　　　　　To Christian intercessors. Follow not;
　　　　　I'll have no speaking: I will have my bond.

Solanio tries throughout Shylock's speeches to interrupt him because the actor thinks that his cue was spoken. This adds to the frustration of dealing with an implacable mind, because Shylock won't let him get in a word edgewise. Finally, at Shylock's exit, he is able to say, literally:

Solanio: It is the most impenetrable cur
　　　　　That ever kept with men.[86]

Impenetrable indeed. Notice Shylock prevents Solanio from continuing by following the cue with "speak not against my bond," "speak not," "I will not hear thee speak," and "speak no more."

When the Nurse, Lady Capulet, and Juliet are speaking of Juliet's childhood, Shakespeare uses the same device, as the Nurse repeats the cue line for them both.

Nurse: And said "Ay."

Juliet and her mother may both be trying to cut off her long story where she speaks the cue line again and again.[87]

Playing the Entire Thought

Sometimes the actors must keep the audience in suspense, as the end of the thought may come after several lines. Hamlet's "To be or not to be" soliloquy has such a question, which takes up six and a half lines beginning "For who would bear the whips and scorns of time," and ending with, "When he himself might his quietus make / With a bare bodkin."[88] The actor must lift the phrases that support his argument as he moves towards the possible solution: suicide with a blade. The actor may ignore the ends of lines and jump immediately into further speech or, instead, raise the pitch on the last stressed syllable of each line as a means of maintaining interest before proceeding to the next line, or to get a topping off breath in between lines which together constitute a longer thought.[89]

　　Cicely Berry uses an exercise that helps the student to feel how the thoughts are living in the brain: using two chairs set six feet apart, she asks the actor to start a speech at one chair and then to move only when they reach a punctuation mark. After they move to the other chair, they continue speaking until the next mark, run back, and so on. They must move quickly – but safely – and must stand still whenever they speak. If a student uses all of the commas, semicolons, dashes, periods, and question marks, the mind seems to be racing just as the student is, embodying the developing changes of thought in individual phrases.[90] If the teacher wants the student to identify and complete larger thoughts, then she may have them move only on the periods or question marks.[91]

A character may speak a series of lines that grow in power, as if they are climbing a ladder with their voice. The speaker lifts each line to a higher volume or pitch or intensity until their point is made.

Petruchio: Think you a little din can daunt mine ears?
Have I not in my time heard lions roar?
Have I not heard the sea puff'd up with winds
Rage like an angry boar chafed with sweat?
Have I not heard great ordnance in the field,
And heaven's artillery thunder in the skies?
Have I not in a pitched battle heard
Loud 'larums, neighing steeds, and trumpets' clang?
And do you tell me of a woman's tongue,
That gives not half so great a blow to hear
As will a chestnut in a farmer's fire?
Tush, tush! fear boys with bugs.[92]

How to Deal with Rhyming

First of all, the actors should think of rhyming as a character choice. A character will show their wit by using the other character's words against them.[93] Therefore the actor should embrace his character's tendency to rhyme and find a motivation for it. The play *Love's Labour's Lost* is full of this device. When first they meet, Berowne and Rosaline exchange a quick series of rhyming couplets:

Berowne: Your wit's too hot, it speeds too fast, 'twill tire.
Rosaline: Not till it leave the rider in the mire.
Berowne: What time o'day?
Rosaline: The hour that fools should ask.
Berowne: Now fair befall your mask.
Rosaline: Fair fall the face it covers.
Berowne: And send you many lovers.
Rosaline: Amen, so you be none.
Berowne: Nay, then will I be gone.[94]

Second, rhyming is sometimes used as a spur to get a character offstage. After Hamlet speaks with Horatio, Marcellus, and Barnardo, he is left alone for a short soliloquy. It ends: "Till then, sit still, my soul. Foul deeds will rise / Though all the earth o'erwhelm them, to men's eyes."[95] Iago concludes a scene with "I ha't. It is engendered. Hell and night / Must bring this monstrous birth to the world's light."⁹⁶ The actor may even head for the exit and disappear after the last word.

Alliteration and Assonance

Alliteration is the repeating of consonants within a line. Assonance is the repeating of vowel sounds. If the speaker remains aware of these patterns, she may find clues as to the stresses within each line.

An example of alliteration:
Romeo and Juliet

Chorus: From forth the fatal loins of these two foes
          A pair of star-crossed lovers take their life . . .⁹⁷

In *A Midsummer Night's Dream*, alliteration is used for comic effect:

Bottom: Sweet Moon, I thank thee for thy sunny beams;
          I thank thee, Moon, for shining now so bright;
          For, by thy gracious, golden, glittering gleams,
          I trust to take of truest Thisby sight.
          But stay, O spite!
          But mark, poor knight,
          What dreadful dole is here!
          Eyes, do you see?
          How can it be?
          O dainty duck! O dear!
          Thy mantle good,
          What, stain'd with blood!
          Approach, ye Furies fell!
          O Fates, come, come,
          Cut thread and thrum;
          Quail, crush, conclude, and quell!⁹⁸

Examples of assonance:

Helena: Love looks not with the eyes, but with the mind,
          And therefore is winged Cupid painted blind.⁹⁹
Hamlet: What is a man,
          If his chief good and market of his time
          Be but to sleep and feed? A beast, no more.

Making the Verse One's Own

Making the verse sound natural to the audience's and the actor's own ears is a challenge that all performers undergo who regularly appear in Shakespeare's plays, particularly when it is heightened or rhyming speech.

Sir Derek Jacobi believes, in speaking poetic verse, the actor must "make the text sound as if it is spoken thought."[100] To make the lines "as contemporary as possible without losing any of the intrinsic poetic quality of the text."[101] He did this with the following formula: "Thoughts occur to you, you pluck them out of the air, you give life to them, you give feeling to them, you give emotion to them, you give thought to them, and you speak them."[102] As people do, characters make up the words as they go along, choosing the most appropriate that aid them in achieving their aims. John Barton noted, "Heightened speech must be something that the actor, or rather the character he's playing *finds for himself* because he *needs* those words and images to express his intention."[103] The actor must "*find* them or *coin* them or *fresh-mint* them. We can use any word we want to describe the idea of inventing a phrase at the moment it is uttered."[104] The key is not to pause every time the character is searching for a word but to, as Jane Lapotaire suggested to John Barton in *Playing Shakespeare*, "Think faster."[105] He agreed that to do otherwise created laborious and slow speech.

Pronunciation

It is a motivational idea to suggest that American students pronounce Shakespeare's language in a mode that is closer to the original, but, as David Crystal explains, this is a myth.[106] This does not mean Americans cannot do Shakespeare without Received Pronunciation, any more than it is true that all British subjects speak the same dialect. Great American Shakespeareans include Morgan Freeman, Randall Duk Kim, Viola Davis, Raul Julia, Meryl Streep, Denzel Washington, Diane Venora, James Earl Jones, Kevin Kline, Condola Rashad, Paul Robeson, Keith David, Liev Schreiber, Ethan Hawke, F. Murray Abraham – the list goes on. Showing these actors in full flight will give the student examples of how deft Americans can be with the verse and in their own voices.[107]

The Music of the Lines

The students need to be encouraged to vary the pitches, the volume, and the weight of the words. Derek Jacobi: "If you listen to young actors approaching Shakespeare, they don't inform the language with any kind of vocal cleverness or vocal interest. They tend to find a pitch and stay on it."[108] Cicely Berry suggests sounding only the consonants of each line or only the vowels. The first gives the speech texture and aids the actor in articulation, the second gives the actor resonance. Ultimately though, Berry notes these isolation exercises "will not necessarily enhance our use of words."[109] The actors should speak slowly, concentrating "on the length and vibration of the consonants."[110] This keeps the language "active and muscular."[111]

Two exercises may help with variety and connection: (1) to have the students sing some of their purple passages of heightened speech, and (2) to ask the student to pronounce each individual, notable noun, verb, adjective, and adverb the way they feel about it. Chiefly, however, the students have to connect the breath with the thought, to "conceive the breath and the thought as one."[112] The actors must have enough breath to finish a long thought in verse; otherwise, the audience may lose the thread of the argument. As Berry notes, "[H]ow we breathe is how we think."[113]

218 *Styles: Shakespeare*

Berry also gives her actors a number of muscular exercises to put the words into the body, such as having a number of participants physically holding the speaker back from reaching a target, adding to the effort the actor must make to communicate.

Shakespeare the Director

What clues does Shakespeare give the actor that tell him what to do in terms of blocking or business? So much of what the actors need to know is provided within the text. When the actors want to know where something is, "this" and "that" tracks a person or prop near the speaker or farther away.

Since Shakespeare's characters swear oaths to the heavens, and the heavens were actually painted on the roof of the Globe above their heads, it is possible the actors raised their hands towards heaven and looked up at God. Swearing had both a gesture and a target. More importantly, a character's actions may revolve around keeping an oath to God; to break an oath was to damn oneself.[114]

When the character should be shedding tears onstage, the crying is mentioned in the dialogue, as in, "What's the matter / That this distempered messenger of wet / The many coloured Iris, rounds thine eye?"[115] or "Lady Beatrice, have you wept all this while?"[116]

The characters describe each other as pale – or "wan" – when the color has drained from their faces – an indication to the audience even if not observed on the actor.

A character uses the word "Soft" as a request for quiet so they can hear something offstage or as a warning to the audience to pay attention because someone is coming. "Hark" is also an injunction to "listen."[117]

Hands are used in greeting or parting – as in "Give me thy hand,"[118] or as a means of restraint – "Unhand me, gentlemen."[119]

"Thus" is a word indicating the character does the thing described. An example from *Romeo and Juliet* is Romeo's "Thus, with a kiss I die."[120] A comic example appears in the Pyramus and Thisbe play from *A Midsummer Night's Dream*: Bottom as Pyramus stabs himself many times as a means of milking his death: "Thus die I: thus, thus, thus."[121] Ralph Alan Cohen suggests the modern equivalent is "like this."[122]

For a reference text on stage directions from the period, the reader is referred to Dessen and Thomason's dictionary of stage directions.[123] Some of the more unusual include: "Hercules shoots [an arrow] and goes in. Enter Nessus with an arrow through him, and Dejanaria";[124] "the *sick-chair* used to transport **sick, wounded,** or dying figures";[125] and "he is killed with a flash of lightning."[126] Two Shakespearean stage directions are so dramatic as to be nearly comical: "Exit, pursued by a bear,"[127] and "Enter Lord Clifford wounded, with an arrow in his neck."[128]

Connecting the Actor's Present to the Past

Ultimately, the rules are of little use if they cannot be put into practice, i.e., unless the actors imagine they are living the lives of vivid and believable characters who fight to achieve what they want, that they convey the meaning of the situations and language to the audience, that they work to reveal the hearts and souls of the beings they inhabit.

The student may not have experienced a life at court, fought in a battle, raised sheep in the countryside, lived in exile, or been mortally wounded, but they have contemplated "the slings and arrows of outrageous fortune": they have been unhappy in love; had their hearts broken; been betrayed by their friends; contemplated the torment or demise – however briefly – of those who have wronged them; been excluded from a group; felt misunderstood; fought with their parents; bent to the will of a superior – willingly or out of expediency; adapted to the physical changes of age; been jealous; been depressed and lonely; been joyful and excited; tried to make people laugh; empathized with the less fortunate; been the object of someone's desires – people who they were attracted to or were indifferent to or repulsed by; been made a figure of fun; made fun of someone else; feuded with another group; lost a loved one; have become a part of something bigger than themselves; worshiped; questioned the meaning of life; shown off; felt immortal; mistreated a person or animal; done something they are ashamed of; had a close brush with severe injury or death.

Twelfth Night, Act I, Scene 5 Discussed

The following is a discussion of Act I, Scene 5 of *Twelfth Night*, beginning after Malvolio's exit and ending before his reentrance. Here are suggestions for how the actors begin to relate to the characters and their situations. In this large section of the scene, Viola – as the boy Cesario – is the first messenger to intrigue Olivia, who has rejected many entreaties of love from Orsino. Because she is secretly a woman, and because she has also lost a brother, Viola can identify with and understand Olivia's behavior and call her on it. Viola has memorized a speech that the actor must identify and separate from her lines of dialogue, as she moves back and forth between studied and improvised speech. She is thrown off – because she is interrupted. Olivia is disappointed that this is yet another proposal from Orsino.

Both Orsino and Viola love someone who loves someone else. Viola keeps the secret to herself and suffers. Orsino is desperate to make Olivia love him, though she doesn't feel the same. Viola has feelings for Orsino, so she can't understand why Olivia wouldn't. Viola's mission is to plead for her master, and she is obligated to do so – to win Olivia for Orsino is a painful task and means failing herself. In describing how she would hypothetically woo someone, she imagines her master and unknowingly impresses Olivia, who has never met anyone like her. This is a much better speech than the one she has studied because it comes from her heart.

If this situation is clear, the actors can identify with the feelings of their characters and have specific actions and counteractions which require various strategies for success. If Olivia's women are added to the beginning of the scene, using other actors from the class, this group can laugh at Viola's behavior, another obstacle to her success. All of the women should be veiled, as this is Olivia's test: can the messenger identify her? Olivia has been dressed in mourning, and Viola insists on speaking to her face, wanting her to remove her veil so she can see why Orsino is so enamored of her.

When Viola brazenly accuses Olivia of being too proud, Olivia is surprised but also attracted. She is used to being the object of attention, and here is someone who doesn't seem to be overwhelmed by her beauty. The moment Olivia realizes how she feels towards Viola as Cesario is a wonderful epiphany and made clear by the changes in the verse. Throughout the scene, the women behave and feel in ways the actors can understand and identify with. Their actions are clear. If the teacher can remind the actors that these circumstances are familiar, the students in class begin to play the essence of the scene. Their obstacles by and large are based on their social standing: Viola is, in this instance, not on equal footing with Olivia as the servant Cesario. Does she forget the basic signs of courtesy? No, chances are she's been practicing at Orsino's court and will bow correctly – as a man. She will know her place, though she has to constrain herself, and eventually speaks her mind beyond her role as a messenger of a lower order. Olivia, though of higher rank, defers to Viola and slowly forgives her impertinence. She also begins to address Viola in a more familiar mode.[129] These manners, unfamiliar to the students, can be practiced. The events that day are unusual: Olivia grants an audience; Viola, having mastered her role as a servant, is so upset with Olivia for dismissing Orsino's attentions – those she herself desires – she drops her servant role and speaks her mind. Olivia, for the first time since her brother died, has feelings she has suppressed.[130]

Picking Scenes

If the instructor can, they should choose scenes from Shakespeare's plays with which the students are less familiar, such as *The Two Gentlemen of Verona*; *Henry VI, Parts I, II, and III*; *All's Well That Ends Well*; *Antony and Cleopatra*; *Titus Andronicus*; and *Cymbeline*. If they have time, they should try a variety of forms: monologues, comedy scenes, and dramatic or tragic scenes.

To give the actors fresh material, scenes can be taken from other Elizabethan and Jacobean writers of heightened language, including John Webster, John Ford, Thomas Middleton, Ben Jonson, Christopher Marlowe, Francis Beaumont, and John Fletcher. Students have done scenes and monologues from *The Revenger's Tragedy*, *The Duchess of Malfi*, *A Fair Quarrel*, *A Woman Killed with Kindness*, *The Changeling*, *Doctor Faustus*, *The Alchemist*, *The Knight of the Burning Pestle*, and *The Roaring Girl*, among others. Although they add a greater number of topical allusions, these playwrights use the same form of blank verse and prose, the characters are fascinating, the situations can be darkly comic, and the characters exhibit fascinating psychological traits.

Resources for Shakespeare's Language

The students can learn the phrasing and different methods for playing with the language by listening to the actors who are famous for it. As an experiment, the teacher can give them various recordings – not from the scenes or monologues they will be doing in class. First, they try to imitate the actor exactly, then they perform the speech in their own voices, free to do it in their own way. The pattern of the speechifying tends to remain either above or just below the surface, instilling in the actor the feel for the phrasing. Some years ago, Caedmon issued recordings of heightened language plays, including *Love for Love* and *Love's Labour's Lost* by actors from the National Theatre who were playing those roles at the time.[131] Other companies continue to add to the number of audio plays available to the student.

To give examples of the staging of the plays, the teacher may refer to clips from the many films made from Shakespeare's works. Ralph Alan Cohen offers a "Personal Guide" to many of them and explains their strengths and weaknesses.[132] A superb example is Dominic Dromgoole's production of *Henry IV, Part One* at the New Globe. The language, in particular the obscure passages, is startlingly clear, through the actors' physical and vocal work.

Here are some questions for the students to consider when dealing with blank verse:

1. What do the words of the play tell you about how the character thinks?
2. How does the verse work with your character in relation to the other characters?
3. Do you have run-on or end-stopped lines?
4. Are your lines less than ten syllables long? If so:
    A. Do you share ten-syllable lines with other characters? (Do you pick up the cues?)
    B. Are the lines on either side of yours ten-syllables each? (Do you discover a pause? Where does it go, before or after the line?)
5. Is your language more "poetic" or filled with metaphor, or is it "simpler"?
6. Does your character elide words or expand them? Does your character have many feminine endings?
7. In each case, why is this so? What do these language choices say about your character?
8. How do you deal with rhyming?
9. What words or phrases are unfamiliar to you? (Beware of false cognates.)

Resources abound about directing, acting, speaking, and serving as a dramaturg for, his works. Some of the great reference texts are:[133]

Playing Shakespeare by John Barton
The Actor and the Text by Cicely Berry[134]
Speaking Shakespeare by Patsy Rodenburg
Speaking the Speech by Giles Block
The Eloquent Shakespeare: A Pronouncing Dictionary for the Complete Dramatic Works with Notes to Untie the Modern Tongue by Gary Logan
Shakespeare's Words: A Glossary and Language Companion by David Crystal.
Mastering Shakespeare: An Acting Class in Seven Scenes by Scott Kaiser

The Shakespeare Master Classes edited by Ron Destro
Shakespeare Lexicon and Quotation Dictionary Volumes 1 and 2 by Alexander Schmidt
Shakespeare's Metrical Art by George T. Wright
The Shakespearean Stage 1574–1642 by Andrew Gurr
Prefaces to Shakespeare, Vols. 1 and II by Harley Granville-Barker
Moving Shakespeare Indoors: Performance and Repertoire in the Jacobean Playhouse edited by Andrew Gurr and Farah-Karim Cooper

Working with the students on Elizabethan and Jacobean scenes allows them to practice all of the tools they have been learning and adds a number of processes of technique. Shakespeare wrote for actors and was an actor himself. He was also a great observer of the human condition; all of his characters are unique individuals, and he peopled his plays with hundreds of characters, each of whom had their own personalities, ways of speaking, and mindsets. To delve into the works from these periods is to explore all types of situations and the characters' attitudes towards them – ways of thinking the modern actor can still understand and play.

Notes

1. In the case of the history plays, scenes from either *Richard II, Henry IV Parts 1 and II,* and *Henry V* reference each other, as do *Henry VI Parts 1, 2, and 3,* and *Richard III*. When the student doesn't have the time to read all of them, the teacher can enrich the rehearsals with examples where necessary. It is given that the instructor will have reviewed the plays beforehand.
2. A classic work that examines *Hamlet* from an Elizabethan viewpoint is J. Dover Wilson, *What Happens in Hamlet* (Cambridge: Cambridge University Press, 1990). For example, it completely changes one's perspective on the Mousetrap scene.
3. *Richard II* was rehearsed for little over a day before it was revived for Lord Essex in 1601. See Andrew Gurr, *The Shakespearean Stage 1574–1642* (Cambridge: Cambridge University Press, 2009), 122.
4. He was one of the few members of the group who shared both the costs and a one-eighth share of the profits of the theatre, as opposed to a "hired man" who was paid on a weekly basis. See Gurr, *The Shakespearean Stage*, 61.
5. Modern editors have added the stage directions for clarity. Later in this chapter, the reader will find examples of lines that direct players to action and emotion.
6. *As You Like It*, Act II.4.
7. The teacher should remind the class that Shakespeare lived in two different eras: during the reign of Elizabeth I and then James I of Scotland.
8. Alexander Schmidt, *Shakespeare Lexicon and Quotation Dictionary: A Complete Dictionary of All the English Words, Phrases and Constructions in the Works of the Poet*, 3rd Revised and Edited Edition, Vol. 1 (New York: Dover Publications Inc., 1971), 246.
9. Schmidt, *Shakespeare Lexicon and Quotation Dictionary*, Vol. 1, 651, definition 7.
10. Schmidt, *Shakespeare Lexicon and Quotation Dictionary*, Vol. 1, 652.
11. See David Crystal, *Think on My Words* (Cambridge: Cambridge University Press, 2008), 1561, for these and other examples. A glossary of false friends can be found at the end of his book, 234–244.
12. Crystal, *Think of My Words*, 157–158.
13. *Hamlet*, Act I.2.
14. Alexander Schmidt, *Shakespeare Lexicon and Quotation Dictionary: A Complete Dictionary of All the English Words, Phrases and Constructions in the Works of the Poet*, 3rd Revised and Edited Edition, Vol. 2 (New York: Dover Publications Inc., 1971), 1331.

15 *Richard III*, Act I.1.
16 Schmidt, *Shakespeare Lexicon and Quotation Dictionary*, Vol. 1, 210. For example, the gravediggers in Hamlet are listed as First and Second Clown.
17 See Eric Partridge, *Shakespeare's Bawdy*, 4th Edition (London: Routledge, 2005). *Measure for Measure* and *Othello* are, according to Partridge, "the most sexual, the most bawdy plays." Partridge, 46.
18 See the tables in Ralph Alan Cohen, *ShakesFear and How to Cure It: The Complete Handbook for Teaching Shakespeare* (London: The Arden Shakespeare, 2018), 13–16. Cohen's book is filled with tips and exercises for the beginning student and professional.
19 When a Juliet begins to look around for Romeo on "wherefore," she has not looked up the word.
20 See Scott Kaiser, *Shakespeare's Wordcraft* (New York: Limelight Editions, 2007), 20–23.
21 See Kaiser, *Shakespeare's Wordcraft*, 23–25.
22 See Kaiser, *Shakespeare's Wordcraft*, 20–21.
23 Petruchio, *The Taming of the Shrew*, Act III.2; Kaiser, *Shakespeare's Wordcraft*, 24.
24 Kaiser, *Shakespeare's Wordcraft*, 24.
25 *Twelfth Night*, Act I.2.
26 See the section on emotional language later in this chapter.
27 See Barton, *Playing Shakespeare*, 27, emphasis mine.
28 Bolinbroke in *Richard II*, Act I.3.
29 Each has a feminine ending.
30 *Richard III*, Act V.3.
31 *Julius Caesar*, Act III.2.
32 *Hamlet*, Act III.1. Is Hamlet less decisive because he cannot end a phrase on a strong stress: "To be or not to be that is the QUEST"? All emphases mine.
33 The first line of Sonnet 130, emphasis mine.
34 Caius Marcius in *Coriolanus*, Act III.2, emphasis mine.
35 Hamlet in *Hamlet*, Act IV.4.
36 Shakespeare's Sonnet 12.
37 Hamlet in Act III.2.
38 *Antony and Cleopatra*, Act II.2.
39 *Romeo and Juliet*, Act II.1.
40 See later in this chapter for a discussion of shared lines.
41 *Troilus and Cressida*, Act IV.5.
42 Barton, *Playing Shakespeare*, 35.
43 *As You Like It*, III.5.
44 See entry on "Od" in Schmidt, *Shakespeare Lexicon and Quotation Dictionary*, Vol. 2, 791.
45 *The Taming of the Shrew*, Act I.2.
46 A theory, never definitively proven, is that Shakespeare adapted Psalm 46. Forty-six words from the top is the word "shake," while 46 words from the bottom is the word "spear." Shakespeare was also 46 years old in 1610, a year before the new Bible was published.
47 Constance in *King John* Act III.4, Lear in *King Lear* Act III.2, and Antony in *Julius Caesar* Act III.2, respectively.
48 *All's Well That Ends Well*, Act V.1.
49 *All's Well That Ends Well*, Act II.3.
50 Brutus in *Julius Caesar*, Act II.1.
51 *Love's Labour's Lost*, Act I.2.
52 *The Merchant of Venice*, Act I.2.
53 The whole passage is in prose, including Nerissa's reply.
54 *All's Well That Ends Well*, Act I.3.
55 The whole exchange between the Countess and Helena is full of antitheses.
56 See William Shakespeare, *Hamlet: Arden Performance Edition*, ed. Abigail Rokison-Woodall (London: Bloomsbury, 2017), xxxiv–xxxviii.
57 See the Arden edition, 124–125. *King Lear* was published in the First Folio of 1623 but also in the quarto of 1608, and many productions combine famous passages from each version.

58 Mary Z. Maher, *Actors Talk About Shakespeare*, (Milwaukee, WI: Limelight Editions, 2009), 201, emphasis Church's.
59 Maher, *Actors Talk About Shakespeare*, 201, emphasis Church's.
60 See the discussion on You and Thou later in the chapter.
61 See the discussions on each topic further in the chapter.
62 This is a variation on Ralph Alan Cohen's exercise in Cohen, *ShakesFear and How to Cure It*, 48–50. He has many more.
63 *The Merchant of Venice*, Act III.2. In the DVD of *Playing Shakespeare*, the actor Lisa Harrow performs this passage in the episode "Language and Character." See Barton, *Playing Shakespeare*, 64–65, and the *Playing Shakespeare* box set from Acorn Media, 2009.
64 Ophelia in *Hamlet*, Act III.1.
65 *King John*, Act III.4.
66 Barton, *Playing Shakespeare*, 142.
67 Helena in *All's Well That Ends Well*, Act I.1. Another example of the use of "O."
68 Here the "his" and the "him" are two different people, Bertram and her father, respectively, and this can be brought out as an antithesis and perhaps with a gesture towards Bertram's exit.
69 Beatrice in *Much Ado About Nothing*, Act III.1. The line is a natural iambic if "fire" and "is" are elided: "What fire's in my ears? Can this be true?" The verse speech continues.
70 See *Hamlet*, Arden edition, xli.
71 *Julius Caesar*, Act III.2.
72 *Julius Caesar*, Act III.2.
73 See David Crystal and Ben Crystal, "Thou and You," in *Shakespeare's Words: A Glossary & Language Companion* (New York: Penguin Books, 2002), 450–451.
74 This does not mean that "you" and "thou" or their variants need to be stressed, but simply that they are clues to the ways characters become more formal or intimate towards each other as a scene progresses.
75 *Hamlet*, Act III.4.
76 *Twelfth Night*, Act I.5.
77 *Henry V*, Act II.2.
78 *Henry V*, Act II.2.
79 Notice the way the speech is launched with an O, indicating Henry's anger and disappointment and the elision of the word "cruel" to one syllable.
80 *Julius Caesar*, Act I.2.
81 Doran, *My Shakespeare*, 337.
82 Doran, *My Shakespeare*, 337.
83 Doran, *My Shakespeare*, 337.
84 See Tiffany Stern, *Rehearsal from Shakespeare to Sheridan* (Oxford: Clarendon Press, 2007), 88–90, for discussions of false cueing in both *The Merchant of Venice* and *Romeo and Juliet*.
85 This is why the collection of lines a character has is now referred to as their "roles," and why the actor knew how big their part was: it was literally a larger or smaller roll of paper.
86 *The Merchant of Venice*, Act III.3.
87 *Romeo and Juliet*, Act I.3. As an exercise, I have given students their scenes in roll form. For the first read-through, I ask one of the students to be the first speaker. Everyone must listen intently to see if they hear their cue. At first, they don't know who is in their scene or even sometimes where the scene comes from.
88 *Hamlet*, Act III.1.
89 This is particularly helpful for performing Sonnet 29, beginning "When in disgrace with fortune and men's eyes," which is all one sentence or thought. The writer thinks of his terrible state but then remembers finally "thy sweet love," allows him to "scorn to change [his] state with kings."
90 The punctuation may vary according to the edition used.
91 Cicely Berry, *The Actor and the Text* (New York: Applause Books, 2000), 282–284.

92 *The Taming of the Shrew*, Act I.2.
93 An excellent example is the first scene between Lucetta and Julia from *The Two Gentlemen of Verona*, Act I.2.
94 *Love's Labour's Lost*, Act II.1.
95 *Hamlet*, Act I.2.
96 *Othello*, Act I.3.
97 *Romeo and Juliet*, Act I, Prologue.
98 *A Midsummer Night's Dream*, Act V.1.
99 *A Midsummer Night's Dream*, Act I.1.
100 Jacobi quoted in Destro, *The Shakespeare Masterclasses*, 6.
101 Jacobi quoted in Destro, *The Shakespeare Masterclasses*, 6.
102 Jacobi quoted in Destro, *The Shakespeare Masterclasses*, 6.
103 Barton, *Playing Shakespeare*, 18. Emphasis Barton's.
104 Barton, *Playing Shakespeare*, 18. Emphasis Barton's.
105 Barton, *Playing Shakespeare*, 32.
106 See David Crystal's refutation of this notion in Crystal, *Think on My Words*, 1–2.
107 DVDs of the plays of Shakespeare are widely available, including Denzel Washington's performance as Don Pedro in Kenneth Branagh's *Much Ado About Nothing*, and James Earl Jones's *King Lear*, as well as clips for the Public Theatre's production of *The Taming of the Shrew* with Raul Julia and Meryl Streep. What might be interesting is to show the students how the original punctuation led to further rhymes and puns. See David Crystal, *Think on My Words*, under "Insights," 143–145.
108 Sir Derek Jacobi quoted in Maher, *Actors Talk About Shakespeare*, 69.
109 Berry, *The Actor and the Text*, 34.
110 Berry, *The Actor and the Text*, 36.
111 Berry, *The Actor and the Text*, 36.
112 Berry, *The Actor and the Text*, 30.
113 Berry, *The Actor and the Text*, 30.
114 This is why, in *Love's Labour's Lost*, once the men have sworn to study for three years and avoid the company of women in the court, they must twist themselves into knots trying to extricate themselves from their promise when the Princess of France and her ladies in waiting arrive in Navarre.
115 The Countess remarks on Helena's tears in *All's Well That Ends Well*, Act I.3.
116 Benedick to Beatrice in *Much Ado About Nothing*, Act IV.1.
117 Schmidt, *Shakespeare Lexicon and Quotation Dictionary*, Vol. 1, 513.
118 This phrase appears in many plays as a greeting.
119 *Hamlet*, Act I.4.
120 William Shakespeare, *Romeo and Juliet* in *The Oxford Shakespeare*, Act V.3. Romeo then kisses Juliet and expires.
121 William Shakespeare, *A Midsummer Night's Dream*, Act V.1. Bottom as Pyramus, ever the ham, stabs himself at each thus, three, or even four, times. The colon may indicate a comic pause.
122 Cohen, *ShakesFear and How to Cure It*, 60.
123 Alan C. Dessen and Leslie Thomson, *A Dictionary of Stage Directions in English Drama, 1580–1642* (Cambridge: Cambridge University Press, 1999).
124 See an entry for "arrow" in Dessen and Thomson, *A Dictionary*, 12, from *The Brazen Age* by Thomas Heywood (1611).
125 See an entry for "chair" in Dessen and Thomson, *A Dictionary*, 46, emphasis Dessen and Thomson's. The audience knew a character was sick, not just from the actor's behavior but from the look of the chair itself.
126 See the entry on "lightning" in Dessen and Thomson, *A Dictionary*, 133, from *The Devil's Charter* by Barnabe Barnes (1606).
127 *The Winter's Tale*, Act III.3.

128 *Henry VI, Part Three*, Act II.6.
129 See the differences between the use of "you" and "thou" earlier in the chapter in the *Twelfth Night* passage.
130 Maria's lines may be cut or kept, depending on a student's willingness to take it on, with the understanding they will be playing a larger part in another scene.
131 Derek Jacobi plays Ferdinand, Jeremy Brett plays Berowne, Geraldine McEwan plays the Princess of France and Ian Holm plays Don Armado. The Royal Shakespeare Company has also released a CD boxset of scenes from their productions, *The Essential Shakespeare Live*, BBC/Opus Arte, 2016. It allows you to hear the changes in verse speaking from the late 1950s to the 21st century.
132 See the Appendix, "A Personal Guide to Shakespeare on Screen" in Cohen, *ShakesFear and How to Cure It*, 347–368.
133 See the Bibliography for full citations.
134 Both John Barton and Cicely Berry have recorded their workshops.

15 Conclusion

Scene study can be a fascinating way to explore acting with students, a standard practice that has the potential for an in-depth engagement with theatrical art as well as an examination of the self while identifying and creating – or re-creating – human behavior.

Great actors have been known to dismiss the idea of acting as a study. Their natural talent and hard work has made attendance at conservatories or public universities unnecessary. They have learned on the job and have achieved great success and attained status in their profession. My view would be that scene study itself can be a form of on-the-job training: creating the conditions for rehearsal without the pressures of delivering a performance to a paying audience. The Actors Center in New York was created by J. Michael Miller to give professional actors a private space to continue to learn and grow away from the public eye. Some of the most highly regarded performers have joined the center because they are unwilling to accept the idea they have nothing more to learn. Under the tutelage of teachers from all over the world, these actors return to basic principles, find new precepts for approaching their roles, and remind themselves of the importance of the work – the art in themselves.

I was able to study with some of these teachers in the Teacher Development Program for two summers in 2012 and 2013 and the Continuing Teacher Development Program in 2021, including Ron Van Lieu, Slava Dolgachev, Fay Simpson, Jane Nichols, Karl Kenzler, Katherine K. Willis, Brandon Dirden, Crystal Dickinson, Kenneth Noel Mitchell, and Hugh O'Gorman. These artists and their leader, J. Michael Miller, one of the great men of American theatre, changed my perspective and my life. Having become depleted by the succession of years in higher education, eventually offering much the same material over and over again, I joined the TDP, a decision that revived me; after that first year, I felt an overwhelming calling to bring these lessons to my students. In particular, Ron Van Lieu's scene study classes were germinal in terms of my own classes after 2012, the real seed for this work.

The teacher's ongoing mission to read, investigate, research, and apply new strategies and pedagogical methods to an acting course need not be a burdensome one, but an opportunity to learn and to play, to avoid stagnation and embrace change. One of the personal benefits I received when writing this book was my opportunity to review and discover what other teachers have found effective and inspirational, to hold my own views and practices up to theirs in ways that brought great improvement to my own work. This ongoing journey to give my students a deeper and more effective process has been an exciting one; if I can share even a small percentage of my enthusiasm, arrest the students' attention in a world of social media, focus their talents and skills on processes for improvement, point to the vast knowledge available to them in and out of the academy, encourage their lifelong pursuit of a craft that brings so much pleasure to so many people, and remind them of the responsibility they have to the art they have chosen as a profession, I will never think of my vocation as a job; I will live to work rather than work to live.

In these pages, it has been my intention to begin a discussion on the uses a scene study may have and the ways in which it might be implemented. What any teacher may believe is a useful habit or one that doesn't serve the actor; what categories of diagnosis should receive attention; how actors should connect with their feelings and those of the character; how a scene should be studied; what kind of material the students should rehearse; how characters should be developed and embodied; what tools should be practiced and when; how the space should be arranged; what the teacher's philosophy is about theatre, teaching, art, and life is really up to the individual instructor. If the reader were to use the book simply as a means for considering their own views on the matter, it will have served its purpose.

Appendix 1
Diverse Classroom Plan[1]

(How do you respond to the items listed below? For example, what diverse plays will you study? What are your values as a teacher that you can offer to your students? How do you connect to the material yourself? And so on.)

1. Approach the subject from a beginner's mind.
2. Establish and list the ground rules before the sticky moments appear. (Ask if you missed anything.) (Agree to procedures such as the "oops" and the "ouch.")[2]
3. Provide resources for the students, both to do with general topics and with specific authors, including the cultural landscape, the biography of the playwright, the breadth of dramatic literature for study, interviews with authors of color – any dramaturgical work that can transfer to honest moments onstage steeped in the traditions of the world of the playwright and the play.
4. Rely on your students to guide you: "What is it I don't know that you'd like me to know?" "What part of your experience do I need to know to help you in this process?"
5. Study/analyze the texts carefully.
6. Find and read diverse plays with your students.
7. Identify the value in your own teaching.
8. Speak from a personal place about the universal values of the plays.
9. Focus on the positive values in the play: find the "sustenance."
10. How will you deal with racist language in the play? (Discussions, compromises, and/or substitutions?)
11. Point out the training to be gained by working on great, diverse literature.
12. Dig deeply into each piece to find the intimacy, the core of the characters.
13. Acknowledge the treatment of the marginalized in our history and society.
14. Honor the intentions of the playwrights.

Notes

1 Brandon J. Dirden and Crystal Dickinson, Notes from the Continuing Teacher Development Program, June 14, 2021.
2 An agreement by the teacher and students that an unconscious bias spoken aloud will be acknowledged rather than avoided. "I bought a car but paid too much: I was gypped." Class: "Ouch." Then, an explanation: "Gypped" is a slur about the Romani people, and "gypsy" is increasingly offensive as it calls up negative stereotypes.

Appendix 2
Open Scenes

SCENARIO A: THE APARTMENT

A: Hello.
B: Hello.
A: Are you going to Mary's tonight?
B: Yes, I am.
A: Good.
B: Are you?
A: No.

SCENARIO B: THE OFFICE

A: Come in.
B: Thank you.
A: I understand you want a raise.
B: Yes.
A: I really can't afford it.
B: Thank you anyway for seeing me.

SCENARIO C: THE STORE

A: Excuse me.
B: What's the matter?
A: You're taking my package.
B: I am?
A: Yes.
B: I'm sorry.

SCENARIO D: AT HOME

A: Good morning.
B: Hello.
A: Where's my breakfast?

B: Are you hungry?
A: Yes.
B: Oh. Sorry. What would you like?

SCENARIO E: MEETING FOR LUNCH

A: What's the matter?
B: What do you mean?
A: You look awful.
B: I feel fine.
A: Are you sure?
B: Yes.

SCENARIO F: THE EMPLOYMENT AGENCY

A: What is your name?
B: Brown.
A: Are you here about a job?
B: Yes.
A: We don't have any openings.
B: You don't?
A: No.
B: Goodbye.

SCENARIO G: AT HOME

A: There you are.
B: Here I am.
A: Where have you been?
B: Taking a walk.
A: A walk?
B: I went over to Jim's.
A: Oh. How is Jim?
B: Fine.

SCENARIO H: THE LAUNDROMAT

A: That's mine
B: It is?
A: Yes.
B: I thought it was mine.
A: No, it's mine.
B: Here, take it.
A: Thanks.

SCENARIO I: IN THE APARTMENT

A: I hate you.
B: I know. I hate you too.
A: What are we going to do about it?
B: What do you think?
A: All right.
B: Let's go.

SCENARIO J: IN THE PARK

A: Do you like me?
B: No.
A: You don't.
B: No.
A: I like you.
B: You do?
A: Yes.
B: Good.

Appendix 3
Grading Rubric for Acting Period Styles

Exceeds expectations In all of the following: A	Students completely embrace process in class: 1. Have specific goals for the scene and ask to work on them. 2. Research language of the play and can define all archaic words and passages. 3. Answer questions demonstrating thorough knowledge of the whole play from which the scene is taken. 4. Incorporate all notes from previous scene rehearsals. 5. Add outward physical work appropriate to the style being studied. 6. Make themselves open to "affect" and react to what their partners give them. 7. Reveal the character's intentions. 8. Move the story forward from the viewpoint of their characters. 9. Serve as an audience for the actors showing attentiveness and support of the rehearsing group and offering constructive comments.
Meets expectations In all of the following: B In some of the following: C	Students are ready to work and commit to process in class: 1. Have defined one or two goals for the scene. 2. Can define most archaic words and passages. 3. Answer questions demonstrating basic knowledge of the play from which the scene is taken. 4. Remember to incorporate some notes from previous rehearsals. 5. Demonstrate basic physicality as prescribed by the world of the play. 6. Listen to their partners and rarely act for themselves. 7. Demonstrate some basic intentions during the scene. 8. Use the character's viewpoint to solve problems. 9. Serve as a good audience for the rehearsing group and offer some comments about the scene.

(Continued)

(Continued)

Does not meet expectations D or F	Students are not ready to commit to process for any of the following reasons: 1. No goals are articulated. 2. Are unprepared to work. 3. Show little knowledge of other scenes in the play from which their scenes are taken. 4. Fail to incorporate notes from previous rehearsals. 5. Demonstrate little physicality of the period being studied in any of the rehearsals. 6. Act for themselves and not with their partners. 7. Act without intention. 8. Demonstrate no awareness of the character's viewpoint. 9. Come late to class. 10. Show inattention to the notes being offered or to the instructor in general. 11. Are inattentive to or ignore the scene being rehearsed.

Bibliography

Ackroyd, Peter. *The English Actor: From Medieval to Modern*. London: Reaktion Books Ltd., 2023.
Adams, Maurianne, Warrant J. Blumenfeld, D. Chase, J. Catalano, Keri "Safire" DeJong, Heather W. Hackman, Larissa E. Hopkins, Barbara J. Love, Madeline L. Peters, Davey Shlasko, and Ximena Zúñiga. *Readings for Diversity and Social Justice*, 4th Edition. London: Routledge, 2018.
Alberti, Joe. *Acting: The Gister Method*, 2nd Edition. New York: Joy Press, 2015.
Alcoholics Anonymous. *Alcoholics Anonymous: The Story of How Many Thousands of Men and Women Have Recovered from Alcoholism*, 4th Edition. New York: Alcoholics Anonymous World Services Inc., 2001.
Allen, David. *Stanislavsky for Beginners*. Danbury, CT: For Beginners LLC, 1999.
Ambrose, Susan A., Michael W. Bridges, Michele DiPietro, Marsha C. Lovett, and Marie K. Norman. *How Learning Works: Seven Research-Based Principles for Smart Teaching*. San Francisco: John Wiley & Sons, 2010.
Anonymous. "Shakespeare at 400 Part II: The Great Sir Laurence," *Life Magazine*, vol. 56, no. 18 (May 1, 1964).
Archer, William. *Masks or Faces: A Study in the Psychology of Acting*. London: Longmans, Green and Co., 1888.
Bain, Ken. *What the Best College Teachers Do*. Cambridge, MA: Harvard University Press, 2004.
Ball, David. *Backwards and Forwards: A Technical Manual for Reading Plays*. Carbondale: Southern Illinois University Press, 1983.
Ball, William. *A Sense of Direction: Some Observations on the Art of Directing*. New York: Drama Publishers, 1984.
Barker, Clive. *Theatre Games: A New Approach to Drama Training*. New York: Drama Book Publishers, 1977.
Barkworth, Peter. *The Complete About Acting*. London: Methuen Drama, 1991.
Barton, Allen. *The Oasis of Sanity: The Study and Pursuit of Acting at the Beverly Hills Playhouse*, 1st Edition. Beverly Hills, CA: Beverly Hills Playhouse, 2017.
Barton, John. *Playing Shakespeare*. London: Methuen Drama, 1984.
Batson, Susan. *Truth: Personas, Needs, and Flaws in Building Actors and Creating Characters*. New York: Stone vs. Stone Inc., 2006.
Belknap, Robert L. *Plots*. New York: Columbia University Press, 2016.
Berne, Eric, M. D. *Games People Play: The Basic Book of Transactional Analysis*. New York: Tantor eBooks, 2011.
Berry, Cicely. *The Actor and the Text*. New York: Applause Books, 2000.
Berry, Cicely. *Voice and the Actor*. New York: Wiley Publishing Inc., 1973.

Berry, Ralph. *On Directing Shakespeare: Interviews with Contemporary Directors*. London: Hamish Hamilton Ltd., 1989.
Beverly Daniel, Tatum, PhD. *Why Are All the Black Kids Sitting Together in the Cafeteria? And Other Conversations About Race*, Twentieth Anniversary Edition, Revised and Updated. New York: Basic Books, 2017.
Block, Giles. *Speaking the Speech: An Actor's Guide to Shakespeare*. London: Nick Hern Books, 2013.
Bradford, Gamaliel. "Joseph Jefferson," *The Atlantic*, January 1922.
Brecht, Bertolt. *Brecht on Performance: Messingkauf and Modelbooks*, edited by Tom Kuhn, Steve Giles, and Marc Silberman. London: Bloomsbury, 2014.
Brown, John Russell, ed. *The Routledge Companion to Directors' Shakespeare*. London: Routledge, 2008.
Bruder, Melissa, Lee Michael Cohn, Madeleine Olnek, Nathaniel Pollack, Robert Previto, and Scott Zigler. *A Practical Handbook for the Actor*. New York: Vintage Books, 1986.
Burton, Hal, ed. *Great Acting*. New York: Bonanza Books, 1967.
Butler, Isaac. *The Method: How the Twentieth Century Learned to Act*. New York: Bloomsbury Publishing, 2022.
Butterworth, Jez. *The Ferryman*. London: Nick Hern Books, 2017.
Caine, Michael. *Acting on Film: An Actor's Take on Movie Making*. New York: Applause Theatre Book Publishers, 1990.
Caird, John. *Theatre Craft: A Director's Practical Companion from A to Z*. London: Faber and Faber Ltd., 2010.
Callow, Simon. *Acting in Restoration Comedy*, edited by Maria Aitken. New York: Applause Theatre Book Publishers, 1991.
Carnicke, Sharon Marie. *Dynamic Acting Through Active Analysis: Konstantin Stanislavsky, Maria Knebel, and Their Legacy*. London: Methuen Drama, 2023.
Carnicke, Sharon Marie. *Stanislavsky in Focus, 2nd Edition: An Acting Master for the Twenty-First Century*. London: Routledge, 2009.
Carson, Christie and Farah Karim-Cooper, eds. *Shakespeare's Globe: A Theatrical Experiment*. Cambridge: Cambridge University Press, 2008.
Carter, Ash and Sam Kashner. *Life Isn't Everything: Mike Nichols, as Remembered by 150 of His Closest Friends*. New York: Henry Holt and Company, 2019.
Chantery, Les. *Life in a Mid-Shot: A Premier Acting Coach's Tools for Auditions and Self-Tapes*. Sydney, Australia: Les Chantery Studio Pty Ltd., 2022.
Chekhov, Michael. *Michael Chekhov's Lessons for Teachers*, Expanded Edition, edited by Jessica Cerullo. Ottawa, Canada: Dovehouse Editions Inc., 2000.
Chemers, Michael Mark. *Ghost Light: An Introductory Handbook for Dramaturgy*. Carbondale: Southern Illinois University Press, 2010.
Cohen, Ralph Alan. *ShakesFear and How to Cure It: The Complete Handbook for Teaching Shakespeare*. London: The Arden Shakespeare, 2018.
Cohen, Robert. *Acting Power: An Introduction to Acting*, 1st Edition. Palo Alto, CA: Mayfield Publishing Company, 1978.
Cohen, Robert. *Acting Power: The 21st Century Edition*. London: Routledge, 2013.
Cottrell, John. *Laurence Olivier*. Englewood Cliffs, NJ: Prentice-Hall Inc., 1975.
Crystal, David. *Think on My Words*. Cambridge: Cambridge University Press, 2008.
Crystal, David and Ben Crystal. *Shakespeare's Words: A Glossary and Language Companion*, New Education Edition. New York: Penguin Books, 2002.
Davis, William B. *On Acting . . . and Life: A New Look at an Old Craft*. Altona, MB: FriesenPress, 2022.
Dean, Alexander and Lawrence Carra. *Fundamentals of Play Directing*. New York: Holt, Rinehart and Winston Inc., 1966.
Demidov, Nikolai. *Becoming an Actor-Creator*, edited by Andrei Malaev-Babel and Margarita Laskina, translated by Andrei Malaev-Babel, Alexander Rojavin, and Sarah Lillibridge. London: Routledge, 2016.

Dennett, Daniel C. *Intuition Pumps and Other Tools for Thinking*. New York: W. W. Norton & Company, 2013.
Dessen, Alan C. and Leslie Thomson. *A Dictionary of Stage Directions in English Drama, 1580–1642*. Cambridge: Cambridge University Press, 1999.
Destro, Ron, ed. *The Shakespeare Masterclasses*. London: Routledge, 2020.
DiAngelo, Robin. *White Fragility: Why It's so Hard for White People to Talk About Racism*. Boston: Beacon Press, 2018.
Dixon, Everett C. "Lloyd Richards in Rehearsal," PhD diss., York University, Toronto, ON, 2013.
Donnellan, Declan. *The Actor and the Target*. St. Paul, MN: Theatre Communications Group, 2002.
Doran, Greg. *My Shakespeare: A Director's Journey Through the First Folio*. London: Methuen Drama, 2023.
Duhigg, Charles. *The Power of Habit: Why We Do What We Do in Life and Business*. New York: Random House, 2013.
Dweck, Carol S. *Mindset: The New Psychology of Success*, Updated Edition. New York: Random House, 2016.
Elmore, Tim and Andrew McPeak. *Generation Z Unfiltered: Facing Nine Hidden Challenges of the Most Anxious Population*. Atlanta, GA: Poetry Gardener Publishing, 2019.
Esper, William and Damon DiMarco. *The Actor's Art and Craft: William Esper Teaches the Meisner Technique*. New York: Anchor Books, 2008.
Esper, William and Damon DiMarco. *The Actor's Guide to Creating a Character: William Esper Teaches the Meisner Technique*. New York: Anchor Books, 2014.
Felnagle, Richard H. *Beginning Acting: The Illusion of Natural Behavior*. Englewood Cliffs, NJ: Prentice-Hall Inc., 1987.
Findlay, Polly. *National Theatre Talks*, podcast, Polly Findlay on *Rutherford and Son*, December 13, 2019.
Fine, Howard and Chris Freeman. *Fine on Acting: A Vision of the Craft*. Los Angeles: Havenhurst Books, 2009.
Fowler, Benjamin. *Katie Mitchell, Beautiful Illogical Acts*. London: Routledge, 2021.
Francis, Carla Claudine. "Preparing Birds to Fly: Lloyd Richards and the Actor," PhD diss., University of Missouri, Columbia, 2013.
Friel, John and Linda Friel. *Adult Children: The Secrets of Dysfunctional Families*. Deerfield Beach, FL: Health Communications Inc., 1988.
Garland, Robert. *How to Survive in Ancient Greece*. Yorkshire: Pen and Sword History, 2020.
Goldhill, Simon. *How to Stage Greek Tragedy Today*. Chicago: University of Chicago Press, 2007.
Gorchakov, Nikolai M. *Stanislavsky Directs*, translated by Miriam Goldina. New York: Funk & Wagnalls Company, 1954.
Gordon, Mel. *The Stanislavsky Technique: Russia: A Workshop for Actors*. New York: Applause Theatre Book Publishers, 1987.
Granville-Barker, Harley. *Prefaces to Shakespeare*, Vols. 1–2. Princeton, NJ: Princeton University Press, 1959.
Gurr, Andrew. *The Shakespearean Stage 1574–1642*. Cambridge: Cambridge University Press, 2009.
Guskin, Harold. *How to Stop Acting: A Renowned Acting Coach Shares His Revolutionary Approach to Landing Roles, Developing Them and Keeping Them Alive*. New York: Farrar, Straus and Giroux, 2003.
Hagen, Uta. *Respect for Acting*, 2nd Edition. Hoboken, NJ: John Wiley & Sons Inc., 1973.
Harris, Mark. *Mike Nichols: A Life*. New York: Penguin Press, 2021.
Harris, Thomas A. *I'm Okay – You're Okay*. New York: HarperCollins, 2004.
Hethmon, Robert. *Strasberg at the Actors Studio: Tape-Recorded Sessions*. New York: The Viking Press, 1965.
Hobgood, Burnet M., ed. *Master Teachers of Theatre: Observations on Teaching Theatre by Nine American Masters*. Carbondale: Southern Illinois University Press, 1988.

Hodge, Francis. *Play Directing: Analysis, Communication, and Style.* Englewood Cliffs, NJ: Prentice-Hall Inc., 1971.
Houghton, Norris. *Moscow Rehearsals: An Account of Methods of Production in the Soviet Theatre.* New York: Harcourt, Brace, and Company, 1936.
Hunter, Madeline. *Enhanced Teaching.* New York: Macmillan College Publishing Company, 1994.
Jacobi, Derek. *As Luck Would Have It: My Seven Ages as Told to Garry O'Connor.* London: HarperCollins Publishers, 2013.
Johnstone, Keith. *Impro for Storytellers.* New York: Routledge, 1999.
Johnstone, Keith. *Impro: Improvisation and the Theatre.* New York: Routledge, 1979.
Johnstone, Keith. "Ten Days with Keith," a Keith Johnstone Workshop, Calvary, July 2017.
Kaiser, Scott. *Shakespeare's Wordcraft.* New York: Limelight Editions, 2007.
Kaufman, Moisés and Barbara Pitts McAdams. *Moment Work: Tectonic Theatre Project's Process of Devising Theatre.* New York: Vintage Books, 2018.
Kazan, Elia. *Kazan on Directing.* New York: Vintage Books, 2009.
Kemp, Rick. *Embodied Acting: What Neuroscience Tells Us About Performance.* New York: Routledge, 2012.
Kogan, Sam and Helen Kogan. *The Science of Acting.* London: Routledge, 2009.
Kulick, Brian. *How Greek Tragedy Works: A Guide for Directors, Dramaturges, and Playwrights.* London: Routledge, 2021.
Laban, Rudolf. *The Mastery of Movement Third Edition*, revised by Lisa Ullmann. Boston: Plays Inc., 1971.
Lecoq, Jacques. *The Moving Body (Le Corps Poétique): Teaching Creative Theater*, 3rd Edition, translated by David Bradby. London: Methuen Drama, 2020.
Leiter, Samuel L. *The Great Stage Directors: 100 Distinguished Careers of the Theatre.* New York: Facts on File Inc., 1994.
Leonard, George. *Mastery: The Keys to Success and Long-Term Fulfillment.* New York: Plume, 1992.
Lessac, Arthur. *The Use and Training of the Human Voice: A Bio-Mechanic Approach to Vocal Life*, 3rd Edition. Mountain View, CA: Mayfield Publishing Company, 1996.
Linklater, Kristin. *Freeing the Natural Voice.* New York: Drama Publishers, 1976.
Logan, Gary. *The Eloquent Shakespeare: A Pronouncing Dictionary for the Complete Dramatic Works with Notes to Untie the Modern Tongue.* Chicago: University of Chicago Press, 2012.
Lovett, Marsha C., Michael W. Bridges, Michele DiPietro, Susan A. Ambrose, and Marie K. Norman. *How Learning Works: Eight Research-Based Principles for Smart Teaching.* Hoboken, NJ: John Wiley & Sons Inc., 2023.
Luckett, Sharrell and Tia M. Shaffet. *Black Acting Methods: Critical Approaches.* London: Routledge, 2017.
Maher, Mary Z. *Actors Talk About Shakespeare.* Milwaukee, WI: Limelight Editions, 2009.
Maisel, Eric, PhD and Ann Maisal. *What Would Your Character Do? Personality Quizzes for Analyzing Your Characters.* Cincinnati, OH: Writer's Digest Books, 2006.
Marcus, Bennett. "Sam Mendes's 25 Rules for Directors," *Vanity Fair*, March 11, 2014. https://www.vanityfair.com/style/2014/03/sam-mendes-rules-for-directors
Martin, Bella. *The Complete Stanislavsky Toolkit.* Hollywood, CA: Drama Publishers, 2007.
McClure, James. *Laundry and Bourbon: A Comedy in One Act.* New York: Dramatists Play Service, 1981.
Meisner, Sanford and Dennis Longwell. *Sanford Meisner on Acting.* New York: Vintage Books, 1987.
Mekler, Eva. *The New Generation of Acting Teachers: More Than 20 Revealing Interviews with Today's Master Teachers on the Art and Craft of Acting.* New York: Penguin Books, 1987.
Miller, Alice. *The Drama of the Gifted Child: The Search for the True Self*, translated by Ruth Ward. New York: Basic Books, 1997.
Miller, Arthur. *All My Sons: A Drama in Three Acts.* New York: Dramatists Play Service, 1974.
Mitchell, Katie. *The Director's Craft: A Handbook for the Theatre.* London: Routledge, 2009.

Moss, Larry. *The Intent to Live: Achieving Your True Potential as an Actor.* New York: Bantam Books, 2005.
Neilson, William Allan, Thomas A. Knott, and Paul W. Carhart, eds. *Webster's New International Dictionary of the English Language,* 2nd Edition. Springfield, MA: G.&C. Merriam Company Publishers, 1943.
O'Gorman, Hugh. *Acting Action: A Primer for Actors.* New York: Rowman & Littlefield, 2021.
Orenstein, Ellen. "Shaping the Independent Actor," *American Theatre,* January 1, 2008. https://www.americantheatre.org/2008/01/01/shaping-the-independent-actor/
Pace, Chelsea and Laura Rikard. *Staging Sex: Best Practices, Tools, and Techniques for Theatrical Intimacy.* Abingdon, Oxon: Routledge, 2020.
Palmer, Parker J. *The Courage to Teach: Exploring the Inner Landscape of a Teacher's Life,* 20th Anniversary Edition. San Francisco: John Wiley & Sons Inc., 2017.
Partridge, Eric. *Shakespeare's Bawdy,* 4th Edition. London: Routledge, 2005.
Ramczyk, Suzanne M. *Delicious Dissembling: A Complete Guide to Performing Restoration Comedy.* Portsmouth: Heinemann, 2002.
Rand, Ronald and Luigi Scorcia. *Acting Teachers of America: A Vital Tradition.* New York: Allworth Press, 2007.
Ranelli, J. "Putting the Actor in the Text," a Workshop at WildWind Performance Lab, Texas Tech University, Lubbock, June 2014.
Redfield, William. *Letters from an Actor.* New York: The Viking Press, 1969.
Richards, Lloyd. *Working in the Theatre #125 Playscript/Director.* City University of New York: The American Theatre Wing Seminars, 1987. https://www.youtube.com/watch?v=WSv-AXg9D0Q.
Robb, Brian J. *Starstruck: Heath Ledger.* Edinburgh: Glencairn Press, 2020.
Rodenburg, Patsy. *The Right to Speak.* London: Routledge, 1992.
Rodenburg, Patsy. *Speaking Shakespeare,* 1st Edition. New York: St. Martin's Press, 2004.
Rodrigue, Jean-Louis and Scott Weintraub. *Back to the Body: Infusing Physical Life into Characters in Theatre and Film.* Beverly Hills, CA: Alexander Techworks, 2023.
Rosenfeld, Carol. *Acting and Living in Discovery: A Workbook for the Actor.* Indianapolis, IN: Focus, 2014.
Rothstein, Dan and Luz Santana. *Make Just One Change: Teach Students to Ask Their Own Questions.* Cambridge, MA: Harvard Education Press, 2011.
Rubin, Leon. *The Nicholas Nickleby Story: The Making of the Historic Royal Shakespeare Company Production.* London: William Heinemann Ltd., 1981.
Rundell, Katherine. *Super-Infinite: The Transformations of John Donne.* New York: Farrar, Straus and Giroux, 2022.
Schmidt, Alexander. *Shakespeare Lexicon and Quotation Dictionary: A Complete Dictionary of All the English Words, Phrases and Constructions in the Works of the Poet,* 3rd Revised and Edited Edition, Vols. 1–2. New York: Dover Publications Inc., 1971.
Schreiber, Terry. *Acting: Advanced Techniques for the Actor, Director, and Teacher.* New York: Allworth Press, 2005.
Scott, Siiri and Jay Paul Skelton, eds. *Stanislavsky and Race: Questioning the 'System' in the 21st Century.* London: Routledge, 2023.
Shakespeare, William. *The Complete Works,* 2nd Edition, edited by John Jowett, William Montgomery, Gary Taylor, and Stanley Wells. Oxford: Clarendon Press, 2005.
Shakespeare, William. *Hamlet: Arden Performance Edition,* edited by Abigail Rokison-Woodall. London: Bloomsbury, 2017.
Shurtleff, Michael. *Audition: Everything an Actor Needs to Know to Get the Part.* New York: Walker and Company, 1978.
Sinden, Donald. *Laughter in the Second Act.* London: Hodder and Stoughton, 1985.
Smiley, Sam and Norman A. Bert. *Playwriting: The Structure of Action,* Revised and Expanded Edition. New Haven, CT: Yale University Press, 2005.
The Southbank Show, "Ian McKellen: Diary of a Year," broadcast on October 20, 1985, by London Weekend Television.

Spivak, Alice and Robert Blumenfeld. *How to Rehearse When There Is No Rehearsal: Acting and the Media*. New York: Limelight Editions, 2007.
Spolin, Viola. *Improvisation for the Theater: A Handbook of Teaching and Directing*. Evanston, IL: Northwestern University Press, 1983.
Spolin, Viola. *Theatre Games for Rehearsal: A Director's Handbook*. Evanston, IL: Northwestern University Press, 1985.
Stafford-Clark, Max. *Letters to George: The Account of a Rehearsal*. London: Nick Hern Books, 1989.
Stanislavski, Konstantin. *An Actor's Work on a Role*, translated by Jean Benedetti. London: Routledge, 2009.
Stanislavski, Konstantin. *An Actor's Work: A Student's Diary*, 1st Edition, translated by Jean Benedetti. London: Routledge, 2008.
Stern, Tiffany. *Rehearsal from Shakespeare to Sheridan*. Oxford: Clarendon Press, 2007.
Stewart, Patrick. *Making It So: A Memoir*. New York: Gallery Books, 2023.
Stone, Douglas and Sheila Heen. *Thanks for the Feedback: The Science and Art of Receiving Feedback Well*. New York: Penguin Books, 2014.
Styan, J. L. *Restoration Comedy in Performance*. Cambridge: Cambridge University Press, 1994.
Tichler, Rosemarie and Barry Jay Kaplan. *Actors at Work*. New York: Faber and Faber Inc., 2007.
Toporkov, Vasili. *Stanislavski in Rehearsal*, translated by Jean Benedetti. London: Bloomsbury, 2014.
Trevis, Di. *Being a Director: A Life in Theatre*. London: Routledge, 2012.
Turner, J. Clifford. *Voice and Speech in the Theatre*, 5th Edition. London: Routledge, 2000.
Van Lieu, Ron. Teacher Development Program Notes, June 2012 and June 2013.
Weimer, Maryellen, PhD, ed. *Grading Strategies for the College Classroom: A Collection of Articles for Faculty*. Madison, WI: Magna Publications, 2013.
Whitfield, Petronilla. *Teaching Strategies for Neurodiversity and Dyslexia in Actor Training: Sensing Shakespeare*. London: Routledge, 2020.
Wilde, Oscar. *The Importance of Being Earnest and Other Plays*. New York: The Modern Library, 2010.
Wildeblood, Joan and Peter Brinson. *The Polite World: A Guide to English Manners and Deportment from the Thirteenth to the Nineteenth Century*. London: Oxford University Press, 1965.
Wilson, J. Dover. *What Happens in Hamlet*. Cambridge: Cambridge University Press, 1990.
Wineburg, Sam. *Historical Thinking and Other Unnatural Acts: Charting the Future of Teaching the Past*. Philadelphia: Temple University Press, 2001.
Winters, John J. *Sam Shepard: A Life*. Berkeley: Counterpoint, 2017.
Woolson, Michael. *The Work of an Actor: Michael Woolson on Technique*. Hollywood: Drama Publishers, 2010.
Wright, George T. *Shakespeare's Metrical Art*. Berkeley: University of California Press, 1991.
Wright, John. *Why Is That So Funny? A Practical Exploration of Physical Comedy*. New York: Limelight Editions, 2007.
Young, Harvey, ed. *The Great American Stage Directors, Vol. 3, Kazan, Robbins, Richards*. London: Bloomsbury Methuen Drama, 2021.

Index

action 16, 17, 20, 35, 43, 50, 61, 63, 64, 71, 72, 73, 92, 93, 99, 100, 103, 105, 109, 110, 111, 112, 113, 114, 115, 116, 124, 125, 126, 128–129, 137, 138, 139, 140, 143, 158, 165, 181, 189, 218, 219
active analysis 73, 76, 111, 113, 114, 116, 117, 118, 124, 132, 181, 236
active listening 92, 93
activities 98, 99
affective memory 20, 21, 25, 98, 105, 106, 108, 109
Alberti, Joe 115, 118, 235
Alexander, Frederick Matthias 32, 98
Ambrose, Susan A. 24, 34, 101, 119, 120, 131, 155, 164, 168, 169, 235, 238
analysis 5, 44, 58, 59, 60–74, 77, 86, 238
animal work 145
anticipating 127

Bain, Ken 15, 24, 235
Ball, David 65, 73, 86, 87
Ball, William 86, 87, 112, 117, 118, 122, 124, 131, 132, 235
Barker, Clive 177, 178, 179, 182, 188, 195, 235
Barton, John 200, 202, 209, 217, 221, 223, 224, 225, 226, 235
Batson, Susan 101, 138, 235
Benedetti, Jean 9, 10, 25, 240
Benedetti, Robert 19, 25, 79, 86, 102, 113, 118
Berne, Eric 147, 153, 180, 182, 235
Berry, Cicely 131, 197, 214, 217, 218, 221, 224, 225, 226, 235
Berry, Ralph 185, 194, 236
blackchild, cfrancis 24, 74, 86, 169
breath 8, 38, 75, 84, 97, 98, 100, 122, 123, 124, 128, 145, 171, 207, 214, 217
Butler, Isaac 25, 172, 236

Caine, Michael 93, 102, 236
Callow, Simon 186, 191, 193, 194, 195, 236
Carnicke, Sharon Marie 9, 61, 72, 73, 74, 106, 109, 113, 114, 116, 117, 118, 172, 181, 236
casting, scenes 54, 56
Cephas Jones, Ron 96, 102
challenges 24, 26, 33, 40, 45, 46, 50, 52, 84, 89, 90, 120, 144, 150, 160, 161, 170, 172, 179, 184, 196
Chantery, Les 17, 24, 68, 73, 236
character 133–154; actions 64, 87, 93, 187; advocate 16, 137, 138, 139; arcs 71, 72, 143; attachments 68, 69; frames of reference 150; history 63, 64; intelligence 143–144; Laban movement efforts 148–149; language 43, 143, 186, 197, 198, 208, 217, 220, 221; mission 92, 93; moral stance 149, 150; music 148; secrets 68, 74
Chekhov, Anton 33, 56, 61, 73, 102, 114, 148
Chekhov, Michael 39, 47, 50, 171, 181, 236
coaching: categories 5, 59, 62, 81, 85, 88–103; methods 5, 79; notes 81; questions 14, 15, 16, 63, 75, 76, 80, 81, 89, 120, 162, 163, 165; side-coaching 36, 81, 85, 94–95, 163, 179; stumbling blocks 80; timing 81, 85
Cohen, Ralph Alan 199, 218, 221, 223, 224, 225, 226, 236
Cohen, Robert 87, 115, 116, 118, 125, 144, 175, 177, 179, 181, 182, 184, 194, 236
comedy 7, 54, 84, 101, 103, 146, 147, 177, 188, 189, 190, 194, 195, 220, 236, 239, 240
complexes 107
conditioning forces 63, 68, 73
counteraction 113, 114, 219

creative hiding 128
Crystal, David 197, 210, 217, 221, 222, 224, 225, 236
cybernetic analysis 115

Davis, William B. 43, 50, 73, 124, 132, 151, 152, 236
defeatist attitude 33, 122, 125, 126, 131
Demidov, Nikolai 83, 85, 86, 87, 103, 130, 132, 134, 151, 173, 181, 236
diagnosis 5, 8, 18, 40, 52, 77, 80, 85, 86, 88–103, 160, 168, 170
Diderot, Denis 142
discomfort, encouraging 75, 76, 83, 84, 85, 177
diversity 33, 35, 229, 235, 240
Dixon, Everett C. 24, 73, 237
Dolgachev, Vyacheslav 73, 227
Donnellan, Declan 19, 25, 29, 34, 125, 132, 135, 151, 172, 176, 181, 237
Doran, Greg 59, 213, 224, 237
Dukakis, Olympia 12, 23, 94

embodying 54, 76, 80, 109, 121, 138, 143, 144, 171, 187, 196, 215, 256, 265, 284
emotions 5, 6, 18, 20, 21, 25, 32, 40, 63, 66, 68, 78, 79, 84, 90, 99, 101, 104–118, 122, 127, 128, 129, 130, 131, 134, 137, 139, 141, 142, 149, 151, 171, 172, 178, 186, 188, 197, 199, 208, 209, 210, 212, 217, 222, 223
empathy 3, 22, 48, 61, 75, 105, 106, 133, 139, 140
endowment exercise 145, 153, 156, 165, 166, 169, 171
endowment of the other exercise 145, 146, 156
ensemble 17, 21, 41, 136, 168, 175, 177
Esper, William 6, 21, 25, 43, 66, 79, 86, 108, 117, 134, 136, 139, 140, 151, 152, 172, 237
etudes 2, 6, 7, 23, 36, 44, 85, 90, 101, 102, 110, 114, 116, 130, 132, 147, 165, 168, 172–175, 180, 181, 188
evaluations 56, 59, 86, 95, 97, 124, 144, 159, 160, 162, 164
events 5, 16, 17, 18, 39, 40, 43, 49, 54, 56, 60, 61, 62, 63, 64, 65, 66, 71, 72, 80, 83, 89, 90, 91, 93, 97, 106, 107, 108, 111, 113, 126, 129, 131, 134, 139, 144, 163, 172, 174, 175, 180, 189, 190, 191, 220
external approach, the 7, 96, 99, 100, 105, 122, 124, 133, 142–143, 146, 171

fear 6, 7, 28, 29, 30, 31, 44, 51, 76, 84, 98, 101, 105, 115, 116, 127, 128, 135, 138, 177, 178, 186, 223, 224, 225, 226, 236
feedback 2, 3, 6, 13, 40, 41, 44, 46, 49, 50, 54, 56, 79, 81, 85, 86, 88, 115, 116, 127, 151, 155–169, 170, 194, 240
Felnagle, Richard H. 92, 102, 237
Findlay, Polly 125, 149, 154, 237
Fine, Howard 106, 107, 117, 126, 132, 137, 138, 152, 237

games 2, 3, 6, 7, 23, 41, 50, 101, 136, 142, 153, 168, 170, 175–180, 182, 184, 188, 195, 235, 240
Garland, Patrick 84, 87
gestures 100, 109, 119, 120, 126, 142, 145, 199, 218, 224
Gister, Earle 114, 115, 118, 137, 152, 235
Gister Method, The 114–115, 118, 235
goals: student 9, 17, 19, 27, 36, 42, 43, 46, 48, 54, 76, 78, 81, 82–83, 92, 99, 109, 112, 113, 115, 125–126, 151, 155, 157, 158, 168, 172; teacher 3, 4, 11, 13, 15, 22, 23, 30, 37, 60, 81–82, 89, 155, 156, 159, 160, 163, 164, 167, 168, 170, 171
Gorchakov, Nikolai M. 59, 102, 132, 181, 237
Guskin, Harold 77, 86, 237

habits 4, 6, 14, 16, 24, 45, 46, 47, 48, 77, 82, 97, 98, 116, 119–132, 142, 144, 151, 155, 179, 183, 184, 228, 237
Hagen, Uta 1, 26, 68, 73, 90, 101, 117, 134, 145, 151, 156, 165, 169, 171, 172, 181, 237
Hapgood, Elizabeth Reynolds 10
Harris, Mark 24, 73, 102, 195, 237
Henderson, Stephen McKinley 29, 33, 34, 35, 65, 73, 101, 118
Hobgood, Burnet M. 23, 25, 118, 237
Hodge, Francis 37, 50, 71, 74, 154, 185, 194, 238
homework 14, 33, 42, 43, 47, 49, 53, 62–63, 64–74, 76, 77, 86, 93, 95–96, 113, 134, 136, 137, 138, 160, 218
Houghton, Norris 100, 103, 238

identification 18, 61, 139–141, 185
imagery 31, 35, 61, 108
Irby, A. Dean 14, 24

Jacobi, Sir Derek 123, 131, 132, 195, 217, 225, 226, 238
Johnstone, Keith 18, 24, 25, 28, 29, 34, 54, 59, 97, 102, 128, 132, 146, 147, 153, 177, 181, 238
jugyōkenkyū 10

Kaiser, Scott 199, 221, 223, 238
Katselas, Milton 89, 101, 128, 132
Kaufman, Moisés 55, 59, 238
Kazan, Elia 24, 30, 34, 38, 50, 86, 112, 118, 238, 240
Kenzler, Karl 227
Knebel, Maria 73, 111, 113, 236
Kogan, Sam 77, 86, 99, 100, 101, 103, 107, 117, 150, 154, 238

Laughton, Charles 22

Magic If, The 106–107, 139
Martin, Bella 100, 103, 117, 238
Mekler, Eva 102, 152, 153, 168, 172, 238
memorization 43, 58, 59, 130
Mendes, Sam 22, 25, 238
Method of Physical Actions, The 35, 100, 103, 109–111, 112, 117, 128, 181
milking 127
Miller, Arthur 74, 91, 238
Miller, J. Michael 227
Mitchell, Katie 61, 72, 73, 116, 118, 237, 238
Moscow Art Theatre, The 29, 73, 111, 129, 181
Moss, Larry 66, 68, 73, 78, 84, 86, 87, 89, 101, 108, 109, 117, 118, 132, 145, 153, 172, 174, 181, 239

Nichols, Mike 18, 24, 31, 35, 64, 65, 67, 73, 91, 96, 102, 189, 195, 236, 237

obstacles 28, 33, 53, 64, 71, 78, 90, 92, 93, 112, 113, 115, 125, 135, 137, 141, 144, 149, 175, 189
Olivier, Laurence 22, 25, 119, 131, 142, 152, 236

paraphrasing 131
personalization. 6, 96, 117
philosophy 2, 3–4, 6, 11–25, 28, 41, 49, 58, 59, 69, 133, 143, 150
physicalizing *see* embodying
presentism 24, 66, 69–70, 73

previous circumstances 7, 39, 44, 56, 60, 61, 64, 66–67, 71, 89–90, 91, 92, 126, 141, 142, 143, 156, 163, 164, 171, 174, 196
pushing 122

Ramczyk, Suzanne M. 192, 193, 239
Ranelli, J 239
rehearsals 2, 4, 9, 15, 17, 20, 24, 25, 29, 34, 37, 42, 43, 45, 46, 48, 49, 50, 58, 66, 73, 75, 78, 80, 87, 96, 100, 103, 110, 117, 121, 125, 130, 149, 152, 153, 158, 178, 179, 182, 184, 188, 194, 197, 202, 213, 222, 224, 227, 233–234, 237, 238, 240; beginning 75–79; first moments 83; pace of 81, 85, 99–100; rules 77
relationships 21, 29, 56, 60, 61, 63, 64, 66–67, 71, 76, 83, 89, 93, 97, 116, 134, 141–142, 144, 145, 148, 172, 174, 188, 210, 212
resisting the condition 132, 149
Ribot, Théodule-Armand 20
Richards, Lloyd 6, 14, 15, 17, 18, 23, 24, 28, 29, 34, 63, 65, 70, 73, 74, 75, 82, 86, 89, 101, 116, 118, 164, 165, 169, 237, 239, 240
ritual 38–39, 48, 76, 190
Rosenfeld, Carol 70, 74, 239
rubrics 159, 160, 165–168, 195, 233–234

Salvini, Tommaso 104
scenes: choosing 4–5, 14, 41–42, 51–57, 220; number of 41–42
Schmidt, Alexander 197, 222, 223, 225, 239
Schreiber, Terry 31, 35, 44, 50, 170–171, 181, 239
Schulman, Michael 98, 102, 140–141, 152, 172
Shakespeare, Verse Speaking 87, 197, 198; alliteration 216; antithesis 205–206; blank verse 200; the caesura 212–214; elision 201–202; iambic pentameter 200–201; myths and legends 199; regular *vs.* irregular verse 200–201, 203; rhyming 215–216; shared lines 203–204; short lines 203–205; soliloquy 209; you and thou 210–212
Shakespeare, William 7, 56, 57, 59, 67, 74, 104, 124, 132, 185, 186, 188, 191, 193, 194, 196, 197, 198, 199, 200, 201, 202, 203, 205, 206, 209, 210, 211, 212, 213, 214, 216, 217, 218, 220, 221, 222, 223, 224, 225, 226, 235, 236, 237, 238, 239, 240

Shay, Michelle 17, 24
Shepard, Sam 53, 57, 59, 240
Shurtleff, Michael 89, 97, 101, 102, 179, 192, 239
Smith, Wallace 11, 13, 23
Spivak, Alice 107, 117, 145, 146, 156, 172, 240
Spolin, Viola 179, 182, 240
Stafford Clark, Max 147, 153, 187, 194, 240
stakes 46, 48, 56, 84, 92, 112, 113, 124–125, 126, 128, 129, 135, 163, 175, 176, 187, 188
Stanislavsky, Konstantin 6, 8, 9, 10, 12, 14, 18, 20, 21, 22, 24, 25, 29, 30, 34, 35, 43, 50, 53, 59, 72, 73, 82, 83, 87, 93, 94, 95, 99, 100, 102, 103, 104, 105, 106, 109, 110, 111, 113, 116, 117, 121, 128, 129, 132, 134, 136, 139, 152, 156, 172, 173, 174, 181, 235, 236, 237, 238, 239, 240
state of being 112, 129
status 54, 59, 63, 74, 146–148

Strasberg, Lee 18, 20, 24, 78, 82, 84, 86, 87, 105, 106, 116, 117, 127, 132, 162, 174, 181, 237
substitution 96, 107–108, 146, 156

tempo-rhythm 72, 74, 99, 100, 101, 103, 131
Toporkov, Vasili 9, 24, 25, 34, 50, 87, 110, 111, 117, 152, 240
Tovstonogov, Georgy Aleksandrovich 66

underplaying 129–130

Van Lieu, Ron 15, 17, 22, 24, 25, 34, 61, 69, 73, 74, 78, 84, 86, 87, 93, 98, 102, 126, 132, 163, 169, 172, 177, 181, 227, 240

warmups 36, 41, 120, 123, 175
Wineburg, Sam 66, 69, 74, 240
Woolson, Michael 46, 50, 139, 152, 240
Wright, John 100–101, 103, 177, 240

For Product Safety Concerns and Information please contact our EU representative GPSR@taylorandfrancis.com
Taylor & Francis Verlag GmbH, Kaufingerstraße 24, 80331 München, Germany

www.ingramcontent.com/pod-product-compliance
Lightning Source LLC
Chambersburg PA
CBHW050532300426
44113CB00012B/2055